A Spirit to Resist

Elizabeth Ellen Gething
Texas Pioneer Woman

By Rose M. Hall

KATE:

> Gentlemen, forward to the bridal dinner.
> I see a woman may be made a fool
> If she had not *a spirit to resist*.
> > William Shakespeare
> > *The Taming of the Shrew*
> > Act III, Scene ii

DEDICATION

to
All Pioneer Women
where frontiers and women
have changed, are changing, and will change.

These three women
of the past, present, and future respectively
have my admiration and love.

Elizabeth Ellen Gething
Texas Pioneer Woman

Justice Patricia O. Alvarez
Fourth Court of Appeals, Texas Courts

Cierra Nicole
Beloved Granddaughter

CONTENTS

Acknowledgements   ix
Preface   xiii

I - GRAPPLING

1 - One Face of Fort Worth   1
2 - Another Face of Fort Worth   13
3 - The Bride's Homecoming   25
4 - Courage   33
5 - Breakfast—Texas Style   43
6 - Llano Estacado   53
7 - Community Church   61
8 - Taking Stock   71
9 - Accident   79
10 - Coming to Grips   87
11 - Charles Rath's Mercantile   91

II – THRASHING ABOUT

12 - Window in a Hole   105
13 - Root, Hog, or Die   119
14 - Mule Train, Mule Train   129
15 - Elizabeth's Journal   141
16 - Mobeetie on the Horizon   149
17 - Expecting   159
18 - Circle of Friends   165
19 - Enter Edward James   177
20 - Indomitable Women   187
21 - Deep Wounds   195
22 - Here Comes the Bride   201

III - RUBBING ALONG TOGETHER

23 - Proving up the Stock   209
24 - Return Trip   223
25 - Unexpected Visitor   235
26 - Put the Wind to Work   243
27 - Cost of Water   253
28 - Watch and Wait   261
29 - Shot across the Brow   273
30 - Fragile Relationships   281
31 - Trouble Nearby   291
32 - The Great War   303
33 - Marmalade Christmas   313
34 - Farewell Arthur   323
      Historical Endnotes and Comments   335

ACKNOWLEDGMENTS

Storytellers earned a special seat in any gathering of my friends and relatives. I admire the gifted storyteller. They have a place of honor in our culture. Elizabeth Ellen (Nana) Gething was one of those to whom I listened with my chin cupped in the palm of my hand. Hers was a fine art! Then, I thank my students on whom I practiced telling stories about Texas Panhandle history.

My personal thanks to many from whom Nana-stories were collected. My sister Judy Smith Neslage stayed with Nana one summer between college semesters while Nana recovered from an illness. Nana retold some of the stories Judy and I knew and presented new ones. Lynne (Followell) Cline, a treasured friend, reminded me of a story Nana told us about the time we graduated from Pampa High School. It became "Shot across the Brow." Lynne read for me along the way and read with valuable comments and suggestions before publication. My very special thanks and appreciation goes to W. E. (Bill) and Mary Ellen Gething-Jones, Nana's grandchildren; they were gracious with their time and met with me many times over the years and gave me oral histories and their insights as Nana's closest living relatives. Their participation was so essential, generous, and extensive that those details are included in the Historical Endnotes and

Comments. My niece Lori Roberts read a number of chapters and gave me encouragement when it was especially welcome.

When I first embarked on this project, I turned to Schreiner University in Kerrville, Texas, and took writing courses with Dr. Kathleen Hudson and Assistant Professor Sarah Hannay in its English Department.

I am blessed with membership in a group of writers. We listened to one another's written works and then commented, asked questions, and reflected upon everyone's in turn. My longest association is with Frances Lovett, R.N. and Rhonda Wiley-Jones, who recently published *At Home in the World*. That group extended to include Garland O'Quinn and George Fischer who published his trilogy of memoirs. Their friendship, encouragement, and support was essential.

Thanks to Donna Snow Robinson for patiently editing the rough draft and counseling me with grace and charm. Good friend and commercial media specialist Wendy Barber [fl1media.com] created my website and photographed Mel Amyx for the cover. Dr. R. Malcolm Brown, Jr., a family friend of the Gethings, is a director of research at the University of Texas, Austin, in the field of Botany; Malcolm graciously permitted the use of his photographs taken on a 2001 "Tour of the Gething Ranch" for my website. The model for the front cover of this book, Mel Amyx, keeps things running smoothly at the circulation desk of the Butt-Holdsworth Memorial Library and was perfect for the front cover; she is a "have gun, will travel" sort of woman.

These libraries and their staffs were accommodating, generous and delightful to work with. Both Fred R. Egloff, writer and librarian and Nan Stover, Research Library of Western Artists of America Museum in Kerrville, Texas, furnished materials. The staff of Butt-Holdsworth Memorial Library of Kerrville ordered books from the Inter Library Loan (ILL) and furnished its conference room for our writers' meetings. On trips back to the Texas Panhandle, Tonie Bolin, with the Lovett Memorial Library, offered their extensive services.

Collecting information and opportunities to see historic materials, I went to a number of museums. The president of the board of the McLean-Alanreed Historical Museum, Nita Riemer, opened up on a Monday and had articles waiting for me to view. Janeane White, Coordinator, of the Charles Goodnight Historical Center gave me a tour of the Goodnight House and grounds, supplied floor plans and photographs for references. Melba Corcoran, Old Mobeetie Texas Association, opened the archives of that fine museum and spent several pleasant hours with me searching for information needed. Becky W. Livingston, Curator of History for the Panhandle-Plains Historical Museum, introduced me to the research staff who gathered materials on windmills. Courtney N. Oxley, Director/Curator, of the White Deer Land Museum of Pampa, Texas, furnished a copy of a photograph of Elizabeth Gething and Vera LeFors, located information, and found books for my research.

This is the first story I remember hearing from 'Nana' Gething: It was about her elopement in 1896 with Arthur Gething to the Texas Panhandle. She told it to my sister, Judy Ann (Smith) Neslage, and me one evening while our parents were playing bridge with Nana's son, Edward and his wife, Lucile, in their house, a short walk from Nana's house on the Gething Ranch.

Rose Maureen (Smith) Hall
Circa 1944-45

Preface

My sister and I called her Nana. She was Elizabeth Ellen Smythe before she married and was then Mrs. Arthur Edward James Gething. Finally, she was called Nana by her granddaughter, Mary Ellen Gething-Jones, and her grandson, William Edward (Bill) Gething, many young people, and others for whom it was a term of endearment. However, her husband always called her 'Kate' a name she suffered throughout the twenty-two years of their marriage.

There is a family belief that Elizabeth's grandmother was a companion or acquaintance of England's strict Queen Victoria who shaped Elizabeth's education and training in the social graces. Whether there was a close association between Queen Victoria and Elizabeth's grandmother, Her Royal Majesty set British social standards during her reign throughout the British Empire that persisted for decades after her death.

Elizabeth eloped with the Welshman, Arthur Edward James Gething near the end of the Nineteenth Century. Little is known about their courtship and marriage. However, Arthur Gething immigrated to America in 1880 and at later date, about 1885, he established a ranch in the Texas Panhandle located near Mobeetie, the town that grew up beside Fort Elliott. Arthur Gething was nine years older than Elizabeth and once served as a barrister in the prestigious Queen's Court of London. In England, there are two tiers of lawyers: the *solicitor* who is not a member of the bar and who may only be heard in the lower courts and the *barrister* who is admitted to plead at the bar in superior courts.

Nana's grandchildren—Mary Ellen Gething-Jones and W. E. (Bill) Gething—assume their grandparents met during the social seasons at court. That is supported by a couple of my recollections. My sister, Judy, and I were pre-school children when Nana told us these stories of her earliest days in Texas; we heard them during WWII when Winston Churchill was in the news often. The first memory was that we once asked whether she knew Winston Churchill. Nana replied that she did, but she was not partial to him. Instead, she preferred his cousin who attended the balls they attended. The second indication that she attended royal balls is that Nana also told us how she brought beautiful ball gowns to

Texas in the anticipation of entertaining her husband's friends—lawyers and business men—and their families. The trains of those gowns were later used in the Texas Panhandle to make clothing for their son Edward.

Elizabeth and Arthur married, left England from the Southampton port, crossed the Atlantic on the steamship *St. Paul* and arrived in New York City, New York, on February 4, 1896. They stayed in New York City at the Astor Hotel before continuing their journey. Nana told us she was seasick during most of the passage and for that reason they stayed a few days in New York City before continuing their journey to the ranch. This is how I recall the story she told.

One evening as Mr. and Mrs. Gething chat in the dining room of the Astor Hotel, a woman across the way does something Elizabeth finds bizarre. Although she does not stare at the woman because it is bad form, she steals glances at this woman from time to time.

Elizabeth and Arthur Gething talk of the train trip they will take to Fort Worth. Elizabeth, always a curious soul, asks questions about the ranch and her new home and Arthur tells her more tales of the West. Still, she watches this woman throughout their conversation.

The waiter serves them a fresh salad that Arthur requests. It is a combination of pale green celery slices, chopped red apple, and fragrant walnut-halves coated in a creamy dressing. The salad's crisp flavors of autumn delight Elizabeth in these mid-winter days. She catches another glance of the woman who intrigues her.

This woman wears a shimmering cerulean gown. Her coiffure is stylish and elaborate and she sits erect on the first six inches of her chair. Each morsel she brings to her mouth in a dainty manner and she eats the meal in leisure. She is doing what proper ladies do at the dining table except for one thing.

There, the lady does it again! She lifts a full ear of corn to her mouth and bites into it. Butter drips from her chin. She wipes it away with her fingertips!

Elizabeth is aghast. In England, corn is fodder for farm animals and *only* farm animals. Ladies and gentlemen never eat corn. A lady uses her dinner linen to blot her mouth—not her fingertips. A breach of manners! *Incomprehensible behavior for a lady! As out of place as a pig in a parlor!*

"Arthur," says Elizabeth, "*who* is that lady across the hall in the blue silk gown?"

Arthur looks to identify the woman just in time to see her bite into the corn-on-the-cob.

"That…is Lady Astor," Arthur chokes. With a twinkle in his watering eyes he continues, "Kate, Americans are fond of eating corn. You may learn to enjoy it as much as Lady Astor does."

Not in my lifetime! Elizabeth rejects the thought.

Married women in England and America at this time had neither property rights nor voting rights and little protection under the law. American women did not secure franchise, the right to vote, until August 26, 1920, under the 19th Amendment to the U. S. Constitution. Elizabeth will live in

Texas more than two decades without voting rights or any property rights. This newlywed couple, Arthur and Elizabeth Gething, entered the new and challenging world of the Texas Panhandle toward the end of the Frontier Period and into the Settlement Period. After their emigration neither his nor her standing in the British class system, no matter how high or low, transferred with them to the United States of America excepting what they might make of it with their education, talents, and financial situation.

Almost as he [Charles Goodnight] spoke there hung over the Plains the shadow of the memorable drought of 1893 – 1895, which practically depopulated the country.

J. Evetts Haley, page 383
Charles Goodnight

1 - One Face of Fort Worth

The steam engine train hisses to a stop in Fort Worth in a stinging blast of dirt and sleet. Black smoke rolls out of the engine's smokestack and cinders fall all about. Along with other passengers, Arthur Gething and his bride, Elizabeth, debark with foreboding.

Arthur feels uneasy about his business partner, Roger Stone, whom he left to manage their fledgling bank. Elizabeth dreads to find what their lodging accommodations will be. As they advance across the country, those seem ever more dreadful. Arthur leaves to claim from the baggage car their many personal effects: several portmanteaux, her sidesaddle, Arthur's crated foxhound, several trunks, and other smaller parcels. She is weary and her eyes smart and sting from battling the grit and ice pellets whipping against her.

Looking on the collection Arthur retrieves, she insists upon checking the condition of her sidesaddle case. The baggage handler tossed it into a railroad car without a proper storage device upon which to rest it.

"Mr. Gething, I fear for the condition of my sidesaddle. Will you ask the porter to check it and make arrangements to find it a temporary perch among our baggage?" Elizabeth requests.

"Kate, there is no time for frivolities. Saddles are made to withstand rough treatment, and yours is in the case. There are arrangements to make for lodging this evening. I must locate my partner, Mr. Stone, as soon as we register in the hotel." says Arthur.

Elizabeth bristles, *Damn! I hate that he calls me 'Kate.' Earlier I accepted it as his way to tease me. Now it annoys me.* She does not answer, ignores his fit of temper, and moves to supervise the collection of their belongings.

"Will you find us a carriage so that we may load our baggage," she says.

"We can manage well enough with one of the streetcars!" Arthur says.

Elizabeth peers down the unpaved roadway adjacent to the depot and shields her eyes from the dirt swirling around and the sleet spitting from above. She sees a mule-drawn streetcar coming toward the train station; its iron-rimmed wheels grind through the ruts and the car hobbles down the street.

Elizabeth thinks, *Great Beelzebub! Loading this pile into that blundering car will just about end my resolve to face off Arthur's high dudgeon.*

"Mr. Gething, you are no longer traveling light and by yourself. Please have the courtesy to accommodate my need for a bit of comfort," she insists above the racket.

"By God, Kate, you would strain the patience of band of angels. Fort Worth is not London; it is an East Texas cow town and as raw as they come. To ride in a carriage here, you must own one,…and I do not. We will travel by streetcar," he says and he walks away muttering to himself. His face flushes.

Elizabeth thinks, *Well, I will leave him to load the entire lot. You would think that hound is more precious than gold the way he caters to it.*

The driver lends Elizabeth a hand up into the passenger car. The streetcar is open, cold, and drafty. New arrivals squeeze in beside her bumping and jostling her and the already-seated passengers in the process.

Arthur addresses the driver, "My man, at your invitation I will join you up top."

The streetcar is so heavily loaded that it is the only possible place for him to sit. There is a tacit agreement between them. The driver snaps the reins, shouts to his mules and the streetcar moves away toward the business center of Fort Worth.

Elizabeth pulls the hood of her cloak around her head and shoulders for some protection against the elements. With her eyes protected by the cloak, she looks about this residential part of Fort Worth. The houses are obscured somewhat by low afternoon light and the dirt blown about, but they are humble, modest dwellings, and some garden space surrounds each one. Some are attractive; others, left to nature. The town's population takes shelter inside; she sees no one on the streets. A blown newspaper goes rolling past. Here and there a window is lit. It is curious to her how small the cottage windows are.

As they rumble along, the scene begins to change toward a more industrial or business area of the city. A wooden overhead protrusion extends over the storefronts that protect passersby on the walkways from rain, sleet, or snow, and the foot-traffic area beneath is a boardwalk. She sees three advertisement signs: Meredith Hotel, Pharmacy, and Trunks. Most of the buildings they pass are two-storied suggesting they may be businesses operated by families whose living quarters are on the top floor. However, some of the stores are ground floor only.

Elizabeth speaks to the woman seated next to her and whom she recognizes as a passenger from the train. "Do you know how much distance we will travel? My husband is sitting with the driver, and we have just arrived. Our hotel is in the center of Fort Worth."

"Yes, we have a bit more discomfort to endure," replies the lady, "You will note when we are near the business district for the buildings are much more substantial. Fort Worth boasts the second electric streetcar system in the entire country and we are learning to call the cars 'trolleys.' Notice its rails run down the middle of the street. It is a much better system for travel but inconvenient when you travel with luggage and trunks. Taking this mule-drawn streetcar is best because the driver takes you to your door."

"Thank you for your information. Traveling in America is a new experience for me. Every change of conveyance surprises me because I come from London where it is different," Elizabeth says.

She turns again to the street scene and sees men moving about holding onto their head-gear to keep from losing their big western hats in the strong wind. The men walk at a brisk pace and seem to have an important meeting or engagement, but it may only be to find a warm shelter. She pulls herself as deeply into her street-length wool cape as she can to retain her body heat. The roadway changes and the passengers no longer sway from side to side, and the streetcar is not dropping hard into large street cavities causing them to lurch about. Instead, there is a steady rumbling vibration because they are rolling on a brick road. Many buildings are substantial ones made of brick and stone rather than wooden structures they passed minutes ago. The driver takes side streets to deposit his passengers in their hotels or residences, and each stop means unloading luggage, trunks, and bundles. The abrasive blowing dirt subsides some and the sleet no longer spits from above.

At one stop, the woman seated beside her motions to a rather imposing building.

"There is the courthouse and it also houses our post office. It is a very fine building and one I recommend you visit," she says.

"Yes, I see it is a building of significant architecture. Is that a church just beyond?" says Elizabeth.

"You are sharp-eyed! Saint Patrick's Church is just there. We are proud of our red sandstone courthouse for it serves many purposes. In addition to the post office, the federal offices are located in it, and there is a weather station under the roof. The best-supplied pharmacy in all of Fort Worth is to your right. They stock everything you may need," says the traveler. "Excuse me, I have not introduced myself; I am Mrs. Sullivan. My house is the next stop…just one street beyond the Courthouse. I pray your visit to our fair city is pleasant."

"You have been very helpful and gracious. I am Mrs. Gething. My husband and I go on to the Panhandle of Texas and the Gething ranch," says Elizabeth.

"Mrs. Gething, I admit my curiosity. You spoke of this as your first trip to America and also of going to the Gething ranch with your husband. Is there more to tell?"

"Yes, Mrs. Sullivan, in January, Mr. Gething and I married in London and I travel to my new home."

"Congratulations to Mr. Gething and best wishes to you. I hope you have a safe journey."

Elizabeth helps Mrs. Sullivan collect some of her small parcels. They wave to one another as Mrs. Sullivan moves toward her mansion. Her staff braves the nasty weather, and the men collect her luggage while she enters her home.

While stopped, Arthur joins Elizabeth and surveys their luggage stacked altogether in the rear of the streetcar. The driver and Arthur had secured the crated foxhound to the rear of the streetcar. The remainder of their baggage along with her sidesaddle case surrounds them.

"Did you and Mrs. Sullivan enjoy a visit during the ride? She is the wife of an influential businessman. He owns and operates Fort Worth's packing and shipping plant. It was a revolutionary idea in its beginning. They ship meat—fowl and pork—in refrigerated railroad cars back east and to points in between. One day I hope they will slaughter and ship beef and save cattlemen the long trail drives that are the only way to move the beeves to market. Even from the ranch, there may be a time I can load my cattle from a shipping point closer than Dodge City, Kansas," says Arthur, but he shows no further interest in talking to his wife.

By the time they arrive at their hotel—the Henderson—it is late afternoon; Arthur makes quick work of giving the porter instructions to put their personal luggage in their room and the rest in hotel storage. He requests that the porter see Elizabeth to their room because he is off to the livery stable where he will leave the sidesaddle and his foxhound; then, he will search for his partner.

Elizabeth settles herself in the room and takes time to refresh herself before going downstairs for a cup of tea. She notices a handbill in the lounge that interests her. It announces a symphony to begin at week's end. As they travel through this vacant region, she grows apprehensive. The poster about the symphony performance reassures her. *Cow town, indeed! Here in Fort Worth, there are cultural refinements.*

The tea room is cozy; one other guest sits at a table. Elizabeth selects a place near the window and studies her surrounds.

A matronly woman wearing a starched white apron over a uniform approaches her table and says, "What'll you have?"

"A pot of tea and some dainty to go with it, please. What do you offer?"

"There are several pies fresh from the oven today …apple, apricot, and peach. Which will it be?"

"I was hoping for a trifle with fruit sauce." She savors the memory of that treat—sponge cake layered with custard and fruit and sherry. "Pie is more substantial than I want."

"You're English, I guess. We don't serve trifle; I'm afraid, but, the peach pie is 'specially good today. C'n I bring you a slice?"

"Please and make it a small portion. My husband and I just arrived; we will probably dine early this evening. Now, can you tell me about the type of musical entertainments you have here? I saw an announcement in the lobby."

"Don't go to 'em myself. There's too much work 'round here. The fine ladies and gentlemen do attend, but there is little I c'n tell you 'bout 'em. 'Scuse me, Ma'am."

Resolving to pursue the matter further, Elizabeth surveys the small dining room. It is clean and Spartan. White tablecloths and napkins are arranged neatly on the tables. She inhales and relaxes, smelling the roast beef and cabbage baking in the kitchen. She notices the only other diner in the room; he is a short rotund fellow. He wears a hat with an exaggerated crown and brim. She chuckles to herself because the hat seems exceedingly large for him. Perhaps she can arrange an introduction to one of the lady guests and learn more of the symphony and opera entertainments displayed on the billboards in the lobby.

The wait-servant returns with a chubby yellow teapot, its matching cup and saucer, and a dish of peach pie. She smiles and places her serving tray on Elizabeth's table and arranges the dishes.

"I'm Molly O'Connor and happy to take care of anything else you need," she smiles.

"It will help if you introduce me to one of your lady guests who may be able to enlightenment me about the musical events in Fort Worth."

"It'd be my pleasure. But there's no one 'bout right now with your same interest. Be keepin' it in mind though."

Elizabeth takes note of the serving before her. *Ahh! Aroma of tea. Swirl of cream. Moisture rises to my face. Nothing erases the cares of the day like a good cup of tea! The peach pie is satisfactory. Entirely too sweet. Americans do love their sugary desserts. Thanks for the small pleasures of life!*

"Thank you! The pie is wonderfully spicy and…quite sweet."

"Welcome, Ma'am." Molly beams and departs.

Elizabeth relishes the quiet teatime and feels restored when she returns to their room.

I am aching for the company of my sister! Where would she be? What would she be doing? Nighttime in London, Alice will dream in her comfortable bed. Imagine awaking once again in my feather bed in the morning with a crackling fire burning in the grate. Hetty would be in to help me dress, brush out, and arrange my hair before I go down to breakfast and join Alice and Grandmother.

I must think ahead of meeting my maid servant on the ranch. Does Mr. Gething have a good kitchen staff and housekeeper? Will I have to school them to my liking? Will they welcome me as his bride and be attentive? Too many questions! They scramble one's thoughts! After we arrive, I will soon know. I hope to be respected by our servants and fair to them as well. Arthur is not here to keep me company so I will make an entry in my journal.

> Travel was arduous today and the weather, foul. Arthur was never attentive and he left almost as soon as we arrived. I was angry about his concern for his partner and his need to locate him straight away.
>
> On our ride to the hotel, I met a Mrs. Sullivan, who was engaging. She spoke proudly of the city of Fort Worth touting its Courthouse and electric street car system. She cannot have been much in Europe or our precious British Isle or she would know both are ordinary.
>
> Mr. Gething tells me constantly that this is a new country and that I should not be critical. It is the land in which we will make our fortune and our lives. Oh, to be in my new home and not merely traveling toward it. My husband does not remember it is Valentine's Day and I am having a grand pout.
>
> February 14, 1896

Tomorrow I may take a trolley about the city. Will it be improper for me to go unattended? Arthur will not be interested, but the conversation with Mrs. Sullivan sparks my interest. I may ride the trolley through downtown until I see something of interest, get off to explore, and then catch the next trolley. This idea reminds me of my last trip to Paris with Alice when we had a similar plan and had some rollicking adventures in spite of our chaperone.

My favorite Paris memory was when Alice and I yelled and waved to warn a lorry driver he was about to back into an elegant shop window. The dismissive driver ignored us and crashed into the expensive display window. We turned heel and walked away laughing and tossing our heads at the embarrassed driver.

Arthur is still away when the electric lights of Fort Worth come on across the city. Elizabeth watches from her hotel window until she tires of the scene. She orders a bath brought up and enjoys its luxury because bathing on the train was only at a wash stand, and there was no privacy. After housemaids remove the tub, she reads from her collection of English Romantic poets for an hour and retires.

Mr. Gething does not return for an intimate meal together in their room as she expects. She waits beyond serving hours in the hotel. She thinks of no reason to explain her husband's delay in returning. Having his partner join them for dinner here would be better than this. He has sent no word of his delay or excuse for it. She tosses and turns on the bed.

As the night deepens, Elizabeth thinks; *Mr. Gething and Mr. Stone must be celebrating their reunion at The White Elephant saloon we passed on the way to the hotel. In London, Arthur spoke of it.*

The exhaustion of the day's travel overtakes her worries, and she falls asleep to dream of her new home. Mrs. Sullivan's mansion drifts through the dream and then subtle changes occur as the Victorian architecture replaces the features of the American mansion with a Victorian style she admires in London. She is in the entrance hall surrounded by the staff in her new home. Arthur makes introductions, several maids bob curtseys and the gentlemen bow to her. Her housekeeper welcomes her and offers a tour through the separate halls.

Arthur engages in business in another and entirely different sector of Fort Worth.

[B]y 1889, the notorious half acre of sin for sale [Hell's Half Acre of Fort Worth] was virtually shut down.

But it refused to die.

Caleb Pirtle, III; and Ellen S. Blakley, ed., page 60
Fort Worth: The Civilized West

2 - Another Face of Fort Worth

Arthur heads to the stable thinking; *Kate is going to be a disaster for me; she is a cosseted woman with no stomach for the West and she does not understand my opportunity in Texas. I can never do as well in England.*

He shoulders her sidesaddle case and leads his new foxhound down the street to the stable. *Why I thought, it would be pleasant to wed an intelligent, witty woman escapes me. She turned harridan on me!*

The blustery weather with its combination of fine sleet and dirt slamming into him compounds his volcanic mood. He jerks on the hound viciously and very nearly topples a passing man.

"Think you own the walkway? Watch where you go!" snarls the tall, angular man in buckskins as he regains his balance and shoves Arthur out of the way.

Arthur storms into the stable and thrusts his hound and saddle case on the stable boy.

"This is a valuable hound from the best breed in England. See that he is bedded down in a proper space and well fed. He will be boarded here for a week or longer. The saddle case is for my wife. Secure it well," he says and turns back out into the street.

"Mister! This here is a stable. We ain't got no room for no hound!" says the stable boy. He receives no reply.

Arthur sets his course for what is known in Fort Worth as 'Hell's Half Acre.' It is where cattlemen, outlaws, cowboys, and hustlers go for the excitement of action disapproved by society.

Men die here, and their murderers are not brought to justice under the law. Instead, it is justice by Law of the West: if wronged, a man gives a public warning to his violator that he intends to take any measures including killing if his adversary persists in the named injury against him. Then, the wronged man may punish, even murder him, with justification.

If men lie dead in alleyways, rumors abound, and the most prominent men of the Acre act as an unofficial jury. They may know the beater or murderer whom they consider the avenger or, if they hold a minority opinion of the situation, duck their heads and raise no objection. It is a dangerous place. Official lawmen seldom enter this part of Fort Worth and let the residents handle their disputes.

When Arthur Gething first arrived, he opened a law office to give advice and pen legal documents, but he failed to secure sufficient clientele. The rough crowd of men living in the Acre ridiculed his tailored British suits and derby hat; they made coarse comments about his manhood. Unlettered men bullied him with malignant humor and vilified his clipped and precise English. He met them fist-to-fist as a college-trained pugilist but lost to these no-holds-barred-street fighters.

With few clients, he encouraged Mr. Roger Stone, an attorney, to become his partner in a real estate and banking venture. It succeeded where the law practice did not and since then Arthur divides his time between his business in Fort Worth and his ranch.

Now Arthur searches for his partner to claim funds he left on deposit for the final leg of the journey to the ranch with his bride. He expects to find him playing poker at their favorite saloon in this disrespectable part of Fort Worth.

Arthur enters the marginally acceptable O'Sullivan Saloon. Tom Morgan spots him and strides dead-center toward him.

"You ol' Son-of-a-Gun, I thought you'd run off with my entire bank deposit!" Tom says.

"Why, my man, would you think that?" Arthur says.

"Hell, I've been searchin' high and low for either you or Stone for weeks now. Some said you'd gone off to England to bring back a bride, but Stone, we hear, left for Australia. Everyone figured we'd been robbed," Tom says.

"Stone is gone? I left him to tend the business," says Arthur.

"Oh, I reckon he tended it all right! Everything is buttoned up tight as…," says Tom. Arthur's sudden silence and drained expression stop Tom mid-sentence.

Tom begins again. "This is a blow! What's the story? My…."

Arthur surges into the street without answering Tom or showing any regard for traffic or other pedestrians; he heads down the boardwalk to the nearby building he and Stone leased for their banking business. He is cold and damp with fear when he arrives at the doorway. Inset in the door is a decorative glass panel on which is this note: OUT OF BUSINESS.

The Knave! Ready to explode with fury, Arthur takes gulps of the cold air and slumps to the boards. For a devastating interval of time, he cannot begin to think how to act. There is no remedy for Roger Stone's disappearance for Arthur took a chance to involve him in the partnership and an even greater risk leaving him alone with their business. But there was no one else in whom to place his trust. *Damn Stone's soul! If I could put my hands on him, I would thrash him.*

Arthur assumes the worst about Stone. That so, there is no time to waste on finding Stone, who is likely an ocean away. Arthur's predicament is critical.

Not enough for the rest of the journey to Mobeetie. What in hell am I going to do now? He pulls out a roll of cash and counts his reserves. *Lady Luck, smile on me as never before!*

He knows a back alley place deep in Hell's Half Acre where his small reserve of cash will seem a fortune. If his luck is good, he may yet overcome this.

Arthur unlocks the door of his failed bank and goes to a back room and changes his British style derby and his suit and vest for a coarse pair of pants and homespun shirt. He pushes his arms into a heavy woolen jacket and pulls on a hat that is slouchy, but somewhat like the hats worn by cattlemen. Its brim is narrow, and its crown of a modest depth compared with those most often worn in this part of Fort Worth. He intends to win some cash, if lucky, at the poker tables tonight. He needs time to put some, even all, of his properties in the Acre up for sale. He pours and swallows a glass of whiskey and then fills his flask from the bottle. The street is dark when he leaves the office. No one is about.

His first stop is not the poker parlors, but it is to visit Fanny LaRue's house. She may be able to tell him where he can find buyers for the properties he owns in the Acre for she knows what happens and keeps an ear to all the gossip here. When he lived in Fort Worth, he gave her sound legal advice on her businesses and other investment matters; he believes she will return the favor.

Fanny spots him from across the parlor where she is entertaining a group of men he knows and her ladies. Interest in him is evident in the group. Gossip travels faster than the Texas wind.

"Well, Arthur Gething, we seldom see you! It is longer than I can recall. How is it you are about this night?" Fanny says.

Brass Murdock says, "Tom, told us you were back. I expect you got the surprise of your life that Stone left."

"I am somewhat puzzled for I depended on my partner to have everything in good shape when I returned," says Arthur.

"Any idea of what has happened?" Brass says.

"Only hear-say! I shall sort it out soon and before I leave for the ranch. My plan was to stay here with my bride for a fortnight, but that may change depending on what I learn."

Murdock seems satisfied with his response and Arthur turns to Fanny. "Miss LaRue, I need a word with you?" says Arthur.

"Excuse me, Ladies and Gentlemen. Enjoy the entertainment and drinks at the bar. I will rejoin you after I visit with Mr. Gething," says Fanny taking Arthur's arm and retreating to her waiting room off the parlor.

"What is your trouble, Arthur?" says Fanny.

"My bride, Kate, is resting in our hotel, but she does not know of this situation. I believe Stone absconded with the entire assets of the bank, I am forced to sell properties until I can cover the accounts of my clients and depositors. Do you know of investors who may wish to buy property for cash?" says Arthur. "I am not interested in selling on a mortgage at interest or trades, only cash."

"Hmm, well you hold some desirable properties. I need to give this some thought and speak with a few who may be looking to buy outright. Your holdings are well known, but it will be difficult to identify the property without giving you away. Should I keep your name in confidence as much as possible?" says Fannie.

"I know I can count on you and your discretion. Keeping my name out of it will be helpful until I determine in what financial situation Stone left me," says Arthur. "I would avoid being tarred and feathered or worse," says Arthur.

"And your bride, how will you manage affairs with her?"

"Her pride and temper match my own. A tar and feathering may be mild to what I face with her. She is high-born and well-educated and is not pleased with the Wild West," says Arthur. "I am in a damnable situation, but you need not worry your adorable head about me, for I believe the situation is manageable."

Arthur embraces Fanny warmly and speaks of his gratitude. Then he returns to the men and women that he and Fanny just left. He acknowledges the group, excuses himself and charges out the door. He braces himself against the cold outside, contemplates the route to the best location for raising funds by playing poker and sets out to a known location.

Reaching a popular hang-out of the young men who work for cattlemen and may be easily relieved of their earnings and least likely to be advanced poker players, he opens the door to Bret's Place. The stench of stale beer and urine well up from the warm rooms. Unwashed bodies and tobacco stench wafting from spittoons envelop him as he edges through the crowd. He is alert to the postures, stances, and expressions of the men. To give himself time to size up the situation, he finds a place at the bar and orders a whiskey.

His eyes grow more accustomed to the dark interior, and he spots poker tables in the rear of the back room. He locates one table with an empty seat backed up to the wall. It is the position he seeks. At such a table, he will see anyone entering and can identify anyone who might be a threat to his purpose: winning money with little effort while remaining anonymous. He pulls his hat down further over his forehead and goes to that table.

Luck seems to smile; he learns that they are looking for another person to sit in their game because the previous player gambled all his money and closed.

"The name's Ed," Arthur says using the diminutive of his middle name Edward rather than the one he would use in other locations. "If you will, I would join your game."

The young men are cautious for there is something off-putting about this stranger with an odd manner of speaking English, and he is a bit too polished for their tastes. He dresses in clothing as rough as theirs, but it is still foreign.

"Whose outfit do ya ride with?" says the bold one to his left.

"I am looking for a new outfit. My last outfit just went broke. You men recommend any cattleman looking for a rider?" says Ed. He hopes that as an older man pretending to need their assistance, they will be flattered enough to override their suspicious tendencies. And he is careful to address them as 'men,' not 'boys.'

"We might. Who you worked for?" the cowboy asks.

"Bob Cator, Billy Dixon, Charles Rath, and Colonel B. B. Groom and his son, Harry. The last man was Will Jones, a small stock farmer, a friend who is down on his luck. I would be surprised if you know of him," says Ed.

"Never heard of your friend! That Groom bunch was the most easy suckered cattlemen in the whole of Texas; they didn't know nothin' 'bout cows. Did you help 'em go broke?"

"No, Colonel Groom and his son needed no help spending money; they spent it all on fine mansions, colored servants, and thoroughbred horses as if it could grow on tumbleweed," says Ed.

"What's became of your friend?" another of the men asked.

"He's gone back to Wellington to move his family back east. Left this morning," says Ed.

The men about the table relax and begin offering their names. It does not escape Ed's notice that they are deep in their cups, and the edge of their clear-headedness wears off. It is the very group he hoped to locate. However, he plays a couple of hands just to size up their card playing skills and is confident he can leave with the cash he requires.

At the end of the night, he wins enough for his immediate purpose. He does not play an aggressive game because he fears they will question his story, so he loses enough hands to eliminate any lingering suspicion. To complete the ruse, he takes away the name of their boss who is due to leave Fort Worth in two days. They leave on companionable terms.

In the morning, he can pay his hotel bill in advance for a week and give the owner of the livery stable cash against his estimated stay. Soon he must face his wife and find a way to avoid her tomorrow while he learns whatever Fanny can tell him and check the books at his closed bank. He owns some desirable properties, and it is a matter of being a tough and crafty negotiator in order to get the full amount he needs. He hopes to finish this business in one week to ten days. He cannot afford to leave town without satisfying his depositors because he will inevitably need to do business here in the future.

Back at the hotel, he finds his wife sleeping soundly. He is careful not to disturb her and falls into a deep slumber beside her.

Elizabeth awakes well into the night because Arthur is thrashing about and grinding his teeth and uttering curses. She is alarmed and listens as Arthur talks in his sleep.

She thinks, *He is not acting like a man married so short a time. Something is afoot! His searching for his partner as soon as we arrived, his returning long after I was asleep, and his reeking of whiskey: all this is unnerving.*

Elizabeth listens hoping Arthur will reveal what happened, but his speech is indistinct and she is unable to make anything of it. Finally, she sleeps again.

At breakfast the next morning, Elizabeth begins the conversation.

"I trust you and Mr. Stone enjoyed a pleasant evening together." says Elizabeth. "And what are our plans for the day?"

"I was unable to find my partner last night and I looked until every establishment was closing. There is a rumor that he left for Australia. I can believe it because he wanted to join a relative there even before I left for England. I must investigate that today," says Arthur.

Well, this throws some light on the problem. "I did wonder what kept you out late last night," says Elizabeth. "I am interested in exploring Fort Worth today if you are engaged elsewhere. I can ride the electric street car and stop here and there to visit the shops and parks. Of course, I will need some money for the trip."

"Shop and explore the entire day, but stay on the street on either side of the electric street car route. Do not wander off on the side streets! I will make arrangements for someone to accompany you. Be careful and return an hour before the stores and shops begin to close. I supplied a handsome sum earlier; it will be enough for your outing," Arthur says.

"Do you suspect foul play from Mr. Stone?" she says.

"Kate, this is none of your affair. I will see you this evening for our meal here in the hotel," says Arthur. "There is much for me to accomplish. Good day!"

There is trouble, but Mr. Gething does not confide in me. If he knew his partner was going to be a problem, it explains his outbursts of temper yesterday. But it does not explain the scruffy clothes he deposited here last night. How much can I trust my husband? He is stingy with his money now, but he was generous before. What happened? My plans will keep me occupied all day; otherwise, I might fret alone in the hotel.

Arthur and Elizabeth go their separate ways during the following days. Arthur solves his financial woes for the time being. Elizabeth shops and explores Fort Worth with *Mrs.*

Fanny LaRue whom Arthur introduces as a refined widow woman of his acquaintance to chaperone her.

Neither Arthur nor Elizabeth is pleased with the delay but, for different reasons.

"The first thing brought before your notice out west is that a [single] man has all the woman's work to do as well as his own."

Thomas W. Cutrer, page 101
The English Texans

3 - The Bride's Homecoming

Arthur says they are near his ranch. Elizabeth struggles for her seat riding sidesaddle on a mule that Arthur named Kate. Riding away from Mobeetie, she only gets relief by alternating between the driving the wagon and riding the mule. No lady rides astride a saddle as Arthur rides Spider.

The gait of the animal she rides jars her and every mile challenges her will to continue. In truth, she wished to go back to London from Fort Worth, but she lacked the price of the return voyage.

Her breath forms a gray mist on this bitter February afternoon. The thick brown wool cape, scarf and riding costume she wears fail to protect her from the snow-chilled wind that gushes through this prairie. But even in these circumstances, her posture announces she is a lady.

The land before her is unchanged from the land behind her. It is not flat but rugged and remarkably treeless.

They traveled by train in some comfort out of Fort Worth. Even then there were interesting changes in the scenery. From Pampa, they took a stagecoach; it is the mail route from Tascosa to Mobeetie. The coach perches on springs that cause its passengers to catapult from their seats when the driver dodges off the treacherous trail to avoid animals and washouts. When the coach detours from the trail and crosses rugged prairie, its clump grasses increase the roughness. Elizabeth believes the wheels of the coach are square. Because she wears a fashionable and tight-laced corset, she is twice miserable. No one visits, for everyone grips any stable means of support.

They arrive in Mobeetie after dark, eat a cold meal, and Elizabeth sleeps before she draws covers about her head.

In the morning, Arthur arranges transportation to the ranch, but Elizabeth does not rouse from the bed for several hours. Meanwhile, Arthur orders provisions for the ranch at the mercantile, a general store. After a hearty breakfast, they leave for the ranch.

After claiming his prized mount, Spider, at the livery stable, Arthur saddles the mule he bought for Elizabeth. Spider walks on a lead alongside the team and Arthur drives the wagon. Seated upon her sidesaddle, Elizabeth will ride the mule that her husband named Kate alongside the team.

She longs for the comforts of London or the Astor Hotel. Their train ride across the American heartland was challenging, but absence of services or hospitality on the sparsely settled Texas Panhandle plain was so foreign that she was both miserable and disdainful.

Homesteaders own the shacks in which they spent the nights, but their unknown hosts might never return, or the homestead family may be away for a few days, or a bachelor might be lodging with neighbors all winter. Doors to these shacks are open and travelers are welcome to the shelter. The traveler must replenish the fuel, feed the chickens, and wash the dishes.

A much-loved tale told by residents of the Texas Panhandle is of a homesteader who put a lock on the door of his shack. Two passers-by took extreme offense! They shot the lock off the door and dropped it on the prairie miles away; although, they did not need lodging.

Arthur halts and sweeps his hand to the north. Elizabeth stops alongside.

"Well, Kate, we spend tonight here," he announces.

Elizabeth winces at the name her husband uses to address her. *Kate!* She feels that he ridicules her with that name. The leading female role in *The Taming of the Shrew* is Kate as she knows. When Arthur courted her in London, she accepted it as a pet name with which she thought Arthur paid tribute to her independent nature. She begins to suspect there are undertones with which the name is used to annoy her. He may even call her Kate to establish that her place in their relationship is subservient.

They are facing a small shack. Elizabeth sighs. *Another night in a crude hut! I long to be home and stop traveling.*

Arthur steps down from the wagon and leaves it, but mounts Spider for the final distance to the shack and the lean-to jutting from the northeast side of it. Once Arthur leaves his horse, Spider enters the lean-to and whiffles and snuffles his muzzle into the feed box.

Elizabeth kicks the mule with determination; it yields to her firm handling and stops at the entrance of the shack.

"Mr. Gething, help me dismount!" *I am damned if I add 'please' to that command.* He comes to stand beside her; she grabs his shoulders and descends awkwardly for her every joint is stiff. On level ground, she stands a half-head taller than Arthur.

"You address me as 'Kate' and eschew my Christian name, Elizabeth. If you do so because you believe I will succumb to your will as Kate did in Mr. Shakespeare's *The Taming of the Shrew*, you are mistaken."

"Kate…, I am head of the house and you will remember it! Come inside."

Arthur pushes Elizabeth through the door. The shack has no window; its black interior stops her. Arthur steps around her and lights an oil lamp on the table chasing the dark away with an ease born of familiarity.

Dust filters down from the roof supported by cottonwood saplings covered with straw and sod. Stale smoke and fine dust burn their nostrils and cause their eyes to tear. The woodstove is cold. Elizabeth chokes and sneezes; Arthur hacks up phlegm and spits.

She sees five items of furniture in this dimly lit room: a woodstove, a table, two benches and a bed. A chamber pot is under the bed. A fuel box stands in a corner near the woodstove and some shipping crates serve as cabinets and shelves on either side of the woodstove. A flimsy stove pipe juts through the roof. A water barrel rests on one of the shipping crates and a dipper hooks over its side. Clothing pegs protrude from the wooden framework at the entrance and a jumble of cast-offs lie in a heap in one corner near the doorway. Worn faded quilts covering the bed are the only softening feature.

Arthur goes confidently to the woodstove and carries kindling, dried cow chips, euphemistically referred to as 'prairie coal,' and sticks of wood from the fuel box. Elizabeth is so chilled she trembles and she watches the tedium of starting a small blaze as twigs and prairie coal are consumed bit by bit. Arthur moves through this shack finding coffee pot, coffee, and tin cups without searching for anything. She doubts she will be warm again.

With the fire set, Arthur leaves the shack to tend the animals.

The next morning Arthur announces, "Well, Kate, this is it."

The gradual decline of civilization and its comforts did not prepare Elizabeth for this, for her hopes and eagerness for the 'fine house' that Arthur promised her rests on her trust in him and expectations she formed in London. The full weight of his words falls into a chasm of disbelief and then erupts as a volcano of anger.

"You brought me on this grueling journey to this shack! Why, in God's name, am I here? This is not the fine house I was promised to manage?" Elizabeth storms and rails at him berating the surroundings.

He turns his back to her and feeds the fire. He counts on her vulnerability and dependence on him in this isolated place to subdue her.

Silence follows killing all that is sacred.

"Kate," Arthur growls, "You married a gambler and an adventurer. You like adventure as much as I. Whether you appreciate it, you are a gambler, too, for you agreed to the elopement. I won this land in a poker game in Fort Worth. It is a prime piece of land because it has two good springs. They flow, year in and year out. They did not cease once in the recent drought. The grass is excellent for cattle. My inheritance gets good interest in London; I improve the ranch by hard work and by investing the interest in it.

"You want your own home. This is not what you expected, but I knew you would not come otherwise. This is a lonely place as you will learn. I want companionship, a helper, and sons. That is why you are here; I need you."

Elizabeth collapses in a faint; Arthur has betrayed her. How long will she need to come to terms with her grief?

Arthur leaves the next morning while Elizabeth is asleep and he goes without a word to her. He drives the wagon toward the north pasture with Spider trailing alongside the team. He expects to find his ranch workers—Jake, Bob, and Green—whom he unfailingly refers to as 'cow-servants.' Finding his first man, Arthur halts alongside Jake, who is checking the bunch of cows for any sign of injury or disease.

"Jake, did we lose any this winter? What is their condition?" Arthur inquires.

"Mr. Gething, glad to see you! None are lost and the heifers are winterin' well enough. No blizzards so far! Hay could hold 'til spring. Do you want to check 'em?" Jake asks.

Mr. Gething does not mention whether he has come home with his bride, but his men learned his intentions to wed before he left by means of the gossip of their boss's friends and acquaintances. Jake is curious but does not inquire.

"I will inspect them when I return. I am on my way back to Pampa to pick up my new foxhound and extra baggage. I expect to be back in a few days."

"Did you find everything satisfactory at your place? I've laid in a good stock of fuel. No sign of anyone around lately! Bob and Green are out looking for strays."

"You will need to replenish the fuel on a regular basis now. Mrs. Gething is going to need your help with other chores. I will see you when I return!"

Arthur dismisses Jake and drives the team southwest toward Pampa. Jake grins at the casually dropped information of Mr. Gething's marriage.

Leaving Pampa and on the return trip to the ranch, Arthur hunts with the new foxhound and carries the rest of their baggage in the wagon leaving Elizabeth alone to accept her humiliating circumstance. He assures himself that this action will succeed if his words did not.

Arthur tests his new foxhound's hunting skills. There is small game—quail, jackrabbits, and prairie chickens.

Besides, Spider and the new hound are a matter of pride for they came at a price and provide entertainment for him. He makes opportunities to impress his neighbors along the way back to his ranch and he plans to pick up a game of poker with friends. He wants to flush out a coyote. Hunting them is a sport many men of the region enjoy. Arthur hopes to spot a den of them or one hunting alone. Adult coyote pelts are a valuable source of supplementary cash because the big cattlemen's associations pay four dollars each. He will take his time returning to the shack; he is in no hurry to face his bride.

Without justice, courage is weak.

Poor Richard's Almanac [1734] January

4 - Courage

Elizabeth awakes to sunlight edging around the door. She arises from a homemade bed and the straw-filled mattress rustles; turning, she faces the center of the shack. The quilts and hard pillows smell of wood smoke, musk, and sweat. Her neck is sore and her muscles scream. She does not remember how she came to bed. She still wears her riding habit, but Arthur removed her shoes and cloak; it disturbs her. There is a keening of the wind. Is this a nightmare? She needs to relieve herself and remembers the chamber pot she saw under the bed. *If only this were a nightmare....*

She sits on the bed with every muscle of her body protesting, locates her shoes, and laces them. Going to the woodstove for some warmth, first she makes her toilet and then stirs the ashes hoping there are enough coals to revive the fire. There are none. In spite of the malodor of the bed; it is warm and she slips into it keeping on her shoes. There she listens for any sound that Arthur is about. The wind moans. She listens intently for a long stretch of time and hears nothing to indicate Arthur is here. *Thank God! The coward has fled!* She aches for the companionship of Grandmother and Alice. She pushes this shack away from her thoughts and concentrates on memories of her London home where Alice and she sat in their cozy sitting room doing needlework. Grandmother disciplined her many times for her misbehavior with tasks of embroidering samplers. She took out more stitches than ever became a part of the finished pieces. Today, embroidering a sampler in that sitting room would be a welcome pursuit.

Tears leak from her eyes. She catches herself in a bitter laugh remembering the time her governess chastised her for flirting with a handsome Catholic priest who went to and fro in the park across the street from their house.

"The priesthood is a waste of mankind," she remembers saying saucily to her governess. The punishment for her impertinence was embroidering still another sampler.

Elizabeth dozes off into a fitful sleep. She comes over a rise and sees before her the house her husband Arthur promised he built for her. It is one of classic proportions with a sweeping drive in front. She stops and lifts her skirts before climbing the steps to the doors. When she looks again, all is gone. Frantically she searches for her home. It is futile, but she hunts for her fine house as a person looking for an escaped gaggle of geese. The nightmare evaporates and she comes out of her sleep...heavy heartbeat by heavy heartbeat. She weeps.

How can I escape this dreadful howling land and my deceitful husband? My dream to create a home and family evaporated. She cries and sobs. Never has she felt such defeat. The wind will not stop its incessant howl. It seems to mock her—not as a nightmare, rather as her personal day-mare.

She watched Arthur build the fire last night and she must attempt it if she is to get warm. There is plenty of fuel in the wood box, but ashes lie in the belly of the stove. She scoops them into a metal bucket. Shivering, she prepares a pile of small twigs, twisted grass, and bark. She locates matches and starts a blaze; first she adds dry disk-shapes Arthur called 'prairie coal' and then small branches. She does not breathe for fear the flame will die. She drops more prairie coal onto the feeble flames. Last she adds the split logs praying with each addition that they catch. The fire sputters, but Elizabeth's flagging hope increases at the birth of each new flame. Her shuddering and shivering subside minute after expectant minute as her first-laid fire spreads.

She dips water from the barrel into a basin and sets it over the front stove plate. Huddling close to the stove, she spreads her hands above the sides of the basin. It will take half the morning for the water to heat. Looking about the single room she searches for a chair or stool so that she can sit as she waits. After taking a drink to fill her demanding stomach, she drags a bench to the front of the stove and almost hugs the stove as it becomes steadily warmer. Bored with waiting for the water to heat, she bundles into her scarf and cloak and shoves the only entry door open. As she steps out, the wind wrenches the door from her hand and it slams behind her.

Outside, she wanders. A lean-to for their animals is attached to the shack, but Arthur's horse, Spider, is gone and so is the mule team. The lean-to adjoining the shed is a poor excuse for a stable. Inside there are feeding troughs and over the earthen floor a scarcity of straw that the wind scatters. She finds a lopsided outhouse on around to the back of the shed and wonders that these strong winds have not already toppled it. Curiously, a rope is extended from the front of the shed around two posts and stretched away from the lean-to and onto the outhouse. The rope seems to have no purpose…another oddity in this cursed land.

Returning to the entrance of the shed, she notes a crude table that she saw on leaving but took no interest in until now. It sits to one side of the doorway entrance to the shack and hanging on a nail above it is a metal wash basin. *Washing of one's hands and face must be a customary practice here before entering the shed because on the table are a dipper, a water barrel, and a lump of what I recognize is lye soap. It was unknown to me before leaving the train, but I found that same soap in some hotels and shacks en route.*

Looking toward a creek, she sees trees and walks to them; they line each side of a dry creek. There is a slope from the bank to the creek bed and a stand of cottonwoods buffer her against the wind. She walks to the bottom and is protected from today's strong wind in this low spot. As she continues her survey of the land around to the west of the shack, she spots a heap of rusted tin cans. This pile gouges a red-orange scar on the view looking away from the northwest side of the shack. Beyond is the rough and scrubby prairie that does not end. Snow is scattered across the land like litter. It settles in the shady places and clings to the base of clumped-together tall dead grasses. The sky is like dirty wool and promises another snow. The lowing of the wind continues. At times, the sound is a high screech and other times a rumble. Whatever the volume or pitch, it is ever present.

Arthur abandoned me for there is no sign of any other person. Arthur is gone and perhaps he will never return. While she cannot bear to see him, she yearns for some kind and understanding soul. There is a vacuum, a sucking space inside her as overpowering as this empty land. Her dream was to be mistress of her home, to create the comfort and happiness she cherished in her grandparents' home. Her husband crushed her dream and obliterated her trust.

Too cold to remain out-of-doors any longer, Elizabeth returns to the shack where she hovers near the stove. The fine house that Arthur promised is this crude shack that appears nothing more than an overgrown packing crate. Arthur's promises…a fine house…entertaining friends…a cruel joke.

She is so hungry that her stomach may cave. She explores the contents of the packing crates near the woodstove. Dust filters through the roof and grit covers all surfaces. There are sacks of flour and sugar, a tin of coffee, and cans of food that will over time increase the hill of rusted cans around beside the shack. She finds nothing with which to open the cans. Her search results in locating a tin of crackers and a round of drying cheese. Removing the cheese cloth, she breaks off a chunk of cheese and dampens the cheese cloth before rewrapping the cheese. She eats the cheese and crackers and drinks another dipper of icy water and then covers the water barrel to keep the dirt out of the drinking water.

I will unpack my trunks while I consider what to do. There will be fresh undergarments and a bar of mild soap.

There was nothing in her trunk or other baggage as warm as her brown riding habit and cape so she removes both, locates her clothes brush, and gives both these items a vigorous brushing before bathing. She finds neither a bathing tub nor a towel, but the water is hot, so she uses the white enameled bowl and sponges herself with her washcloth and her fragrant bar of lavender scented soap. Competent to care for herself, Elizabeth copes without tub, towels and screens—the bathing accouterments she had in London, and she takes the first step to regaining her sense of confidence, task by task.

After she finishes her all-over sponge bath, she dresses in fresh underwear and warm outerwear. In the next hour, she brushes and pins up her hair and plans her next undertaking within the shack.

Assessing her need for cleanliness and order, she decides to find a place for personal items—brushes, combs, hair pins, soap, washcloths, undergarments, and handkerchiefs. From the time she left London, she carried them in her portmanteau, a large leather suitcase that hinges open to form two compartments. Now she puts this assortment of toiletries in a tray in top of her trunk. She reorganizes her personal items, and she will not expose them to the filth of this shack.

In her search for these items, she disturbs two of her ball gowns. One is the cranberry red velvet she planned on wearing for winter entertainments with her new neighbors. It is soft and pliant so that merely sliding her hand upon it is soothing. Another gown is a brilliant blue silk satin that complements her auburn hair. Many, including Arthur, admired her when she wore it. There are many other ball gowns, gloves, corsets, hoop shirts, bustles, and stockings. There are morning dresses and day dresses she considers wearing, but none of them will be warm enough in this drafty hovel. Finally, she refuses to contemplate what-might-have-been, but she cannot bear unpacking any of the dresses or ball gowns in this fetid place. She slams the lid shut and locks the trunk as firmly as she stores away her dreams.

How could Arthur proclaim his love for and care for me and yet betray me? He told tales of the English investments that were pouring into this promising cattle-raising country; he spoke of wealth and a promising future for the two of us. How many times, Arthur told her of the Capitol Syndicate that built the Texas Capitol building just so it might control a major portion of its fertile grassland?

I did not think to question the integrity of an English barrister. As I listened to all Arthur told me, I could envision the prairies whose grasses ripple and toss in the wind much as the wind moves the water across the ocean. I could imagine riding across that land with excitement and vigor. How was I completely misled, so foolish, so damned foolish? Damned! I listened to the seducer's tale of loving companionship, my home, adventure, and I believed him.

Grandmother would be appalled to learn that the well-bred young woman she took to France as part of her education is now living in a shack.

Elizabeth tries to remember the gardens, shops, and galleries of France. Those happy memories juxtaposed with the reality of the shack cause a new flood of tears.

A memory of a visit with her grandmother who was occasionally asked to serve Her Majesty Queen Victoria returns to enchant her. When her grandparents returned from their tour in South Africa, the Queen wished to learn of her colonies there and to hear the gossip from that corner of her Empire. The Queen hinted to advance Elizabeth's case as the possible bride of a widower, one of the Queen's favorites. That hope of marriage was short-lived; she learned the prospective suitor was the age of her grandfather! *My God, can I ever stop crying! Can I ever go back to my home there? It would be a scandal for me and my family. I cannot think I can ever have a future there, but will I survive here in a lonely hopeless land with the world's most despicable husband?*

She adds fuel to the fire, undresses, and goes to bed. Perhaps she can take respite from her incredible situation if she can sleep. Warmed she drifts into a shallow sleep. She hears a roar; it mocks; fear overwhelms her. She runs over a cliff and falls…falls…falls. She jerks and wakes herself crying out. The nightmare is over and she sleeps at last. This time an angel with her grandmother's voice whispers to her, "Courage, my child, I am watching over you."

Elizabeth spends the first few days in a shack in the Texas Panhandle in this manner. She thinks, *I am crying enough tears to float the battleship Maine down the Cantonment Creek.* Her guardian angel comes again and again to whisper 'Courage' in her ear. Her head tells her that tomorrow will be no different unless she takes action. But what action…?

Too late she realizes that Arthur trapped her. His fraudulence cripples some part of her. Memories of her family in London are cruel comfort because her mind cannot accept this place to which Arthur has brought her, but more damaging is the realization that this man, her husband, cannot be trusted. In her family, the men and women are trustworthy. She expected her husband to be of this same moral character…to have integrity, to be responsible and compassionate, and altogether trustworthy. He is none of those. She clings to her innate courage for now and it must be enough. She must trust that Arthur is the exception among men and she must trust that she can outwit him.

She takes harbor in the recesses of her soul. Black depression visits her and she cries bitterly, but, after a time, she is no longer able to cry. She feels lost and doomed. It is not possible to hang onto the past and she has no future to which she can yet look forward. She manages to make for herself a little routine of rising, feeding herself, caring for herself, walking, wandering, and mentally searching for some way to overcome her present circumstance. Elizabeth cannot explain how she continues from day to day.

Circling her mind are these questions. *Can I escape? Can I survive this? On which course will I find my way? Escape or survive?*

Am I but a fly caught in an orb web whose spider is wrapping me in its silken threads so it can feed upon me later?

"Cowboys are the gentlest, most well-mannered people. They're not mean and rough as a lot of people think."

Mrs. E. E. Gething, *The Pampa Daily News*,
Sunday, April 22, 1962.

5 - Breakfast—Texas Style

Elizabeth wakes the fourth morning in the silent shack. Leaving the lumpy bed that crackles from the straw under its padding, she finds the little bachelor stove barely warm and nothing to eat. Her hunger commands her attention as it has for days, but she cannot open any of the cans of vegetables or fruit on the shelves. She wonders, *Am I left to starve?*

There is water so she drinks a dipperful. In her grandparents' London home, she did not appreciate the fire started in her room each morning before she awoke. Her maid took care of it.

Elizabeth started a fire for the first time several days ago and has set one to warm herself every morning since then. On this frigid February morning, she wears her heavy woolen riding habit. A sound alerts her. It is the sound of wood splitting. She grabs her cloak.

Outside, she follows the sound with her eyes. A whip-thin youngster leans over to retrieve the length of wood; he works in a clearing near the creek among cottonwood trees.

"I'm Jake…come back to check the wood supply," he says extending his right hand.

She does not extend her hand; he drops his own and bobs his head.

"Welcome, Ma'am. I've did everything Mr. Gething told me. Is something on your mind?" he says cocking his head to one side.

"Where is Mr. Gething?"

"Ma'am, I reckon he'll be back in a day or so."

"I asked: where is he."

"He has gone to Pampa for the extra luggage and to bring his new hound, Ma'am. Is there anything you need?" he says.

Too late, Elizabeth realizes that she has just revealed to this boy that her husband is not at home and she is unaware of his whereabouts or his plans. She hesitates about whether to let him also know of her desperate need for food.

"I found nothing to eat. Is there someone to cook and clean? No one seems to be about," she says halting at each thought. *It is necessary to keep up the appearance that Arthur expected someone to provide for me.*

"Well, Ma'am, I thought you would be doing the cooking and cleaning for Mr. Gething. 'Bout all the cooking and cleaning we cowboys do is…," he says.

"Our service staff always did the cooking and cleaning. I cannot manage without them. Oooh…," she says, her voice quavering.

Tears well up in Elizabeth's eyes and she struggles to keep from spilling them.

"There, there, hold on, Ma'am," Jake urges. "I can stir up a fair batch of sourdoughs. I can do that for you. You'd pick that up quick. With a pot of beans and a batch of sourdoughs feller can go a long way."

Elizabeth is unable to hold back her tears any longer and turns away.

"Mrs. Gething, you can go on back. Soon as I finish here, I'll be right up," he says.

Elizabeth goes toward the shack, nearly sprinting. She needs time to her to staunch her tears and calm herself; then she hears the logs clatter into the wood box outside the door.

"Mrs. Gething, are you ready?" Jake calls.

Elizabeth comes to the door and stands in the entrance a moment too long to be welcoming. It is not appropriate for her to entertain a man—even a boy who is nearly a man—alone in a room.

Finally, Jake says, "I'm not handy around a woodstove and that little bachelor stove is not much count. I'll dig a fire pit away from the shack and cook like it's did on the trail."

"Jake, biscuits are something sweet to enjoy in the middle of the afternoon with tea. I cannot imagine the combination of biscuits and beans," she says.

"Ma'am, these biscuits ain't sweet. You'll see they ain't strange at all and go good with beans. Mr. Gething don't keep tea, but I know he's got coffee 'cause I restock and sweep out his place. We can prepare a pot of beans to cook tomorrow. Now, there are things I'll need from your place."

"Very well, what do you need?"

"There's a coffee pot; it's on the stove. Look for the Dutch oven, the only pot on the floor near the stove. The Arbuckle coffee, flour, crock of sourdough starter, lard, canned milk, and salt should be on the shelves beside the stove. See if you can find a can of peaches. Don't forget to fill the coffee pot with water," he says.

Jake leaves and collects some tools from the lean-to shed. He uses a pick to break up and a shovel to scoop out the winter-dried grass turf. Then he lines the depression with stones. Finally he makes quick work of starting a hearty blaze in the pit.

In a while, Elizabeth returns with the filled coffee pot and the tin of Arbuckle coffee. Jake sets the water to boil and when it is comfortably warm he pours some of it into his cupped hands and scrubs them with lye soap he retrieved from the wash stand at the entrance to the shed. He instructs her to pour a heaping handful of coffee into the pot once it is boiling. The coffee will cook until it is strong enough before moving it aside to a warm spot, but he cautions her not to let it boil anymore.

"Jake, the flour, salt, and Arbuckle coffee were easy to find, but I cannot locate the crock of sourdough starter, the lard, or the canned milk."

"The crock of sourdough warms on the back of the stove, the lard is in a bucket on the bottom shelf to the left, and you'll locate the canned Carnation milk by looking for it on the top shelves," he says.

She makes another trip to assemble the rest of the ingredients. Jake sees her struggle under the burden of the Dutch oven loaded with these last items and comes to help her.

Jake explains that sourdough is the leavening agent and the most important ingredient. He stresses it must be kept warm; doing that was one of his additional chores while Mr. Gething was away. He instructs her to replace the used portion of sourdough with some of the newly-mixed dough every time she makes a new batch of biscuits.

Jake, Bob, and Green made sourdough biscuits in Mr. Gething's place while he was away. Jake figured that was the best way to keep the sourdough working. However, he and the boys slept in their dugout a mile away from Mr. Gething's place and out toward the sand hills. It was a treat to cook inside the shed rather than out-of-doors.

The lesson begins. Jake shows her how to mound up a couple of handfuls of flour, to dash in some salt, to add a glob of lard, a scoop of sourdough, and a measure of canned Carnation milk. Then, he mixes it in a large bowl with his hands and presses it out on the floured packing box before cutting the biscuits with a tin can. Jake removed the top and bottom of the can. He returns the remaining bits of dough with the sourdough starter in the crockery jar.

The round biscuits lie on the surface of the box he uses as a tabletop. Jake moves to the heavy Dutch oven, a large deep iron pan with three stubby legs and a heavy lid having a wide upturned lip all around it. He lifts and sets it near the fire checking the progress of the fire in the pit.

The fire has not burned to good white coals yet, but Jake tosses in more cow chips.

"I do not recognize this 'prairie coal' you are using. Mr. Gething has a large supply of it in the fuel box," she says.

"Most folks calls 'em 'cow chips'; they're dried cow-plops we collect from the prairie," Jake grins.

"No!" Elizabeth pulls away and dusts off her hands vigorously. Her face is contorted with revulsion, for she has just brought them to the fire pit.

Jake laughs, "Ma'am, Look around! They's blessed few trees and they's lots of cow chips."

They begin to catch fire and Jake explains that they will, when glowing with heat, go on top of the Dutch oven lid. The upturned lip that surrounds the entire top of the lid prevents the glowing cow chips from falling off or onto the baking biscuits.

Jake checks several times on the fire. After the cow chips begin to turn white, he secures the lid over the base and lifts the oven by is over-arching handle. He settles it into the fire pit. Then, he removes the lid and drops a lump of lard the size of a plum inside the Dutch oven and watches it melt. Next he squats beside the fire pit, removes one biscuit at a time from the floured box top, turns both sides of each into the melted lard, and arranges all the biscuits in the bottom of the Dutch oven. The lid goes on top and Jake selects a short-handled shovel from the tools he has used to build the fire pit and piles the glowing cow chips over the lid.

"There! They will bake in about half an hour. Meantime, we'll drink a cup o' that coffee you've brewed. I drink mine 'barefooted'—without milk or sugar. You?" he says.

"Barefooted! You Texans say so many unusual words; they amuse and astound me. Cow chips, indeed!"

"Ever heard of a dugout? It's a place to live in that's dug into the side of a hill with a wooden framed-up front opening. A roof of saplings covered with sod completes it."

"A place to live is…*a hole in the ground*? Jake you are teasing me," she says.

"Naw, I was raised in one on the homestead my folks built near Fort Worth. It was real comfortable," he says.

"A hole in the ground cannot be a comfortable place to live," she says.

"Sure it was! Mom knew how to make it nice. She made a plaster of gypsum and covered the walls with it. It keeps out the dirt and varmints and it's a heap cleaner than dirt walls," he says.

"What did she do about the roof? The roof of this shed lets in so much dirt that it covers everything and sweeping and dusting cannot do much to keep it really clean," she says.

"She and Dad stretched canvas under the roof to catch the dirt and grasshoppers, scorpions, ants, and such; every spring she washed it and they put it back," he says. "The only other problem is heavy rainfall 'cause the roof leaks."

"How did your mother keep the floors clean? If the floors are dirt, it seems useless to sweep out dirt," she says.

"We all worked to stretch burlap bags over the floor and pegged the edges into the ground. We spread straw over the burlap and spread fine mud over all of it to make a smooth surface. Some women manage to cover the dirt floors with rugs," he says.

"Jake, I did not know people live in holes in the ground," she says.

"Mrs. Gething, most of us live in dugouts you call 'holes in the ground.' They are much warmer in winter and cooler in summer than anything on top of the ground. We live in dugouts because lumber, nails, and glass are shipped by ox-freight or mule-freight and at a terrible price. Ain't many men can pay for a house on top of the ground."

"Jake, I do not believe I can do those things your mother does because I neither cook nor bake. We hired cooks, bakers, housekeepers, and gardeners—the service staff—to do that. I was taught to manage the household by overseeing the staff. Everything was different in London," she says.

"There are lots of ladies who do what my mom did right around here. They also plant gardens and raise chickens. My mom does all of that *and* picks wild plums for jellies and jams *and* dries apples and apricots. Say, the ladies at the community church are right helpful to newcomers and you ought to meet them," he says.

Jake is educated in the ways of survival if not in school, she thinks and finds him chivalrous and good-hearted. *With his help, I believe I can learn enough to manage until I decide what I must do.*

She watches Jake carefully while he finishes breakfast. She is determined she can do this and next Jake will teach her how to make a pot of beans. The breakfast of biscuits, peaches, and coffee should soon be ready and she cannot wait to sit down to eat.

Jake says, "This is a good time to sort and soak them beans. We'll need a small bowl of dried pinto beans and another bowl twice that size or larger."

Eager to finish her first cooking lesson, she fetches these items. Jake shows her how to spread the beans on the box top and remove any stones, dirt clods, and irregular beans. They pore over the beans to sort them and scoop the sorted beans into the second bowl.

"Take the beans back to the shack and cover them with water and stir in a heaping spoon of baking soda and soak them overnight. In the morning the beans are going to be twice their size. Then pour off the water and cover them again with clean water."

"Why do I add the baking soda?"

Blushing, he says, "Beans make a lot of gas in the stomach and the baking soda keeps everyone from bein' uncomfortable after eatin' 'em.

"Also look for a large crock jar with hunks of salted pork packed in lard. Tomorrow morning dig out one piece of salt pork and add it to the beans and cook them over low heat in the Dutch oven. You'll know when they're done when they pop easy in your mouth. Stir in salt until it tastes the way you like it. If you got onions, chop one of 'em up and add it at the beginning. Gives 'em a good flavor!" he says.

To Elizabeth, these sourdough biscuits smell like the yeast bread that her Grandmother's baker served. She imagines them dripping with butter as Jake removes them from the pit. He sends her to the shack with them, the cooking supplies, and ingredients. He brings the coffee pot and the opened can of peaches.

"How did you open the can of peaches?"

"With a butcher knife, it takes muscle, but Mr. Gething keeps it right here on the shelf."

"Will you join me for breakfast, Jake?"

"Thanks for askin', but I got chores to do. Bob and Green are waitin' for me to help 'em work the cows. I'll just bring up some more water from the spring before I leave."

"I enjoyed our visit and your lesson in cooking. It was good to visit with you; it is lonely out here. Jake, will you be coming back often?" she says.

"Mr. Gething told me to keep the wood box filled and said I'd do other chores about the place. So, I'll be back when you need help," he said. He leaves the shack briefly before returning with buckets of water and bids her farewell.

The sweet scent of peaches and the moist yeasty steam of the biscuits waft under her nose as she sets them on the table. She seats herself at the table and sips the hot coffee. Tea is her preference over the pungent coffee which is strong and it is as black as a chimney sweep's brooms. She has a ravenous appetite and dines on breakfast like a gourmand.

Mrs. Exxum, a newcomer to the Texas Panhandle from Tennessee, asked another Tennessean Mrs. Henry, "…just what she thought of this Panhandle country anyway?"

Mrs. Henry replied, "Well, I tell you, Old Mrs. Banks had it about right, 'It's heaven for men and cattle but it's hell for women and horses.'"

Millie Jones Porter, page 334
Memory Cups of Panhandle Pioneers

6 - Llano Estacado

Elizabeth bakes a batch of sourdough biscuits in her Dutch oven over the fire pit and by midday brings them inside. The dough was stiff as she worked it and they did not rise as high as those Jake made yesterday. Inside, the pinto beans that soaked overnight in the crockery bowl are simmering in a pot on the bachelor stove. They are well-done and smell inviting.

Stopping and listening, she hears a rider in the distance. It will be a while before she can tell who it is. She waits and listens as the rider nears the shack. It is the walking gait of Spider! *The Devil returns.*

Elizabeth sets the biscuits on the table and carries the bean pot to the table. The coffee is only lukewarm. *It is good enough for him.* She is damned if she will heat it.

As Arthur steps inside, he looks around. "Well, Kate, I see you came to your senses. Pour me some coffee. I could use a meal."

Elizabeth moves to the table, sits ignoring his command for service and serves herself some beans and biscuits. *The brazenness of his coming in as casual as sin!* She observes that his eyes are red-rimmed and haggard. He does not brag about his poker winnings, as she expects, or his success in hunting either, so she is sure he has been drinking and has lost money, too.

"What? No word of welcome for your weary husband?" slurs Arthur.

Silence stretches like a tightly wound clock, another twist away from snapping. After a long time, a red-faced Arthur settles himself at the table with coffee in hand. He serves himself and begins to eat. He bites into the biscuit.

"Kate, your damn biscuits are tough." he says.

"You need not eat them!" she replies. With a swoop, she dumps the entire plate of them on the floor and stomps on them, crushing them into the dirt.

Out the doorway she sails, grabbing the cloak from the peg as she passes. She makes her way to the lean-to where Spider stands unsaddled.

Names both me and his female mule, Kate, to aggravate me and to remind me he plans to tame me as Petruchio did Kate. Those biscuits will stay there until hell freezes over, she thinks.

Trembling with anger, she finds the tack; Spider accepts the bit and allows her to bring the bridle over his ears. He stands still while she arranges the thick woolen blanket on him. The saddle is a problem because these Western saddles are heavy and cumbersome. It takes three attempts to hoist it onto Spider's back and then she cinches it as tight as possible for she realizes Spider is swelling to keep the cinch to his liking.

Elizabeth finds a box to stand on in order to mount. Spider is an English thoroughbred and trained to jump. His long graceful legs and black color gave him his name.

She wishes women wore trousers, but arranges her full skirt like a loin cloth and mounts Spider. They are away, but she studies the position of the sun in the sky and searches for scarce landmarks. During their courtship, Arthur regaled her with tales of travelers losing their way across the Llano Estacado. She is alert and plans her strategy for returning.

"Damn him! He'll be sorry he ever deceived me," Elizabeth promises. *There is no name harsh enough for him; he led me to believe that we would receive the same sort of friends and take pleasure in entertainments we enjoyed in London. On one hand, he lied to me and, on the other, he allowed me to assume my life would continue much as it was. And I believed his every word. Before emigrating, he argued before the bar at Queen's Court in London and his father owns coal mines in Wales; I assumed he was trustworthy. How could he so completely deceive me? That shack is unbelievable! He must be a pauper.*

She trots alongside the Cantonment Creek and feels she can reverse her course and return to the shack. Then, her eyes consume the treeless prairie with its wide expanse of land beyond the creek. At first, it seems colorless and most of the plants are less than a foot in height. Some strange spherical bushes, released from their roots, go rolling across the prairie pushed by the wind. It is somber; the dead winter colors are umber, gray, and black. This stretch of flat land welcomes her and she fancies a full gallop across it and into the horizon. She wishes to be as free as those odd wind-blown bushes. Veering due west, she canters and keeps the cottonwood trees along the Cantonment Creek in sight. She plots a straight line toward and under the westward moving sun.

She rides out her anger galloping across the prairie. This land gives rise to a new-found freedom. At this moment, there are no dreary rules to bind her and no Arthur to thwart her. She is a superb equestrienne and the ride exhilarates and relaxes as her cares flow behind her. Spider's smooth rhythm becomes her own. Feeling free relieves her of her recent temper; she gentles Spider from cantering to trotting, walking, and halts him.

She dismounts and strokes Spider's neck and shoulders. He is content to graze. She weeps silently as she encircles the neck of her mount. With the release of tears, Elizabeth relaxes and wraps the warm cloak around herself and stretches out on the prairie even as cold as it is. She watches as clouds flow like buttermilk across the sky.

The frigid ground holds less fear than Arthur's lies and indifference and she slumbers.

Aroused by Spider's whinny, she is alert to her situation. The sun is lower in the west and she judges there are only a few hours of daylight. She knows she is in danger and was foolish to ride so far in this unmarked territory. She remounts and follows Spider's and her own shadow back to the east. Their pace is slower going back, for she is looking for elusory landmarks. The light has changed and everything has a different appearance. That which seemed a recognizable feature on the flight away from the shack now seems altogether unfamiliar. Fear takes over and she urges Spider into a trot. She is in real danger of spending the night alone and freezing on this endless tract of land.

There is nothing familiar in sight. Spider slips into a canter as a loved hymn glides into her thoughts. She, Spider, and the hymn are as one in rhythm. After the second stanza swings through her mind, the third stanza erupts from her throat in song:

> Perverse and foolish oft I stray'd,
> But yet in love He sought me...

and she sang it to the end...

> Good Sheppard [sic], may I sing Thy praise
> Within Thy house forever.

She takes strength from this hymn and has the idea to attract attention by singing. Now, she chooses a hymn to buoy her courage and one to attract someone's attention.

> Guide me, O thou great Jehovah,
> Pilgrim through this barren land;

She sings full-throated as the sun nears the horizon and she urges Spider to pick up the pace. She begins singing again with urgency even though her voice is becoming hoarse.

> Death of death, and hell's destruction,
> Land me safe on Canaan's side.

She loses count of the number of times she has sung the entire hymn. But, then....

Riders approach. Although she is leery, she canters toward them and then she recognizes...Jake!

"Did you hear me singing?" she rasps.

"I can't be sure 'bout the singin'; we thought we heard coyote pups howlin'." Jake answers.

"Are you criticizing my singing, Jake?" she says.

"No, Ma'am," Jake blushes.

"Which way back to the shack?" she asks. "I fear I am lost." *Blast it all! I hope Arthur never learns I lost my way and was frightened. I must never allow him to intimidate me.*

57

"Ma'am, it's easy for a greenhorn to lose the way out here. I'd slow up and rest for a spell," says Jake. "You should meet the rest of your cowhands.

"This here is Green; he goes by his last name 'cause he don't like the name his folks give 'im and he won't tell it."

Green dips his head and Elizabeth perceives he is shy. He tips his gray hat slightly; it is deep crowned and wide brimmed. The crease down the center of the crown is just where he grasps it to put it on or take it off. The brim is not shaped but worn as level as when it was new. The dark stain testifies that it is a well-used hat. He wears a kerchief knotted around his neck and a light colored full-length duster. His pants are of a crisp canvas fabric. He sits casual in the western saddle, and he keeps his lariat looped over the saddle horn.

Green says, "Howdy, Ma'am, pleased to meet you."

"I am pleased to meet you, too, and very glad to find the three of you to direct me back," says Elizabeth.

"And this here is Bob," Jake continues, "He never met a stranger and will talk your ears off if you give 'im a chance."

Bob takes his hat off in a flourish and says, "Jake ain't done you justice and it's my pleasure finally to meet you."

"My pleasure as well and my luck that all of you are about today," says Elizabeth.

Bob is the oldest of the three and has a florid full face that surely wears a smile day in and day out. His eyes twinkle and wears a hat brim shaped so that the sides curve upward slightly and the crown is shaped in a roll all around and tipped slightly forward in the front. He wears his hat away from his face and to one side in a jocular fashion. Instead of a jacket he wears a thick sort of blanket with a place in the center to slip his head through, but it is sewn together down the sides from underarm. He wears an impressive pair of heeled boots and spurs and the same sturdy pants these cowhands seem to favor.

With introductions completed, they tip their hats again and grin. Thus uniquely attired, their wide-brimmed deep-crowned hats shade their faces. They wear bright colored kerchiefs around their necks. Their spurs jingle pleasantly and their saddle leather creaks as they change positions.

"Did Mr. Gething send you looking for me?" Elizabeth says.

"No, Ma'am, we're hunting and thought we'd come upon a den of coyotes," Green answers.

"Please, never tell Mr. Gething that I lost my way back!" she says.

"You got our word on it," guffawed Bob. "If asked, we'll only say we never could find that den of coyotes we heard."

"Mr. Gething warned me about getting lost on the Llano Estacado, but I planned how to find my way home." *"Home?"* She jolts. *This God-awful land is never going to be my home!*

"You done a fair job, but Spider knows the way home if you just give him his head. You are pointed toward the Cantonment Creek and from there you'd find it," Jake says. He indicates the right direction. "Keep on that same line for 'bout a quarter-mile, you'll be home afore you know it," he says.

"Jake, I am attending church on Sunday because of your advice about meeting the ladies. Tell me how to find it? Will I find my way back without trouble?" she says.

He looks at his two companions. "Boys, let's take her to church! We never miss a chance to eat a woman-cooked meal and there is always a big spread after the preachin'."

"We'll do it! 'Sides, Ol' Green," chuckles Bob as he thumbs toward Green, "...he has another reason to attend. Betty is sure to be there!" He wiggles his eyebrows.

Green ducks his head. "Aw, h...! Ain't you ever gonna letup on that?"

"Be ready about nine o'clock. The ride takes the better part of an hour. All the ladies bring a dish; you may want to bring a pot of them beans, Mrs. Gething," says Jake as they spur up their horses.

Beans! Well, no one would enjoy eating my biscuits, Elizabeth says to herself. *The biscuits were as tough as hardtack of the Royal Navy. Arthur, when you promise me a fine house and a well-trained house staff, you better give me both or get ready for an endless supply of tough biscuits.*

She returns to the shack before the last light.

In summary: Newton Willis recalled when he was 'in his old age' that no church existed in Mobeetie in 1881. Although a Presbyterian minister arrived a year later, he died about a year afterward. Other denominations did not follow for over a decade.

Pauline Durrett Robertson and R.L. Robertson,
pages 202-203, Panhandle Pilgrimage

7 - Community Church

Elizabeth ignores Arthur and decides to attend the community church. Because families consider it too far to travel, they do not attend church in Mobeetie. Instead, the neighbors along the east and west Cantonment Creek hold non-denominational services in the schoolhouse with circuit-riding ministers of several denominations supplying the pulpit.

The preparation of her single menu is not as daunting as it was the first time when she scorched the skirt of her brown riding habit while starting the fire in the pit. Humming a jaunty tune, she takes stock of the remaining food and checks the fuel box.

Arthur glowers at her, "Mr. Gething," she says, "Jake, Green, and Bob offered to accompany me to church on Sunday morning. Attending church will give me an opportunity to meet the ladies. I would like to ride Spider."

"Kate, you run away with Spider at any whim and waste my bread in your bad temper. I will require the beast on Sunday…and all other days! I must tend the cattle."

A rat scurries from behind the woodstove to its burrow behind the bed and goes unnoticed by these two. It feasts on the bread crumbs it has pilfered.

Elizabeth thinks, *Arthur does not need to tend the cattle. He left the cowhands in charge for three days while he went to Pampa gambling, drinking, and hunting. His cowhands inspect the cattle whether he is here or off somewhere. Arthur, in fact, invents a task to deprive me of taking Spider.*

She is not one to quail before confrontation and answers with an unruffled voice, "Since you betrayed me and brought me here with lies and false promises, I am due the peace offering of a horse and, as you are unable to provide it, Spider is acceptable. In answer to your reference to the wasted bread, it was better than you deserved. You promised me a fine house with a full staff. This run-down shack is not fine and Jake is not house staff." She continues without hesitation.

"You knew that I was educated to conduct a household befitting a lady. I am not schooled to bake or cook or keep house. My first attempt was critically received and under these circumstances it is a testament to my restraint that I did no more than waste a pan of the damned bread.

"The ladies at church may be able to assist me in learning some domestic skills, but first I must meet them. I claim the horse on Sunday, Sir!"

"When pigs fly, Kate!"

"I deserve a horse then!"

"Humph!"

"You will, then, learn to enjoy an endless provender...of beans and tough biscuits for that is all I can put on the table."

The days before Sunday advance. A grating stubborn silence exists between Elizabeth and Arthur. Elizabeth pretends cheerfulness and lack of concern toward Arthur. He affects a hard and unyielding manner. She serves him tough *unsalted* biscuits daily.

On Sunday morning when Elizabeth awakes, Arthur is gone. It does not surprise her, but her need for companionship subverts her pride of mount. She decides to attend church as planned. She will ride on the mule that Arthur acquired when they left Mobeetie.

Elizabeth chooses a warm blue wool skirt and weskit from her trunk. It contrasts sharply with her auburn hair which she piles high and elegantly on her head and holds it in place with pins and ivory combs. She is carefully groomed and ready to ride when her escorts arrive. She dons a matching blue hat and veil and a pair of gray kid gloves. She is confident of her appearance.

The three cowboys arrive as promised and their eyes drink the vision of her as they might to a warm fire after riding the fence line in deep snow. Each removes his hat, but then they stand dumb for a moment before Jake speaks.

"Ma'am, we will be the envy of all the men today. You are a sight to see. I never seen any peacocks as fine feathered."

Green offers, "Ma'am, I'll carry them beans for you."

The gregarious Bob loses the art of speech and simply stares.

Elizabeth hitched and saddled the mule in the lean-to beside the shack early this morning. Now Jake helps her mount the sidesaddle as she deftly arranges her instep-length black cloak and its hood.

The time passes as unnoticed as morning dew evaporating while they ride and visit. Elizabeth inquires, "How did you become cowboys?"

Bob says, "My parents died during a flu epidemic within days of one another. I figured I was old enough to set out on my own and hankered to ride and work cows. Got a few jobs with ranchers and learnt the ropes."

Elizabeth says, "What about you, Green?"

"Well, Ma'am, Maw works all the time with my brothers and sisters. Paw cain't work after the accident 'cause he's crippled. My older brothers like farming; I don't so I left. Truth is: there ain't nothin' else to do here about to keep body and soul together."

"Green's the most honest of us," says Bob, "Cowboyin' is about all there is for ol' boys without two nickels to rub together."

Jake says, "You know my parents helped me get started by givin' me some of our calves to raise and sell. Like Bob and Green, I ride and work on ranches. I'm a horse wrangler—keepin' the remuda for the rest of the hands. One day all of us reckon to have our own places."

Elizabeth thinks, *I understand your plight more than you know. Women do what they must, too. But we cannot own property or use laws to our advantage.*

"Jake, what is this remuda you keep as a wrangler?" asks Elizabeth.

"The job of a wrangler is to drive all the cowboy's strings of horses—up to ten in each string—to the next camp during a roundup or cattle drive. The wrangler is usually the youngest cowhand, but he's got t' know horses. When the horses are altogether—maybe a hundred horses—they're called by the Spanish name—remuda. The wrangler moves along with the coosie, the chuck wagon cook. He's always second in command after the boss," says Jake.

"We're lucky t' get this job with Mr. Gething. Few cowboys are needed on ranches in winter. The bosses keep their ranch managers and a few top hands on the payroll 'til spring when cows start calvin' and then more hands are needed to work the cattle. The bosses will need plenty of cowboys 'til the fall roundup is over," says Bob.

Elizabeth is fascinated that they avoided what they call 'riding the chuck-line' this winter due to their agreement with Mr. Gething for permission to establish their dugout on his land, draw half-wages and full-grub in exchange for work. She learns that riding the chuck-line is way of saying what out-of-work cowboys do to survive the winter. They ride from cow-camp to cow-camp, accept the hospitality of meals from its chuck wagon cook, stay about three days, help the boss or coosie, and move on to another cow-camp. Others do like Arthur's three cowhands and shovel out their dugouts on the prairie and fend for themselves. In spring when most ranchers are ready to hire on additional hands, Jake, Bob, and Green will leave for better jobs.

Bob loves to talk and senses Elizabeth is interested. He says, "The biggest ranches like the XIT are beginning to sell off some of their land."

"Why?" asks Elizabeth.

"The Englishmen were drawn to the Llano Estacado as soon as the Indians and buffalo was gone because of this unendin' grassland. They brought in big money to set up windmills, better breeds of cattle, and barbed wire fences....Well, other improvements, too! Even their money did not prepare them to deal with grassfires, droughts—long periods of little or no rain—and the blue northers and blizzards."

"Others took advantage of them?"

"I can't say anyone took advantage of them, but they lacked any experience raisin' cattle in such a dry land. Some wouldn't listen to good advice. It takes an old frontiersman like Charles Goodnight to get it right. He tells ever'one who'll listen that this land is jest only for small stock farms like Mr. Gethin's got."

"So that is why you, Green, and Jake plan to own ranches?"

"Yes, Ma'am, we know the 'mportance of learnin' from the best while we get the know-how an' cash an' cattle t' make a go of it."

Elizabeth says, "When we came through Fort Worth, I met the wife of a man shipping meat to eastern markets in refrigerated cars. Mr. Gething told me he looks forward to the time that he, too, will take his cattle to a nearby rail yard instead of driving cattle to Kansas."

"Railroads is makin' a difference. They need our cattle and grains for markets all around the country, but the freight cost is too much for the little stockmen. There is a demand for beef back east and the government buys beef to feed the Indians on reservations in Oklahoma, New Mexico, an' Arizona Territories," continues Bob.

Jake says, "Colonel Goodnight established a ranch in Goodnight, Texas, after he and John Adair dissolved their partnership on the Palo Duro. He's after breedin' cows as tough as Longhorns at his new ranch, but he's lookin' to breeding stock with fleshier meat for the folks back east."

Green interrupts, "The Colonel and Mrs. Goodnight give common-sense learnin' for youngsters—men and women—at Goodnight's College. Got a cousin in school there!"

"Mrs. Gething," says Jake, "the whole blame' country's changin' and we aim to be part of it."

At the church, the cowboys introduce the newly-wed Mrs. Gething to the neighbors. The worship service is unlike those of the Church of England for they do not follow the Book of Common Prayer. Instead, there are simple original prayers, unfamiliar hymns, and a fiery sermon delivered by an itinerant preacher—a Baptist this time. It is followed by his stirring call to the congregants to repent their sins and join the church.

After the service ladies are eager to chat with Mrs. Gething. The ladies she meets are wearing dark dresses of serviceable material; they touch the soft wool of her dress with pleasure and admire its style.

She is interested in the dishes of food that they are spreading out for the noon meal. Elizabeth says to Mrs. Joe Harrah, "Your dish of chicken and dumplings is delicious. I am no cook, but I want to learn to make it."

"My daughter Louella made this. She'll be happy to show you how."

Elizabeth also enjoys an apricot cobbler made from dried apricots baked by a neighbor, Mrs. Perry LeFors. Elizabeth's pot of beans is well received and she is proud of her recent accomplishment. In addition, spread on the table, there is a variety of pickles, roasted root vegetables, boiled eggs, and canned tomatoes.

Mrs. Harrah introduces her oldest daughter, Louella.

"How was your journey from London?" says Louella

"The crossing was rough and I was ill from the motion of the ship almost from the time we embarked until we arrived. We stayed in the Astor Hotel in New York City several days for me to recuperate. We traveled overland by train and it was arduous and tedious."

Elizabeth smiles with introspection, "It was not until we left the train that I fully appreciated its comforts. Since Fort Worth, we traveled first by train, next by coach, and finally by riding our animals. I fear I cannot survive here."

"This is a hard life for us, Mrs. Gething. There are few women on the Llano Estacado, but we help and support one another. If my family and I can help you, we will. Do come by the next time you go to Mobeetie to get supplies and we can visit."

"I welcome your invitation and look forward to calling on you."

When the Harrah family departs, three women she has not met approach to visit with Elizabeth.

Sally Sites introduces herself and says, "Louella's family has been here for many years. Her parents are Joe and Emmogene Harrah. They came when no towns existed and no settlers lived here. Her father was a buffalo hunter at first and her mother traveled with him. It was before Fort Elliott was established. Theirs is a large family and they know how to make the best of this land."

"Do go visit with her! She'll love the company. Louella no longer attends school, but that family works together and they are generous to their neighbors," chimes in Annie Polk.

"Jake has already suggested I will find help among the ladies here at church and I welcome your offers of friendship. I admit the only meal I can provide is beans, biscuits, and coffee. Jake taught me to do that and I will learn it."

"The Harrah family dugout is not far from your place. Mrs. Harrah is fearless; she can ride and shoot with the best and has seven children. Louella is the oldest," says Maude Rives.

The ladies clear the table and their husbands join them to prepare to return to their homes.

Arthur's cowboys accompany Elizabeth to her mule and take charge of the empty bean pot. She expects to accept

Louella's invitation to visit her for she is tired of her unvaried diet and hopes to learn from the Harrah family.

"Jake, Bob, and Green, thank you for escorting me to the church today. It helps to begin meeting neighbors."

"We want to eat all them dishes the Harrah family offered to teach you," says Green.

"Do tell, Green! I guess Betty is not inviting you to sample her cooking!" says Elizabeth.

"Aw, Ma'am, I ain't even talked with Betty," says Green flushing and ducking his head.

Bob and Jake laugh at Green's embarrassment.

Bob slaps him on the shoulder and says, "Betty peeked at you off an' on all afternoon. You oughta talk with her about somethin'."

"You can practice talking with me, Green," says Elizabeth. "It will be no different talking with Betty. Tell me more about your plans to own your own place. It is easy for you to talk about that."

Jake says, "Tell Mrs. Gething about the six little doggies Perry LeFors is letting you graze free on the Diamond F."

"I am interested, Green. Mr. LeFors showed his confidence in your work when he put the calves in your care." encourages Elizabeth.

"Aw! Those little doggies' mamas was sold off afore they's ready to fend for their selves. That's the only reason I got the job bottle feedin' em."

"That sounds like a responsible job to me. I believe Mr. LeFors recognized you were the man to do it," she says.

"You think a girl like Betty cares about me acting as momma for a bunch of doggies?" Green scoffs.

"I am. Betty will want to know about it, too?"

Bob says, "She would, Green. Ever'body in the whole country is interested in gettin' a herd of cows!"

"She will be interested in your cousin who is attending the Goodnight College," adds Elizabeth.

The visit continues and Elizabeth learns that school lands are put up for bids by the state and men with little money get them at fair prices. These cowboys stay informed about the laws regulating land sales and the free grass ranges of which all of the bigger cattlemen take advantage. Some of them are generous to their cowhands and they encourage them to start building herds. These three cowboys seek out cattlemen with generous natures who help promising cowhands get their starts.

Back at the shack, the monotony of beans and biscuits is nothing beside her refusal to accept her living conditions. She begins to clean the one room to make it more livable, but her isolation here is the most difficult of all. Arthur is seldom around during daylight hours, but that is not something she regrets. She copies favorite poems and posts them around the shack so that she can memorize them as she works. It reassures her to hear a human voice, even if it is hers. She looks forward to Sundays at the Community Church and the visits with the cowboys and her neighbors.

Trying to fix meals [on the frontier] with meager equipment was difficult enough, but finding something to cook was sometimes an even greater challenge.

Sandra L. Myres, page 148
Westering Women and the
Frontier Experience 1800 – 1915

8 - Taking Stock

Elizabeth does not wait until it is time to make a trip to Mobeetie with orders to replenish their stocks and supplies. Instead, she plans ahead for the evening meal she will serve Arthur and saddles the mule for a visit to the Harrah family. Jake is going to escort her there before he fills the wood box. Arthur is away today and Jake can return in a few hours. Arthur may never know Jake took her to the Harrahs' place.

Mrs. Harrah, Louella's mother, opens the door to her and invites her inside. "My, you are shiverin' and chilled to the bone. Come stand by the stove and warm yourself."

"Mrs. Gething, we hoped you'd take us up on the invitation," says Louella Harrah who is up to her elbows in flour and doing the family baking for the week.

"I could not wait to come, but I had to wait until Jake could show me the way. He does not come to our place every day," says Elizabeth.

"Will Jake be staying?" says Miss Harrah.

"No, he must work with the cattle for Mr. Gething as soon as he fills my wood box. I'm counting on finding my way back."

"Jake needs to come inside to warm hisself before turnin' back. I'll call him in!" says Mrs. Harrah. Going to the door, she sees Jake watering his horse and motions to him.

"Jake, come in this house! We've a pot of coffee and a warm spot by the stove," she says.

Jake takes no time joining them. He says, "Louella, whatever you're bakin' smells like heaven?"

"Bread, you flatterin', flirtin' feller. The first loaves'll come out in minutes. Bet I can talk you into butterin' a slice or two to eat with a cup of coffee."

"Yes, Ma'am!"

The four of them settle around the kitchen table visiting. Soon Jakes speaks up. "Louella, ever' time you talk with Mrs. Gethin', you gonna be so stiff and la-ti-da? I always call her 'Mrs. Gethin', of course, but she's my boss's wife. You ladies don't do that 'mongst yourselves, do you?"

Mrs. Harrah laughs, "Now, Jake, we need her permission to call her by her Christian name."

Elizabeth says, "I would love you to use my Christian name. It's Elizabeth and among friends I prefer it."

"Elizabeth, call me Louella."

"I answer to 'Aunt Em', says Mrs. Emmogene Harrah.

"Well, now, Ladies, this is what I call real friendly-like! But, daylight's burnin' and I gotta get! Thanks for the breakfast, Ladies! The bread and butter hit the spot!"

"Welcome, Jake!" says Louella.

"Mrs. Gething, I'll come back for ya if you'd like," says Jake, "We don't want ya gettin' lost out here."

"No, Jake, my mule will know the way even if I do not."

"If you're not sure, one of us'll ride back with you," says Aunt Em.

After Jake leaves, Aunt Em laughs again. "Our Jake doesn't stand on ceremony. Elizabeth, it's good that you're our neighbor. We women are on a first-name basis when we are together. In public, we are more la-ti-da, as Jake said."

Elizabeth says, "I miss hearing my name since I left London. Thank you for including me in your family."

"We can't wait to visit," says Louella.

"I can't wait to learn how to make sourdough biscuits that are not like hardtack," says Elizabeth. "Also, I need some dresses in which I can do my work. I changed one I brought with me, but most of them will not serve my purpose.

"Lucky, we can visit and bake and study on dresses the rest of the day!" says Aunt Em.

While the ladies ask about London and Elizabeth's family, Louella makes a pan of sourdoughs for their noon meal. She shows Elizabeth how she mixes them so that they are light and fluffy. Louella passes along her secrets of making sourdoughs to Elizabeth. Aunt Em brags on her daughter.

After they eat, Aunt Em goes to shelves of books and catalogues and brings the current year's Sears, Roebuck Catalogue for them to look through. "Elizabeth, we tend to wear the simple dress of prairie women, but pictures of the fashions that city women wear may be more to your liking."

For an hour or more, they look at the Sears-Roebuck catalogue. Elizabeth explains that she never made her dresses because Grandmother hired a seamstress to dress her. Elizabeth thinks the six-gored skirts and weskits are smart, but Louella and her mother point out the simpler design of their clothes and recommend them to Elizabeth, who will make her first dress.

"That is sound advice. While I use needle and thread, it is of the decorative sort—embroidery for samplers, handkerchiefs and scarfs," she says.

"Look at patterns for dresses in our box," says Louella, "and you may find one that you can use."

Aunt Em says, "Bring our sewing box to the table, Louella. Elizabeth can decide."

They show Elizabeth their collection of patterns and offer Elizabeth the loan of several. Aunt Em and Louella will help Elizabeth adjust the pattern, cut the fabric, and after she sews the dress, they will help her fit it. This offer encourages Elizabeth who knows she needs their experience.

The rest of the Harrah family are working with their father and return mid-afternoon after their farm and ranch chores are finished. Most of the rest of the family is introduced to Elizabeth; they are: Mr. Harrah, who is 'Uncle Joe' to friends and family, and the children are Mary, Oren, Etta, Josie, and Herbert.

Em says, "You'll meet our daughter, Bertha, another time. She and 'Boots' Wechesser married only months ago. It was the day after Christmas. They live nearby on the Cantonment Creek."

It is time for Elizabeth to leave for her own place. The family gives her baked potatoes wrapped in newspaper to keep inside her muffler for warmth. Finally, Elizabeth saddles her mule, Kate, and true to its nature, Kate, the mule takes Kate, the bride, home.

The dugout is too cool to be comfortable without her cloak and the wood fire is turned to white ashes. Elizabeth removes the ash and sets a new fire in the stove taking care of her clothing.

She lays the potatoes on the rough table near the water barrel and begins to consider how to make an enticing dinner with these common foods. Arthur enjoyed excellent meals in London when he courted her, but nothing in the stock of food for their dinner can equal them. There are the endless pots of beans with sourdough biscuits. She is weary of the tasteless bread she bakes; it is time stop serving the tough biscuits.

Elizabeth watched every step as Louella prepared a batch of biscuits during her visit. Her friend handled the dough very little and used more of the sourdough starter in the batch. The biscuits they ate with stewed apples were light-textured and fluffy.

Well, it cannot hurt to try imitating what I observed Louella doing.

The space around the stove grew warmer and Elizabeth changed from her warm riding habit into a dress in which she found it easier to work. Then setting out the ingredients for biscuits, she follows the methods she learned from watching Louella.

She cuts the through the sourdough, lard, and flour combination with a couple of knives by sliding them blade to blade across the other. She repeats this cutting action until the mixture of flour, sourdough, salt, and lard has the appearance of cornmeal; then she adds just enough canned milk so that when she turns it with her fingers it comes together in a soft ball. Louella never squeezed and pounded it as she did. Then, she sprinkles just enough flour to prevent the dough from sticking to the table surface before she flattens it with her hands as Jake did.

Louella used a rolling pin to flatten the ball of dough, but Elizabeth does without it. She slips several tablespoons full of lard into the cast iron skillet and lets it melt in the hot oven. Next, she cuts out the biscuits with her homemade biscuit cutter Jake made for her. Finally, she retrieves the skillet from the oven and turns each biscuit over in the melted lard until all the biscuits are pan-ready for sliding into the oven. She adds some water to the pot of beans and places them on the hot stove top. Noticing the potatoes, she places them at the back of the stovetop to warm. They will be a welcome addition to their usual diet.

Her supply of canned goods is dwindling and after surveying the contents, she decides to open a can of tomatoes and adds chopped onion to them along with salt.

The very notion that all of the supplies in the larder are down is an excellent way to begin her conversation with Arthur. A trip to Mobeetie is necessary in order to restock the staples and canned goods. Arthur cannot deny that they need to restock the food. This puts her in Charles Rath's store where she can shop for calico. How will she present her own need for appropriate dresses to Arthur?

She sits at the table to study the paper patterns she has borrowed from Louella. One design is especially simple and she believes it will be easy to move about in it here in the dugout and out-of-doors when she cooks over the fire pit.

This little bachelor stove is much too small for anything except warming small amounts on the top and holds only one pan of biscuits in the oven. If there were meat and vegetables to roast, it is not adequate. The biscuits make a pleasant aroma throughout the shed and Elizabeth sets the paper pattern aside. She is tired.

Arthur arrives when it has turned dark outdoors. He smiles as he enters because Elizabeth is napping on their bed and their dinner is simmering on the stove top. The mingling of the smells of beans, biscuits, and tomatoes welcome him and he is hungry. He helps himself to a cup of hot coffee and watches Elizabeth sleeping. The table is not yet set and he sees an envelope with the illustration of a woman's dress on it.

Kate has been out. I suppose she called on the Harrah family. They will guide her to be practical. It is about time this proud wife of mine realizes that the fancy dresses she brought here are the height of foolishness. Arthur smiles, pleased with himself, he looks through the packets of dress patterns. He adds wood to the stove. He clatters about the wood box until Elizabeth wakes.

Before Elizabeth sets the table, she sees the envelope with the paper pattern and tucks it away inside her cloak pocket hoping it has gone unnoticed. She soon announces that the meal is ready and they begin their dinner.

"Mr. Gething, I called on Mrs. Harrah today. She sent me home with the potatoes to keep my hands warm. They are a nice addition to our meal tonight."

"Kate, the dinner you are serving is very nice and I notice you are not serving those 'tough biscuits' again. These are an improvement!"

"Mr. Gething, you knew when we married I was not trained for this life. Your compliment is appreciated and there are some things to consider that will be helpful in making a home for you. Very soon we need to restock our supplies. Also, I need dresses for working in at home. Mrs. Harrah tells me that the general store in Mobeetie has all those things and also a fair selection of calico fabric for dresses. How soon can we make the trip for these necessities?"

"Kate, I am pleased that you are taking all of these things into account and you can plan on the trip this next Saturday morning. Jake will take you. You can put the supplies on my account with Charles Rath…the calico, too."

"I will make plans accordingly," Elizabeth replies barely able to contain her joy. "In order to make the dress I will need a few other things…scissors, pins, thread and perhaps ribbons."

"You should be able to find all of them at Rath's place."

That happened so easily! Elizabeth thinks. *I must learn how to duplicate that outcome.* She has been so focused on creating a situation in which she can take care of herself that she did not remember how her grandmother managed with her grandfather.

Thinking it through later, Elizabeth recalls: when Grandmother needed things for the home and Alice and me, she ordered the cook to prepare Grandfather's favorite meal—roast pheasant with creamed turnips and apple torts. It was Grandmother's unwavering habit in winter to greet Grandfather with a warm fire and a glass of sherry at the end of his day in surgery. The meal was followed with a brandy for her husband and then the needs of the family were discussed and plans were made.

The lesson was demonstrated in London; it was forgotten by Elizabeth for a time in this raw country and in her difficult new life. However, this event distills Grandmother's lesson. In the future, she thinks to herself, *I will neither undervalue the importance of providing comfort to my husband nor prevent his belief in his illusion that he is always right. No, only that he is right when it serves my purpose!*

[Elizabeth] lost her first baby with a miscarriage when she fell as a mule colt ran between her and the mare she was about to mount.
Darlene Birkes, Eloise Lane, and Elleta Nolte, eds.
page 278, *Gray County Heritage*

9 - The Accident

Vigilance is the stance of Arthur and Elizabeth. Winter blizzards can easily rob ranchers of the cattle so that stockmen take precautions—even feeble ones—to prepare for them. Hay reaped from the playa, shallow lakebeds, and stored in a small Soddy barn is a survival plan along with a dependable source of water from their two springs. Winter impresses upon Arthur his tenuous hold on the land. So, normally more prone to pleasure, he abandons card games and trips to Mobeetie to stay with the cattle.

Arthur thinks, *the cattle are my most-pressing responsibility now. It is another day of inspections and keeping warm and dry. Jake and his friends are responsible enough, but their wages are a steady draw on my cash reserves.*

Between them and Kate, this winter is the most comfortable since I arrived in 1885. When I am back at the shack, the water barrel is filled, laundry is spread out on the pegs and benches and her chair drying and there is something to eat—more than just biscuits, beans, and hot coffee. The biscuits are good now—not those hard bricks of flour. I was right to let her know my place as head of the family from the beginning.

But the winter always robs a body of its reserves; we are all feeling the strain of long hours and limited food.

Kate seems withdrawn and listless; she reads and memorizes poems to distraction. She reworked another of the dresses she brought with her. She adjusts better than expected for a well-born woman, but now she knows the loneliness of this prairie. She and Louella are inseparable and when there is the opportunity Kate is off to see Louella.

Elizabeth is awake before daybreak either tending the fire or setting a new one because the cold invades the shed and keeping the fire is the first business of each day. The training of household management from her grandmother serves her in keeping the shack well stocked. She looks at her hardened dry hands and sometimes cries. The demanding work of washing clothing and linen on a rub board, carrying water from the spring, and sweeping out the shack is thankless and never-ending. Preparing their simple meals is now a routine with its pleasures, but there is seldom any variety in what she puts on the table. Sometimes there are gifts from Louella's cellar; they are treasures. Arthur has come to the stove for warmth.

"Kate, my long underwear is still damp! Can't you arrange to get it dry before morning? It's freezing enough out there without having to go out half wet!" *Damned inconsiderate woman!*

"It is not that damp, Mr. Gething! Back up to the stove and turn around until it is dry. You stand over that stove for half an hour every morning whether your underwear is dry or damp. Next time, feel free to launder and dry them yourself; doing it yourself should make you happy." She reflects upon her marriage.

Mr. Gething knows not Mr. Shakespeare. He casts me wrong in this role he assigns me. Arthur Gething patterns his ideal husband after the groom of the old Spanish folktale. That man shot all of his stock animals because they did not do his bidding in order to throw fear into his bride. I am a fool who eloped with such a one. These thoughts lead to bitterness, and I will not embrace them, but he will not correct me as if I were a child either.

Elizabeth does not give her thoughts any more attention and continues to prepare the biscuits for the oven. This morning she has prepared a pot of porridge that is almost ready to serve. As she expects, Arthur is out of the shack soon after breakfast, but he followed her directions to finish drying his long johns while wearing them. It was that or take over the laundry. He knows she means it. There are other ways to serve 'tough biscuits.'

Elizabeth establishes a routine of housekeeping that is becoming less daunting and she is more competent than she was. She brings the water from the spring herself, sweeps the earthen floor, washes both clothes and linen, and, on warmer days, she prepares some of the cooking outside. The highlights of each month are the regular trips to church or the Harrah place to visit Louella. She is taking an active part in deciding on the supplies they will need and manages well enough. Louella is her ally in this and her reliable source of information.

She knows that she carries Arthur's child and begins planning a dress—a Mother Hubbard. Again she will get Louella's help with the paper pattern and the fittings. She has not shared her condition with Arthur yet. She worries about the birth. There is a doctor in Mobeetie, but he is not always available due to the many calls on his time and the distances he must travel to care for the families in this sparsely settled land. What if he is away when it is time to deliver her child?

March is just around the corner. She has a list of seeds she wants for her spring garden. Jake assures her that he will set up a fence of Cottonwood saplings and plow a garden plot for her. He also reminds her that in the spring, the big ranchers will be hiring and then he, Green, and Bob plan to get work with their former bosses. *How will she manage without their help? Will Arthur take care of chopping the wood and gathering the cow chips and keeping the wood box filled? If not, will she be able to manage while carrying her child?*

The days are uneventful and her concerns lengthen them. In the future, she needs to disguise her pregnancy with the Mother Hubbard dress. Sewing the dress will keep her mind from lingering on the troubles she foresees. In her trunk she finds a treasured book of English poets for reading. She continues to copy her favorite poems on wrapping paper from Rath Mercantile and props them up on the table to memorize them as she sews. These distractions and her daily routine are planned to keep her worries and cares at bay.

The shack is cold as Jake warned her it would be, but it is too dark with only a kerosene lamp to light it. She is thankful for a better door, a gift from the LeFors family. It keeps out most of the cold, and she arranges herself near the little stove which dances about and threatens to dislodge itself from the fragile roof while the fire roars. There is no window for which she prayed, but there is another 'window' upon which she depends.

She sings her favorite hymns and reads Scripture to keep her faith and courage. She seldom dreams of her grandparents' home now for when she goes to bed she is thoroughly tired and sleeps immediately. Sometimes she dreams Alice's face, and they begin to visit, but the scene vanishes before she can share her concerns with her sister. At other times, her grandmother whispers encouragement to her. Elizabeth hears, "Take heart!" "Be strong!" Or, "We love you!" Perhaps it is only the incessant whistling wind that sweeps out of the North, but she prefers to believe it is the Spirit of her Creator.

Unable to bear her isolation any longer she plans a visit with Louella. Her brothers and sisters are in school, and there will be time for an unhurried visit. Aunt Em will be there, and she will ask about the doctor, the birth of the baby if he is not available, and how to prepare for the baby. She learns that Aunt Em is a trusted midwife and can answer many questions.

Elizabeth finishes her preparations for plenty of food on their table so that her absence for the day will not be a problem. Their diet is not much changed. Sourdough biscuits can be made ahead and warmed along with the beans. Louella showed her how to make an apricot cobbler with her gift of dried apricots. She hoards a jar of green beans, another gift from Louella.

Every step of her day away from the dugout must be carefully planned. Now she only has to saddle her mule. Then, she will come back inside to warm herself before leaving. She folds potato-sized rocks, warmed on the stove, inside her muffler and blanket. She wraps several in her cape pockets and more in the blanket to place at her feet. She wears extra stockings on her feet for more protection from the icy wind.

The mule waits for her. The Jenny stands hitched to the post and her colt frolics about them. Just as Elizabeth steps forward and reaches the sidesaddle, the colt breaks between

Elizabeth and Kate, the mule. The colt knocks her to the ground with such force she cannot move. Showered with pain, she cannot catch her breath for a time. Stunned, dizzy, and unable to move for several minutes, Elizabeth pulls herself up by the sidesaddle and holds onto the mule until she feels she can walk.

Her hand and foot warmers tumbled away and she knows it is impossible to visit Louella. She is unable to take the saddle off the mule, Kate. It takes all her resolve to return to the shack. She adds fuel to the stove and goes to her bed. She bleeds and stretches out and cries herself to sleep.

When Arthur returns after dark, he is annoyed that Elizabeth's mule stands saddled next to the lean-to barn. He unsaddles, rubs down, and feeds both Spider and Kate. He finds the dugout lifeless, no supper ready and Elizabeth sound asleep in their bed. This alarms him for it is a complete departure from what has been her habit. He begins a fire in the stove to make coffee and Elizabeth rouses from sleep.

"What is the problem, Kate? How is it you are in bed?" he demands.

"Mr. Gething, I am ill. I was on the way to see Louella when the mule's colt rushed between me and the mule and knocked me down. It took me a while to return here. I fear I lost a baby! Please bring Louella to me," she sobs.

Arthur stands silent taking in the unexpected news.

"Kate, the coffee is made. Can I get you a cup? Do you want a bite to eat before I leave? What can I do for you? You never told me about a baby," he accuses.

"Just some coffee! Please go quickly. I really need her. I am frightened."

Arthur feels robbed of this information and uncertain about what to say or do. He brings Elizabeth a cup of coffee and leaves from the shack without delay. Unprepared for this news, Arthur is bereft and chokes on his anger. He hopes for sons. He loses no time riding to the Harrah dugout.

Speaking of the often seen statues of men on horseback in public parks, Will Rogers said, "Women are twice as brave as men, yet they never seem to have reached the statue stage."

Susan Butruille, page 145
Women's Voices from the Oregon Trail

10 - Coming to Grips

The hole in her heart is so vast Spider could sail through it and never touch what remained of her heart. Elizabeth knew she no longer carried a child even before she sent Arthur to bring Louella. She needs the comfort and quiet presence of her new-found friend who returns with Arthur. Louella tends to Elizabeth with quiet understanding and loving care throughout the evening. Elizabeth falls into an exhausted sleep before Arthur drives Louella to her home.

But it is then—when Arthur takes their neighbor home—that Louella gives her English friend a sustaining gift.

"Arthur, you married a good strong lady, but she is not likely to recover from this unless you take very special care of her. She is not like me and the other American women who live in this land. We have mothers and grandmothers and aunts to teach us how to survive and make homes. You lived here long enough to court and marry an American woman, but you chose an English wife. The prairie is a hard, hard land, and many American-born women die or return to homes back east because of it. Elizabeth is a lady used to servants and a comfortable life. Surely, even you appreciate what she is faced with out here on the prairie."

Arthur does not reply.

"She is a treasure, Arthur. Do you want her? Care for her?"

"You take a lot of privilege with my private affairs, Miss Harrah," Arthur growled.

"I grant that you would only be satisfied with a wife of refinement and education and society," flatters Louella.

"I am a Welsh gentleman and you judge my expectations of a wife accurately!" Arthur spits his reply.

"Then, I tell you there are a number of things you must do for her."

Arthur turns to face Miss Harrah and moves in to intimidate her. "What are these things you deem necessary, Miss Harrah?"

Louella turns to Arthur, not budging as much as one-eighth of an inch, thrusting her head and shoulders even closer to Arthur. "Keep her close company now for she will experience black days filled with tears and sobs. Be patient and show her how cherished she is," said Louella.

"You don't mind speaking your mind!" said Arthur.

The two glare at each other sitting on the jostling spring seat of the wagon.

"No, Arthur Gething, I don't. Next you must build her a dugout so that she can rear a child. Your rickety shack is not a respectable home.

"Elizabeth needs a half-human dugout. Most of it should be below ground to protect her from cold in winter and heat in summer. But she needs a framed house above ground so that she has a window or two to see out. The walls must be prepared so that they can be plastered. There needs to be enough lumber brought to frame up the top of it and window glasses and a good tight door instead of that flimsy one from the LeFors family even though it is an improvement."

During this lengthening exchange, Louella Harrah started by wagging her forefinger at Arthur and now she is poking him in the chest.

"My God, Woman! Do you intend to run my entire life?"

"Yes, if that becomes necessary, Arthur Gething! You brought that fine young woman half-way around the world to a shed. She has lost your first child, and I dare say you do care for her because she is English and proud and brave and strong,…but you will surely lose her if you don't follow my instructions to the letter! Besides, I will spread the news far and wide that you are a worthless scamp and worse if you don't. I promise."

Arthur Gething and Louella Harrah are nose to nose by the end of the exchange.

Arthur Gething breaks into a roar that turns into laughter. "By God, you've got me Louella! And while you are right, you are the most-troublesome woman I know besides Kate!"

"And, who in thunderation is Kate?"

"You call her Elizabeth; I call her Kate! How I address my wife is none of your concern. Kate, she is and Kate, she'll remain!"

"You, despicable, man! No wonder she is so miserable!"

Arthur roars with laughter again.

"Your wife better be much better when I see her next. Understand me, Arthur Gething!"

They drive up to the Harrah place. Louella hops off the wagon without a backward glance and slams closed the door of her family's dugout behind her as she enters.

She addresses her father, "You are right about Arthur Gething. He is an old reprobate!"

"Not to your liking, eh, Daughter?" says Joe.

"Worse than a scalawag! I am so angry!"

Louella reports her findings at the Gething place and a summary of her part in scolding Arthur Gething. They listen solemnly with concern for their friend Elizabeth. She has allies.

Arthur is not laughing when he turns toward home. Louella gave him a grander tongue lashing than he ever got from his father who excelled in put-downs. *Who would think a woman so much younger than I would reproach me with such gall?* He thinks deep and long about what to do because he realizes, and Louella leaves no doubt: Elizabeth is at a turning point.

Louella is a practical person and respected in the county and beyond. Her family is as formidable as she is. Her family will back her demands. Her words are not idle threats.

Building a dugout is a good idea. The lumber and supplies needed cost enough to beggar a man. I cannot consider it for as much as another year for the expense and the spring and summer requirements of the cattle. Next autumn is the earliest I can do it. Maybe the dugout now while I've help and convert it to a half-human dugout next year.

Damn she is such a stubborn woman! How do I demand the respect of one as proud and determined as Kate?

He has no clue.

Summarized from the Preface (pages v – vii) of *The Rath Trail* by Ida Ellen Rath, daughter-in-law of Charles Rath: Rath owned many wagon trains and hired freighters, but he was rarely in his mercantile stores. Instead, he was in partnerships with a number of local store owners/managers. Rath spent his time supplying products to the many stores and organizing and maintaining his freight lines. The competition of railroads in time, replaced animal-hauling freight lines. Rath's final property was in Mobeetie, Texas. [until 1879 it was Sweetwater, Texas.]

11 - Charles Rath's Mercantile

Bam-kersish-clatter!...bam-kersish-clatter!…bam-kersish-clatter…! The rhythm of wood splitting outside invades the kitchen. Jake is here! The day she has prayed for, Saturday! Quickly she surveys the room. She is ready for the trip to Mobeetie; she wraps her cloak about her shoulders, ties on her bonnet. Retrieving the shopping list and stuffing it in her reticule, she leaves in a rush.

Outside she sees a mule-drawn cart—a two-wheeled conveyance. *Mr. Gething owns such a vehicle? But, of course, it is necessary for fetching auxiliary supplies.* When Mr. Gething brought her to the ranch as his bride in February 1896, only three months past, they packed supplies on a mule-drawn wagon out from Mobeetie.

"Hello, Jake!" she waves enthusiastically to Mr. Gething's cowhand.

"Mrs. Gething, I'm here to take you to Mobeetie. Are you ready?" Jake says and helps her into the cart.

"Oh, Jake, I cannot tell you how ready I am. I looked forward to this all week! Tell me all about Mobeetie," Elizabeth says. "Mr. Gething and I stayed overnight there when I first came to the ranch, but it was the end of an exhausting trip, and I was not interested in it then. Louella tells me that Rath Mercantile stocks supplies and fabric for dresses."

"Yes, Ma'am, Mr. Rath has everythin' and I can tell you're eager to go to town," says Jake.

"Tell me more about the town and the people there," Elizabeth urges, curious and hungry for conversation.

"Charles Rath is mindin' the store, I hear. It is unheard of for 'im to be such a long spell here. Talk is, he's 'bout broke. He is a nice man and a good one…liked and respected. He used to do business all over Kansas, Indian Territory, Texas, and as far west as the Rockies," says Jake. "I 'spect he is or was one of the most 'mportant men in this town."

"Are those rumors credible?"

"Well, Ma'am, it just ain't like him to stay in one place this long. Ever'one knows he's been selling off his land, buildings, and cattle; he's owned a lot of property in and 'round Mobeetie."

"Mr. Gething spoke of this and, like you, spoke highly of Mr. Rath."

"Ma'am, if he ain't busy, get 'im to tell you some of the tales that he's sent to my ears. Ask him about his buffalo-huntin' days. He tells eye-poppin' stories."

Elizabeth falls silent for a long spell and Jake takes note of it.

A Spirit to Resist

I did not write a letter to Grandmother and my sister. If I can buoy my courage, I will. My problem is admitting how devastating my choice to elope with Mr. A. E. Gething was. I cannot admit to them the circumstances of my life here…. I cannot return to my family in London….

"Ma'am, you must've got a lot on your mind this mornin'," says Jake. "I was hopin' you'd tell me 'bout your folks in London. Ever since we've met, I been wantin' to ask. Seemed stranger than anythin' to me that you'd never cooked a meal and lived in a house so big that others did all the chores. I reckon your family is consider'ble rich."

"I never think of them as being wealthy, Jake. My parents drowned in a sudden storm off the coast while they were on a boating excursion," says Elizabeth.

"Terrible thing to happen, Ma'am," says Jake.

"Father was a banker in London and he was not as wealthy as many; he was an educated professional. After our parent's deaths, Alice, my sister, and I lived with and were educated by my grandparents. Grandfather is a physician in London; he is of the professional class, too. Alice and I were fortunate; we were educated to entertain and manage a household with staff for a prospective husband. Mr. Gething completely swept me off my feet with his tales of the West and his confidence in his future here," says Elizabeth.

"So, you didn't know a-tall that you'd live as you do now?"

"None, Jake. Your lesson in cooking and bread-making was my first and it saved me from hunger and even despair."

"An' Mr. Gethin' never said nothin' 'bout the place he was bringin' you to or the hard work you'd do?"

"Jake, he implied I would entertain all the leading citizens in and around Mobeetie. I did not even consider we

93

would live in that shack; I expected household servants—a full staff. I ask many questions about the house Mr. Gething built for me because I wanted to know how grand it would be." says Elizabeth. She swallows and clears her throat.

"Why, Ma'am, I swan," Jake says shaking his head in commiseration.

As they roll along toward town, they talk about friends and acquaintances, the weather, and activities on the ranch. Jake and Elizabeth drop the topic of her life. Elizabeth does not tell Jake that she eloped with Mr. Gething; she is ashamed she did not marry at home with her family in attendance. She knows her impetuous and trusting nature belong to her alone.

In time, the shacks, soddies, dugouts, and windmills of Mobeetie come into view. Elizabeth focuses on the squat buildings as they ride into town. Jake's description of this place is accurate; its appearance, very nearly nothing. There are two windmills, a surprising number of boarded-up bars or saloons, a millinery shop, Rath Mercantile, two churches, several nondescript houses, ant-hill like dugouts, a sheriff's office, a collection of offices—one for a doctor and several for lawyers, a hotel, a restaurant, and a livery stable. The buildings are weather worn and unpainted. Like aged men they lean against each other for support.

"Jake, there is not one saloon on the entire street!" says Elizabeth.

"No, Ma'am, it ain't been the same since the Baptists and Methodists brought to town a revival preacher who made 'bout 300 converts. Then, with 'Cap' Arrington, the new lawman in the county, holdin' such a tight rein, they closed down all the good ol' bars in town," Jake grins.

As they pull up in front of Rath's Mercantile, Elizabeth steps first down onto the street and then up on the boardwalk in front of the store. She forces herself to remember the promise of a respectable selection of fabric. Entering, it is too dark to see the merchandise clearly at first, but then a shadowy figure standing behind a counter emerges. A distinguished man of more than sixty years becomes visible in a few moments.

"Good morning! What can I do for you today?" he asks.

As it becomes easier to see, Elizabeth notes the greeter is a balding gentleman of graying hair. He wears a beautifully tailored suit and a cravat.

"I am Mrs. Arthur Gething and I am here for supplies and other purchases."

"Well, well, I am pleased to make your acquaintance, Mrs. Gething! I am Charles Rath. I heard that Mr. Gething brought home his bride, the 'Lady from London,' but I missed your first visit. It is my pleasure to make your acquaintance."

"Mine, as well. I looked forward to our meeting. Here is a list of supplies Mr. Gething needs. Jake is here to load them in our cart. I want to look at your fabric. My friend Miss Louella Harrah told me you carry a selection of calico."

"A friend of Louella, are you? She is a fine young woman. She works along with her mother raising her brothers and sisters. Joe Harrah and I are old friends…known one another a long time," says Mr. Rath.

Mr. Charles Rath has an appreciative eye for a well-turned-out woman. All of his wives witness to that. He enjoys visits with comely women; however, he is aware that Mrs. Gething is intent on her purchases so that, instead of detaining her for more conversation, he nods toward that area of the store.

"Follow me to the dry goods and you can find what you need while I fill your order," says Mr. Rath.

He leaves Mrs. Gething with the selection of calico and returns to the task of filling the order she gave him.

In my experience, calico is white! The cotton calico cloth in the mercantile display is mostly prints that tend to black, brown, navy blue, and dark green.

She recalls the ladies she met at church and their choices. After a search, she finds one calico pattern that is a lighter blue with yellow and red florets. It is the least dark in overall design.

This one must be my choice. Then she examines the other shelves for scissors, pins, needles, and trimmings. *Mr. Rath is charging twenty-five cents for a packet of needles. An exorbitant price! These three needles may as well be gold. The trimmings offered here are limited and are also dark in color.* She takes her time making her choices, then she gathers her selections and goes to the counter where Mr. Rath has filled Mr. Gething's order.

"Well, did you find everything you need? How much of that calico do you want?"

"I am buying all of it. The packet of needles is overpriced. And, I did not find many colors in your trimmings. Only a few dark shades! I wanted something cheery."

"No, Ma'am, these are the colors used by the women who shop here and we don't keep the bright ones. This is all we offer. Our stock is down some at present. The price of needles is due to the high cost of shipping. Tell me again, how much of this calico do you want?"

Did I not just say all? "All of it, Mr. Rath." *He was not paying attention.* "This will complete my order. Mr. Gething said these should go on his account."

"I will be happy to add this to Mr. Gething's account. However, as I will soon close my business and leave the country for Kansas and then California, I will appreciate Mr. Gething settling his account as soon as he can," says Mr. Rath.

"I am sorry to hear that news; your mercantile is highly recommended to me and you are going to be missed," says Elizabeth. "In view of your plans to leave, Mr. Rath, and because Jake encouraged me to ask you about the days you were buffalo-hunting in this country, I wish to hear of it if you are willing."

"Ah, yes… Louella's father and I hunted buffalo together years ago." Mr. Rath looks out the window collecting memories with the concentration of a child catching fireflies. With a lurch in his voice, he clears his throat and begins. Moisture rims his eyes.

"Mrs. Gething, that was many years ago. I was about young Jake's age then and my family moved to Kansas from Ohio where my family farmed."

Mr. Rath is a proud man. I am aware that my request was insensitive.

"I left in 1855 and found work as a bull-whacker and drove one team of a wagon train for a man in the freighting business out of Dodge City. The wagons were loaded with goods of all kinds and we followed trails into the Rockies calling at Indian trading posts, mercantile stores, small towns, ranches, and road ranches—primitive way stations— all along the trail."

"Was it as dangerous and difficult as I imagine?" says Elizabeth.

"It is hard to tell what you imagine," Mr. Rath smiles. "The trails were somewhat established so we camped near water and fuel or road ranches and trading posts. The oxen and wagons required constant care. Fording streams and rivers and climbing through mountain passes during any weather was the job of a bull-whacker."

"What about the Indians? Did they attack the wagon trains?" says Elizabeth.

"Sometimes they did, it was the practice to trade for our goods. As matter of fact, I lived among the Cheyenne after trading with them. They taught me how to hunt and track; I became a skilled marksman. I dealt fair when I traded among them and earned peace with most of them. I was among them long enough to learn many of their tribal languages. It is an advantage in trading," says Mr. Rath.

"I thought Indians were blood-thirsty, war-like, and horse thieves," says Elizabeth.

"Yes, they can be, but I made deep friendships among them. Many I count as dear as my brothers. They will fight, like any man, to protect themselves or avenge their people. Living with them, as I did, gave me the advantage of knowing what they were most likely to do in a fight or raid. That served me many times because I could anticipate their moves. Now, most are on reservations in Indian Territory."

"Jake said you were a buffalo-hunter and you tell 'eye-popping' stories."

"Mrs. Gething, the buffalo are mostly gone today along with the Indians who survived by hunting them. Back then, herds were so large that they could be seen from my hunting stand all the way to the horizon in every direction and so thick that once they passed the grass all across the prairie was gone. They migrated south in the winter and north in the summer. One day I recall having killed 108 buffaloes from a single stand. I hunted a year or more until I sold enough hides to begin my business as a freighter."

"Of what use were buffalo? Why were they valuable?"

"Their hides were tanned with the fur on because everyone back east wanted two for their buggy, carriage or wagon because they are so warm. One was used to cover the seat and the other one to wrap around the knees and lap. Others were made into great coats with high collars to keep out the cold wind and rain or snow. Many were tanned without hair and were made into industrial belts for machinery here and in Europe. We ate and sold their meat, especially the humps and hams. The tongues were a delicacy; I shipped carloads of smoked tongues back East by rail."

Mr. Rath is not going to tell me his exciting adventures as I hoped. This wide prairie took its toll on him, I think.

"I did not know they were used for the manufacture of those products," says Elizabeth.

"They are used to manufacture products today. Since those early days, buffalo and cattle bones dried and bleached out all over the prairies. Settlers proving up their homesteads eke a meager living by gathering those bones by the wagon-load. I bought many a carload and shipped them back East where they are ground for fertilizer or made into buttons," said Mr. Rath.

It is a wonder he can talk about this knowing his business cannot last long. My heart would be breaking. I think his is.

Jake steps inside to signal that the supplies are in the cart just as Mr. Rath wraps up the bolt of calico and notions Elizabeth chose.

"Mr. Rath, thank you for helping me and taking your time to share what must be a life of rich memories in this land. As you know, I arrived only a short time ago…since February. I find myself longing for London. Your story has been a gift and I wish you well!" says Elizabeth.

Mr. Rath nods his acceptance and turns away, disappearing into a back room, before Jake and Elizabeth gather their bundles.

When they are back in the cart, Jake says, "Ma'am, I apologize if I'm outta line, but what are you goin' to do with that bolt of calico?"

"Well, I took your advice and accepted Louella's help. She will show me how to make a good practical dress for working at home. Why do you ask?" Elizabeth says.

"I am jest thinkin' that Maw never needed more 'n five or six yards of material for a dress and there must be 'bout 20 yards on that bolt," squirms Jake.

"Great Jumping Jehoshaphat! Jake, I think I will never know all the right questions to ask about Texas! Or, even when to ask or to stop asking questions!"

Jake cannot contain his mirth and bursts forth in laughter.

"This way, no one will ever know when I put on a clean dress! They will all be the same," Elizabeth rollicks with laughter.

"Jake, Mr. Rath told me of his various occupations throughout the prairie and even into the Rockies. Even with his brotherhood with the Indians. I find it incredible he was always warned of Indian uprisings and raids by his Indian friends?" says Elizabeth.

"The story goes that his first wife was the Cheyenne squaw, Roadmaker. Her name didn't mean she built roads; it means she was very strong-willed and bent others to her own purpose. He lived among that tribe for years and traded with both Indians and frontier families. Mr. Rath prob'y left that out because he was talkin' with you, a fine lady."

"I think I admire this Cheyenne wife, Roadmaker. Was she was so difficult that Mr. Rath did not stay in the marriage?" says Elizabeth.

"Well, if she was bossy or not, I dunno. Mr. Rath's first wife was Roadmaker and he told me he lived with the Cheyenne, like he was a brother to 'em. Anyhow, he managed to save his skin many times even after he walked away from Roadmaker. He was respected for his bravery and fair dealing by his Indian brothers and the frontiersmen."

"What do you mean 'fair dealing' with the Indians? Do you mean he did not cheat and sold quality goods to them?"

"Well, of course, it must be that, but this is what I heard from the men who was his partners and friends. The Indians thought so well of him because he never called the military on 'em even though there was disputes with 'em or even when they made raids against him and his partners. Instead he took care of it himself."

"Tell me more about Mr. Rath leaving Roadmaker. I imagine that the divorce did cause bad feelings with the Cheyenne and especially Roadmaker's family."

"Among Indians, the end of a marriage is a casual event and not at all like divorce between men and women on the frontier. Ah, it may be an everyday thing among the Indians, I can't say," says Jake.

"Queen Victoria is opposed to divorce and proper English women do not consider it. There is a common saying about the role of English wives—'Suffer and be still!' I would make a good Cheyenne wife who could hold her ground," Elizabeth laughs.

"No doubt, you would!" Jake grins. "I 'spect you got the same grit as my Maw."

"Jake, can we eat before we leave? I am hungry and thirsty," says Elizabeth.

"Good idea! I could use some grub, too. How 'bout us stopping at Bertie's Café? She makes a great peach cobbler," says Jake. "It's a few doors down."

Bertie waves them inside; her remaining customers are finishing their lunches. Bertie and Jake exchange greetings when she comes to their table.

"Bertie, meet Mr. Arthur Gething's bride, Mrs. Gething; she came out with him in late February," says Jake.

"Oh, we've hear'd all about you, Mrs. Gething. Guess you've taken on quite a job there on th' ramshackle Gething place.

"Folks, there is still plenty of chili and cornbread, but the peach cobbler's gone. You ought 'a try my pound cake with wild plum sauce. It's good and I've plenty to serve you both," says Bertie.

"That's good for me," says Jake. "What, for you, Mrs. Gethin'?"

"Fortunate for us that we have arrived no later. Jake recommends your restaurant so, please serve me the same," answers Elizabeth.

"Saw you just come from Rath's store. How does he seem to you, Jake?" says Bertie.

"Lower 'n a snake's belly, I'd say," says Jake.

"He told me about his life when he was about Jake's age. My request was ill-timed and I regret asking him." says Elizabeth. "Jake told me about his Cheyenne wife. Did he ever marry again?"

Bertie says, "He married twice after that. The first was Carrie Markley and their children are grown; Mr. Rath and Carrie lived in Dodge City, and then Osage, and then here. Mr. Rath kept her in silk dresses and finery and let her travel back East as often as she liked. She liked his money well enough and spent it as if she'd never see the end of it. She seldom saw Mr. Rath and they divorced years ago. Could be she didn't care to be separated for such long stretches of time. Funny thing, when he and Carrie Markley Rath were divorced, he married her friend, Miss Emma Nester, soon after. Word is that now Mr. Rath and Emma are at odds with one another."

Jake, looking across the table at Elizabeth, winces. Elizabeth drops her gaze to her slice of pound cake. The exchange between the two goes unnoticed by Bertie who barrels on with her tale.

"People who ought to know around the county thought this marriage would survive because he was home more with Emma Rath than he was with Carrie Rath, who was quarrelsome and demanding. He stayed in Mobeetie purty reg'lar until 'bout five- or six months ago. Now he's always at the store. I heard news of trouble between Rath and Emma only recent-like. Could be his change of fortune has somethin' to do with it. Seems Mr. Rath in his youth and middle years couldn't be still…was always on the move, making deals, bringin' in new businesses and new partners in the mercantile trade, buyin' land and cattle. Jest makin' money hand o'er fist," says Bertie. "It's a puzzle to me how he can be broke!"

Bertie bustles away to clear tables and straighten the chairs.

Elizabeth says, "I think his life has been both full of adventure and…well, he is so courteous even as troubled as he must be now. I cannot tell you how meeting him affected me."

"He's broke, Ma'am," Jake says in a soft voice, "broke in ever' way a man can be broke. He's a broken man. A lot of his mercantile partners left him with all the debt owed others; well, altogether it seems it's led to his present troubles. I say, Rath is respected and stands up to bad breaks and is a-tryin' to take care of the debt both he and his partners owed. He won't be a-stayin'," says Jake.

Mr. Rath and I are proud. I am too proud to return to London; he is too proud to stay here. But, to be a broken woman…no! I must resist.

"Jake, I begin to understand how precarious life with its fortunes and misfortunes are in this land."

"How is it that you know so much about Mr. Rath?" Elizabeth adds.

Bertie interrupts from nearby, "Well, it's all the people in Mobeetie are talkin' 'bout, Mrs. Gething. When Rath pulls out, everyone is gonna be hurt for he was the strength of the town after Fort Elliott closed down. 'Sides he's well-liked all 'round."

Jake and Elizabeth finish their meal, pay, and escape the café owner's gossip.

A pioneer should have imagination, should be able to enjoy the idea of things more than the things themselves.

Willa Cather, page 48, *O Pioneers!*

12 – Window in a Hole

Elizabeth settles on her one chair, removes Arthur's shoes from her aching feet, and slides his shoes under the front of the bachelor stove alongside her slippers. There are only red embers and gray ashes inside; she does not add more cow chips from the bottom of the fuel box.

She returns from the lean-to where a covering of snow hid frozen puddles between the shack door and the lean-to around the corner. It was treacherous for her to plot a path to feed the two mules and Spider. She slipped and slid, but she fell just once. This late March snowfall caught them unprepared.

Her hands are stiff from feeding the animals and she cups her fingers and blows on them to rid them of needle piercing pain. Her feet ache and she ignores the discomfort.

This snow storm invades the prairie just as the *shinnery oak*—a toxic locoweed—turns green while the grass is still brown. So Arthur shifts his work and that of the 'cow-servants' from destroying the *shinnery oak* to hauling hay to his herd. Cattle, unlike horses, do not use their hooves to scrape away snow to graze on dry grass. Arthur and the cowhands must keep ample hay on the ground to divert his cattle from the greening locoweed. Freezing temperatures make other demands.

Arthur chops holes in the ice around the ponds surrounding the springs so that cattle can drink. He returns to the shack to eat breakfast before leaving again to check the herd with the cowhands.

This fragile shack creaks and whistles as it attempts to turn aside frigid wind. Elizabeth is a little warmer inside. Moving closer to the stove, she sits and pulls her knees to her chest and huddles inside her riding habit and cloak.

"Oh, God, is there no other way except to resign myself to living in a dugout…some dank hole in the ground? It is humiliating to live like a hedgehog! Yet this cold and fatigue force me to it," she whispers between chattering teeth.

Dear Lord, I not only protest to living underground surrounded by earth and dirt and crawling bits. What I truly dread is lack of sunlight because the winter on this land is so cold and dark. What I pray for is a window in a hole…impossible maybe, but if Thou move mountains, I need sunlight…so I need a window in a hole. Amen!

Elizabeth turns to practical considerations as soon as her prayer rises.

Deciding whether to live in a dugout, proposed first by Jake and then recommended by Louella and their LeFors neighbors, is what I struggle with each day. This late snow storm comes as the fuel supply is so low that I must ration fuel and supplies of beans, salt pork, canned goods, and other staples like a miser. Arthur, our cowhands, and I exhaust ourselves with effort needed to do essential chores. Arthur bursts into a temper often; only the hard-edged humor of our cowhands relieves tension of Arthur's frequent tantrums. I can no longer postpone a choice because I cannot face another winter in this cold drafty shed. So… some relief must be found and another solution does not present itself.

My pride needs to step aside. Acting now will insure that there is plenty of help from Jake, Bob, and Green before larger ranches hire them for spring rounding, branding, and marketing. My decision is made for me by circumstances, I think. Well, it must be done. So as soon as sun melts this snow, I hope that work on the dugout commences. Simply deciding this lifts a weight from me. It is time to speak with Arthur.

Elizabeth measures out a few cow chips and one split log from the wood box and adds them to the belly of the stove. Then, she makes another pot of coffee; she prepared porridge and sourdough biscuits before she left the shed.

Arthur comes in and stands near the stove with his tin mug of coffee and samples the sourdough biscuits warming on the stovetop. They eat breakfast without conversation. Both are intent on nourishment and keeping warm. Arthur leaves to harness the mules and saddle Spider.

She hears the protests of the mules and the slap of reins as Arthur secures the harnesses. Old Jack, the mule, protests and he stubbornly resists Arthur's effort to get him out of the lean-to. There is a crack of the reins and Jack's rump slams against the outside wall bringing down a scattering of dust and snow inside. She hears Arthur leading them around the shed to hitch Jack and Kate to the wagon loaded with hay. The jangling of the bit lets Elizabeth know Spider will be saddled. The horse blanket plops on the horse's back and she hears Arthur mutter to Spider while he heaves the heavy Western saddle. Sounds of hooves are muffled by the snowfall, but Elizabeth knows Arthur is leading Spider out to the wagon where he will be reined along beside the mules until they meet with the cowhands and their day's work begins.

Again there is her constant companion: solitude. Arthur and the cowhands leave by sunup and return by sundown. Then it is time to eat and sleep for all of them. But she is in that small shack during most waking hours accompanied only by silence or an orchestra of the wind.

She prepares their daily meals…now routine chores. Housekeeping is simple and she does not allow regret into her thoughts. She plans for her next Panhandle winter. It is uncharted territory. She gives survival her entire effort and has since she arrived, she tackles every obstacle with confidence. No longer the callow bride of a few months ago, she has recaptured her self-reliance with support of her neighbors. If Arthur Edward Gething snatched it from her, he never will again.

Her last job before she can rest is trimming wicks of the two kerosene lamps and cleaning glass chimneys that protect their flames. Then she pours kerosene to fill the reservoirs of each lantern and does it with precision so that none of the precious fluid spills.

After feeding the animals, she removed Arthur's shoes and went barefooted, but now she puts on her slippers warmed under the stove. Her toes cramped because his shoes are too short for her and too wide as well. Her own shoes sit atop her trunk. She saves them because there are holes in the soles. After each time she wears her shoes, she traces around them on cardboard saved from boxes, cuts out shoe-forms and places them inside her shoes so that she has her own shoes to wear in public.

She often wished for another pair of serviceable shoes. In her flurry, to pack and elope, Arthur insisted there was no room for the portmanteau filled with her shoes. The shoes she planned to bring from London, she knows, are useless here. In London she packed shoes she would wear in drawing rooms of the prosperous neighbors and entertainments at social events Arthur promised she would enjoy. Entertainment was her life in London; survival is her life in Texas. She concocts a plan for replacing these worn out shoes with a pair costing $1.25 in the Sears-Roebuck catalogue and will speak of this plan with Arthur.

The Miami Chief, the town of Miami's newspaper, contains articles about the money to be earned by raising chickens; it guarantees that one can begin with only a small investment. She reads it for the tenth time or more. There is a good market for eggs or so the article reports. Louella tells her to use chickens to rid the garden of insects and when she compares her larder to that of the Harrah household, she knows that her experienced neighbor gives reliable advice.

Raising chicks to create a flock can give her fresh eggs and chickens so that she can serve a nice chicken and dumpling dish from time to time. Extra eggs can be sold in Mobeetie. Well, with energy saved from collecting and saving the fuel as she must in this shed, she will live in a dugout and devote her time to raising chickens. What a livestock farmer she aspires to become! Buying sturdy shoes for herself is only the beginning of planned purchases.

She prepares the main meal for Arthur and the cowhands for today. Beans, beans, beans, beans! Of course, there will be strong black coffee and sourdough biscuits. If only she can find a can of either peaches or tomatoes. She finds neither but notes a dwindling supply of coffee and adds it to her list of supplies for their next trip to Mobeetie.

Glory! If there is little to prepare, it takes little effort to accomplish it. I must appreciate the advantages of poverty! It gives me time today to make an entry in my journal. It is a blessing to spend time on my own pleasure.

She opens her journal, wraps a quilt around herself and snuggles up to the stove.

> I accept the need to live in a dugout. I shall be a mole in a hole and adopt a droll humor! If Mr. Gething will invest in chicks, I will learn to be a stock farmer—a fowl deed! With a husband like Arthur, I rejoice in a wealth of good friends— Louella, Jake, Green, and Bob.
>
> March 12, 1897

Four hungry men—Arthur and his 'cow-servants'—arrive at dusk and it is dark before their animals are fed and rubbed down. Elizabeth hears their animals snort and blow and grind away at their oats. A modest meal is hot and ready to serve by the time they wash up in warm water she supplied for them at the outside washstand. Jake enters first and hands her a bag.

"Mrs. Gething, the boys and me brung somethin' for you." The men enter behind Jake.

She peeks inside and there are six cans—three each of tomatoes and peaches—and way down inside is something cold. A whole round of frozen butter! She could almost hug them.

"Jake, Bob, Green! This is wonderful. I promise peach cobbler for tomorrow!"

Green pulls out a tin canister of molasses and sets it on the table. He says, "This'll go great with them buttered sourdoughs, Ma'am."

"Thank you for sharing this. I never met a man as fond of molasses as you are, Green."

Elizabeth plates the butter and sets their meal on the table. Meanwhile, the men stow their coats and wraps and pull up to the table. They eat in silence as only very tired and hungry men do and she counts her blessings a second time that day with a promise to herself to add an entry to her journal as soon as she can. Jake faces Arthur and lifts his chin.

"Mr. Gething, how soon do you think one of us can make a trip to Mobeetie? We can pick up more supplies and the mail."

"The weather always decides it. If the snow melts soon, I judge a trip can be made within the week. Somewhat…it depends upon birthing of the new calves for we will need to be sure they are up and their mothers are taking care of them especially after cold temperatures brought by this unexpected snow. Other than that I don't see a problem," says Arthur and Elizabeth enters their conversation.

"I wrote several letters to mail to my family and I would like to go with the wagon for there are things on which I must check."

"Anything special?" Arthur asks and cocks his left eyebrow.

"Louella has talked with me about a garden which I spoke with you about; it would be helpful to know what is available at Rath's Mercantile, for I may need to order additional materials. It would be good to be away for a day trip."

"Kate, I talked with Bob and Green about your plans and Jake told me what is needed based on a garden he made for his mother; they gave me a general idea of materials required and cost."

Bob interrupts with another need. "That ol' mule Jack needs to be re-shoed and his hooves trimmed. We don't need 'im to turn up with a sore hoof in the middle of a job. B'sides he don't need much excuse for bring on a limp an' holdin' up."

Arthur, eager to end the conversation, looks around the table. "Is there anything else? Once we go we can't go again until we return from driving the cattle to Fort Worth."

Green sums it up, "We orter be a-checkin' all tools, supplies and brandin' med'cines o'er the next few days."

Arthur nods in agreement and turns to Bob, "Tell us about that recent visitor out at your place."

Bob begins, "I can guess who passed along that news you're speakin' uv. But, well, Mr. Benson, manager of the Quarter Circle, came around searching for Jake 'cause he's been a-working for him for a year now. Seems Jake has a real knack for countin' cattle for a drive. Mr. Benson asked Jake to operate as his outside man for this spring drive," says Bob.

"What is an 'outside man,' Bob?" says Elizabeth.

"He's a hand Mr. Benson hires to work outside the Quarter Circle home ranch to contact other stockmen an' invites 'em to join his boss' cattle drive. Other stockmen who join him must brand and round up their cattle at a chosen place on Quarter Circle ground just before spring drive begins. Stockmen who join the Quarter Circle arrive with their herds then it's his outside man's responsibility t' count cattle in each stockman's herd and recognize every brand. As you'd reckon, an outside man's needs the respect of all the stockmen and be dad-gum near perfect at countin'," says Bob.

"That is quite an honor, Jake," says Elizabeth. "But how do you manage to be so accurate?"

"Oh, Ma'am," says Bob, "that ain't nothin' for a sharp feller like our Jake. He jest counts their legs and divides by four."

As the men hoot and holler, Elizabeth realizes she has just been set up for the telling of this joke and laughs with them.

"Jake, are you really Mr. Branson's outside man?"

"No, Ma'am, but Bob knows it's a spot I'm aimin' for. So far I'm Branson's wrangler, but I been studyin' how I can get to be his outside man," says Jake.

As the cowhands make ready to leave for their dugout, Jake says, "Mrs. Gething, take a look here," as he motions to the wood box outside the doorway.

Elizabeth follows and in the light from the lantern Jake is holding ahead of them and she sees the wood box heaping with split logs.

"Bob cut wood in a trade for 'em at Rath Mercantile on our las' trip to Mobeetie," says Jake.

Tears well up in Elizabeth's eyes and she does not even try to hide them.

"You weren't s'posed to say nothin'. I planned it for a surprise in the mornin'. That's the reason we was so quiet loadin' the box," says Bob.

Jake grins. "Some surprises don't need no waitin' on," he says.

"Bob, this is the best surprise ever. Thank you for your generosity. Green, the molasses you brought made a fine dessert tonight. All of you are to be rewarded tomorrow with a dish of tomatoes with onion and a peach cobbler made from Louella's recipes," says Elizabeth.

The cowhands leave in a circle of light given off by the lantern Jake is holding shoulder high. They pick their way back toward their own dugout, minus a stack of wood. Elizabeth brings in several split logs for tonight and Arthur follows.

Arthur says, "Kate, those are good 'cow-servants'."

"They are exceptional *cowhands*, Mr. Gething. Please stop referring to them as 'cow-servants.'" Arthur laughs; he knows this is a sore point with her and he loves aggravating her.

As Elizabeth clears table and washes dishes, Arthur says, "Kate, this is an example of hospitality and goodness of Panhandle people. These three appreciate you including them for our evening meal and they enjoy what they call a "woman-cooked" meal. I do too, Kate, dear!"

"Thank you, Mr. Gething. A word with you, please. I made decision today that we should prepare a dugout for our living quarters. I object to living in the ground, but I do realize its benefits in saving fuel in winter and providing a warmer place in winter and a cooler place in summer. Still, I encourage you to plan on a well-built home above ground. I cannot do well living in a dirt hovel."

"Just keep working with me, Kate, and someday you will have your fine house as I promised. It was my plan to bring you to one when you first arrived, but years of drought here made my plans…a failed promise. Your efforts in these circumstances are exceptional and deeply appreciated."

Mr. Gething, you conveniently forget that your promise was bringing me to a fine house where I would entertain community leaders and our Congressman to the capital of this state.

"I shall continue to do my best for it is in my interest, too. I have made another decision today. It is to become a stock farmer."

"A stock farmer! Kate, I am the only stock farmer in this family!"

"You would not object to my raising chickens, would you? Louella assures me that they keep a garden free of insects and will provide eggs and chickens for our table and additional eggs to sell in Mobeetie. It would not be such a fowl deed, now, would it?"

Arthur throws back his head in laughter. "Kate, you are indeed a clever wench! How much of an investment do you require?"

"It is supposed to be a modest one, but I need to learn more of what is required. I will depend on Louella's help for its management. Besides the chicks and pens there will be grain and other things. Will our cowhands set it up for me as well as the garden and the dugout? It seems like a lot to ask since they are eager to return to work on the big ranches soon."

"They are all quite fond of you so that I think they will agree to it. I will ask them tomorrow. Now, let us get to bed and rest, Kate. It has been a long day," says Arthur, placing arms about her.

A Spirit to Resist

Yes, Arthur, to bed it is. Rest will be postponed, I am sure.

"Mr. Gething, I want first to add something to my journal about this evening. It will only take a moment."

"I am washing-up before bedding. Keep your journal entry to a sentence or two," Arthur directs as he places an enameled metal bowl of water on the stove top for bathing.

Elizabeth surveys her kitchen and sees that everything is ready for preparing their breakfast tomorrow. Then she retrieves her journal and sits at the table with pen in hand and writes:

> So many of my worries at the beginning of this day have vanished—diminishing fuel and food are relieved by our cowhands' generosity. Arthur will supply money for my chicken farm and I have put to rest my resistance to a dugout. Arthur has that amorous look in his eye and is even at this minute washing himself before bed. I will not be ruled, thank you, Mr. Gething. I write *five* sentences!
>
> March 12, 1897

Mr. Arthur Gething, you need to produce more than a small compliment, a flowery word and an excuse for your deception to regain my trust. A new pair of shoes for me would be a start! In addition, you could cease calling me 'Kate' and address me as Mrs. Gething or, in private, Elizabeth. My options are few, but I shall make my own

117

advantages. Beware! Trust is easily lost and you will need a long time to regain it with me.

Like most frontiersmen, freighters were inclined to be multifaceted and multi-talented individuals (jacks-of-all-trades).

C. Robert Haywood, page 117
Trails South: The Wagon-Road Economy
in the Dodge City-Panhandle Region

13 - Root, Hog, or Die

Change comes timidly to the Panhandle. It knows that winter clings to the land and bullies spring if it can. This warm morning invites Elizabeth to sit in front of the dugout. The tall grasses are the string instruments of the wind that strums and plucks through them. The prairie creatures play an accompaniment. The sunrise colors are flagrant from purple to red-orange to golden.

Elizabeth sits at the doorway with her cup of coffee to warm her hands and listens to the symphony of the land. It is here in the steadiness of the turning of the seasons that she decides finally to stay with Arthur rather than to ask her grandparents for return train tickets and passage. Wrapping her warm cloak about her, she reflects again, as she has for the past months…nearly a year…since her loss of her child, upon her options.

It is a multi-facetted decision. The loss of her child is close to her; it amazes her that its short life within her has left such emptiness. A child to care for here where she is often alone she anticipates with such pleasure. She worries about another child—whether she will give birth to a healthy child and how the birth will affect her. Some women die giving birth, but that was true in London as it is here. Will she manage the birth without the attention of a doctor if it should come to that? Her growing circle of women friends invites her to take courage and these are dependable, reliable women. Many women did this before her so she gambles that she will also accomplish it.

Arthur reassures her that the cowboys and he will complete her new dugout: one safe for children. The hired men will prepare a garden plot before they leave. He has already made an order for the lumber, plaster, window glasses, and hardware needed. The cowhands are digging and plowing and fencing his promise.

A new home is not her only consideration. She knows life in London where she left comforts and entertainments and friends. London offers its treasures but for a select set of its citizens. Men with titles must be first-born and control substantial wealth to live well. Ladies must marry well to enjoy wealthy society. Arthur is no Lord; she is not a Lady of substance. It is a fact of their lives that they must create their wealth and station in life. Many young couples are setting their hopes for the future on other lands in the British Empire or underpopulated lands like the United States of America. Too, her situation if she chose to return to London would be beset with problems. Everyone in her social set will know that she and Arthur eloped and she would be a divorced woman…not a desirable prospect among the gentlemen of her class if she chose to marry again. Her prospects might lead to a much lower station if she were single…housekeeper, governess, seamstress…and nothing toward which she aspires.

Elizabeth admits Arthur is right about her. She does love adventure, but she is not one to gamble so much as him…or so she thought. But she is gambling everything for a place of her own. She likes what she is experiencing in this new land. There is a freedom here that rises from the land itself. The exacting rules, laws, and class constraints of England do not exist here. She can carve out her life and be part of the creation of a new country. It excites her and at the same time it terrifies her. She experiences the cost from sunrise to sunset.

Bob teases her daily that first thing each morning in the new dugout she must examine every inch for bugs, snakes, scorpions, mice, and other interloping creatures. He torments her saying a single scorpion sting will teach her to place her shoes upside down on the benches and shake them vigorously before dressing her feet. He tells her that no matter how cold she is, she will do that before building a fire and making their coffee and breakfast. Bob's razing is his way to teach her what is to come. She knows her established routines will become new routines in the dugout.

She expects to use the balance of each day doing laundry and cooking on an open fire pit and the project she has chosen of planting and tending more trees. Too, there is a dream of having flowers around the entrance of her new place. For this dream, she is sacrificing her soft hands and attention she once gave to making herself attractive and well dressed.

Arthur has been much more attentive since she lost their first child; he does not stay away for such long periods, but she is oddly lonely whether he is present or absent. She is a necessity in his world, not a friend, not a companion, not his beloved wife, and she knows it. Her role as she perceives it is that of a business partner only. It is her newly made friends and the cowhands that give her the strength to take on this new land and life, for she admires their fortitude.

When she is finished with her meditation, she returns to sweep out the shack and set it to order. She cleans the oil lamps and trims the wicks, airs the bedding and cleans the cooking implements in the kitchen, so they are ready for their next use.

The cowhands she is so fond of will be here again this morning to carve the new dwelling from the prairie. The mules stand ready to pull a scoop to hollow into the southern exposure of a hill—actually but a hillock. The team stands harnessed near the dugout; she and Arthur are driving them to the location of the dugout. She takes the shovels, picks, and wheelbarrow to the Murphy wagon while Arthur hitches the team.

As she tends to these chores, she is also reviewing her plan for a small garden which will be for tomatoes, green beans, onions, potatoes, and carrots. And perhaps watermelons, but then pumpkins might be a better choice because they can be stored in a cool root cellar, a shallow cave or depression, with the onions, potatoes, and carrots for the winter. Her plan is to wrap the root vegetables in newspaper and pack them in sand to better preserve them. Five- or six plants will be adequate for a beginning gardener for she must learn the process and then continue to weed and water it. It is difficult to carry water from the springs to the garden and also to the trees she planted for future shade, for it will add hours of hauling water. Sometime soon she needs to learn what is necessary to keep chickens. The cowhands agreed to complete both the dugout and garden before leaving in late March or early April. She hears the scraping of earth-moving and knows the morning's work begins. Bob's voice follows in song.

> I'm a lonely bull-whacker
> On the Red Cloud Line,

Arthur has ordered a door for the new place. The ladies of the church sewing-circle are saving their seed catalogues and ladies' magazines for her new home. She has a plan of what the two rooms will be like…especially the window that will let light into them.

> I can lick any son-of-a-gun
> Can yoke this ox of mine.

She sets about making lunch preparations and fills buckets so she can carry water to the men during the day. The noon meal will be the standard, but Elizabeth has made them a cobbler with canned peaches today from Louella's recipe. She wants them to know how she appreciates their extra dedication to the improved dugout they are making.

> If I can catch him
> You bet I will or try,

Bob's voice continues leading the song. The work is measured by the cadence of it. Elizabeth's work indoors profits from the rhythm of their song and digging noises. Arthur comes to the door.

"Kate! We're going to need a bucket of water. It's a thirsty work we're about," yells Arthur from outside.

> I'll lick with him an ox-bow,
> Root, hog, or die.

"Yes, Mr. Gething, I'm on the way with it."

123

She hauls two covered buckets at a time at the end of a human yoke until there are four in the wagon.

Sitting in the wagon Arthur says, "Move it along, Kate, these men cannot work any longer without water."

Then, Elizabeth climbs into the wagon and together they return to the work site. She greets the men with the water buckets and a dipper. The men stop, drink deeply and return to work. She stays to watch the progress they are making. They take turns working with picks, shovels, and wheelbarrow. She brings water throughout the morning and lays out their noon meal on an even plane in the shade of cottonwood and hackberry trees.

After they eat, there is a period for all of them to rest. She is pleased that all of the men took a second serving of her peach cobbler and told her how good the meal was.

"Bob, I heard you tell you were a bull-whacker. Tell us about the song you are singing," Elizabeth engages.

"Oh, Ma'am," chuckles Bob, "I earned my way once as a bull-whacker. It is a rough way to live. The six-cornered cussin' we yelled would blister your ears. Once a Christian General I hauled for made us stop cussin,' but within 50 miles the animals came to a complete stall. So he ordered us to commence with the 'cussin' as usual.' The other part of the job is using a twenty-five foot long bull whip to keep the oxen or mules on the move. It takes both to be a teamster— hard cussin' and being handy with the bull whip—and they do this standing in the wagons just behind the wagon tongue.

"Bob, this land is so full of stories. Sometimes I think they are more exaggeration than truth," says Elizabeth.

"Mrs. Gething, Bob brags and loads up his stories a heap, but what he's telling about being a teamster is just like he says," interjects Green. "Take a look-see when your supplies arrive and then you won't doubt him a minute."

Bob continues, "Oxen or mule teams were the only way to move materials into the Panhandle plains before any railroads were built. Mr. Gething tells me your supplies are ordered."

"At the price I will pay, I expect they are charging by the curse-word instead of by the pound," Arthur Gething sighs.

"Mr. Gething," says Bob, "I judge that even today the price of ox-freight is none too high. There was a time in the 80s when mule and ox teams were meeting one another on the Jones-Plummer Trail many times in the trip. Traffic like that is gone today, and I know wagon masters are paid $70 a month, which is high compared to cowhand wages of $20 to $30 a month.

"More than 20 years ago," says Arthur, "I recognize the teamsters prepared to be waylaid by outlaws and Indians. The outlaws took money any goods they wanted or needed and stock while the Indians were interested only in the horses and mules, but they burned out the shipments. Today most of that threat is gone yet the wages remain high?"

"I've did some time as a teamster," says Green "There are still thieves who will relieve a wagon train of its shipment. We used our bull whips as weapons and we carried guns out of necessity. There are renegade Indians who slip off the reservations in Indian Territory to hunt, and when government does not deliver the beef they won by treaty, they will attack the oxen or mule trains. We also survived any weather throw'd at us and sometimes thirst and no grub. Teams and their teamsters froze to death on these trails."

Jake says, "I've been told three teamsters traveled together and one was the wagon master or wagon boss. Each of the oxen teams pulled three high-loaded wagons with the sides planked up. Then there could 'a been 20 mules in a team because of the loads they pulled were that heavy. Today I see loads pulled by mule teams of only six, eight, or twelve."

Bob says, "I did all that as a younger man in order to get a stake on a place of my own, but it is not something I'd do again. I admire what you and Mrs. Gething are doing and by next spring, I'll be ready to go out on my own. Did you know that this sort of freighting was the way Charles Rath got his start and he was also a buffalo hunter for a spell?"

"I understand that, Bob, and I do not disregard the dangers of freighting or the courage of the teamsters, but the cost of materials and services can also be devastating," says Arthur.

Everyone returns to his work. Elizabeth walks back to the shack and leaves the men at the site of the new dugout.

It is fascinating to learn of the way men make a life for themselves on these high plains. Bob is a good storyteller— always a swashbuckling tale to tell—and until today I realize I never thought of him except as a cowhand. He is ambitious and now I wonder about Jake and Green. They plan to homestead or start their ranches! I liked the way they let parsimonious Arthur Gething know how they view the freighting business...and did it in a manner so that Arthur could not get in a temper about it. These men do not put up with Arthur's views silently even if they take his wages. That's Texans for you and part of the reason I am coming to love this country. I think the flaw my grandmother saw in me for speaking my mind too freely will be an advantage here. It seems our cowhand Bob and I are both due for a change in our lives. God, bless us both!

Amused about this Elizabeth leaves and hears Bob's work-song follow her home,

> You may whip and you may holler,
> If you cuss it's on the sly,
> Then it's whack the cattle on, boys,
> Root, hog, or die.

I suspect it's not just the boys who must "root, hog, or die." Perhaps I should learn to cuss like a teamster. Arthur is in some ways like an ox but better handled as our cowhands talk with him than he would be managed with a whip and curses. I take lessons from them!

There is a different relationship between the married couples I know here than those in London. The wives do not depend upon their husbands as Grandmother did upon Grandfather for there is no staff of servants who can cook and clean and make comfortable homes for the husbands so that in this land husbands are equally dependent upon their wives. The wives I meet can do much of the work their husbands do and single men must also cook, clean, mend, and make a home for themselves. These men value their wives more than others I knew in England. There is a kind of justice in that and perhaps I chose well indeed.

She acknowledges that she uses her favorite, "Damn," more here than she ever did in England. She thinks it is a succinct way to display one's feelings, and grins at her recent insight.

By 1890, however, freighting was no longer a major industry. By then the growth and development of the Region [Dodge City-Panhandle], which the wagons had sustained, had become dependent upon the new mechanized modes of travel [railroads].

C. Robert Haywood, page 141
Trails South: The Wagon-Road Economy
in the Dodge City-Panhandle Region

14 - Mule Train, Mule Train

Crisp cool November approaches. Arthur goes to work early before the sun clears the horizon; Elizabeth places her only chair outside the dugout and she listens to the morning sounds of the land once the sun rises. Quail are running down by the creek and their 'Bob-bob-white' whistles roll up to the doorway. The cricking insect songs play in the background. A sparrow surveys his territory and sweeps away to another perch. Locusts buzz for a seeming eternity and then fall suddenly quiet. She cradles her tin coffee cup between her hands and enters into this soothing morning reprieve. This is her favorite part of the day for she feels closer to God here than at any church service.

At the end of her worship, she pulls a travel valise into her lap and slips the contents out. Here are the treasured clippings from seed catalogues, magazines, and sundry advertisements that will become wallpaper in her two-room dugout. The neighbor ladies add to her collection at each and every quilting party. She smoothes out the picture of the flowering dogwood that is a favorite; it will go with other floral clippings to grace the seating area. For the cooking area, she cut out pictures of fat purple eggplant, red tomatoes, cauliflower, green beans, and fruit. A third selection is of babies' faces that she thumbs through with both regret and hope; these sweet visions she is saving for the bedroom area that she calls her 'pregnant room.'

The paper treasures she squirreled away over the year will soon decorate the wooden portion of the half-dugout above the ground. Layers of newspaper will be pasted down for backing and these hoarded and decorative bits will go on over the news-papered walls. It keeps the wind, dirt and dust outside and her family safe and comfortable inside.

Arthur made our order for everything needed for the larger wall-plastered dugout. The plaster should keep unwelcome intruders—insects, rodents, and snakes away. The whole past year I felt unclean and frightened of what I might find coming from the walls or slithering across the dirt floor. It seems we will never get into the new place. Bob tells of rattlesnakes moving into dugouts but partly to scare me I am sure.

There is not a breath of air stirring and chores call her indoors. It is Arthur's promise of a new home that sustained her in this tiny cave with its tow-sack covered walls and dirt floor. The inside temperature is better here, but the dirt, scorpions, rodents, and snakes that she stomps or slashes or traps make the dugout a questionable improvement.

Mid-afternoon, she hears a clattering boisterous rider approach.

Green gallops past the Gething dugout and yells, "Mule train's a-coming! Yee Haw! Let's ride!" A trail of dust follows him as he plows toward Mobeetie.

There is a telegraph office in Mobeetie, but 'fence-line news' travels faster than the news by telegraph. Somehow cowboys know the latest news first. It never fails to amaze Elizabeth.

The materials for their 'half-human' dugout are in this shipment. She flies to the barn raising her skirts and sails in a manner that betrays her eagerness to carry the news to Arthur.

"Mr. Gething, the mule train is coming to Mobeetie," Elizabeth gasps.

"I'm not deaf, Kate!" Arthur barks.

"Oh hurry, our shipment is here."

"Not ours, Kate. Don't you remember, I ordered it sent out by ox-freight? There is no reason to get in a tizzy."

"Mr. Gething, you know ox-freight takes almost twice the time to deliver goods. Surely, you did not choose ox-freight."

"Of course, I had it shipped by ox-freight; it costs almost half. The lumber alone is costing me a fortune. Our shipment will come later."

Mule trains carry fodder for the mules and oxen eat prairie grass. Ox-freight is slower than mule train, but it is a necessary economy of many. Some ship their freight by rail; it arrives in Miami sooner and sometimes for less, but ox-freight can bring it all the way to Mobeetie because the former Rath Mercantile continues to do business with a network of his former business associates. Arthur weighed his options and chose ox-freight although few oxen or mule trains continue to do business on the old Jones-Plummer Trail.

Damn your eyes! Elizabeth holds her lips in a tight line of determination. Then, "I'm going anyway if only for the excitement, Mr. Gething. Everyone says it is a grand sight and our neighbors will be there."

"Aw, hell, Kate, I just unhitched the wagon." He hesitates and wipes his inner arm across his face to mop the sweat. He heaves a long sigh and proceeds to hitch the mules back to the wagon. As he does this, he recalls their short marriage and thinks on it.

Kate's preparations for our new dugout following the loss of our first child restores her spirits. She pours herself into the planning of the new 'half-human' dugout which she proudly announces to all will be half above ground...with windows. Perhaps she will no longer complain of living like an animal. Going to Mobeetie will shelve her disappointment about waiting for our shipment of materials. She is eager to improve the new living space which the hands and I made for her last year; I do support her ingenious plans...even if Louella were not so eager to tarnish my reputation with the neighbors.

Arthur finds himself grinning at the lecture he got from Louella last year.

Once they are underway, Arthur surveys his bride. She wears her handmade blue calico print cut from the paper pattern Louella loaned her. The sunbonnet matches her dress and a tendril of her auburn hair escapes her bonnet and curls down her back.

The change she made as a bride from London Socialite to prairie wife amazes me and I am awed and proud of her. She still carries her tall slender body as regally as when I first met her and sits as if expecting others to pay her court. She is stunning in the print dress and she is a credit to me among the neighbors, for she is their favorite companion and guest.

The ride is slow because their animals already put in a day's work, but Arthur does not urge them to a brisk pace so there is time to take pleasure in the land. Only a mile away from their home, Elizabeth is aware of a sweet, sharp breath on the air.

"Mr. Gething, that smell is almost succulent it is so refreshing. What is it?"

"We cut the hay there only this morning for animal feed during snowstorms and blizzards. Notice that it grows from the dry playa. It is also called a 'plate lake' because it is shallow and holds water after the rainy season."

"It seems almost level which is unusual in this rugged land. How is that possible?"

"Only twenty years ago the buffalo migrated through this area. I'm told by the buffalo hunters that one could see their furry humps in an almost solid line all the way to the horizon. When the beasts found a marshy pond, they rolled in it as horses do, and they carried away the mud and soil in their long shaggy coats. Each year the buffalo wallows held more runoff water. It means a good crop of hay for cattle."

Quail and prairie chickens are beginning to make their soft whirring sounds and roadrunners zip along beside the wagon to feast on the insects that the wagon disturbs. The sky is clear and untroubled as they roll and pitch along. The tumbleweed are turning brown and dry and the first big wind storm can send them rolling across the prairie like croquet balls blasted askew. Leaves of the mesquite hang limp, testifying to how low the moisture drops below the surface. A great flock of white-winged birds wheel and turn above showing their wings black in one direction and yet white in the other.

"Tell me how your work goes, Mr. Gething."

"Our herd is branded and rounded up for the drive to Dodge City. If the drive is a good one and the prices I hear spoken of hold until we arrive, we should do well enough. I will go along with our neighbors on this drive, but we should be home before hard winter arrives."

"Living in our old shack again, I am wondering about our new dugout. Is it near completion? I want to see it."

"It's ready to finish as soon as our supplies arrive. I will walk over with you to see it whenever you will. Jake can take over the finishing now; he, Green, and Bob will be back this winter just as last year so there's nothing to fear in that regard. That should ease your mind and make it easier for you to water the trees you are tending, for it is near the springs."

"I do not look forward to this long separation. I do wish I had a horse; it helps to ride out on the prairie just for the joy of riding and it would be easier to visit our neighbors. Is it possible?"

"Kate, I know how you long for a good mount and I'll keep that in mind. You do understand that increasing the herd and having more to take to market must come first. It is not possible for me to make you a promise, but it is a consideration for the future."

They continue speaking of the work they must do on the land, gossip of the new neighbors, and what they know of their friends' activities and plans.

As Mobeetie comes into view, they see mule teams stretched out beyond the end of town.

Farmers and ranchers lay in supplies at this time of year to get through the winter. Everyone gathers about the wagons and the families from the outlying areas hurry into town. Saddled horses line both sides of the dirt road along the hitching rails. Women wear their most presentable Sunday dresses and a yellow hat or bonnet and red shawl dot the crowd here and there. The mule skinners are announcing the names of people with freight on their wagons.

Shouts of the recipients and their neighbors' affirming cheers make the street festive. Men make their way to freight wagons, claim their merchandise and settle their accounts.

The lead teamster and its wagon master shouts, "Henry Ivy, rocking chair and organ. Julius Ward: crib, barbed wire, and butter churn. Arthur Gething: lumber, plaster, hardware, and window glasses. Will Abbot: churn and sewing machine…"

"Mr. Gething, Mr. Gething, our order *is* here," crows Elizabeth.

"By, God, this is a huge mistake. I will take care of this!" Arthur strides toward the wagon master. "My shipment was ordered sent by ox-team. It is an outrage. I'll not pay the difference in the freight charges."

"Just who are you?" the wagon master inquires.

"I'm Arthur Gething, who is to receive the building materials. It was to be sent out by ox-freight, not mule train."

"It's shipped the way it's ordered. The stock clerks fill the orders in Dodge City. You owe freight charges of $115. Take it or leave it!"

The wagon master stands before Arthur with one eyebrow raised, a sheaf of papers in his left hand, and his arms crossing his chest. The two stand on the street and the wagon master glowers at Mr. Gething. Arthur glares back and balls his fists. Neither blinks. The crowd grows silent.

Suddenly Arthur raises fists in the stance of the trained pugilist that he is and he advances crouching; he goes first left and then right of his opponent. He is stopped cold half the distance between him and the wagon master. The over-towering muleskinner has thrust his outstretched right hand squarely in the middle of Arthur's forehead and he holds Arthur at bay. Arthur flays about and his feet churn to make purchase of the ground. He tries ducking and weaving and slashing out at the big man's arm.

"Rotten thief! Move your damn hand" rages Arthur.

"Ginger-headed, bow-legged little snot!" teases the wagon master.

Then name calling turns serious; it is so serious that a number of ladies cover their ears.

The gathering of neighbors begins to snicker; then chortle and guffaw at Arthur's predicament; his face turns as red as his hair; he twists, ducks, backs away, and melts into the crowd to stand in bowed defeat near his team.

"Sir," Elizabeth says stepping forward, "My husband, Mr. Gething, was unnecessarily embarrassed. Before we left home, he declared our order would come by ox-freight and I was not to expect it on this mule train. It should be obvious that a mistake was made in the shipping orders.

"I trust you are a fair-minded man. You will please make some mutually acceptable arrangement with him over by our team." Elizabeth addresses the muleskinner calmly.

"That's the way to go, Mrs. Gething!" a voice in the crowd bellows.

Elizabeth identifies the man who called out as their neighbor Perry LeFors.

Freight is a luxury on the treeless Llano Estacado. Families sacrifice for lumber and a few comforts. Those meeting the mule train understand the necessity of using ox-freight for they generally prefer it.

"Hip, Hip, and Hooray!" Mr. LeFors shouts out and the crowd joins him.

"At your service, Ma'am," the teamster grins and makes his way toward Arthur Gething. The crowd encourages their meeting with a shout; then, it turns to the business of claiming its shipments and socializing with neighbors.

Dear Lord, I thought my heart would leave my chest confronting the wagon master like that. Bless Perry LeFors! He backed me against the wagon master and drew the crowd in our favor. Perry is a good neighbor!

After a few uneasy minutes, Elizabeth sees Arthur; he and the teamster visibly relax. Elizabeth watches from the crowd where Ginny Jones joins her. The two of them walk away together and stop in front of Christine's Millinery Parlor, the ladies' hat shop favored by the women and girls. They admire the hats on display and speculate on the ones they prefer and then retire to Mrs. Carlson's Café for a visit and refreshment.

When Elizabeth was expecting their first child, she had sent a letter to her sister in London asking for her help in sending information from her grandfather's medical library. She had found the anatomical diagrams and pictures of men and women of great interest as she came into young womanhood and she was curious about the birth of babies. Her letter was a request for Alice to make sketches and copy or summarize the text that told about the pregnancy and the birth. She was worried that no doctor would be able to accompany her child's birth and she felt the books contained the information she needed. Other young wives confided they had the same concerns.

"Elizabeth, did you hear from your sister? I am hopeful that you got the letter because I find that I'm in the family way," says Ginny.

"What happy news! And when do you think this grand event will occur?" says Elizabeth.

"Mother and I believe it should be mid-to-late March, but I should see a doctor before I plan on a date," says Ginny.

"No, Ginny, no answer yet. My sister cannot know how important this is to women so isolated on this prairie. Perhaps I should write another letter stating our urgent desire to hear from her. I can ask my grandmother to assist me. I will post a letter before we leave tonight."

Their talk continues at length about the preparations for the baby Ginny expects and soon Arthur walks into the café to join them.

"Well, Kate, you will be happy to know that I made the teamster see the error of his company's ways and we packed materials for your dugout in the wagon," Arthur boasts.

"Mr. Gething, meet my friend Mrs. Jones. Mrs. Jones, my husband Mr. Gething," Elizabeth says.

"My pleasure, Mrs. Jones," Arthur says.

"Mine as well," says Ginny.

Elizabeth notes that Arthur is beaming with pleasure. He levels a gaze at Elizabeth and inquires, "Elizabeth, what did you say to the wagon master, Josh Vander Zee?"

"What you told me…before hitching our team…that we would not be getting our order by mule train but instead by ox-freight. Do you suppose the company shipping clerk made an error?" says Elizabeth

"Exactly so! After I had talked to him, Vander Zee was forced to the same conclusion and he made me an apology as well. He accepted the original price plus a minimal charge for animal feed. Between us, our supplies are ready to finish the human dugout, Kate."

"Elizabeth, how brave of you to speak up to the teamster as you did. You are courageous!" says Ginny.

Elizabeth demurs and raises her hand in protest.

Grandmother raised no fool. Now, we shall be able to finish the dugout well before winter. With good prices from the sale of our cattle, Arthur may buy a horse for me. A fast gallop across the prairie will help me manage the loneliness.

15 – Elizabeth's Journal

The morning sky is crystal blue as only a winter sky can be and it is not necessary for Elizabeth to wear her heavy cloak to gather more firewood and cow chips for the indoor wood box. A pleasant winter morning! It begins Elizabeth's third winter on the Gething ranch.

By midday, there is a wind shift! Now a blast comes from the northwest and, as rapid as ripples on a pond, ribbons of clouds scuttle across the sky. By noon, the temperature plunges and even Elizabeth's sturdy brown cloak provides little warmth. As she gathered her dried laundry from the garden fence over an hour later, she saw to the north an immense mountain ridge balanced on the horizon in navy blue where there are no mountains. All the time, her teeth chatter uncontrollably.

The men are away. I made no preparation for this abrupt drop of the temperature. I heard our cowhands and neighbors tell of 'The Great Norther of 1880.' Elizabeth follows some nearly forgotten advice and ushers her fluffed-up flock of chickens, gathering in front of the entrance of their fragile hen house, inside. Coming back with a pan of hot yellow cornmeal mush laced with cayenne pepper, she thrusts this feed into the hen house and fills another pan with water for them. With a sense of unease and foreboding, she re-enters the half-human dugout that her husband had built for her.

Sounds like brushes on a drumhead rouse her from tending the stove. Stepping out the door, a sting of sleet sears her face, *Gather in more fuel! I must be quick!*

The sleet turns to snow. Severe and snow-laden cold whips her breath away as she makes three trips to the wood stacked outside and piles the fuel all about the indoor wood box.

"Hands and feet are like ice," she mutters to herself as she slumps down onto her rickety chair. She sleeps from exhaustion until the chill temperature awakens her; she must tend to the stove. That accomplished; she prepares the basic ranch meal—beans, sourdough biscuits, coffee, and she adds, as a treat, two cans of sugar-laced tomatoes thickened with left-over biscuits. The tomato dish will warm in a pot on the back of the stove until the men return.

Hours pass before Arthur and his men come in to feed and rest their horses. They drain the coffee pot as they stand around the stove and then eat a hearty meal before resupplying their saddlebags with provisions. Finally, they punch out into the storm with their hat-and-scarf covered heads butting into the torrent.

While there is daylight and before a blinding snowfall stops all their efforts, Arthur and his men search for the herd scattered on the range in bunches. After the storm passes, they must carry hay to cattle trapped in the arroyos and breaks. Cattle can and do step off onto a snow covered arroyo as they are pushed in front of the storm, then they become trapped there. Some break their legs in the fall. Some, caught on the flat prairie and away from breaks or any shelter, pile up against barbed-wire fences and freeze. Arthur is fearful of these and other storm-inflicted losses.

As night descends minute by minute upon the prairie, the wind screams in its high-pitched whine. This 'blue norther' sweeps in and covers Elizabeth's dugout with drifting snow all along the back and covers most of the stove pipe and the puncheon roof.

She sequesters herself inside where the snowdrift protects the north end of the dwelling from the wind. Whiffs of snow invade near the roof line whipping in beneath its shingled roof. The warm air rising from the stove begins to melt the portion of the snow bank close to the top of the wall and sends rivulets of water down the wall. Below the drifted snow outside, this moisture re-freezes forming a glaze on the wall in a band. Near the earthen floor the deep snowdrift beyond the wall insulates the indoor space and the wood stove radiates a cozy heat.

She prepares beans, bacon, and sourdough biscuits in large quantities for the return of the weary men. There must be a pot of thick black coffee warming on the back of the stove. Elizabeth saves energy; she does not fetch water from the spring. Instead, she collects buckets of snow from outside the door and nests them beside the black cast-iron stove; they will melt there, the warmest place in the shed.

While the fire warms the inside, Elizabeth retrieves her journal from the folds of her cranberry red ball gown inside her leather trunk. She strokes its velvety softness and whispers, "Once an English lady; always an English lady!"

She moves the chair she found years ago in the lean-to and places it close to the front of the stove. She moves the brightest burning kerosene lantern to the packing-crate cabinet beside the stove. Wrapping a quilt around herself, she moves the chair before the stove and props her feet on the stove shelf jutting from the face of the stove and opens her journal. First she reads the entry she wrote after they left Fort Worth more than year ago and almost two.

> A few days ago we boarded the Ft. Worth and
> Denver City train and traveled as far as Washburn.
> Our destination was to the north so we transferred
> to the Atchison Topeka railroad toward Panhandle
> City. We traveled only as far as Pampa today and go
> from here by stage coach in order to connect from
> the Southern Kansas Railway of Texas (SKRRT or
> also the Atchison Topeka) into Miami. Then we
> will go to Mobeetie, the town nearest our ranch.
> February 25, 1896

Mr. Gething was irritable when we left Fort Worth. He told me he sold all his valuable properties and settled accounts with all the depositors at his start-up bank, but he said his financial situation was weak. I did not know what he meant and he refused to tell me. Once we took the Atchison Topeka north the train was a combination of freight and passenger cars. There were a few farm wives, their husbands, children, and crying babies along with dozens of cowboys—a rough and weary lot covered with travel dust.

> In Pampa, we stay in a room of the Holland House.
> It is clean, neat, and unadorned. There is a bathing
> tub! The proprietor gave me kerosene for a
> delousing. Halleluiah! Perhaps it is unnecessary,
> but I find that my scalp crawls, but after this treat-
> ment I am less concerned. Few of the Texas hotels
> in which we took lodging was as well appointed
> as this. Arthur said the room was $2 a day including
> meals. There is a fine grand piano in the lobby. Most
> of the other guests are traveling salesmen who are
> pejoratively referred to as 'drummers' and a few of
> the guests are travelers as we are.

Another place where we stayed on our journey
in order to transfer from the Fort Worth and Denver
to the SKRRT was slovenly and louse, flea and
bedbug infested. I was also suspicious of the
seating in passenger cars of the trains.
    Mr. Gething told me that the hotel lodging
facilities are often so limited that several men
sleep in a common bed. The guest turnover at that
hotel, I learned, was often great. Little concern was
given to cleanliness or prevention of an infestation
so I chose to sleep in a wooden chair.
                                        February 26, 1896

The Holland House was fine. It was such a comfort because
we stayed in one in Washburn; it was not a proper hotel, for
nothing was clean and the handles of the knives and forks
were greasy. I found bedbugs in the linens and did not sleep
in that bed. I remember being so tired that moving was an
effort.

Mr. Gething announced we were on the last
leg of our journey. I am so near exhaustion
that the announcement gives me assurance!
He reserved passage on the stage coach to Miami
and again by stage coach to Mobeetie. Mr. Gething
explained that when he traveled to and from London,
Spider, his own high bred mount, was stabled in
Mobeetie and was waiting there for the final
leg of our journey. However, his newly purchased
foxhound remains in Pampa. He'll go back for
that damn hound and will haul it back to the
ranch. This barrister husband of mine has more
regard for his horse and hound than his wife!
                                        February 27, 1896

We arrived in Miami by train and took the stage to
Mobeetie. When Fort Elliott was closed, the track from
Miami to Mobeetie was taken up. We stayed in a crude

shack in Miami. The owners abandoned it and the custom is to use whatever shelter is available. The land was dry and we heard of the drought they endured for many years. It was a dismal place. People moved away from Mobeetie to Miami to take advantage of commerce the railroad brings. She reads the next entry.

> The stage coach was the roughest ride we took. I was sure my brains would rattle so that no thoughts would ever again be possible and my corset seemed a torture vise. We passengers jostled, jammed, and tossed into one another for the entire trip. We stayed the night in Miami, an insufficient town, and we left by stagecoach early the next morning. I asked Arthur how much further and he grew more contentious every day. His only response was 'soon.'
>
> February 28, 1896

I thought I would die before we arrived in Mobeetie late that evening. I was so cold that I could no longer feel my feet move. The wagon we took from Mobeetie to the ranch the following morning was more comfortable than that insufferable stage coach.

No more entries follow this one. Odd!

In losing consciousness after she learned the shack was to be her home, Elizabeth shielded herself from reality. Over time, she recalls all the events that transpired in that void. She wandered, explored, and cried. The fragments of her memory come back to her, but she parts company with her journal and rarely writes in it from that day. Now, almost two years later, this 'blue norther' strips control away from living things, but Elizabeth Ellen Gething muses over her journal knowing there is that something deeply ingrained within her that does not admit defeat or self-pity.

There was never the option of returning to London. My pride would not allow it! I eloped and it followed that Victorian society would either scorn me or deny my existence. I might be turned out as a governess or housekeeper in another's fine house, but never be mistress of my own. Arthur Edgar Gething professes he is master of this place. But, I am its mistress. What an adventure I am having! Mr. Gething was right in his assessment of my love of adventure, but he knows me very little for I will endure and I will prevail. There is a leap from adventure in the imagination to adventure in the raw elements. Here I am, like it or not!

Elizabeth settles back in the warmth of the stove and the comfort of the quilt and recalls those dark days. She passed through them without knowing how. She revisits them today as if living them with a renewed spirit.

Robert Benjamin (Ben) Masterson was a cattleman and landowner in the Mobeetie area and, also, in Greer County, (once part of Texas but now Oklahoma). He served as the sheriff of Mobeetie (once named Sweetwater) until after this tornado in 1898. He enjoyed the reputation of a family man and law enforcement officer but moved his family to Fort Worth following the tornado that nearly wiped out Mobeetie. Later oil and gas were discovered on his land and years later he moved his family to Amarillo. He served as a director of the board of the First National Bank of Fort Worth and served in other economic and civic duties of distinction. This chapter is in part about Robert Benjamin (Ben) Masterson and his family.

Ben Masterson might be confused with another sheriff of this same frontier town whose name was once Sweetwater but was renamed Mobeetie. However, William Barclay (Bat) Masterson served as its sheriff almost twenty years earlier when the counties were still being organized and district judges made regular visits into the Panhandle to hear all manner of legal cases.

Rose M. Hall, author

16 - Mobeetie on the Horizon

The last day of April in any year ought to be time to celebrate spring's arrival, but it is a tossup time of year! May 1, 1898 is not yet unwrapped. Who can tell you what will happen tomorrow or even in the next breath?

At the Gething place, the routines are predictable. Arthur must tend the herd; Elizabeth must weed the garden, tend the chickens, do laundry, and prepare meals. But, Arthur notes as the day advances that the stock are restless…even skittish…and, he, a farmer and stockman, looks always to the sky. Nothing visual. Just an unease that causes him to check the sky again and again. The prairie is heating and the grasses are coming back, but the air is a bit off. Arthur and Elizabeth go about their separate chores and duties keeping to one necessary task after another, but both are watchful. Those dear cowhands who squatted in a dugout on the sand hills during the winter and kept them company now work the roundup on the Frying Pan ranch. Arthur and Elizabeth continue as they do throughout each day.

But the evening brings on low hanging dark clouds accompanied by a thunderstorm and fierce lightening. That distinctive smell of ozone announces the natural forces are mixing up something spectacular. After penning up the domestic stock, Arthur is uneasy and returns to the dugout.

"Kate, some bad weather is coming; it looks dark enough to be a hailstorm."

Elizabeth steps outside to view the horizon. "I need to pen and cover the chickens. That old wagon tarp can go over the coop. I need you to weigh it down with something heavy when I finish?"

"Let's go! The wind is whipping all about with a vengeance."

Before they return to the dugout, hail stones pelt the ground. They peer out the door for a few minutes, but the darkness comes early and there is little to see. The puncheon roof takes a beating. Elizabeth takes up her mending and darning; Arthur steps outside from time to time, but he cannot see anything but distant flashes of lightening.

Someplace beyond the horizon is also under this storm. Ben Masterson, Sheriff of Mobeetie, and his cowhands drove cattle to Miami and will load them onto freight cars in the morning. He keeps his eyes on the skyline and suspects a severe thunderstorm with possible hail. The cattle are restless and the men circle them in an ever tighter bunch to keep them from breaking away and scattering as the rain, lightening, thunder, and hail assail them. They work throughout the night using cattle calls to quiet the herd. At dawn a rider lopes toward them. It is George, the former 'buffalo soldier,' an Indian name for the Black troop in the cavalry. Masterson left George in charge of his family, his wife, five children, and relatives.

George yells to Ben Masterson that his infant son died in the cyclone (a tornado) that levelled Mobeetie.

The tin mug that Masterson holds in his hand drops and spills coffee on the ground. George rushes to mount a fresh horse and the two speed back toward Mobeetie. After miles of hard riding, they see tree branches and building frames strewn on top of mesquite brush and glass shards glitter in the morning sun. A chill runs down Masterson's back from scalp to toes. He plunges ahead; he is a vessel of fear.

The headline of the next issue of the *Miami Chief* will be: **Mobeetie is Gone; Seven Dead**. The dead are named with dates of their funerals in the paper. Their sheriff's announcement of his unexpected absence from Mobeetie states: "Ben Masterson leaves Mobeetie for Fort Worth with his family following the burial of their six-week-old baby, Flato, and Mrs. Masterson's father and Wheeler County Judge, Frank Exxum. The family expects to return after it recovers from the sharp pains of grief over its losses." But stories of people in the cyclone sweep ahead of print.

Friends in outlying land all around arrive with food, materials, clothing, and comfort. Those who were beyond the reach of the storm piece together the Mobeetie stories as Arthur and Elizabeth will do. A number of survivors tell their experiences during those dreadful minutes when the destructive wind hit.

On their way to help their neighbors, Arthur and Elizabeth see uprooted trees; bark stripped from standing trees; some trees split apart. Branches of trees twist now in unnatural shapes. Homes and businesses are levelled. Debris and litter are strewn about the prairie. When they reach Mobeetie, it shocks them. Only one soddy, a building made of bricks of prairie sod, and part of another are standing. Churches are gone, along with most of the businesses. The wagon yard is in shambles. Many of the stock were killed. Their unburied and bloating carcasses lie strewn over a wide stretch of the prairie.

The Gethings enter what is left of the J. J. Long Mercantile with their bundles of supplies to give to the town folk. Mrs. J. J. Long greets them. "Oh, you've heard of our cyclone, then!"

Elizabeth hands over their bundles of blankets and clothing to Mrs. Long. "I made some things to eat…the usual things. Arthur is behind me with beans and sourdoughs but also canned vegetables. You should know who needs them most and help yourself to them."

"Oh, how generous! I'm ready for a sit-down; I can never find a stopping place with so much to do." She offers a chair to Elizabeth and pulls over another for herself.

Arthur comes with a wooden box packed with cooking pots and newspaper padded jars and crocks. He asks, "Where do you want this?"

"We've scavenged this old counter top. It's a good place," says Mrs. Long. She locates a bench for Arthur. She continues, "I wonder if we can recover. Everyone was.... I don't know. Just not able to believe it happened."

"Tell us about the Masterson family," asks Arthur. "We hear they are leaving the country."

Mrs. Long stops a moment, "Ben and Anna Masterson are leaving after they bury their baby son, Flato, and Anna's father, Judge Exxum. Mrs. Exxum lives but she was crushed by the big cabinet that fell on her. She is unconscious and if she lives, I won't be surprised that she's crippled the rest of her life."

"Ben's been a good sheriff for the town," says Arthur. "Is the news true: they won't return?"

Mrs. Long says, "Mr. Gething, their soddy is gone and Anna doesn't really accept the death of their baby and her father. They need to get away and will go Fort Worth, but we hope they will return."

Elizabeth places her hands about her midsection because she believes she is pregnant. "It is a wonder she can continue."

Continuing her tale of destruction, Mrs. Long says, "The poor woman! That cyclone hit their place with such a force that the sod bricks crumbled into dirt-like powder. She heard it coming, she said, as if it was a train and knew it couldn't be a train. She crawled from her bed to the corner where the baby's crib stood and Flato was covered with silt—as fine as flour. Unable to uncover Flato, Anna gathered her remaining two children to her and headed for a point of light blocks away. The family in that soddy were injured and in pain and the kitchen was the only room standing.

"Big Johnny Jones came to them after finding Uncle Johnnie Stroker dead. Big Johnny is the Masterson's hired man. He met her and the rest of her children leaving that house and asked her to stay and offer them comfort. He insisted Anna and her children go next to his house—one of the few left. Then, Johnny went to check on the Masterson's soddy and finished uncovering Flato. A piece of glass was found on Baby Flato's chest but no scratch on his skin. Reverend Wright, newly married minister, also died when the wall of wind hit.

"I cannot imagine!" exclaims Elizabeth.

Mrs. Long pours out her story, "Before Johnny found Anna Masterson she had gone to her parents' house where her father lay trapped and unable to move and her mother was unresponsive. A cabinet pinned down her daughter Annabelle and son 'Little Ben', but she and her other two children couldn't lift it.

"Big Johnny assured her he'd take care of lifting it off them. It was the only way he could get her to stay with his wife in his half-dugout. Johnny took care of everything, but it fell to him afterward to deliver the news to Mrs. Masterson that her baby was dead. Johnny said to me, 'I think she knew but didn't know.'"

Arthur asks, "How did you manage to stay alive? Your store is gone."

"I left in the evening to sit up the night with ol' Mrs. Jordan who's been ailing. I stopped by to visit Anna on the way. She was feeding her chickens because she'd sent her daughter Annabelle to stay the night with her Grandmother Exxum. In the absence of both their husbands, the sisters, Anna Masterson and Martha Anderson, planned to stay the night in the Masterson house, but Martha changed her plan and stayed with her parents.

"So you escaped because you spent the night in old Mrs. Jordan's dugout?" says Arthur.

"Yes, I went out before the strength of the wind passed, expecting to learn what the damage was. I went a short distance before it blew me off my feet. I fell to the ground and tried to find something to hold onto and finally grabbed around a big clump of bear grass, yucca plant. I was flopped around considerable even then. See, it's how I got these bruises.

"The oddest thing happened. I stopped by the Exxum place before the cyclone hit, Annabelle was there tending her Grandmother's setting hen that was nesting inside a discarded cast iron stove. Annabelle showed me how they kept them safe from coyotes and wedged a twig in the fuel door to give the brood plenty of air. Do you know that after the storm that old hen and her chicks were still there? Safe as could be!"

"Oh, I do not think I can bear to hear any more," says Elizabeth.

"So sorry, Mrs. Gething. I didn't mean to go on and on like that. Going through a thing like that will do that to you. It's almost like talking about it will keep the nightmare away."

Arthur says, "We're sitting here with a good dinner. How will it be to gather everyone around to eat it?"

"That will be good for everyone! I'll ring my old school bell to bring them out," offers Mrs. Long.

When the town folk gather, Elizabeth finds a moment to speak with Mrs. Masterson. "If I can do anything to help you get ready for the services tomorrow, I am happy to do whatever you need."

"Thank you, Mrs. Gething. My sister and I prepared the bodies already. There was not one scratch, one bruise, or one broken bone on my little Flato, but he was gone. Just like that!"

"There is nothing I can do for you?"

"No, nothing. Thank you though."

Arthur speaks with Mr. Exxum's son Frank, a frail young man, during the meal. "I hear you were with your father during the storm."

"Yes, sir. Annabelle and I were. Father told us to check on Mother because he said he was all right. We thought she fainted because she was breathing. I did not know Father was dying; he was only concerned for Mother. She is still unconscious so we don't know about her yet."

"So Annabelle has lost her Grandfather and you, your father?"

"Yes, sir. Annabelle has also lost her baby brother and I, my nephew—Flato."

"I'm sorry, Frank. Call on my wife and me for anything. Your mother may come around soon."

"Yes, sir. We'll all go to Fort Worth after the funerals. There are doctors there. We plan to take Mother to one."

Grandmother Exxum regained consciousness before the funerals of her husband and grandson, but in spite of the doctors in Fort Worth she remained crippled. The Ben Masterson family returned to Amarillo years later, but not to Mobeetie.

Mrs. Easley who ran a place to eat and Postmaster Jack Montgomery also died after the cyclone but as result of injuries sustained during the storm. Judge Frank Exxum also died later and according to court records, he was ill and unable to preside over the called meeting of the

Commissioners Court on May 2, 1898. His burial was two days later, May 4.

Incredible survival stories persisted. The youngest daughter of Zulu Bowers, Mulkins, survived, but the cyclone blew her through a seven-strand barbed-wire fence. A local comic credited her survival to her skinniness. Zulu thought her baby was dead and took the infant to her brother Newt. He jostled the child enough to waken it.

All the members of the Husselby family lived, but Big Johnny did not recognize Mrs. Husselby when he searched for news of the family because of the dirt and blood on her face and her wild-blown hair. After the storm passed, she gathered her family outside the Husselby Hotel, but she knew they were near a large hand-dug well and halted their movement until a lightening flash revealed they were on the rim of the well, the cover of which no longer existed. That caution saved the family from falling into it.

Elizabeth resolves to hold every waking moment precious. Her own parents and an unborn child were taken from her as suddenly as this cyclone has taken others. She cannot think how sorrowful these families must be.

The population of a thousand declined after the tornado. It destroyed thirty-two homes, most of the business section and it damaged the Wheeler County Courthouse and jail so that it was necessary to make extensive repairs. This catastrophe followed by years the closing of Fort Elliott, the bankruptcy of Charles Rath, and the lack of interest in Mobeetie on a permanent railroad trunk line across the Texas Panhandle.

Children were particularly valued in the frontier family, isolated as it was from distant relatives and past friends. With their easy laughter, the children brought humor to difficult times; with their energy they brought lively companionship; with their strength, they brought helping hands to the family's labor. Altogether, they provided a comforting source of family continuity and security.

Joanna L. Stratton, page 144
Pioneer Women: Voices from the Kansas Frontier

17 - Expecting

Elizabeth's day is well underway, she fed the chickens, the beans, bacon, and sourdough biscuits cook and bake; she swept the earthen floor clean, and the dugout is tidy. The comforting scent of bacon and beans and coffee are reminders of the confidence she now owns as a competent housewife. In the privacy of the dugout, she opens her London treasure trunk filled with her ball gowns and lays them out across the bed to consider how she can use them. Their vibrant red, blue, green, and lavender are as delightful to her as an English garden in spring.

Her belly is swollen with the child she expects at year's end. It is good to rest a moment while she makes this decision. Nothing is wasted on the prairie and she is preparing for the birth of her child. The softness and beauty of the fabrics still give her pleasure. She strokes the velvet, satins, and silks with her rough chapped hands and daydreams of London, her stylish wardrobe and social events. She considers the elegant trains of these gowns that flowed and swept across the floor behind her as she moved across the floors of drawing rooms and ballrooms.

She wonders whether there is sufficient fabric in the trains to make clothing for her child. She is a fair seamstress and judges well how much fabric a garment will require. It will be enough. She chuckles as she remembers the entire bolt of calico she bought for making her first dress. For appropriate patterns, she will turn to her friends, especially Louella, who is always the most dependable for sound advice.

Her most pressing need is for cotton flannel to be cut and hemmed for the baby's napkins, infant diapers. She is buying more of the flannel each time she has extra coin, but there does not seem to be enough. Before Charles Rath sold out and left, Elizabeth used Arthur's account with Rath's Mercantile, but now she saves her egg money for expenses beyond the staples required for food. Some of her neighbor ladies confide that they save the flour sacks and boil them in a lye soap solution to soften and to whiten them and thus prepare them for use as nappies. So, she is collecting and preparing them too. All these preparations demand her time and there is little daylight left after the essential chores are completed so she sews in the evening by the light of kerosene lamps. Each morning then these chimney lamps must be washed clean of the soot that forms inside them and the wicks must be trimmed. "A stitch in time," Louella reminds her.

Once her child is born, she must add to her chores the time for nursing, cuddling a fretful baby, scrubbing of the nappies, and keeping enough of them dried by the stove so that plenty are ready for use. She frets, as a childless wife, how she will manage with a child. She sighs and packs her treasures away for another day with the reverence of a priest setting aside the chalice and bread after serving Eucharist.

The weather is uncertain and the temperature a bit nippy; however, Elizabeth leaves the dugout for a brisk walk. The spacious prairie feeds her soul for the freedom she desires. She carries with her a hoop skirt with a bustle attached which she has stored under the bed. She has not worn it since leaving Fort Worth when she first arrived.

In preparation for the baby, Elizabeth will need to box the unused dresses and ball gowns and store them under the bed and the hoop skirt and bustle are in the way. She looks for a place to dispose of them in one of the eroded places along the Cantonment Creek where she can anchor it with large rocks. She visualizes them sailing across the prairie in a strong wind as the tumbleweed do. The embarrassment of having her under things in the public view is a serious concern to her.

She wanders through the creek bed, which is dry now, trying to find the ideal place to bury it. She forgot to bring along a shovel and refuses to go back for one so she continues to look for a crevice back in the bank on the side of the creek bed and inspects several before finding a place at the base of a cottonwood tree where the soil has washed away behind the exposed roots of the tree. Stuffing the stays into the hollow so that they do not spring out again takes some patience. She becomes breathless with the weight of the child in her womb and with this effort. Once this is accomplished she carries selected rocks to the opening and wedges them in the front of the cavity. Pleased with her work she strikes off for the dugout.

Her mission is accomplished and there is time to do a bit of stitching to hem a square of flannel before she must revive the fire in the stove and make fresh coffee for the evening meal she will serve Mr. Gething. Once inside the dugout the bed is too inviting to ignore and she naps. The hemming she planned will wait until she lights the kerosene lamps tonight. She dozes and dreams of buttered bread made into cucumber and watercress sandwiches and served with a pot of English tea. A steady rain begins to fall and croons to her like a lullaby. It is a wide-spread rainstorm extending to the west where the headwaters of the Canadian River arise.

In the days ahead, nesting continues to be Elizabeth's central activity. She turns again to her trunks of clothing brought from London. The baby will out-grow its clothing often and she recalls Louella's offer of infant clothing from her family. These are passed around to friends with infants until they are no longer serviceable. Therefore she continues to concentrate on having plenty of diapers or nappies. Then she begins boiling flour sacks, opening them, and securing the edges with a hem.

Her other preparation is making soft warm baby coverlids. She pieces fabric scraps for the quilt top and thick flannel yardage from the general store for its backing. Between these, she will sandwich cotton batting to give the quilt warmth.

The rain falls for several days and it is welcome, but it also causes the creeks and rivers to rise making crossing them dangerous and travel restricted. Flash flooding occurs and subsides. The men and older boys are out to find their cattle. Mr. Gething cooperates with their nearest neighbors to find the cows who waded into swollen streams, rivers and lakes to drink and many will become stuck in the bogs. The men must lasso the stranded cattle and then tail them up and pull them out. Tailing is just that—holding their tails up on one end and roping around their horns at the same time in order to pull them out of the bogs. Two men work together getting cows out of bogs. Otherwise, the cattle will slowly starve. Some do, of course, if they are not found in time.

One day after the flash flood crisis passes, a neighbor's young son, Leo, comes to their dugout holding circles of bone and metal connected with strips of cloth. When Elizabeth comes to the door, Leo holds it up and says, "Mrs. Gething, this floated up beside the Cantonment near your place but on our land. I figure you won't want to lose it. Looks to me like a new-fangled rat trap."

Elizabeth takes a closer look. It is her hoop skirt and bustle! The one she thought was secure back in the cavity under the exposed roots of an old cottonwood tree along the bank of the creek. *Oh, my, we will both be embarrassed if I reveal its actual use!*

"Leo, how good of you to rescue it! We are in your debt for returning it." Elizabeth invites the older boy inside. Flustered, she tries to tamp down her amusement. "Do come in for some coffee and a bite to eat."

Arthur sits before his mid-day meal and motions Leo to join them at the table. Arthur goes to the stove to fill a cup with coffee and shakes with mirth before he can return with a plate of food and the cup of coffee for their guest.

Leo is alert to the reactions of both Mr. and Mrs. Gething. He wonders whether he is the butt of some joke and it is evident to them because of his defiant lifted chin and questioning countenance.

"Leo, this thing you've returned isn't a rat trap. We are glad to have it, but it is a personal item fashionable women wear to hold out their full skirts," explains Arthur.

Leo wrestles with this information and picks the bustle up by the cloth ties at the top and blushes furiously.

"You must not be embarrassed, Leo. I meant to discard it and thought I buried it," Elizabeth explains further.

Everything becomes clear to their young neighbor in a moment. All laugh until their sides hurt and enjoy the meal. Their friends are never sure which of them—Arthur, Elizabeth, or Leo—enjoy most the fun of retelling the tale afterward. Laughing at their own social blunders and misunderstandings lighten the burdensome daily tasks of surviving on the prairie.

18 - Circle of Friends

By fall of 1898, Elizabeth faces late winter in the Panhandle of Texas and the birth of her child. She and her husband Arthur are living in their half-human dugout that they furnished and stocked. There is a new stove! It is a Charter Oak stove of steel that has four plates on top for cooking, a good-sized oven, and water reservoir in which to keep water hot. Elizabeth cans homegrown tomatoes, wild plum butter, and green beans throughout the summer. She trades some of her canned tomatoes for Mary Hastings' canned peaches. The canned peaches and green beans are lined up on the packing crates alongside the jars of plum butter and tomatoes. Arthur brought more crates to store the growing number of canned goods.

Elizabeth improves her home and food supply only to discover she must do more as result of adding the half-human dugout above their entirely earthen dugout. Along with preserving some of their food and making her clothes, she now maintains a garden, prepares meals, does the laundry, and tends to the domestic stock.

While the original dugout was entirely below ground and was only a refined cave carved into a hill, this improved structure stands above ground with two windows. It is wooden, not earthen. The windows and wooden structure earns it its name—half-human. This addition is twelve feet wide by sixteen feet long. It is separated in two parts—sitting room and kitchen—which merge into a single space. Just inside the door is the sitting area and beyond it, the kitchen.

It is many months since she has visited with her friend Louella. Now she wishes for her company more than ever. The effort she and Arthur are putting into this new shelter will end soon. It is the middle of the week; tomorrow the church ladies' sewing circle meets at Louella's family home and she will rejoin it.

Elizabeth spends her time each evening making a poke bonnet to wear to the quilting party. She borrowed a pattern from Louella and uses the fabric left from making her dresses. Perhaps one day she will use all of that bolt— twenty yards—of calico she bought from the Rath Mercantile. It is a standing joke among her friends that all her clothes will be made from the same bolt of fabric.

She thinks the poke bonnet's brim is ingenious because it has narrow pockets all along the length of it into which she slides strips of cardboard. They hold the brim stiff and will make ample shade for her face. A caplet covers the crown of her head; the brim attaches in front and a gathered flounce covers from the neckline halfway down the back. It will protect her neck and upper back from sunburn. Ties fasten the bonnet under her chin with a bow. She will wear it when she joins the ladies tomorrow.

The women of this group collect pictures for Elizabeth that they cut from seed catalogues, advertisements, magazines, and any source of pictures of fruits, vegetables, flowers, and babies. The creative way she explains she will use them amuses her friends.

Elizabeth papered the walls in the wooden part of the half-human dugout with newspapers and when the paste is dry, she will use the picture collection of flowers she is saving to paste over the newspaper surface to give the walls the appearance of wallpaper. It is her sitting room; she insists upon referring to it as her parlor. The walls in other half of the space, her kitchen, she will cover with the pictures of vegetables and fruits. She collected boxes of pictures and her friends will give her more tomorrow. In the plastered underground part of the dugout, she will arrange the baby pictures. To the amusement of her circle of friends, she christens it her "pregnant room."

Today she leaves to plow up the garden; tomorrow will be a holiday with her friends at church. Whipping an old poke bonnet off the clothing peg, she leaves with a loaf of bread wrapped up in a clean flour sack under her left arm and a pair of leather gloves in her right hand. Kate, the younger mule, she harnesses to the plow and commands it into the first row of the garden.

As they proceed to plow the garden, Elizabeth is protected from the sun by the bonnet and from the pull of the reins and plow handles by the leather gloves and from her need for nourishment with the loaf of bread under her arm. Elizabeth curses the mule! She is sure this mule, Kate, is not as easy to drive as a horse would be. Her baby is turning somersaults in her abdomen and, by noon, her clothing is wet with salty offerings from forehead to feet. Stopping to rest, she splashes water over her face and drinks from a dipper. She hangs on the fence while Kate drinks water from the bucket. She finishes her loaf of bread before returning to her gardening.

Her work will not be complete until she loads layers of hay and manure into the cart and spreads it over the garden. She is proud of the sturdy fence their cowhands have set around her garden. Stopping more frequently to rest as the day advances, she tosses hay from the cart first and shovels muck on top and finishes it off with another layer of hay.

Both legs and both arms are trembling by the time she spreads manure on this plot of ground. Once she opens and closes the gate letting the mule-drawn plow leave the garden, she must remove the harness from Kate, set the plow in the lean-to, rub down the mule, and fill her water bucket and feed trough.

Her work in the garden ends until later this fall when she intends to plow it under to set it up for her garden next spring. She has no strength to prepare a hot meal for herself and Arthur. Hot coffee, cold sourdough biscuits, cheese, sliced tomatoes, and peaches will be their evening meal.

The day for meeting with the ladies for quilting and lunch finally arrives—Thursday morning. Elizabeth dresses in her new calico creation—a Mother Hubbard, the preferred dress of pregnant women, and her new poke bonnet made of the same calico pattern—and is satisfied with her appearance until she examines her hands. They are rough and calloused in spite of the lavender scented glycerin she creams into her face and hands day and night to protect them. Doing hand laundry with lye soap on a rub board and plowing behind a mule conspire against her efforts to keep her skin smooth and soft. She sits down in an uncontrolled temper at her loss.

"Bloody Damn! I hate being a farm wife," she sobs and cries until her face is blotched with red-and-white patches.

After some time she rises and presses a water-cooled cloth to her face. She hopes that by the time she arrives at Louella's there will be no evidence of her crying. Before leaving, she uses her glycerin and lavender skin treatment again. She bridles and saddles Kate before dressing for the ride to the Harrah dugout.

When her preparations are complete, she leaves and enjoys riding through the prairie and seeing the subtle changes autumn brings. She passes small plots of cultivated fields where her neighbors harvested their oats and corn, and pumpkins decorate the doorways and gardens. Some farmers are getting their land ready for the next growing season. She arrives in an improved frame of mind.

Louella meets her at the door. "Do come in, Elizabeth! Our friend, Emma LeFors is already here. What a lovely jar of tomatoes! That warm loaf of bread smells like it just came from your oven."

"Louella, how very good to see you!" says Elizabeth as they embrace.

Elizabeth smiles to greet Emma, sets her part of the covered dish luncheon on the sideboard and joins Emma. She admires and respects Emma and Perry LeFors, who have lived here many years with their large family. They enjoy sterling reputations throughout the eastern Panhandle and graciously encourage new homesteaders. Emma is one of only a handful of women who during the last drought toughed it out when most women and their families either returned to the eastern part of the nation where civilization and plentiful water are available or they moved further west.

"Emma," begins Elizabeth, "It's good to see you again. Louella sent me word you are bringing the log cabin pattern for us to quilt. I have some calico from this, my new dress, to contribute."

Emma chuckles merrily, "How many yards do you have on that pretty bolt of blue calico?"

"Oh, Emma," Elizabeth tosses her head and answers, "I think Arthur will bury me in a frock made from the calico on that bolt! I am pleased to part with some of it today for the quilt."

"Elizabeth, your home is a real standout. Mr. LeFors told me after our visit last week that he could not believe the changes you've made. Mr. Gething built a sound structure. Both of you must be ready to rest. We are so glad you are joining our circle again," says Emma.

"I could not wait to join you today! I am looking forward to learning to quilt."

Louella checks the chicken and dumpling dish that warms on her stove and joins Elizabeth and Emma. Mary Hastings and Ginny Jones come next. The ladies exchange greetings as they arrive and they add their covered dishes to the sideboard. Margaret Hansford causes a stir when she whirls in with news that she and her husband are going to be grandparents.

Before long all twelve ladies have arrived. Each one brings a bag containing her stash of fabric remnants, thimbles, pincushions, needles, pins, and scissors for the quilt making. Deciding on which calico fabric they will use for each block of the quilt comes first so they take the fabric stashes from their bags. Their practice is to piece two blocks each.

"Ginny, look how your brown and gold calico goes with this yellow and gold floral and Judith's orange and blue-green," suggests Ellen.

"Yes, that's good but I think we need a bit more contrast, maybe this would work," says Dorothy as she hands over a green-on-dark-green print.

"I like it!" encourages Louella.

"Notice how it must go together in the log cabin pattern," insists Emma. "We still need two more fabrics that complement and contrast with these. Keep looking, Ladies!"

"We have it," Lacey purrs, "except for the center piece of some medium color that looks good with both the light and dark sides."

"Let's try this," asserts Roz.

"This may look better," adds Joan.

They puzzle it together for about half an hour until there is agreement. Emma begins to set out the pattern pieces for the cutting. After lunch, the ladies will form an assembly line to cut all pieces exactly on the straight grain of the fabric to avoid any bias cuts that cause puckering. With everything organized for the afternoon, they take time to eat and visit.

"The J. J. Long Mercantile has spices—not only ground pepper and dried chilies—all kinds of spices!" Mary Ellen announces. "They come in time before the winter holidays! Mother sent me her cornbread dressing recipe and we'll have sage, rosemary, thyme, and oregano for the roast chicken at Christmas. I checked and the mercantile has all of them! I've the recipe here to share." Mary Ellen lays it beside the lamp on the stand along with paper and pencil.

Mary Hastings rejoins, "Not to be outdone, I remembered to bring that recipe for getting grease spots out of clothes. It is water, ammonia, saltpeter, and soap. Shake well and let stand a day or two. You just cover the grease spot, rub it in well, and rinse with water. It can also be used for shampoo and to kill bed bugs and it will take paint off anything!"

Emma laughs until tears run down her cheeks. "Mary Ellen, is there anything that mixture won't do?"

"Emma LeFors, "You can just laugh all you like, but this does everything I say it does. Remember that itinerant preacher who stayed with us! He left unwanted guests. I promise: it killed all his tiny menagerie. Everyone needs to copy this recipe!" She sets it out for the women to copy when they have free time.

Laughter, cajoling, and teasing subsides. Then Roz, who is boarding the new teacher, announces, "Miss Todd will put on a Christmas program at our school. All the children will have parts in it. She is willing to carry on as Miss Lewis did when she taught our children."

Before returning to piecing blocks for the quilt, Louella passes a stationery box and each of them adds a clipping for Elizabeth's 'wallpaper'. She cannot wait to search through these additions and delights in each of them.

"Julie," says Elizabeth, "where did you find these brilliantly colored flowers?   There are snapdragons, peonies, and chrysanthemums; each bunch of flowers is a separate picture!"

"My husband brought them back from his buying trip in Denver for you," says Julie.

"Roz, this baby's picture makes me want to order one just like her," Elizabeth continues. The ladies are rewarded by her words and the glow on her face as she continues examining each addition to her collection.

"I cannot wait to get home and begin pasting them on my walls," Elizabeth says after displaying the last one."

Following that, the women lay out their fabric on the long dining table and begin cutting the exact number of pieces they need for each and every block of the log cabin pattern. Elizabeth exchanges greetings with some she has not met and listens to the stories of the women who are neighbors. Once the women cut the quilt pieces, they begin sewing their quilt blocks. All of them visit and admire the various color schemes in the log cabin pattern. The ladies group themselves in pairs or triples and continue to sew, gossip and share bits and pieces of information so that many conversions warm and gentle the air.

"Ginny, your block is lovely," begins Elizabeth.

"You are kind to say. I have been eager to visit with you. You have been here almost two years. I'm wondering how you like it."

"I am determined to like it and to stay in spite of anything—like Emma LeFors. It is wonderful coming together like this," replies Elizabeth.

"Yes, I agree. My daily wish is to have neighbors nearby for company. John and I expect our first child in February," Ginny sighs.

"Do you have someone to call on when it is time for the birth?" Elizabeth asks gently.

"No, I am inquiring about a mid-wife in case Dr. von Brunow is not available. Do you know of anyone?" Ginny replies.

"I can recommend Louella." Elizabeth tells her. "I had an accident that caused me to miscarry over a year ago. I sent Mr. Gething to fetch Louella.

"Mrs. Gething, I was not aware of your loss. Please forgive me for asking," says Ginny.

"There is no need for you to apologize, Ginny. I prefer 'Elizabeth' to 'Mrs. Gething' if you will.

"Thank you, Elizabeth, I'd like that!"

"I recommend Louella. She is my friend and a constant source of information. Even though she is younger and unmarried, she helped and comforted me," says Elizabeth.

Ginny frowns, "I hesitate to ask her because of her responsibilities to 'mother' her brothers and sisters. I wonder if she'd be able to leave them on short notice."

Elizabeth says, "You will find her accommodating. Her mother taught her so much. Like you, I cannot imagine how her responsibilities for her family increased since her mother has taken ill. She takes it all on with cheerfulness."

Ginny continues, "Elizabeth, I spoke with you because I guess you are also in 'a family way.'"

Elizabeth laughs, "You are observant! Or, does my Mother Hubbard frock give me away? I expect to have this baby in December or January."

"I didn't mean to pry; I'm looking for help…encouragement, too! I'm frightened, actually. What will you do when it's your time?"

"I wish I had not mentioned my miscarriage. I have written to my grandmother and sister in London to copy information from Grandfather's medical books. I can let you know when I hear from them; I expect to get their letters with the information soon."

"Your grandfather is a doctor?"

"He is and I wish the dear man were here."

"Please, let me know. Maybe you'll have their letters and copies they are making by next month when our circle meets again," says Ginny.

Louella's brothers and sisters troop through the door at the end of their school day. They are full of tales about school events and checking out the sideboard for something to eat. The ladies visit with them and offer the food—bread, butter, pickles, and plum leather. Later, all the ladies begin to gather their dishes and bags of sewing fabric. Emma suggests that the quilt blocks can be sewn together to complete the quilt top next month if everyone returns with two finished blocks.

The circle of friends departs one by one. They are invigorated by this social gathering that lifts their spirits. These women feel their isolation keenly; the men have responsibilities that take them away from the homesteads to buy or sell and arrange for collective business or government activities of many kinds. Each woman here returns to her homestead and its chores that cannot be easily set aside. A family, whether it is large or small, consumes a woman's time and energy. The primary role of women is a homebound one with few needs or opportunities to travel beyond the home. In spite of the extra effort this event demands, a circle of friends is as essential to the women as air and water.

Childbirth itself was often the most difficult time of all. For the most part, women struggled through labor and delivery with little assistance. While a practicing physician was occasionally available, yet all too often the woman isolated on her homestead found no medical help forthcoming. Instead, she relied only on the assistance of an anxious husband, a concerned neighbor or an older son or daughter.

Joanna L. Stratton, page 86
Pioneer Women: Voices from the Kansas Frontier

19 - Enter Edward James

Snow drifts are so deep upon the ground that Elizabeth guesses at the location of the hay stacks in the corral. She brushes aside the wet snow with both hands and claws clumps of dried grasses into piles at the base of the mound of snow. If a pitchfork is around, it is covered with snow and will take longer to find than doing this by hand.

Arthur is invariably negligent with tools and all manner of essentials.

Elizabeth is breathless and, from time to time, she pauses and takes gulps of air before exerting herself again with this task. She trudges through the snow for a mile or more before she starts her work of strewing the hay for the cattle. Once she completes this task, she must retrace her tracks to the dugout. Standing to relieve her back, she lurches forward a half-step.

Merciful Heaven, I must get home. My back feels as if it is grasped by an enormous fist. Agh! The scattered animal fodder is not enough, but all I can do.

Elizabeth holds her right hand to her back and looks back at the foot trail she has left through the snow and urges herself to go back to the dugout. Resolutely she sets out, but she moves slower now. Each step tires her. Long-limbed, she stepped with a lengthy stride going to the barn, but her stride is shorter now; she is unable to step into the already laid snow footprints, left earlier when she seemed full of energy. She forces herself to move constantly forward at a deliberate pace and stops intermittently to take deep breaths through the blue woolen scarf wound around her neck and shoulders.

Smoke wisps from the stove pipe punching through the roof of their dugout. It is as if a misty sugar loaf hill were her home. Encouraged that the fuel continues to burn, she pummels forward toward the door. Inside waits warmth and rest. All along she struggles against the agony of cramping muscles that come and go. She thinks ahead of needing to add more mesquite and cow chips to the stove and then she can stand over it and warm her numb hands and feet. The entrance to the dugout is not too distant now.

Dear Lord, I wet myself! I must hurry or I will be frozen before I reach the threshold.

Panicking, she missteps, stumbles, and lurches forward. The steady restraint she accomplished while pushing forward is abandoned and she moves as swift as skittering quail flushed from underbrush. She claims the door and is inside.

My frigid clothing will wait until I replenish the fire.

Elizabeth grabs the side of the fuel box as a cramp immobilizes her. She holds tight to the rim for a fracturing, elongating moment until she is confident she can release her hands without falling. Then she unwinds her blue scarf, tosses it aside, spreads her cloak, and fills it with fuel. That completed, she hauls her loaded cloak to the stove. Next she releases the catch of the belly of the stove and shovels in fresh fuel; it causes sparks to spew forth from the remaining burning wood and embers. She slaps the fuel door shut. She sits abruptly on the bench and huddles near the stove before she begins tearing her outerwear away and removing her icy soaked undergarments.

Oh, the wetting is the beginning of my labor, not piss! Why did I not realize that until now? I am alone here…. Lord, help me! Twit, get into dry clothing. Go slowly, slowly, slowly! There is time to plan.

Elizabeth disciplines her breathing and accepts her level-headed advice to slip into her soft white flannel nightgown and warm herself in the aura of warmth before her. Her hands and feet are in pain; they sting and prickle. Her severely chilled and puckering skin warms in torture. In an hour, it is again flush, smooth, and supple. She is drowsy. To bed. Sinking. Out.

Her breath is gentle and shallow and her sleep is undisturbed for a half-hour or more. The cramping begins again slowly until she is awake and she waits until the episode passes. She leaves her warm cocoon and checks the fire. Finding it adequate, she fills a pot with water on each of the four stove-top covers. Next she finds towels, some cotton batting left over from quilting and her sewing scissors. She arranges them on another bench near the bed. Finally she pulls over the only chair in the dugout and lifts it onto the bed.

She experimented weeks ago with the positioning of this chair with the top of its back and the front edge of the seat resting on the bed and the legs slanting upward near the head of the bed and that side of the dugout. The new quilt—the log cabin pattern—presented to her by friends of the quilting circle will pad the chair's back and hind legs so that she can rest against them in a semi-sitting position. It is not a birthing chair, but it will serve as one in the latter stages of her labor.

Grandmother, bless her, strongly advised me to use a birthing chair because she used one herself. "Men cannot know," she wrote to me, "what that position does to ease the pain of birth!"

Alice responded to her request for the information on childbirth last year. In her sister's elegant handwriting, there is a full copy of that article and another on nursing a baby from her grandfather's medical library. She knows the material as well as the date of her birth. Everything she expects to need is at hand. Now she has only to rest between contractions and pray that Arthur will be home in time to send for the doctor in Mobeetie or be there to assist her in the birth. Silence reigns outside and inside. Elizabeth only leaves the bed now to add fuel to the stove and does that between her contractions. She sleeps as often as she can. The afternoon is long.

It is her strategy to stay with the events of her labor as they occur rather than to allow herself a plunge into fear. Elizabeth reminds herself that countless women give birth and she will manage also.

The long shadows of the afternoon vanish and it is time to light one of the lanterns. Elizabeth moves cautiously toward the table in the center of the dugout. She deliberately lights one lantern, adds fuel to the stove, and crawls back into bed.

Arthur, do not be late tonight! Would that my husband were dependable!

The sound of the wind kicks up, but its growling howl is muffled because of this underground location. It is warmer than the old shed was and for that Elizabeth is grateful in spite of her aversion to living like a hedgehog.

Elizabeth is growing accustomed to the contractions. She notes the intervals between birth pains and she naps relaxed between them throughout the afternoon. She begins to wish to complete the birth, for she has dreamed of holding her child in her arms and having this small companion for constant company in her isolated dugout. Then she hears Arthur approach. It will not be long before he has sheltered Spider in the new barn. She will no longer be alone.

The snow has drifted against the door since she returned late this morning. The scraping of the shovel alerts her that Arthur is at the door. The door creaks open and the cold air invades.

"Kate, Perry is with me.!" says Arthur. "We just finished checking the fence line and breaking the ice at the tank."

"Mr. Gething, you must take care of Mr. LeFors. The baby is coming and I need your help."

"Perry," calls Arthur from the opened door, "Kate is having the baby. Will you go for Dr. von Brunow?"

Perry's answer is snuffed out by the wind.

"Mr. Gething, you must set out something for Perry to eat before sending him out this late and in the dark," calls Elizabeth.

Arthur leaves to speak with Perry. They return in several minutes.

"Mrs. Gething, thanks for the chance to eat first," says Perry. "We took care of the horses with a good rub down.

Once mine feeds on the oats, I'll get the Doc. It will take hours. Can you manage?"

"You are a good friend, Perry," says Elizabeth.

Who knows whether I can manage? I must manage!

In record time, Arthur and Perry eat and Arthur prepares a lantern for Perry to carry with him back to Mobeetie along with extra clothing and a bedroll with emergency supplies rolled inside.

Once Perry leaves, Arthur busies himself about the stockpiling of extra fuel from outside and offers his wife some bean broth from the stove and a dipper of water. The contractions seem to subside and Elizabeth takes the soup and later some coffee.

"How are you feeling, Kate?" says Arthur.

"Not too uncomfortable. I want you to know what to expect so that you can assist me if Dr. von Brunow does not arrive with Perry in time for the birth. My sister copied the birthing information from Grandfather's medical books and you should read them and keep them handy for reference," says Elizabeth as she hands them to Arthur.

Silence follows as Arthur reads the article Elizabeth has given him.

"When did this begin?" says Arthur.

This morning as I fed the cattle my back began to ache horribly. I did not make it back to the house before my water broke. I knew that I could expect the contractions to go on for hours...even longer...before they became harder and much more often. I took time to set about the things we will need. Be sure there is always plenty of hot water available. Towels, the cotton batting, and scissors are all right here on the bench beside the bed. I set the chair as it should be for use as a birthing chair, but I want you to tie my new quilt firmly to it so that it covers the entire chair's back. Later I will also use pillows from the bed to cushion it."

"I can take care of it. Is there anything more you need?" says Arthur.

"Let me rest for now. The hardest part is yet to come. I am glad you are here," says Elizabeth. "I doubt I threw out enough hay for the cattle. I could not stay any longer. Tomorrow you may want to put out a little extra."

"You did fine, Kate," says Arthur. "I will see to the cattle tomorrow."

The night passes in constant vigil for Arthur. Elizabeth wakes and rests, then, wakes again. Deep in the night hard contractions wake her and they increase in frequency. Arthur takes directions from both the copied article and Elizabeth with impeccable care; he rests and sleeps throughout the night as he can.

Contractions are hard and come in waves of pain. Elizabeth is no longer silent; she moans, groans, shouts, and screams. Her anguish unsettles Arthur. He readies the chair and lifts her onto it in an attempt to do something to calm himself. Before the sun breaks through in the morning, the top of their child's head emerges and Elizabeth pushes hard and loudly three times as she gives birth to their son Edward James.

Arthur is standing by her in awe. Elizabeth directs Arthur to wrap their son in the cotton quilt batting. In less than an hour, they hear pounding at the door. Dr. von Brunow enters first, then, Perry.

"Well, Mr. Gething, it seems you've done my work for me. You have a healthy boy. Leave the rest to me. I'll need some of that water from the stove and the towels."

Drowsy, Elizabeth hears their conversation, *Gentlemen, I've done the work of this birth!*

The doctor surveys the items laid out on the bench beside the bed and scowls.

He opens his bag and replaces the sewing scissors with a gleaming, sturdy pair of surgical scissors, a strong cotton cord, and a shallow pan to receive the afterbirth. He ties off the umbilical cord with the thick cotton twine and turns to Arthur.

"Would you like to cut your son's cord?" he asks.

"Tell me what I must do, Doc," says Arthur.

"While I hold the cord like this, you just cut it off right here. You'll need to put some muscle into it for that cord is more resistant than you expect. Simple to do but not easy!" says Doc von Brunow.

Arthur accomplishes this task and is pleased with his part in the event and himself. He relaxes now and a broad smile testifies to his satisfaction as he watches his newborn son.

Elizabeth instructed Arthur to wrap their son in the cotton batting before the doctor's arrival. When Dr. von Brunow inspects their son, he laughs and says, "Mrs. Gething, babies arrive in a heavy coating of mucous. It will take time to remove all that cotton batting sticking to him. I cannot remove much of it."

"Let your son begin to nurse. It will comfort him and he'll begin to know what he's to do," smiles Dr. von Brunow. "I see you've an article about nursing mothers here on the bench." The doctor scans it as he sponges their infant son. "It's sound advice. How did you come by it?"

"My grandfather is a physician in London. My sister copied it from one of his medical books and sent it to me," says Elizabeth.

"You've a good head on your shoulders, Mrs. Gething. Now you just leave this to me for a while. Then I want you to rest and sleep until you need to nurse your son again."

Elizabeth is content nursing her son Edward James Gething on this fourteenth day of December 1898. Her eyelids are closing. She needs no encouragement to sleep.

Arthur tends to the infant with Doc's directions on changing a diaper and holding him.

"That's the longest baby I ever saw, Doc," says Perry, "and I've a house full of LeFors babies to judge him by."

"Takes after his mother," says the doctor, "He'll be tall like Mrs. Gething." Dr. von Brunow chuckles, "Arthur, you've a fine son!

If I were asked to what singular substance do I mainly attribute the prosperity and growing strength of the American people, I should reply: To the superiority of their women.

Alexis de Tocqueville
Democracy in America

[Circa 1898], a young woman named Levella [sic] B. Harrah became the town's first known resident photographer. The daughter of Joseph and Emmagene [sic] Harrah, Levella [sic] was born in Kansas in June 1877. …In the 1900 U. S. Census Levella [sic] listed her occupation as "photographer"—one of the few women associated with early Panhandle photography.

John Miller Morris, page 83
*Taming the Land: The Lost Postcard
Photographs of the Texas High Plains*

20 - Indomitable Women

Edward is over three years old and plays about his mother in their improved dwelling. Edward clings to the idea of sleeping in the subterranean dugout. He hates the howl and screech of the wind and he cries staying awake at night when it is on a rampage. Her son's preference surprises Elizabeth, who accepts the sounds of the High Plains wind as part of living here.

Elizabeth works in a comfortable, light-filled space near the window where she makes clothing for Edward and herself. She remakes one of the dresses she brought from London using the trains and flounces from a white percale gown to make a proper young English boy's outfit for Edward. Finally, she reworks the rest of the gown to make a three-tiered skirt with bodice for herself. The occasion for making this finery will be a portrait of Elizabeth and Edward that Louella Harrah will photograph and develop in her Photograph Shop in Miami.

Elizabeth hums as she sews buttons on Edward's white shirt and short pants that extend to the tops of his knee-high boots. Edward plays with wooden spools empty of thread that roll about as pretend wagons or carriages. Elizabeth stops from time to time and redirects her son's activities. When Edward tires of rolling the spools, she shows him how to lather one end of the spool with a bowl of water and a sliver of soap. She demonstrates how to blow through the dry end of the wooden spool to produce bubbles. Edward works at the new activity until he makes bubbles. With her son happily occupied, she finishes attaching the buttons, and then tries the garment on her son. After a bit of pressing with the flat iron, they are ready for their trip to Miami.

Elizabeth and Edward will not wear these clothes en route. Instead Elizabeth wraps them in paper and packs them in her portmanteau so that she and her son can change in the photography shop and make crisp fresh appearances.

When the day arrives, Elizabeth mounts her little mare, rides sidesaddle and holds Edward in front. Riding her horse reduces the time it would otherwise require to travel in their farm wagon. The leather luggage with the clothing they will wear for the portrait, Elizabeth straps onto the sidesaddle.

Louella steps out and greets them as soon as she sees Elizabeth ride up in front of her studio and holds up both hands to receive Edward. "Elizabeth, hand over that young man and I'll get your baggage."

"Be my guest, Louella! It was a long trip and I need to stretch and to walk. We dismounted a number of times so I could get some relief." In a few minutes, she hitches her mare and regains circulation especially in her right leg. Riding sidesaddle, most of Edward's weight rested across her right leg. Elizabeth needs time to move about before entering.

"Edward, I'm so glad you and your mother are here. It's so good to see you both." The women embrace before Louella takes Edward by the hand, enters her studio and shows him her camera. "You and your mom are going to stand in front of this box so I can take pictures of you." She lets Edward explore it before continuing. "It will make a bright light every time I make your picture, but it will not hurt you. It may make it hard to see for a few minutes afterward. You won't be afraid, will you?"

Edward stares at Louella in wide-eyed wonder without speaking.

Refreshed from her ride, Elizabeth enters the shop and watches Louella and her tongue-tied son, "Louella, I suggest we let him watch while you take my picture first so he can learn what to expect."

"Just the thing!"

"We need to change our clothes before we begin."

Louella takes the portmanteau to the back room of the shop, sets it inside and leaves Edward with his mother.

While her friends are changing in the back, Louella talks through the door, "Mrs. Morse was in town shopping and asked me to help when she delivers her baby. I can't attend the births as I did before opening this shop."

"How is Mrs. Morse?" asks Elizabeth

"She's as active as always and making plans for their first child."

"Edward," says Elizabeth, "you are ready except for combing your hair. Go on out to Louella and I'll be ready soon."

When Edward comes out front, Louella says, "Elizabeth, he's adorable in that suit you've made. This portrait is an Easter gift for your family, isn't it?"

"Yes, it is and why I want it to be exceptional. Louella, will you comb his hair for me. I'll be out once I repair my rumpled coif."

"Of course!" Louella answers Elizabeth. Then she turns to Edward. "Sugah, come sit on this stool and I'll comb your hair for your mother. Sit still and I'll give you a strip of fruit leather after we make the photographs."

Edward remembers these dried strips of fruit leather he got from the glass jars on previous visits and needs no encouragement. "I want the wild plum!"

"That's what you always want...not apricot or peach...always wild plum. I will give it to you as soon as we take your photograph."

When Elizabeth joins them, Louella smiles as she examines her friend's dress, "Why, you look like you stepped right out of *Vogue* or *Woman's Home Companion* magazine. What a fine seamstress you are!" Edward fidgets and Louella turns her attention to him. "Edward, sit right here so I can show you how I take pictures." Louella lifts Edward onto a tall stool behind the camera and just to her side.

Elizabeth sits on a fainting sofa while Louella directs her to assume several poses and takes several shots. "Now, Edward, it's your turn."

Edward stares at the glass jar filled with fruit leather and points, "Give me the wild plum!"

Edward protests waiting for his treat, but his mother tells him, "We want our photograph made together. It will take a few minutes and, then, you get the wild plum."

He stands beside his mother for a couple of shots and does well enough with the explosion of the camera lights, but he rubs his eyes and complains of the blinding effect. When all is completed, Edward's reward is a strip of fruit leather. Louella slips another one to his mother for later. After they change to their travel clothes, Louella again speaks of Mrs. Morse's request of her.

"Elizabeth, I need your help. The combination of keeping this shop open and managing for my family means I must stop acting as a midwife. Will you consider taking my place?"

"I never acted as a midwife," says Elizabeth.

"On the other hand, you almost single-handedly gave birth to your son because your doctor arrived too late. You prepared yourself with the instructions from your grandfather's medical books sent from London. Dr. von Brunow praised you to the skies."

"Well, we women do a lot of things because we must, but I never attended another."

"Elizabeth, you are better equipped than I because you gave birth and experienced what all mothers must accomplish."

"It is not the same: you ask me to go into woman's home while her husband and family wait until their baby is born."

"Believe me, the families welcome help—especially husbands! I can recommend you to Mrs. Morse and her husband for so many reasons. I trust you because you will follow the procedures of English doctors. Your calm presence and cleanliness are my main reasons for asking you. I can go with you a time or two if you want."

"With Edward now, I cannot leave him or take him along."

"You can get the help of one of your neighbors to stay with him while you are away. I know you are the best woman to do this. Dolly—Mrs. Morse—needs you. I promise to be there with you."

Elizabeth chuckles and her eyes sparkle with humor, "Well, when you put it that way, how can I refuse? Do speak with Mrs. Morse about this and I will find a neighbor who will stay with Edward."

Elizabeth contacts a neighbor lady—the widow Clark in Laketon—who agrees to stay with Edward. Louella sends word that Mrs. Morse agrees with the arrangement Louella and Elizabeth made.

The day Sam Morse telephones to tell Elizabeth his wife is about to deliver the baby, Elizabeth has her kit of materials—surgical scissors, a bottle of whiskey with which to sterilize them, a ball of heavy chord, chamomile tea, scented lotion, and a new set of diapers—packed and ready. Widow Clark moved in with the Gethings days ago; she is here to tend to Edward when the telephone call comes from Mr. Morse. A rider goes to Louella, who meets Elizabeth at the Morse home.

There is no telephone line to Miami, but the neighbors surrounding the Laketon Post Office use telephone boxes among close neighbors by stringing telephone lines between fence posts alongside the top strand of barbed wire fences. Their neighbor, Mr. Stump, purchased many telephones when on business in Chicago and brought them home to Laketon.

At the Morse home, Louella takes a moment to speak to her friend alone, "Elizabeth, you will be in charge and I will stand beside you so you can ask questions or I can make suggestions."

But, that is not the way it happens. They put Sam Morse in charge of boiling pots of water for a supply of warm moist towels to comfort Dolly and to keep the bedding clean and deal with the afterbirth. Beyond that, it is waiting; it is holding Dolly's hand and telling her it is worth it by action rather than words. They make Dolly as comfortable as they can, engaging her with a variety of topics of conversation, supplying her with cups of tea, and soothing her swollen abdomen, arms, and legs with lotion. Dolly's body knows what it must do and it is simple. Just not easy and not painless! It is the overture to motherhood. The final effort is those long, loud, repeated pushes.

The birth amazes Elizabeth. With Edward, she was on the pulsing, pushing, palpitating end of giving life. Today she witnesses a miracle, an awesome event that evokes a spiritual ecstasy which she never imagined. She decides that every day she must observe a host of marvels and mysteries. Perhaps she misses them because she expects merely the mundane. Her world shifts this day and she is reborn with a spirit of adoration.

As soon as this new life rests in her care and she promotes his cry in order that the baby fills his lungs and his breathing begins. Then she performs the routine of separating this baby boy from his former cord of life. "Yes, little one, I would be angry, too if I were you! Cry and rage at the indignity! But instead, joy pours from me for the wonder of you!" says Elizabeth.

Sponged and bundled, he lodges his miniature hand in his mouth. Elizabeth presents him to his mother, Dolly, who gifts him to his father, Sam. The parents choose to call him Samuel Bogan Morse; he shares his father's first name and his mother's family name. The infant needs no physical cord; he depends upon a stronger chord—his parent's love and commitment.

After leaving the new family in the bedroom, Elizabeth says, "Louella, I did not know it would be so grand. Thank you for insisting on this."

"Elizabeth, no poetry can tell another of this. You are a natural, by the way!"

These two ladies give the needed assurances to the young mother and answer a few of her questions. Young Samuel Brogan Morse's parents accept their son with joy and the responsibility for his dependence and growth toward independence.

The midwives return to home and shop where they will finish all the work they must do this day. It is forever the blending of the miraculous and the mundane. These three ladies—Dolly, Elizabeth and Louella—are some of the indomitable women that the frontier produces.

21 - Deep Wounds

Arthur will keep his hounds penned now. One chased and killed Elizabeth's rooster and Arthur's hound came to its end. He cannot believe his wife killed his best tracker until he sees it lying by the chopping block down by the creek where he went to bury it.

Elizabeth earns money in several ways besides selling milk and butter. She raises chickens to sell eggs. Over many months, she saved her money and bought a rooster so that, in time, there will be chicks to sell. When the hounds start chasing her hens, she runs outside, chases them away or grabs and pens them in their rude kennels. This morning she and Edward were ready to make their regular marketing trip to Miami when the rooster screeched and squawked through the yard, but she was too late to save it.

The ax bears witness to the manner of the hound's death. Elizabeth and Edward are blood stained. Edward cries and sobs.

I did that before I thought. I was furious. ... It was as if I were blind, Elizabeth thinks.

Elizabeth trembles, "Edward, we must go back into the house." She takes his hand and they return. Inside, she changes her son into clean clothes again this morning and also her own. Their blood smeared and speckled white garments are put to soak in cold water and she drives the wagon into Miami.

How was I strong enough to hold that animal by its scruff and whack it in the head? There will be the devil to pay when Arthur finds that hound!

She manages to calm herself and Edward on the way to town and she sells her eggs, milk, and butter. They return and wait well into the evening for Arthur to come.

He is not aware of the loss but notices the hounds are penned. Usually, some of his pack of dogs race to meet him baying all the time. Elizabeth meets him at the doorway.

"Mr. Gething," she says, "Your hound, Rowdy, is dead…I killed it."

"You what?" he gasps.

"It killed my rooster!"

"My best tracker?"

"Keep those hounds penned!"

Arthur's temper erupts. He goes at her in a rage.

"The chickens feed us!" Elizabeth holds her hands above her head and turns her head.

"NO! Father!" screams Edward.

Arthur throws his hat on the floor and kicks it out the door and slams the door behind him. Yelling profanity after profanity, he gives vent to his rage. With his curses spent, he races to the barn and rides away.

Elizabeth and Edward stand quaking in awful fear in the center of the room. She reaches out to comfort, to soothe her son and needs the same herself. She goes about the evening routine and tries to put this behind her.

When in control of herself, she calls Edward to sit with her.

"Edward, I am sorry you saw these terrible things. That kind of anger never happened to me before. I was terrified, but your father left; he…did not harm us. He will be back when he can."

"Moms, I am scared. Both of you made me want to run away," Edward says backing away in tears.

"I am sorry, Son. I wanted to run away, too. I think your father ran away because he is too angry. Go onto bed and I'll sing you to sleep." Elizabeth lulls her son to sleep and goes to sleep sitting by her son's bed.

Arthur races Spider away to release his fury. When Spider is exhausted, he blows and humps and staggers. Arthur slips out of the saddle and walks about. "Sorry, Old Boy," he says stroking the horse's neck and withers. I must think…. Kate speaks her mind…never violent before. … I am. …Our son thought I'd…beat his mother. I promised he would never know that fear. My brothers—Hugh and Stanley—and I knew it. Kate spoke truth; she defended her flock to feed us.

He walks Spider home to the barn and stops often making allowance for his recovering horse. *I will call on Perry LeFors tomorrow. Tonight I will speak with Kate.*

He finds her beside Edward's bed and kneels placing his hand on her shoulder to avoid waking their son. She stirs and wakes as if from a drugged sleep.

"Kate, you can't sleep here all night. Let's get ourselves to bed. I'm all right now and wish I could undo that."

"Mr. Gething, our son wanted to run away from both of us. I never felt so alarmed."

"Well, the two of you stayed; I ran away. We'll take care of this. Come on we need our rest. Tomorrow's a new day."

Elizabeth tucks the covers around Edward's head and shoulders and leaves with Arthur.

After breakfast and chores, Arthur buries the hound. For a moment, he stands leaning on the shovel and sobs dry sobs. At last he rides out to call on Perry LeFors, who is easy to talk with about most anything.

He finds Perry at the barn and, with effort, tells him the entire episode. Kate has killed his hound over the loss of her only rooster. Then, how he came close to striking his wife in the presence of his son.

At length, Perry says, "Arthur, you were scared as never before, I guess. Tell me: what kept you from venting your rage on your wife and son."

Arthur does not answer until he gets himself under control and it is with a number of false starts for his emotions run high.

"Perry, I could not...bring upon them...what I, my brothers...even my...mother and sister...suffered...at the hands of my father. Taking a deep breath and stopping, Arthur, then, continues with more control. "I keep a distance between myself and my wife and son so that doesn't happen, but I came damned close.

"You didn't deserve that treatment as a child, Arthur. Neither did your family. You are not the first man I've known who struggles with it. In my cowboy days in the Panhandle and later as ranch manager, I knew some who ran away from it as a solution."

"What happened to them?"

"I can't say because I don't know about most of them. It doesn't seem a satisfactory answer, does it?"

"Guess not."

"Arthur, you did not act on your anger. ...Why not?"

Arthur struggles to continue. He breathes heavily. "I've put my wife through…so much…and she cannot be…replaced. She makes my ranch what it is. She can be tough; she makes me pay when I…."

"We are indebted to our wives and families. I am, to Mrs. Lefors; you are, to Mrs. Gething. They make the harsh life out here worth the grueling labor."

"Yes, I agree."

"Arthur, you bring much to her, too. And you share your information with all of us and not only the legal and political information. It seems to me you are more in control of your temper than when we first met. Trust in that."

"You think so?"

"Did you share this knowledge about your father with your wife?"

"No, I couldn't."

"Well, give it some thought," says Perry. "She may need to know."

Arthur lifts his head and offers his hand. "I will and thanks, Perry."

Arthur returns to his place and gives Perry's words his consideration. He, at the end of his trip home, can see ways to be more thoughtful. To begin, he will keep his hounds penned, but he does not know how to humble himself before his wife. How does he remain head of his house and bend to her? His father controlled his family by force and intimidation. Some part of him admired his father. However, he cannot create the kind of warmth he observes in the LeFors family. He doesn't know how to duplicate it and believes it out of his reach.

Deep wounds are not easily healed, if ever.

22 - Here Comes the Bride

Louella sits at the counter of her father's Cap Rock Café. She and her father, Joe Harrah, enjoy lunch and talk with neighbors who are in town from outlying ranches and homesteads and those who live in Miami. The door opens and the customers turn to check out who is joining them.

Here is a newcomer with two girls about three and four years old whom he ushers in before him. Joe Harrah comes around the counter to greet them. "The name's Harrah, Joe Harrah. I don't reckon I've seen you around before."

"T. J. McEntire is the name. These are my daughters, Kathleen and Palesteen; they are taking the train to Fort Worth tomorrow with my mother. My wife passed a couple of years ago and my girls are out visiting me. I'm Sterling Clark's ranch manager and been there a spell…seldom in Miami. Mr. Clark does most of his business out of Canadian."

Louella joins her father to welcome these little girls who are shy and cling to their father. "Kathleen and Palesteen, what beautiful names!"

"Mr. McEntire, may I bring your daughters glasses of lemonade and something to eat?" offers Louella. She is helping her father raise her two younger brothers and two younger sisters since her mother died. Two sisters, younger than she, are married and no longer live with the family. When her mother died, her father ran a variety of businesses and he elected to remain near Miami until his youngest finishes school. He continues stock farming and tending his orchards and also opened this café for additional income. "Mr. Harrah is my father; I'm Louella Harrah the owner of the Photograph Studio in town."

"That'll be right helpful, Miss Harrah," says T. J. My mother will be along in a few minutes. She's doing some shopping for their train ride tomorrow."

"Girls, tell Miss Harrah what you want to eat, but my mother will insist they drink milk."

Dainty and shy Palesteen says nothing, but her older sister Kathleen says with all seriousness and primness, "Both of us want milk and apple pie, please."

"I will bring it," says Louella. Then she helps them into their chairs and goes to bring their order while their father joins some friends of his at the counter. While these two young girls enjoy pie and milk, Louella sits with them and visits.

While the girls eat, their Grandmother McEntire arrives with bundles and joins them. Louella stands, "I am Louella Harrah. My dad owns this café and I'm visiting with your granddaughters who know milk is best for them."

"Thank you, my dear. My son, Thomas, teases me about my insistence that the girls drink milk, but I don't forbid them to drink other beverages. Louella, thank you for taking over for me. Thomas doesn't know how to be both father and mother to these two. He lost his wife before Palesteen was a year old and he's been separated from them for a while now."

"I understand; I'm helping Dad raise my brothers and sisters. Mother passed not long ago. Tell me what you'd like in the way of something to eat and drink and I'll get it for you."

"That pie looks good. I'll want a slice, too, but I'll drink tea."

Kathleen quirks her eye at her grandmother, "Gran'mother, milk is best!"

Palesteen giggles, "Gran'mother's a growing girl."

"Make hers milk, too!" instructs Kathleen.

"Oh, straight from their father's mouth to my ears," laughs Mrs. McEntire. "I should set a good example; milk for me, too."

T. J. raises his glass of beer to toast his family. "Drink up!" he winks at the men at the counter who enjoy his family's banter about the superiority of drinking milk.

"Ladies, I need to get back to my photography shop down the street so I must leave you. You are welcome to drop by when you leave the café. I might find a small treat for the girls to take along on their trip back to Fort Worth."

T. J. cuts his eyes around to Louella with a gleam in his eye. "That is not an offer Kathleen and Palesteen will let us forget. Thanks for taking over."

Less than an hour later, T. J. takes his family to Louella's shop with the thought that he would like a photograph of his daughters before they leave tomorrow. He wants another opportunity to see the kindhearted proprietor of the shop, too. His girls, he thinks, are not the only ones interested in a treat.

Louella looks up as the McEntire family enters her shop. "Oh, you did decide to come to my shop. I'm so glad! Girls, come here to see what's in my big glass jars. I've rock candy and fruit leather. You can make your choices."

"Miss Harrah, I want photographs of Mother and my daughters to remind me of what pretty women they are. Can you do that today?"

"Of course, that's exactly why I hang out my sign. Let me see...do you want a group portrait or each one separately."

"The group one is good. That way I can see them all at once."

Louella sets about with Mrs. McEntire combing and brushing hair, arranging curls and smoothing the girls' dresses. They sit on her studio couch and Mrs. McEntire stands behind them. The McEntire women are all smiles and make charming subjects.

"Mr. McEntire, wouldn't you like me to make one of you for your family in Fort Worth?"

"Son, this is an excellent suggestion. The girls and I would like your picture, too," says Mrs. McEntire.

"What do you think, girls?" asks T. J.

"Oh, yes, Papa!" The girls chorus their reply.

"Miss Harrah, you've made yourself a sale. Now, how long until they'll be ready?"

Louella thinks, *I could stay late and get them ready to go with the girls by the time they leave on the 11:52 train in the morning. But if Mr. McEntire comes to town anyway, I will get that new order with the photograph finishing preparations that preserve the prints so well.* "Mr. McEntire, some of the supplies I need to finish the photographs won't arrive by train until next week. I hope the delay of another week or more will not inconvenience you. I'm sorry it can't be done sooner."

"I can live with that. Girls, I'll mail them to you in a few weeks."

Louella smiles, *I was hoping to see Mr. McEntire again so this will work out better than I thought!*

Kathleen and Palesteen are gazing at the big jars of rock candy. "Miss Harrah, we've decided on the rock candy," says Kathleen.

"I want the red one?" says Palesteen.

"I will get it for you, Palesteen," says Louella. "Which do you want, Kathleen?"

"The yellow one, please," Kathleen answers.

Kathleen and Palesteen enjoy their rock candy while their father poses for his portrait. "Papa, smile for the camera!" Kathleen instructs, parroting the instructions she and her sister received from Miss Harrah.

After Louella shoots the portraits of T. J. McEntire, she selects the chosen red and yellow rock candies from her jar and sacks them for the girls. Mrs. McEntire says, "The girls love them! Thank you for making this a special day for them." She stows the bag of candy in her purse.

When the train pulls out the following day, the McEntire girls return to Fort Worth to live with their grandmother. But T. J. McEntire gets his photographs and a date with the kind and lovely Louella Harrah. Their courtship continues for more than a year. A ranch manager and a woman with a business and the responsibility of her father's family cannot see one another as often as they would like. By late the following summer, they set their wedding date for September 26, 1906 and town gossip spreads the announcement as fast as a cowboy throws a lariat. Everyone gets an invitation and no one is surprised by the news these two will marry.

The women whom Louella counts as friends gather around her to offer help with the wedding plans. All the women Louella helped when their babies were born want to be part of the event.

One of the women eager to assist with the wedding is Emma LeFors. She recalls her wedding day, "An excellent dressmaker in Old Mobeetie made my wedding dress, and Perry imported champagne for the celebration that followed the wedding ceremony. We were married in the Husselby Hotel where our guests danced the night away; everyone in the country came. My brothers-in-law went all out to show the hospitality for which they are famous and my sisters cooked and baked for the wedding feast."

Elizabeth adds, "That reminds me of the wonderful meals Mr. Gething and I ate at the Holland Hotel when I arrived here as a bride. It was the most wonderful hotel. We did not stay in a nicer one anywhere in Texas.

"Louella, I especially want to be included in your wedding! I did not enjoy making my own wedding plans because I was eager to come to the frontier with Mr. Gething, but all of us want to make your wedding an occasion to remember for the rest of your life. How can we do this?"

"Elizabeth," says Louella, "you are in charge of helping me with my wedding gown!"

This covey of women insist on being part of Louella's wedding plans. Those with gardens of fall flowers decorate the Methodist Church. The best cooks and bakers are taking over the feast for the bride and groom; they will spread it after the wedding. Joe Harrah bankrolls whatever is needed or wanted by his daughter. Elizabeth and Louella pore over the women's magazines choosing the most beautiful gown for the bride.

Louella chooses a dazzling white silk and the fittings of the patterns and the sewing of the gown follow. Elizabeth embroiders the bodice with an elaborate and delicate floral design of forget-me-nots and roses. T. J.'s mother, Mrs. McEntire, makes her granddaughters' dresses in Fort Worth so that they can be flower girls in the ceremony. T. J. recruits his boss Sterling Clark to advise him on the duties and attire as bridegroom and Mr. Clark will act as his best man. Perry and Emma LeFors arrange for and furnish the finest champagne to be found.

Kathleen and Palesteen arrive with their grandmother weeks before the wedding date and fall in love with their step-mother all over again. Many years later, Palesteen would say she and Kathleen never considered her a step-mother and never felt she was any other than their own mother.

When the wedding day arrived, it seemed the whole of the eastern Panhandle celebrated along with the bride and groom. It was a dream come true for all of them, but for the newly-married Mr. and Mrs. T. J. McEntire it was perfect.

Mr. Sterling Clark's wedding gift was a honeymoon trip to Denver combined with a cattle-buying for the ranch. On their return a house on the Diamond F would be ready for them. Grandmother McEntire is with her granddaughters until her son and daughter-in-law return. Then, she makes her goodbyes on the platform of the Miami depot before boarding the train to Fort Worth without Kathleen and Palesteen.

"Gran'mother," says Kathleen, "promise you will come for Christmas!"

"I wouldn't miss it, Sweetheart!"

"Love you, Gran'mother," says Palesteen.

"Love you both," cries Grandmother McEntire, "Be good girls. I'm happy for all of you!"

Louella says, "We'll take very good care of them! Thank you for all you've given them."

"I know they are in good hands, but, oh, I'll miss them so!" says their Grandmother.

Tom kisses his mother, "You are the best, mother and grandmother. We will miss you, too. We expect you for Christmas!"

When the train pulls out of the station, the McEntire family waves until the caboose is only a speck at the end of the track. Many families in the Texas Panhandle are formed and then reformed due to the deaths of mothers or fathers.

23 - Proving up the Stock

Arthur and his neighbor's fourteen-year-old son, Emmett LeFors, face each other across the corral fence as the cooing sounds of evening descend. Emmett leans into one of the Mesquite posts strung with four strands of barbed wire and rests his left shoulder against it. Arthur stands inside the corral with his arms crossed over his chest. Any passerby would conclude they discuss a matter of importance and settle the matter.

"Hungry?" Arthur asks nodding toward his family's half-human dugout.

"Yeah," Emmett drawls, "tomorrow we make an early start. Before daybreak, I judge."

"Packing light is the way to go. We can take care of that after we eat."

"Grass is greening so there is plenty of grazing on our return."

Arthur leaves the corral and closes the gate; he joins Emmett and they head uphill together. They scrub their hands and faces at the wash basin outside before they enter. Five-year-old Edward Gething climbs onto the bench at the table where their meal waits just as the men enter.

"Edward, we wash before we come to the table," Elizabeth reminds her son.

The door slams shut behind him on his way to the washstand outside. Elizabeth motions to Arthur.

"Mr. Gething, your son has his heart set on going with you."

"Kate, he is far too young. Emmett and I will be doing all we can to manage getting a bull home. Do you know how dangerous that could be? Our son cannot be part of this!"

"The likelihood of your being able to come to an agreement to buy a bull from Charles Goodnight does not appear likely considering what there is to spend. Instead, it is a great opportunity for Edward to learn from his father how to live on this land."

"This is no conversation to spill out with a guest present."

Edward peers through a crack in the door where he has been standing long enough to hear the disagreement. He opens wide the door and stands there. He is a tall wiry boy and lightly freckled. His hair is cropped short and it lies in tight waves the color of ginger. Meeting his father's eyes, he grins!

"I'm a great rider and go with Mother everywhere she goes. I promise I won't be any trouble! Please?"

"It is too dangerous. Bringing the bull home is all Emmett and I can manage. If there is trouble, how can we take care of you?"

"Mother gallops full out riding side-saddle…"

Emmett erupts in laughter, "Blamed, if she don't!"

"…and I never fall off! Emmett lets me ride his cow pony, Mischief."

Elizabeth turns away to hide her laughter, recovers and instructs the men and her little man to sit to dinner.

Their meal begins in uncomfortable silence, but Emmett relieves it with a bit of palaver.

"Well, Edward, how is it coming with that lasso we made for you?"

"I practice just like you showed me. I can loop it around that cow skull you set up on the hay most times. I'm going to get it down perfect."

"That's the spirit! Keep at it."

Elizabeth inquires about the stock and tells about the progress of her garden plants. They gossip about their neighbor's comings and goings. Then, they speculate about what the neighbors seem to be planning. The family and friend around this table keep in touch with one another; they also stay aware of their neighbors in the community.

When the meal is finished, the men lay out supplies they will pack in their saddlebags and suggans, a cowhand's travel bedroll. Packing light means they need a skillet, tins of canned beans, bacon, and bags of flour, sugar, and coffee. This rounds out their road pantry. The other essentials are rifles for shooting game as they travel so that they escape the limits of packed foods with rabbit, prairie hen, or turkey. Canteens of water will get them from water hole to water hole.

Elizabeth notices that listless look slipping onto her son's face. "It's your bedtime. Get in your bunk."

"Aww, Mother, I ain't sleepy."

"Tomorrow is another day. Go on!"

Emmett stretches and rises. "I'll bunk around by your lean-to. Mr. Gething, let's get our gear out there now so that our work in the morning is almost done." Picking up their saddlebags and bedrolls, they leave the dugout.

"Mr. Gething, walking your bull back here is a lot less dangerous than you figure. The trip back is probably going to take longer than you planned though. 'Cause this bull wants just two things—grass and water—with plenty of time to take on both. If we spot the water holes going out, that's covered coming back. Since the spring grass is a-plenty, then we'll only borrow trouble if we move the beast too fast coming back.

"That son of yours can handle himself on Mischief and I'd admire being the one to take him along with us. Just give me the word and I'll fetch the pony for him right away."

"By God! I can't put my foot down in my own house without interference from my neighbor!"

"Now, Mr. Gething, this choice is yours! You asked me to go along 'cause my dad and I did this a number of times. I'm telling you what I've come to know. You and my dad are friends for a long time. And he took me along on his travels when I was no older than Edward. Dad always says there's more than one way to prove up your stock and the most important way is bringing your sons up alongside you. You've asked me along to help. Edward can do it. Up to you!"

Arthur pauses for a long time; he drops his head and then looks up toward the horizon and sky and thinks of Perry's advice when he asked for it, even over his lost temper about the rooster and foxhound.

"Well, a barrister knows enough to ask advice and hopes to be wise enough to determine whether it's good advice. You say that your father took you on adventures like this at Edward's age? Is Edward that good on your pony?"

"Yes, sir, on both counts. You won't be sorry."

"We'll give it a go. Get your pony! Let's pack some tins of canned tomatoes and peaches in Edward's saddle bags. They quench the thirst on the trail and he can pack some. We will be glad for bringing them.

"See you in the morning!" Emmett says.

He will fetch his pony for Edward. The trip home and back with Mischief means he will return deep in the night. *Won't get a lot of sleep tonight.*

Meanwhile, Arthur reviews his decision. *Perry LeFors never steers me wrong. Elizabeth and Edward win a victory with this arrangement. They love out maneuvering me. The three of them—Emmett, Elizabeth and Edward—are as wily as bandits, but the rewards I care about will be mine.*

Inside, Arthur slips into bed and whispers to his Kate that Emmett rides to get Mischief so that Edward can go with them. A husband's rewards are sweet. He anticipates breaking the news to Edward in the morning. All is well under his roof.

In the morning, the pungent aroma of brewed coffee drifts throughout the dugout and seeps into the lean-to. Elizabeth notes the earliest signs of the rising sun. A sprinkling of stars and the new moon, like a trimming from a thumbnail, defy the day while the dark of night prevails. She slices cheese and wraps it with yesterday's sourdough biscuits for a midday lunch for the travelers. Bacon spits and pops in the skillet and creamy oatmeal warms on the back of the stovetop. Arthur goes below to awaken sleep-saturated Edward.

"Wake up, son. Time to get up." Edward struggles to rouse himself. "Let's go buy a bull. Mischief waits, saddled and ready to go."

"Now? Right now! And no joking?"

"No joking! Get dressed and go eat your porridge."

"Yippee!" Edward hugs his father's neck and his feet hit the floor as he scrambles for clothes and boots.

"Mother! Mother! I can go with them. Father just said so. I'll ride Mischief all by myself!"

Elizabeth swings him around and around and scoots him onto the bench in front of his bowl of porridge. She gives Arthur a sparkling smile and Emmett, a conspirator's wink. Her son explodes with excitement and cannot seem to sit still long enough to eat the oatmeal. Never was he so excited! Not even on Christmas day.

There is a tinge of blush along the eastern horizon as the trio rides away and Elizabeth waves her apron above her head until the undulations of the landscape fold them inside. *Edward won't be tied to these apron strings long. This is the beginning of his becoming a man. His father wants that Hereford bull; he is ever eager to impress our neighbors.*

Later the men skirt below the bluffs of the Llano Estacado's easterly side and travel south in order to stay off the higher, dryer land, and stay in regions of dependable grass cover. Forage for the animals is now that delicate yellow-green of spring that deepens into a lush green grassland that has nourished native and domestic cattle for centuries. It is not time for small talk as they navigate broken land. These riders and horses pick their way between landforms, thorn-bearing plants, and unforgiving brush.

When the sun is at its high point, they seek shade and water and give their horses a rest throughout midday. When the saddles are off and the horses staked, they eat the biscuits and cheese Elizabeth packed and talk only when necessary. Edward curls up on his spread out bedroll with his head in the saddle for a pillow studying whatever Emmett does and carefully following his lead. Initially they swat away insects with their hats, but soft snoring soon follows. They covered their faces with western hats to anticipate the moving shade. Their hats also thwart the ever-present insects.

By day, the sun is the only timepiece they need and by its two o'clock position, they are in the saddles again and winding their way below the escarpment as before. Their progress again demands their constant surveillance and attention as it did in the morning.

Before dusk, they locate a pool of water by a grove of cottonwood trees and camp for the evening. They remove saddles, blankets, saddlebags, and bedrolls after the horses drink. Tethering them in patches of grass completes the first chore. Next they make camp and collect firewood from among the trees. Their supper is coffee, bacon, and beans. The coffee pot goes on the campfire before the skillet allowing time for the water to boil. Night brings out the stars and cooling breezes and the enjoyment of one another's company. The tempo and pattern of days to come establishes itself with these routines. Passing homesteads, farms, or settlements, and a change of weather can interrupt this manner of travel.

The morning fire crackles and Emmett rattles the coffee pot and skillet. He breaks into a sing-song cry, "Wake up Edward; hoecakes a'bakin'; the ol' bull's a-waitin'." This cry wakes Edward each morning, but Emmett changes the last phrase often in order to tease or cajole. By the third morning, Edward sings out his lyrics, "Wake up Emmett; hoecakes a'bakin'; your ol' bones a-achin'." Father and Emmett chortle at his banter. Encouraged by their reaction, Edward cries another ending phrase. "Wake up, Father; hoecakes a'bakin; your butt's a-achin'." This time he earns a swat on his rump from his sire. They leave the camp in a rollicking mood.

"Edward!" Emmett alerts his companion. "We're likely to come up on a prairie dog town soon. Stay right behind your dad now. It's important to learn what to look for at all times when crossing this country."

Edward watches intently. Arthur says, "We will hear them first so…slow up when you hear whistling."

It seems to Edward that they are joshing him because he hears nothing and they travel a good distance. When he hears a sound more like a screech than a whistle, his eyes grow round and he slows behind his father.

"Now, son," Arthur speaks in undertone, "They hear us coming so keep your eyes open. We need to spot their town and give it a wide berth. They live underground, but if Mischief steps into one of their holes, he is sure to break a leg. But, we will try to get close enough so you can watch them before we move on."

Edward knows he is on trial with his father and he follows instructions from him without fail. He longs to be part of the workforce on the ranch. Emmett and Mother encourage him at every turn.

Emmett speaks softly, "Stop a while. It may trick them into staying still and you'll spot them before they go underground." They wait patiently keeping their mounts motionless. The whistling stops until only the wind lulls across the prairie. Then, Arthur leads them forward in near silence. He slowly palms to the left up ahead. Stops again. No sound.

Edward scans in that direction and sees the first prairie dog sitting up straight, then another and finally several. He is breathless. The prairie dogs sit on top of mounds of earth where these animals stripped the surrounding space of plants. Time passes, but all too soon for Edward, his father sweeps his hat off to the right and clatters away sharply in that direction. A chorus of whistles trill and the prairie dogs all whip into holes.

"That was something! They barked when we rushed away!" Edward beams.

"That bark is their warning sign," Emmett says.

The men agree during the midday rest that they expect to arrive at the Goodnight place by evening and they turn in a southeasterly direction. Goodnight's spread is located near the Salt Fork of the Red River. White clouds billow above and there is no hint of rain. Nothing prevents their progress until they hear a cussing that would make a mule skinner blush. The one cursing eases into more coherent deliverances after his initial outburst.

"You worthless jackass! Sightless as a tick-infested, eye-blind steer! You've trampled my dugout! Buried my biscuits and beans! You damned fool idiots!" a bearded grizzled old man rails at them. The riders and horses collapsed the rear of his dugout because the sod-covered roof is overgrown with brush.

"Damnation!" Arthur wheels Spider; Emmett and Arthur haul back on their mounts. "Mind your tongue in front of my son! We saw no signs of a dwelling and we'll make amends. Now, stop your rant."

The wizened old man, exhausting his wrath, puffs, and scowls at the three. "You know how to rile a man. Come on now…light and hitch! I expect you to fix this mess so I got a roof over my head."

All dismount and begin to examine the damage.

"Mister, we didn't mean to smash your roof," Edward says.

"Aw, Boy, I know you didn't, but you scared me witless and I'm in a predicament without a roof. People just call me "Irish". What's your name, Little Pard?"

"I'm Edward Gething and this is my father and our friend. We can fix your dugout 'cause we made our own."

There are introductions and handshaking all around and then a discussion of what to use for support beams to repair the sod roof. Arthur and Emmett spend the afternoon hauling saplings from the creek, setting new supports for the roof and replacing the sod. With that accomplished, Irish and Edward scoop and sweep away the disorder inside.

At dusk, Irish invites them to camp next to his place tonight and makes an offer they cannot pass up—cool buttermilk that Irish stores in a deep pool in the stream near the dugout and a fresh batch of corncakes he fries up for them. Edward offers two tins of canned peaches and Emmett brews coffee and heats the beans and bacon.

Irish, an isolated settler, relishes the company and they entertain one another with stories of life on the plains. As they leave the next morning, Irish invites them to come this way again. He knows the Goodnight spread and suggests landmarks to direct them.

After leaving, Edward addresses his father and Emmett, "We're a whole lot like those prairie dogs. Dugouts are a safe place to live if strangers don't come crashing in. Irish barked just like those prairie dogs." The men both laugh until tears come to their eyes. Edward's expression tells them he does not understand what is so funny.

The trio passes through the Goodnight gate midday and spot a cowman walking the path and stopping occasionally to pick up something. Arthur hails the gentleman, "Greetings, did you lose something?"

"Picking up nails! I'm averse to waste. What do you want?"

"We've come to see the Hereford bulls Mr. Goodnight sells because of the reputation his livestock enjoys. I'm the stock farmer from near Mobeetie that Mr. Goodnight's expecting. The name's Arthur Gething."

"I'm the man you've come to do business with— Charles Goodnight. I received your letter of inquiry. Guess you got my answer. I recollect we met some years ago when Mobeetie was the main place in the eastern Panhandle for all legal work…beginning with the establishment of the counties. And who are your friends?"

"These are my son, Edward, and my friend and neighbor, Emmett LeFors." Each shakes Mr. Goodnight's hand as introduced.

"Mr. LeFors, you'd be Perry LeFors' son if I take your measure right. You men, take care of your horses at the corral. Should be someone there to help you. I'll meet you at the house and Mrs. Goodnight will fix us some lemonade. Your young cowhand looks like he can use some refreshment."

Edward flashes him a smile to remember. "Yes, sir, Mr. Goodnight!"

Mrs. Goodnight, a hospitable woman, delights in her guests especially Edward. She serves the lemonade with gingersnaps and attends to each guest. "Tell me about your trip, Edward. How many days are you from your home?"

"Nine days, Ma'am. We'd made it in eight, but we bashed in an old man's dugout and had to fix it back up. We rode around a prairie dog town, but later on we came upon his ol' dugout that seemed like just only a creek bank. Boy, he was some kind of mad until he could see we were going to help get his roof back in place."

Mr. Goodnight's wife, Molly Goodnight, chuckles; Emmett and Arthur grin, their eyes reveal suppressed amusement, but Charles Goodnight sits forward in his office chair full of curiosity.

"Saw prairie dogs, did you? Now, that's a right interesting creature. I've studied them a good deal during my life," says Mr. Goodnight.

Edward walks to Mr. Goodnight and props his elbows on Mr. Goodnight's knee as if they are the only two in the room. "I never saw one before yesterday! They stand up straight just like they're froze in place and whistle. When they hear our horses, they bark and all zip underground so fast you ain't sure they was ever there."

Goodnight cocks his head and leans forward and Edward moves even closer establishing instant camaraderie. Goodnight, well over six feet tall, lifts lanky Edward onto his knee as they talk. "You got a good eye, young man! That's just how they act. Since I've been watching their towns in this country, I've seen them migrate at least 150 miles from the original towns."

"They do? That's a really long way!"

"That's moving a town many times over years. Hard workers, those prairie dogs! They leave one town and move on. Maybe because rabbits and snakes start moving in with them. I've seen rabbits kick dirt into snake-filled holes to bury them alive."

"Wish I could a' seen that, but we didn't stay around. We were coming here!"

"Interesting as they are, you never ride a horse into one of their towns. Your dad knows to avoid their towns. You like animals, do you?"

"Yes, sir. I especially like Emmett's pony, Mischief. But I like watching the prairie chickens that come around and grasshoppers, horned toads, and spiders, too. Mother likes the birds because they sing. Wild turkey run around our place. Oh, we see lots of other wild animals. Sometimes deer and antelope!"

"Did you ever see buffalo?"

"No, sir, but our friend tells stories about killing buffalo for their hide and meat. He says he's too old to hunt buffalo now."

"It happens that I have a herd of buffalo. Would you like to see it?"

"I sure would!" Edward slips from his perch on Goodnight's knee and pulls him by the hand, ready to go.

"Gentlemen, I believe I started something. Will you join us? We can also take a look at those Hereford bulls you've come to talk with me about."

Molly Goodnight laughs and pulls her bonnet on and the party follows Edward and Mr. Goodnight. Edward makes a conquest...maybe two.

Once Edward has seen the buffalo herd, his dad and Mr. Goodnight go to another pasture to examine the Hereford bulls. Mrs. Goodnight takes Edward to see the Cattalo, a cross between the Angus cattle and buffalo.

"Mrs. Goodnight," observes Edward, "You are short; Mr. Goodnight is tall. My mother is really tall and my father is short...but not as short as you."

Molly laughs, "You've noticed that, have you? Let's go back to the house to wait for the men."

"Mrs. Goodnight, I've never seen a big house like yours before. My parents used to live in a dugout, but now we live in a half-human dugout. But I like to sleep in the older part of the dugout because I can't hear the wind howl. I don't like that sound."

"Mr. Goodnight and I lived in a dugout for many, many years when we ranched in the Palo Duro Canyon and I know what you mean about the sound of the wind."

"You lived in a dugout, too? Well, I'm going to build my mother a big house like this when I grow up. I will put in those pocket doors between the little room and this big room…just like yours."

"We'll go into the kitchen and we can visit while the cook and I begin our evening meal. I'll show you the other rooms downstairs before that."

"Let's do it!"

They use the front door and step into the entry-way again. Edward gets to open and close the pocket doors with Mrs. Goodnight's help. They go into the parlor off to the left and return through the receiving room where they gathered when they first arrived. The large dining room is just to the right of the receiving room. Next they go to Mr. Goodnight's office and finally into the kitchen to begin cooking.

While they are engaged in the kitchen, the men return and go to Mr. Goodnight's office to conclude their business. With an invitation to the evening meal, all dine on beef steaks and garden vegetables and apple pie in the elegant dining room. The candelabra dazzles Edward, but he is soon yawning and his father thanks the Goodnights for their hospitality and they remove to the guest bedrooms upstairs for the night.

It is a memorable day for Edward and his father who has bought the Hereford bull Mr. Goodnight recommends. Mrs. Goodnight revealed this secret to Edward: Mr. Goodnight refers to his office as his 'War Room'. Edward pledged to keep her secret that sometimes men get shouting angry in the 'War Room'. Edward guessed there was no war today…just men talking.

He [Goodnight] bought cattle far and near. He crossed [Longhorns] with Durhams, but the result did not please him. Black Polled Angus were better in blood and shorter in horn, but he did not like the cross it gave him, either. Then he tried out one of the fine Hereford bulls that O. H. Nelson was transporting from England. The crossbreed he got from them had the stamina of the Longhorn and the self-reliance and hardihood of the Hereford, with good color, good form, and shorter horns. He bought two hundred of these high-priced bulls and intensified his efforts.

Laura V. Hamner, page 47
Short Grass and Longhorns

24 - Return Trip

It is a high point for Arthur when he negotiates an advantageous price for a Hereford bull with Charles Goodnight. With this bull, he will improve his herd and it increases his standing with neighbors because Goodnight has led in breeding excellence in parts of four states for decades.

O. H. Nelson, staunch friend of Goodnight and experienced cattle rancher, introduced and promoted the Hereford breed throughout the area for a long time and, beginning from 1882 through 1889, dealt exclusively in Herefords, selling them from the Bar 96 bull ranch he owned. At some time during that period, Nelson sold 200 of these high-priced bulls to Charles Goodnight, who preferred the Hereford bull in his cross-breeding enterprise.

Arthur Gething admires and seeks quality breeds in cattle, horses, and hounds. As a stockman with a relatively small ranch, he also enjoys an association with lawyers and cattlemen so that his standing within the eastern Panhandle area is modest but significant.

He turns his attention now to the return trip. Emmett encourages him to return by the same overland route, but Arthur is a loner in both travel and relations with others. Having high status among fellow stockmen is his consistent priority. His son's attentions to Emmett and the Goodnights vexes Arthur. He is jealous; it rankles. Seemingly unable to enter his son's world and patiently teach him the ranching skills, he remains rigid in his relationship with Edward.

Arthur's world is hunting coyotes and wolves for monetary reward; riding Spider, his thoroughbred horse; improving his own small stock ranch; and maintaining contacts with lawyers in Mobeetie. Those men sought and appreciated his advice while they established counties in this part of the state at a time when establishment of law on the frontier was still in its infancy, but most of his former legal colleagues left as Mobeetie declined.

Riding the entire return trip and leading the new bull between himself and Emmett, is work beneath his station. For him, a Welsh barrister's proper life ought to be supervising 'cow-servants' and expanding his leisure time to hunt wild game and sail over fences or other barriers on Spider. So he decides to load his bull on a freight car of the Fort Worth and Denver City Railroad and return in a good deal less time than the slow progress Emmett tells him to expect if they make the entire journey on hoof. Emmett's estimate of making only between ten and fifteen miles a day plus the prospect of other disasters such as happened at

Irish's dugout cause him to reject Emmett's advice to return as they came.

He feels smug because he paid below the fair price on the bull. This landfall he estimates will cover a good part of the rail freight and tickets. He congratulates himself on his ability to take advantage of the affection the Goodnights bestowed on his son.

"Emmett, the town of Goodnight is on the Fort Worth & Denver City road and at Washburn we can transfer to the 'Pea Vine' toward the ranch. We will return by rail."

Emmett is perturbed because he knows Charles Goodnight built up his spread and standing in Texas by frugal management of resources and sharing his knowledge. The young men and women from all the area ranches come here to Goodnight College to learn from them. He took Edward around the campus and around the men and women's dormitories and met some of the students. At only fourteen, Emmett will not voice his concern. However, Emmett thinks that Mr. Gething throws his money away.

Edward looks up at his father, "Are we going to ride home on the train?"

"About time you rode on a train! We will lead the bull to the railhead so you see how it is done. After the train trip, we will take my new bull from Pampa all the way home. That is enough travel-time for us."

"Emmett, this is going to be fun!"

Emmett recognizes something like a bribe passes from father to son.

The trio arrive at the railhead beside the town of Goodnight to purchase freight passage for the bull and tickets for themselves. Arthur locates and engages the onsite manager. On hearing what Mr. Gething requests, this site manager swipes the inside of his right arm sleeve across his face to remove the sweat. Arthur interrupts the manager as he supervises his crew that is loading cattle up the chutes into freight cars.

"That's a roundabout trip to even get close to Mobeetie, Mister," the general manager informs Arthur. That ol' 'Pea Vine' road was never but just a little ol' spur line from Washburn to Panhandle City. Amarillo is set to be the real railroad center instead of Panhandle City. The Santa Fe bought the 'Pea Vine' road in 1898 and allowed the 'Pea Vine' to lease Santa Fe roads until the 'Pea Vine' started cutting into their cattle freighting revenue. The Fort Worth and Denver City owns the 'Pea Vine' now. Its crews been a-pullin' up that track for use elsewhere. Your best bet is to go into Amarillo and switch from the Fort Worth & Denver City to the Santa Fe and on into Pampa. I'd be surprised if anything goes closer to Mobeetie now."

Arthur traveled only within the Panhandle and Great Plains since he brought Kate to his place and the loss of his lucrative banking and real estate dealing in Fort Worth make his once customary travel to England rare. He is unaware of the current removal of the 13 mile 'spur line,' a temporary railroad track built for a specific purpose. He doubts the *Miami Chief* newspaper carried this information; because such area news is limited. Even from Pampa, it will be two long days' travel to the ranch, Arthur realizes.

"Aw, hell! These western railroad lines are here today and gone tomorrow," Arthur protests.

The manager uses his hat to fan himself, "Yes, sir, that's the politics of it. Judge O. H. Nelson sold his bull ranch and plowed his money into the Finch, Lord, and Nelson Townsite Company. Lost his shirt, he did, 'cause Amarillo is becoming the railroad center, not Panhandle City!

"Dammit, it will be a long trek from Pampa to our place."

"Tough break, you've got…getting your animal home. Now, you might consider bunking in the freight car with the bull and save the price of three tickets. Stockmen do that to take care of their animals."

"Walking a bull overland can take three days. A considerable chore! I need some time to consider other options." Arthur dismisses the manager with a curt nod.

Emmett is silent and hustles Edward away, diverting his attention to the wooden corrals onto which a herd of cattle continues loading into freight cars. Gething voices a volatile vocabulary equal to or greater than that of Irish's. Emmett expects a string of invectives to flow from Arthur that will shame all everyday swearing and does not misjudge. Mrs. Gething does not approve his language, especially in her son's presence and Emmett respects her wishes. He and Edward stay out of ear-shot until Arthur vents his anger and exhausts his diatribe; afterward, Emmett and Edward join him.

"Mr. Gething, the only faster way is by wagon, but we didn't bring your Murphy farm wagon. Mr. Goodnight may have some advice," suggests Emmett.

"Yes, I'll talk with him," puffs Arthur. His face is flushed.

Together they locate Mr. Goodnight at his place and Arthur tells him his dilemma.

"Mr. Gething, that's unfortunate. The old 'C.O.W. track,' the Choctaw, Oklahoma & Western Railroad, was bought by the Rock Island coming out of Oklahoma City; it runs east-west, not the right direction for you.

"Your only other option is walking the bull north to a Rock Island railhead—three days—and ride that railroad east into McLean, and then lead the bull to your place. That is even further than the distance from Pampa to it—surely three days."

"That wasn't what I hoped to hear."

"You may know that the Rock Island stops at every gate where there's a barbed wire fence so the engineer has to stop the train, put one of his crewmen off to open each ranch or farm gate. Once the train passes, the rear brakeman has to close the wire gate and run to catch the last car. It entertains or annoys the passengers, but if saving time is your objective, taking that line is no advantage."

"Thanks for the information."

"Seems to me with all the travel from here to the Rock Island, you'd be just as well off by hoof on the same route you came. Going into Amarillo from here and then to switch to northbound Santa Fe into Pampa is expensive and also slower combining rail and hoof travel than you expected."

"Leading him overland seems the only way. Well, Emmett, Son, we need to use the rest of this day traveling."

Goodnight says, "Edward, come with me; your dad, and Young LeFors should be gettin' their ropes on your bull. Mrs. Goodnight will be along soon."

"I'm proud, I can tell Mother and my friends about your herd of buffalo and your cattalo. They are something!"

Goodnight smiles at Edward. "Building a good, hearty herd is an important undertaking.

"On the way home, you'll find your bull is fairly easy to handle. This bull isn't going to be a problem. The bulls are used to this country—sudden storms, other animals, and brush country. Pay attention to the bull, keep him comfortable, and mosey him along gentle like.

"Your dad may trail you behind them so your biggest problem may be with the dust they stir up. Do you carry a neckerchief or bandana?"

"Yes, Sir, Emmett told me to put some in my suggan."

"Start wearing one around your neck. If the dust gets bad it'll be handy to pull up around your head to cover your nose and mouth. Get it out and let's get it tied on now." Mr. Goodnight shakes his head and thinks, *Young LeFors uses the word 'suggan' wrong. This group carries bedrolls, not suggans. Cowboys on cattle drives rolled up extra clothes, blankets and comfort items in canvass to keep out rain and snow. Suggans were so large they were rolled and carried on the horse wrangler's wagon. Guess Emmett pretends they are on a cattle drive to amuse the boy.*

Mrs. Goodnight arrives with a package just in time to help with Edward's neckerchief.

The animal is already penned. Arthur and Emmett ride to either side of the bull and each man loops his lasso around both of the bull's horns. Leaving the pen, they ride ahead of the bull and keep just enough tension on their ropes so that the bull follows. They gradually move the bull along taking care that he obediently follows their lead. Setting a good rhythm of travel is most important in the first days—not too fast, not too slow. They must graze, rest, and water the animals each day. Cattle seek shade in the heat of the day as they are unable to sweat in order to cool themselves. After the bull becomes accustomed to the pace, they can relax their ropes to allow for him to graze and lie down for the midday break but still keep his head up.

None of the three is enthused about the return trip. Arthur is disappointed because he needed to abandon his plan; Edward, because he lost a train ride; and Emmett, because Mr. Gething ignored his advice and others persuaded him. The attention from Mr. Goodnight, however, changes Edward's outlook and the train ride is forgotten soon enough.

"Edward, you take the lead only until we get back to the railroad siding where we were this morning; you know the way," Arthur counters Goodnight's suggestion that Edward follow them.

"Put these ginger snaps in your saddlebag for later," Mrs. Goodnight hands a brown paper package tied with twine to Edward.

"Thanks, Mrs. Goodnight!" Edward says taking the lead and waving his hat in Emmett's manner. He sits tall in the saddle relishing this position as leader of the men and the bull. He is sure of the route to the siding.

It is near noon and they must replace the traveling food pantry, so they go first to a railroad siding and mercantile store operating from boxcars and catering to railroad crews and homesteaders.

Canned beans, bacon, and sacks of coffee, flour, and sugar are basic goods in these establishments and they eat their midday meal bought from shelves stocked with crackers, cheese, pickles, dried fruit, canned sardines, and salmon; they relax and listen to the crews visit and gossip. The bull is hobbled in a shady grassy area within sight until the sun is well beyond its apex. Their attitudes improve with rest and nourishment. They travel the rest of the day in silence; all of them are focused on breaking the bull to the trail. Edward follows and learns by watching.

Toward evening Irish sees their approach and sets a pot of coffee and beans bubbling before they arrive. "Hallo, Strangers! Light and hitch!" he hollers going to meet them.

"Oh, my! That is some beast! One of Goodnight's pure Herefords, I reckon. Congratulations! Now, you take care of your animals and join me for grub. Awful good to see you again!"

It was a long afternoon and evening settles around them. Irish's hospitality is welcome and they enjoy it. Edward makes quick work of taking care of Mischief and wrestles his saddle and 'suggan' to the entrance of the dugout. His reward is a tin mug of cold buttermilk and he offers his gingersnaps to Irish for the evening meal.

"Mrs. Goodnight made 'em for us! They taste as good as they smell! Guess you're glad we didn't tromp down your place this time. How'd you get buttermilk without a cow?"

"Well, 'Li'l Pard', I tend a garden for myself and keep my near-neighbor in fresh vegetables in spring and summer with plenty of root vegetables to store for winter. My neighbors keep a cow and give me buttermilk, milk, cream, and butter just about year 'round. And that's how you can drink buttermilk even if you don't own a cow."

Two weary men join them and drink coffee while Irish fries up some corncakes to go with their meal. Once they've eaten they tell about their visit and dealings with the Goodnights. Emmett hums a few tunes and Edward joins in the singing, but he is soon silent and nestles in his bedroll…asleep. Everyone else follows as soon as the campfire is out and bedrolls spread.

The second day out begins just before daybreak with good wishes from Irish and a breakfast of soda bread and wild plum sauce added to the usual fare. Their task is to continue to train the bull to follow at a steady pace. His horns are a bit tender and he will avoid being uncooperative, but they make no attempt to urge a faster pace. Edward observes prairie dog town again. The whistles alert him; he looks for their earthen mounds at the center of a grass free circumference. This time he recognized the town from a distance and it thrills him to hear their barks and watch their rapid disappearance.

The days follow the routine they established when they were outbound. The days of travel are filled with talk and fun. All eyes and ears seek the best passages while keeping the bull in a gradual north northeastern direction, but the bull is trail broken, used to the trail routine. No other people cross their path nor do they see human dwellings. Edward is riding 'drag', bringing up the rear, but he seldom needs to use his bandana to avoid trail dust. The midday rest breaks are as good for him as for the bull, he thinks. He becomes exhausted with the travel and nods off from time to time. A rising wind and booming rumble shake him out of his lethargy; he looks about; the sky is overcast. A light shower becomes a heavy downpour and they move forward slowing a little. The laundered and sweetened air cools and refreshes men, boy, and animals. The dampness and a light breeze preserve the comfortable temperatures even after the sun shines through the clouds again.

That evening Emmett pulls out his pocket knife, opens the blade and tries a variety of ways to flip the knife so that it sticks in the ground softened by the rainfall. First he curls his fingers so that the row of smallest knuckles rests against the heel of his hand and the pocket knife handle lies between the knuckles and the heel pad of his hand. Then with a swift underhanded and upward arc toss, he buries the blade into the ground. He continues this maneuver; it mesmerizes Edward. Then, Emmett tries the same toss with his other hand. He executes a variety of more difficult tosses, each new toss is done first with one hand and then the other and each toss is more difficult than the last.

How'd you learn to do that?" asks Edward

"Aw, this is part of a game called mumblepeg. Started learning these tosses on the playground at school. Lots of cowboys play it at the end of the day. The one who can do all the tosses and bury the blade every time is the winner; he gets to pound a wooden peg into the ground with three strokes using the handle of his pocket knife. Then everyone in the game tries to bury his knife blade using the series of tosses—first with one hand, then the other. The loser has to pull the wooden peg out of the ground with his teeth. If the peg is buried deep, the loser has to plow up the dirt with his nose so he can bite down on the peg and he can end up with dirt in his nose and mouth, too.

"Can I try it?"

"You need your dad's permission."

"Edward, Emmett is free to teach you any manner of things…if the tools you use in the process are no sharper than a rope," Arthur replies.

"That's fair enough, Edward. Some of the things your dad and I do are better learned over time and when you're older," Emmett chuckles. "I can teach you new tricks with your lasso though."

These evenings are memorable because Emmett encourages singing and star gazing and spinning tales. Edward's dad enters in these activities and points out the constellations and tells the myths of many of them. By the seventh day, the land is looking familiar and discussion turns to how much longer until they will be home. At dusk on the eighth day, they spot a familiar window aglow with a lantern light. Elizabeth sits in the threshold enjoying the cool and quiet evening when she sees them.

"Heavens, they are leading a bull! I cannot wait to hear all that happened," Elizabeth cries. Arthur promised her he would buy her a fine horse as soon as he brought home a Hereford bull. She knows of a mare with good breeding that is for sale.

25 - Unexpected Visitor

By mid-November, the Gethings enjoy a reprieve from the heat and heavy work of summer. Elizabeth's canned goods sit on shelves and her garden is almost setup for spring planting. Last week Arthur and the cowhands finished branding and storing feed for the winter. While not ever at leisure, they work at a slower pace. Ed goes to school again. This morning, Elizabeth hangs fresh laundry on the fence and bushes outside. Arthur works in the barn loft making room for additional hay storage. Resting on the hay rake and from the advantage of that height, he looks out on the Texas Panhandle horizon.

"Kate, a rider is on the way!" He calls to her and directs her to look in the direction he points. Someone traveling fast from the northeast stirs up a dust trail. "Can't tell who yet."

"This is a good day for a visit. Our noon meal will be on the table soon. I will tend to it; our visitor is welcome."

From Arthur's advantage of height in the barn loft, he observes the man rides a good mount and with a military bearing. By the time the visitor rides inside their gate, Arthur is back on the ground and he acknowledges the man.

"Light and hitch, Stranger!" says Arthur.

The stranger accepts this customary invitation to dismount. He says, "The name is Brown—Montague Kingsmill Brown. Would you be Arthur Edward Gething?"

"I am the same, Mr. Brown. How is it you know of me?"

Rose M. Hall

"Two men—T. D. Hobart and Tom Coble—suggested I make your acquaintance. Mr. Hobart employees me with the White Deer Land Company. I am returning from the T—T Ranch, Mr. Coble's outfit."

"Pleased to meet an Englishman! My wife is expecting you for our noon meal. Will you join us?"

"I am happy to accept your invitation, Sir."

"You ride a fine horse, Mr. Brown.

"I win a number of matched races with her.

"I may challenge you on Spider. He's there in the corral."

"Always like to examine a competitor! Mind if I take a closer look?"

As they walk to the corral, leading Mr. Brown's mare, a number of Arthur's foxhounds come from their kennels up to the barn and surround them.

Mr. Brown says, "You hunt with excellent hounds, too.

"They are from the finest breed in England. My neighbors and I enjoy the sport of hunting coyote."

"I hunted fox with family friends in London waiting for my discharge papers from her Majesty's Army.

"At your leisure, but I'm ever serious about racing...perhaps a hunt, too?" Arthur grins with expectation, tilts his head, and lifts his chin in an undeniable challenge to another sportsman.

"I look forward to both. Let us not keep your wife waiting and join her for the dinner."

"Excellent! There is a basin, soap, and a towel beside the doorway for our convenience before we sit to eat our meal. Please help yourself." The men wash and enter.

Arthur says, "Kate, meet a fellow Englishman, Mr. Brown."

"Mrs. Gething, thank you for your kind invitation."

Elizabeth says, "What a delightful surprise this is! Do sit at table! I need a few minutes to finish serving."

"Kate, Mr. Brown is recently from London and employed with the White Deer Land Company in Pampa."

"I am curious! How did Mr. Gething and I come to your attention, Mr. Brown?"

"My employer, Mr. Hobart, suggested on a number of occasions that I should meet you especially as we are countrymen," he says.

Elizabeth's meal is simple and she finishes setting the table with haste so that she does not miss the conversation. Having visitors is always a treat and having a visitor from England is rare.

"Mr. Brown," asks Elizabeth, "when did you begin with the White Deer Land Company?"

"It is over six months now, Mrs. Gething, I arrived during the last days of April," says Brown.

Arthur says, "We seldom talk with anyone from England and never from London. Mrs. Gething and I both came from London, but my family is Welsh."

"We are honored with your visit, Mr. Brown," says Elizabeth.

"Most Englishmen come by way of either New York City or New Orleans. Where did you enter the country?" asks Arthur.

"I received my discharge papers from the Army on August 30, 1902. I was home in London with my family when Mother's brother, Mr. Kingsmill, encouraged me to come here. I took the cheapest route; it was through New Orleans."

"That was my customary port of entry for the same consideration," says Arthur.

237

Elizabeth glances at Arthur, "Well, once he came by way of New York City. That was just after we married. Traveling west was a unique and enlightening experience for me. Where in London did you attend school, Mr. Brown?"

"My brothers and I attended Magdalen College School with its traditional relationship with University College of Oxford. However, my father, a banker, went broke. When he could not afford additional higher education, he found a position for me as an office-boy. Not long afterward, my uncle Andrew Kingsmill, who was head of a big Scottish bank, found me a position with one of its branch banks. I held a position there for six years beginning from when I was fifteen."

"My father was a London banker," says Elizabeth hoping there may be a connection. But, Mr. Brown does not know of Elizabeth's father. It is a long time since her parents drowned, and they cannot establish a connection between their fathers.

After they eat, the men invite her to join them to saddle up and survey the range, but Elizabeth says, "No, the two of you go. I must be here when our son returns from school. It is a long ride back to Pampa, Mr. Brown. Stay with us tonight and continue your journey tomorrow."

"That is a generous offer, Mrs. Gething, but I am traveling light and used to camping out."

Arthur says, "We request your company for a while longer so that you will meet our son, Edward."

Elizabeth adds, "You are welcome to spread your bedroll in the parlor. It is the custom among neighbors. Do whatever suits you, but you are most welcome."

"Texas hospitality is impossible to resist. I look forward to extending my visit and meeting your son," says Mr. Brown.

After this casual conversation, the men ride out together so that Arthur can complete his rounds and chores. Mr. Brown is pleased to accompany him to enlarge his knowledge of the region.

Elizabeth begins to prepare something special for their guest's evening meal. Arthur slaughtered a beef days ago selling most of it to the railroad crew in Miami, but reserving a portion of it. Elizabeth will serve steaks and selections from her garden—squash, corn, and tomatoes. For dessert she will prepare gingerbread with stewed apples. It became Ed's favorite dessert after they bought the Hereford bull from the Goodnights.

When Ed comes in from school, Elizabeth is so engaged in the meal preparation that she does not hear him return.

"Mother, something smells…like gingerbread!" Surprised, Elizabeth turns as Ed places the basket of eggs beside the water barrel.

"Ed, a visitor came from Pampa. Mr. Brown is recently from London and will stay over tonight before returning. He and your father are riding out now and taking care of the usual things. You should do your homework now before they return."

"What's Mr. Brown's business? Father must like him since he asked him to go along. Dad always likes men who are excellent riders."

"I was impressed with him, too; he is more than a good horseman. He joined the White Deer Land Company that started advertising its land in Gray, Roberts, Carson, and Hutchinson Counties. This should bring more settlers."

"You'd like that, wouldn't you?"

"Yes, especially families with children. Maybe more classmates for you. Now, your homework waits. Put your books on the table and begin."

"Must I?"

Elizabeth answers with only the motion of her head toward the table.

During the evening conversation, Mr. Brown talks of his duties with the land company. He is its accountant and is included in most of the excursions with Mr. T. D. Hobart throughout the company's lands. Mr. Hobart, the company manager, wants him to become well versed in all the details of the business and the land it has for sale.

Elizabeth listens eagerly for news of London. However, they only learn that the English owners of the White Deer Land Company is the Cunard Steamship Lines. Mr. Brown tells of his recent journeys and he seems a world traveler to Elizabeth and Ed.

Mr. Brown impresses Arthur with his integrity, connections, and his willingness to accommodate his associates. Since Mr. Brown spoke of serving in the British Army, Arthur asks, "Where did you serve?"

"It was in South Africa—the Boer War. I was keen on making my fortune in one of the colonies. When the Dutch farmers (Boers) declared war on England, the country was forced to fight a cavalry war because the Boers were predominantly a cavalry force with few infantry troops. England, then, called up its yeomen forces (farmer soldiers) from the counties to match the Boers cavalry in battle because the regular English Army needed a reserve of mounted troops.

"I determined to emigrate once I was twenty-one. It made sense to me to enlist to get free passage to South Africa rather than pay it myself. I expected to determine whether I would stay there after I served in the Army."

Arthur says, "What was your regiment? I lost two brothers fighting in South Africa."

"I volunteered with the Yorkshire Yeomanry, commonly referred to as Lord Scarborough's Yorkshire Dragoons. We were in the area of Vryburg, Orange River, and headquartered at Graaf-Reinet."

Arthur rises, speechless, from the table. He goes to his old trunk and brings to the table an article from the *London Times* which he hands to Mr. Brown to read. Mr. Brown studies the report about a pair of lieutenants who were speeding away from Vryburg after claiming their unit's pay and mail.

Mr. Brown says, "My unit went into Vryburg, a small railroad town, for that same purpose because my regiment, the Yorkshire Dragoons, was six months without its mail or pay. I took two others with me to claim those. We sorted it out as soon as possible. Our orders were to return with all speed in order that our regiment could move ahead without delay. Mr. Gething, if I am not mistaken, you are related to the Gething in this article?"

Arthur says, "Yes, he was my brother."

"My sympathies, Mr. Gething! When my corporal, sergeant, and I returned from Vryburg after collecting our regiment's mail and pay, we came upon two lieutenants who galloped passed us a short time earlier. Your brother was thrown from his horse and broke his neck. We stopped to offer assistance, but they waited for their physician and medics advancing close behind and said there was nothing for us to do. Later we learned your brother, Lieutenant Stanley Gething, died of the injury."

"Mr. Brown, it is a small world indeed," chokes Arthur. "I am pleased to learn you were there, I assume, before he died."

"Yes, he was in rough shape; I was there, indeed. Would you care to step outside? I carry a fine bottle of Scotch in my saddlebag and we should toast your brother."

"That is a fitting tribute, Mr. Brown. I accept your offer." The men depart for a private moment.

Elizabeth looks to Ed and says, "Your father was deeply attached to this brother. It is a providential coincidence, I believe."

Ed says, "I've never seen my father cry before, Mother."

26 - Put the Wind to Work

"Kate, the Webb family is putting in a well. I leave to watch the well digger and talk with him. Word is that he drills where there is water. He brings in water most of the time, seems to be able to 'read' the land. You need to take care of the stock while I am away. Could be several days," Arthur says.

"Do you plan to drill wells here?" she asks.

"With the purchase of two more sections, the cattle in our far pastures walk off a lot of weight going back and forth for water. A windmill is a possibility!"

"You say several days, but often it takes longer. Do our close neighbors know you plan to leave?"

"Just drive the mule and cart or ride to a neighbor if something comes up you cannot handle alone. Everything should run smoothly. The grass is good everywhere; calves are not dropping now, and water is plentiful even in the shallow lakes."

Mr. Arthur Edward Gething! There are some problems that can arise that will not give me time to go to either neighbor's place. Your interest is in more than in drilling wells. Meanwhile, I pray nothing happens here that I cannot handle. Edward is seven now and too old to tie to my apron string as I did when he was two while I tended the garden and fed the chickens. He rides beside me on his paint now when I check the stock. Still....

Windmills hold Arthur's undivided attention. Week after week, he goes up and down a five county area following that digger. Each time this well digger and his mule complete a well, the windmill crews are fast on their heels to make a pitch to the landowner for selling and installing a windmill. Arthur visits with the men of both the driller and the windmill crews and counts on using those acquaintances to his advantage.

The very next morning, Elizabeth rides into Mobeetie with Edward. She enters the J. J. Long Mercantile with Edward by her side and says, "Mrs. Long, tell me about these windmills here along the road."

"Mrs. Gething, not a word of 'Good Morning! How are you?' Right away it's, 'Tell me about these windmills!'" Mrs. Long teases.

"I must know how they are set up and how they work. I crave water piped into my kitchen so I'm no longer the 'water mule.'

"Edward, do not wander away. Stay in sight!" she admonishes Edward who is edging his way toward the saddles and tack gear.

"Mrs. Gething, I can't say I know, but there is no customer to wait on now so my man, Martin, can handle things for a little while if someone happens by. Let's go over to the café. There's bound to be someone who can give us some information."

The women enter the Mobeetie Café and before they take a table, Mrs. Long spots Thaddeus Jones, who is a close friend to their mayor.

"Thaddeus, you've been in Mobeetie a long time. You know about the windmills put in along our main road? Mrs. Gething is eager to find out."

Mr. Jones looks up from his newspaper, "Is Mr. Gething thinking of getting a windmill on your place, Mrs. Gething? With those two good natural springs I wouldn't expect he'd need one."

"He thinks it can be an advantage for our cattle on the far range, but I'm interested in whether it is possible to pipe water into the kitchen. I want to learn how they operate and get water inside my kitchen."

"After the tornado almost wiped us out, we had to repair both of them; new ones were out of the question. The galvanized steel models are an improvement on these wooden ones. You need to talk with someone with a lot of experience with wells and windmills. That new Englishman with the White Deer Land Company, Mr. M. K. Brown in Pampa, is the fellow you need to speak with, says Thaddeus. "The English syndicate has him digging wells and erecting windmills all over the land he manages for them."

"He made a call on us not long after he arrived when he learned we were English. Thank you for the advice," says Elizabeth. "Mr. Brown happened upon my husband's brother when they fought in the Boer War and he brought us news of the death of Mr. Gething's brother."

Mrs. Long says, "Mrs. Gething, would you like coffee and something for Edward so we can chat. It's been ages since our last visit."

She and Mrs. Long order a cup of coffee and Edward, a glass of buttermilk, with a slab of cornbread while they share family news and the progress of their own lives. When Edward becomes restless, Elizabeth says, "Mrs. Long, let's return to the mercantile. I need some stationery and a few other things. With Mr. Gething away, I must check on and care for everything before dusk."

They finish their conversation in the store. Mrs. Long collects information from her customers and acts as the town crier so she will garner whatever she can learn about the Gething household. Informing Mrs. Long is a valuable way to communicate for everyone in the community and she is careful not to dabble in gossip. Elizabeth, on the other hand, is intent on writing a letter of inquiry to M. K. Brown so that she can post it before they return to the ranch. She cuts short her visit and wastes no time returning to the ranch.

When they return, there is someone is sitting on the porch stoop with his horse grazing nearby. "Jake! Oh, Ed, it is Jake!" Jake stands with a big welcoming grin as he waits for them.

"Mrs. Gething, I'll take over the horses for you and your son can help me," offers Jake. "I've already fed the chickens and penned them up for the evening."

"Jake, feed your horse and put him up in the corral if you can stay," offers Elizabeth.

Edward asks, "Jake, do you know my mother?"

Jake answers, "Edward, I was one of the first people who met your mother here at the ranch and I saw you when you were only a few days old. I used to work for your dad. You must be about seven now, right?"

"You're a good guesser, Jake!" Edward grins.

Elizabeth interrupts, "Jake, it is splendid to see you again. We spent the day in Mobeetie. I can put a meal on the table in no time. Do join us! I want know whatever you can tell me about windmills. Can you stay?"

"Heard Mr. Gething is following our well digger and stopped by to check on you and the boy. I'd be proud to pull up a chair to some of your sourdoughs and beans," he teases.

"Jake, you are in luck. There are fresh garden vegetables, beans, and sourdoughs ready. I can make a cobbler in no time. It is so good to see you. It must be seven, eight years since you taught me how to make sourdough biscuits, coffee, and beans."

"Naw, Jake, you didn't teach Mother to cook," says Edward in disbelief.

"He definitely did, Son. I could not cook or bake anything when I came to Texas," Elizabeth smiles.

Jake takes Edward with him to get a fire started in the pit outside where cooking and baking are done in spring and summer to avoid heating the dugout. Jake shares with Edward more about the time he worked for Mr. Gething. Edward helps gather firewood and they strike up a friendship. When they go back inside, Jake brings Elizabeth up to date.

"Ma'am, the boss at the Diamond F Ranch way back then let me run my own little bunch of cattle—31 head—on the free grass range with his. I started with money I'd saved and a signature loan at a bank. Now I've got a place of my own and the future looks good," Jake tells Elizabeth.

"I've heard of your success, Jake. You always thought ahead and planned carefully. You never stopped until you finished a task. This stock farming is demanding."

"Mrs. Gething, the other reason I stopped by is to ask you to my wedding next month. Janet Spears has agreed to be my wife and I 'specially want your family to attend. Janet gave me this invitation for you." Jake grins as he hands her a crisp envelope.

"This is grand news, Jake. Oh, how wonderfully everything is turning out for you!" says Elizabeth reading the wedding invitation. "You can count on our attendance in Pampa next month.

They continue their visit over supper and sit together in the dugout while a peach cobbler bakes in the Dutch oven over the fire pit outside. After they enjoy dessert, Edward yawns and goes to his bunk.

Jake begins, "Mrs. Gething, you know after Green, Bob, and I spent the winters in our dugout out here near you, Green moved on to work on both on the XIT and the LX. Those ranches were the first I know'd of that digged wells and set up windmills on top, so he'd know about windmills, but I can't say about piping water into your kitchen. If it could have been did, they piped it into their headquarters for the cook. You'll get more information from Green on that score. He was there last time we talked. If I cross his path, I'll let him know you could use his help."

Elizabeth asks, "Where do you go when you leave?"

"Headed to Mobeetie where you've come from. Figured on finding a place to throw down my bedroll in your barn tonight if it suits," answers Jake.

"Oh, you are always welcome here. I am going to write a note to Green before I go to bed. Will you post it in Mobeetie for me?"

"Much obliged, Mrs. Gething! Set it under the wash basin outside so I can pick it up when I leave and I'll post it for you.

"Now here is my idea of how the windmill works. You can hold water in a soda straw by putting it down into a glass of water and then putting your thumb on *top* of the straw. Try it next time you're in town at the café. You'll see water stays in the bottom portion of the straw and flows out when you take your thumb off. A windmill holds water in the pipe by a sort of gate at the *bottom* of the sucker pipe; it don't work like water in a soda straw.

"The way a windmill works makes it possible to set another pipe, called a 'sucker,' inside the casing, or outer 'guard' pipe that protects the sucker pipe against cave-ins from the sides of the well; The casing sits in the well water. The sucker pipe is sort-a like a plunger sitting inside the casing. On the down-stroke, the sucker pipe fills with water, but on the up-stroke the flanges drop against the leathers, sealing off the first collection of water. It holds the water inside the pipe on the up-stroke; then, on the next down-stroke, *down* goes the sucker pipe again to fill itself with another column of water. The first water in the pipe is pushed further up by the column of water behind it. And so it goes! The power of the turning windmill keeps going down and sucking up more water to the top. The continual action keeps water flowing into another pipe going to a stock tank and it waters cattle. Windmills are a marvel to watch!

"Get Mr. Gething to explain it to you since he's getting' acquainted with the windmill crews all around. He'll tell you more than you want to know about it," grins Jake. "I picked up a bunch from him after I learn't he loves to talk about anythin' that he knows and is interested in."

Oh, Jake, you are a clever young man. Mr. Gething and I count you a special friend. Thanks for sharing what you know about these windmills."

"I'll turn in now and let you write that letter to Green," Jake says and withdraws.

Several weeks later, Elizabeth hears from M. K. Brown and Green. M. K. Brown sends a diagram of the windmill operation and excellent information on the ones he recommends. He prefers three quality windmills—Eclipse, Fairbanks-Morse and Aermotor. Green sends a chatty letter and assures her she can pipe the water inside. Louella drops by with information after a visit with Mrs. Long. Louella names three of their neighbor ladies whose windmills are pumping water into their kitchens. She tells that the windmills generate enough power for indoor electric lights, too.

One day afterward, Arthur comes in pleased with the progress on the ranch, Elizabeth asks, "Tell me what you know about these places where they are erecting windmills. It must be a complicated operation."

"Kate, it is not complicated, but these new Aermotor windmills out of Chicago are designed better. Windmills are an ancient invention from the near East and before that China. For centuries, the Dutch used them for grinding wheat, corn, other grains, and also for controlling water in their dikes."

Elizabeth diverts his attention from a history lesson, "What is special about the Aermotor?"

"They are made of galvanized steel and the blades on the circular fan are curved to catch the wind more efficiently. The old windmills in use are wooden and the blades are flat like the slats in a window shutter. Also there is a 'tail' attached to the back of the fan which keeps the fan turned into the wind automatically; it works sort of like a weathervane. There is a weight that functions to tilt the fan aside when the wind is strong enough to cause damage."

"How long does it take to erect this windmill? Elizabeth asks leaning forward.

"A good crew can set it up in a day usually. First they erect a tower with a ladder up one side of the tower. A man has to climb up once a week to grease the gear at the top.

Once the pipe is installed it is not difficult to run another pipe to the cattle tank near the base."

"Must be as expensive as sin, I guess. Will you drill a well and set up a windmill on the far range?" asks Elizabeth.

"One of the windmill crewmen says the biggest problems is wasps! They favor making their nests under the platform at the top. Because someone climbs to the platform to grease the gears every week, it can be dangerous," Arthur laughs; he attempts to divert her attention.

"Are you going climb to the top of our windmill and battle wasps?" asks Elizabeth.

Now, Kate, the profit on the ranch is better because I am managing our herd well. That Hereford bull was a good investment and we can ship our cattle from Miami or Panhandle now which eliminates the long drives to market. I am confident we can buy a windmill without you worrying."

"That is a relief, Mr. Gething. I am proud of your hard work and fine management of our assets. You need to make another investment. This time in the health of your wife. Three of those people you witnessed putting windmills in are our neighbors, the Webb, Black, and LeFors families. All of them also put in a windmill near their houses and ran water into the kitchens so their wives did no longer need to haul buckets of water. Windmills also generate electricity; I want these, too."

"Lord, God Almighty, Woman! There are two bubbling springs only steps from our door. We do not need two windmills!"

"Mr. Gething, I haul water for cooking, washing, laundry, bathing, watering the garden, and the domestic livestock not to mention the trees I planted. You are concerned for the weight cattle lose traveling miles to water.

I am concerned about our family. If I become too frail or sick to do all the work I do on the place, are you going to take over in my place? When you are away for long periods, I do your work and my own. I work right along beside you and this is something I need."

"Dammit, Kate! You drive a hard bargain and you always spring these things on me."

"Dammit, Mr. Gething! I never drive as hard a bargain as you do and this windmill near the house with piped water and electric lighting into the house is as fair a deal as you will ever get."

"I never heard of piping water into the kitchen," fumes Arthur.

"You never concern yourself with how the wives of your friends manage; all of them now use hand pumps on the sides of their kitchen sinks...and have for almost a year."

"I suppose it is one of those times I better get you a windmill or suffer years of "tough sourdough biscuits!"

"Mr. Gething, you are so perceptive!" Elizabeth laughs and Arthur grins, chortles, gives her a hug, and a smack on her bottom.

27 - Cost of Water

John Jameson's windmill crew camps out on the East Cantonment Creek tonight. Jim Logue's son, Mark, and his drilling rig move to find a promising well site on the far range. Mark drilled a good well near the dugout as expected, for it is beside the creek and their two gurgling springs. Locating a sufficient underground water source may challenge Mark's ability to bring in a well out on the Gething range.

The Gething family is awake before sunrise. Arthur leaves to prepare for the windmill crew. Elizabeth and the ladies will feed the crew and neighbors their noon and evening meals today. She puts porridge, honey, and bacon on the table for her family's breakfast and then arranges her kitchen to cook for all the workers who will be coming. Arthur comes back inside for coffee and breakfast. He puts his hands on Edward's shoulders.

"Son, you are to stay away from the crew today. Watch all you like, but from the safe distance of the hay loft above the barn. My friends and I will set up the windmill tower and holding tank rather than the crew because it saves money."

"Sir, I could watch from the shed. I promise not to get in the way! It's hard to see from the barn loft," pleads Edward.

"No, your mother and her friends are going to be busy all day cooking for the crew and our neighbors. We use the shed for tools and pipe. The men need plenty of space to work. It's too many people and too much activity for children to be underfoot! Watch from the barn and mind Mildred whom we are putting in charge of the children."

"Blast!" says Edward pulling a face and then he cocks his head. "Can Mildred take us down to the pond so we can swim?"

Arthur hesitates, "Maybe, I will discuss it with Mildred when she gets here with her family."

Arthur turns to his wife, "Kate, let me put your mind to rest about the other well because you do not need to fret about it. I am confident Mark Logue will find water in a central section for the second windmill. I visited with all the well diggers around and I am confident in Jim's son because he learned well-digging from his father, one of the earliest and a successful driller. Mark is competent and carries on the business. He reads the land as well as his father did."

"Mr. Gething, exactly how does one read the land?" asks Elizabeth.

"Let me give you an example of how I found others who did that about the time I first arrived here. There was a successful Negro cattleman, Bones Hooks, who could tell by the depth of the buffalo and cattle trails whether there would be surface water. If those trails were deep and became deeper because they were laid down over hundreds of years of use, Bones told me he knew he could also find water beneath the surface in those locations. If that fails, I can hire a water-witch." Elizabeth cuts her eyes at Arthur.

"Mr. Gething, the next thing you will tell our son is: you will hire a Gremlin!"

"Father, you are trying to fool Mother!"

Arthur grins, "No, water witching is a time-honored way of finding underground water. It's called dousing, and it's done by walking over the ground holding a green willow limb and when the branch tips down they are sure the well-digger will find water. Many swear by dousing!"

Elizabeth answers, "Seeing is believing! You did well to buy that used Eclipse windmill in Amarillo. It amazes me that the families in Amarillo do not need windmills because the city has a water system. You managed all that so well that we will have two windmills and I will have water pumped into my kitchen and electric lights. It is going to be wonderful!"

"Your reasons for having a windmill here are valid. The expense that I cannot predict is how deep the other well will be and whether they will find layers of sand that cave into the hole and then have to make a much deeper 'bottom well' in order for it to be productive. Stock farming is as risky as predicting tomorrow's weather. Good thing, I am a gambler!" Arthur smiles.

"I appreciate your accommodating the needs of our family along with those of the herd." Elizabeth leans toward Arthur and pats his hand.

"Well, daylight is wasting! Edward, give your Mother a hand with the chores—fuel and water. The other families will be here soon."

Racket outside tells them the windmill crew is preparing to go to work. The neighbors and hired hands arrive and the work begins. The neighbors assemble the windmill on orders from the crew boss. The women are cheerfully preparing the midday meal. Mildred organizes games for the children in the barn after they tire of watching the men put the windmill sections together. About midmorning, the women take a break. Elizabeth walks to the work area to learn how much longer before the men can stop their work to eat. She returns to join the women.

"Ladies," says Elizabeth, "It will be a while before the men are ready to eat. Our meal is ready to spread on tables outside and the pot of coffee waits for us. Let's sit for a while." The women come and enjoy mugs of coffee while sitting on the benches near where they will serve the noon meal. When her neighbor women rest, she leans toward her friends and smiles, "I am so thankful for your help today."

Emma LeFors speaks up, "Elizabeth we are happy to be part of this day with you!" The other women chorus their agreement.

"When you put in your windmills and piped water into your kitchens, why did I not help you?" Elizabeth quizzes and tosses a hurt look to Emma. The women are neighbors and friends. Emma's husband, Perry is mayor of Lefors, the county seat of Gray County.

Emma says, "We thought because we were taking your husband away so often to get information on wells and windmills, we should not take you away from your place, too."

"I could have left it a few days from time to time," says Elizabeth.

"Yes, you could have, but wasn't Arthur away most of the time following well-diggers and windmill crews?" asked Emma. "It seemed only right not call you away from your work."

Louella says, "You were not in Texas back when the men organized Wheeler County. That was, I judge, fifteen years ago. Mobeetie used to be thick with lawyers. My father told me all those lawyers who lived in Mobeetie asked your husband for his advice; he helped them out of the bogs in the law. He, also, entertained them with stories about how the English Assize judges dealt with problems like their own. Back hundreds of years ago, English law was developing as ours still is."

"Yes, Elizabeth," said Emma, "he is very good at tracking down legal information and knows where to go to find about things like improving the stock, drilling wells, and raising windmills. Mr. LeFors still talks with him about his problems as mayor."

Louella says, "He helps us in these ways the same way we teach you about dugouts, gardens, chickens, and cooking. It's life here on the plains. Families take care of one another."

"We never shut you out, my dear!" says Emma, "We think you and Mr. Gething hold up your end…and more. At the time, our husbands were not chasing windmills! But your husband does these things for us that we can't do for ourselves easily."

"Oh," Elizabeth says, "in the ten years I have lived among all of you, I realize more each time that you bless me as my neighbors. All of you have made this possible for me! And I understand it more all the time,"

Louella adds, "Elizabeth, we learned these ways to survive from our mothers who grew up on this dry land. You did not know how, but your enthusiasm and openness to our friendship makes you very dear to all of us."

Timid Ginny Jones reaches for Elizabeth's hand to claim her attention. "Do you remember the quilting party where you and I met? John and I were expecting our first child. I was so frightened about not having a doctor available when I'd need one. After you had Edward, Dr. von Brunow praised you on having everything ready to deliver Edward by yourself, even using a birthing chair. I was so happy you recommended Louella to act as mid-wife for our first child."

Ella Mae Ivey says, "Not everyone has a London physician for a Grandfather and a sister and Grandmother to copy his medical texts! How many babies have you brought into this world?"

"Not enough, yet," replies Elizabeth, her eyes glazing with tears, "the Panhandle needs many more. I can never deserve such wonderful friends!"

The day is woven with work and enjoyment of being together in a land where isolation is normal and chances to work with neighbors are rare and always cherished. After the noon meal, everyone gathers in the shade of the cottonwood trees surrounding the springs and cattle tanks. The children are playing and splashing about in the water and the heavier work is done. Later this afternoon, the finishing work begins.

There are extra pipes and casings that Arthur ordered from a supplier in Miami. It is loaded in their farm wagon and Arthur appoints Elizabeth to return it to Miami. The rest of the women have the evening meal well in hand and Louella will see to Edward after Mildred leaves with her family.

This errand is Elizabeth's alone and she drives their team hauling the pipes steadily toward Miami. It is a time she can dream, reflect and enjoy the land.

I cannot wait to have water in my kitchen and a water tower to store water for use for the house and another tank for domestic stock. I have a plan to irrigate the garden. My work load will be greatly reduced. Maybe I will be able to grow melons and watermelon like they do in McLean. They ship them to Trinidad by refrigerated cars on the Rock Island.

She rattles along with the pipes clinking and clanking behind her; she keeps a moderate pace and she looks over the country mile after mile. Hours later, she sees the windmills and church steeples of Miami. The team picks up its speed. She looks down upon the scene. They roll faster! The pipes begin to ping with a metallic ring. The cacophony of the loose pipes excite the team. The gentle incline dips steeply. The heavily loaded wagon pushes the team downhill.

A silent alarm surges through her! To check the team, she alights down onto the floor of the wagon to gain control. Even as she hauls back on the reins, she knows her strength is not a match for the frightened team as it surges forward. The pipes slam into the front of the wagon, slide underneath the seat where she stands. An erratic side to side movement of the wagon across the trail rolls and bounces the pipes that crisscross around and over her feet. She jerks her feet away but drops the reins. The frightened team lunges forward. More pipes roll back and forth. It is a runaway!

To keep her feet away from the crush of these heavy rolling pipes and casings, she holds onto the bench with one hand and the front rim of the wagon with the other. When she braces her feet on the wagon rim in front of her, pain envelops her. She screams. The maneuver to protect her feet was too late.

"Oh, God! Help!" she shrills. The scene going into Miami blurs before her. People are scattering out of the road ahead.

A bunch of cowboys mount horses from hitching posts on both sides of the street. Two men take the lead and race alongside the team. Onlookers go silent. This pair of riders leap on the backs of Elizabeth's team. They grab the traces of her team. With the traces in hand, they lean forward and snag the reins. A victory holler goes up as they pound down the street. The clatter and clang diminish; the runaways come to a halt far outside downtown Miami where Elizabeth's rescuers bring the team to a halt. The horses are still wild with excitement and Elizabeth is near to fainting.

Some level-headed onlooker rushes Dr. von Brunow to the wagon and team.

"Mrs. Gething, are you hurt?" he asks.

"My feet...the pipes!" she mumbles. Another team comes along side and others lift Elizabeth out to carry her into the doctor's office where he tends to her. The cowhands gentle and soothe her team. They move the wagon to rest near the railroad siding, unhitch the team, and take them to the livery stable.

Word is sent to Mr. Gething that there has been an accident and that his wife's feet have been broken and crushed. She can return to the ranch when the doctor says it will be all right. He will notify Arthur when he can fetch Elizabeth.

The cost of water goes up. Elizabeth will be off her feet for a long time afterward.

28 - Watch and Wait

As soon as Arthur learns of Elizabeth's accident and knows she is in Dr. von Brunow's office, he asks Louella to take Edward to her home and rides to check on his wife. The neighbors and windmill crew finish the work and depart. Arthur arrives in Miami after dark. He makes arrangements for them to stay in Miami seven days in a boarding house because Elizabeth will elevate her feet until the swelling is down. Arthur barters with Widow Sikes for their lodging in her boarding house; he will deliver half a beef in exchange.

Dr. von Brunow reduces the laudanum he administers over the period of a week. He speaks with Arthur explaining how important it is that Elizabeth be off her feet for three weeks more. He explains that her feet cannot be set and splinted as leg and arm bones; it is impossible to set the many small bones. They will heal in whatever way they do. Thankfully, the ankle bones are not broken. Elizabeth believes she avoided more damage by lifting her feet when she lost control of the team.

On the day the Gethings leave Miami, Elizabeth's friends make her bed in the wagon; it as comfortable as possible with straw and quilts. Dr. von Brunow oversees the departure along with friends who brought the straw-filled ticking mattress pads, quilts and blankets to cushion Elizabeth's ride home.

The doctor stands in the group and wags his head; he thinks, *What possessed that man to send his wife to Miami alone with such an unstable load? That long steep slope into Miami is well known and everyone knows extra precaution is needed. He is not the only person in Miami to make that observation.*

In a day or two Elizabeth is bored with inactivity. So she plans to use the daylight hours seated outside so that she can watch Curly and Joe bury the pipe from the storage tank on the elevation above the house down to her kitchen. Arthur directs the two men he hired as they work.

Edward attends his mother by bringing her the noon meal and fetching whatever she needs. When he is not needed by his father, he visits with her. But Edward loves to go off with a sling-shot to hunt prairie chickens and rabbits. When he can slip away, he does.

Charles Goodnight made a long lasting impression on Edward and he is keen to study plants and animals in the way Mr. Goodnight took time to observe how they grow and what habits they have. Ed is especially observant of snake movements and their habits because of related dangers or benefits. A rattler can poison or kill you if you wander unawares into its surrounds. A bull snake can keep down the mouse and rat population in the barn or get into the chicken coop and consume eggs. Edward figures he can learn by watching the same as Mr. Goodnight.

"Mother, how much longer do you have to be off your feet?' asks Edward.

"Another ten or eleven days, I think. Why do you ask?" replies Elizabeth.

"I miss your cooking and baking. With Father cooking, we get beans, porridge, and canned tomatoes. I wish he'd make something else like…sourdough biscuits." Elizabeth laughs before answering.

"He would not dare make biscuits. I would have too great a story to tell on him if they were not fluffy and perfectly baked."

"Why?"

"He criticized my first attempt too harshly and I do not let him forget it! Be patient for a few more days. You need to learn something about making a few meals yourself. Roundups make it necessary for men to know some trail cooking. Many are great cooks. Remember when you met Jake? When we met he was still practically a boy, but his parents saw that he knew how to cook. Learn all you can."

Curley and Joe are working for Arthur again. After the windmill crew left, they did not stay, but they returned once Arthur brought Elizabeth home from Miami. They are back now to dig ditches in which to bury pipe below the frost line to protect the pipes in below freezing temperatures of winter. The original plan was to set up a tower for the water tank about twenty-five feet above ground beside the windmill. This gravity flow will insure enough water pressure in the half-human dugout and downhill to the big round metal stock tank for the domestic stock inside the corral and for the cattle that come to drink near the barn. This metal tank is, half-way in the corral and half-way open to the range. The men continue to dig the ditch. Talk is free. So Elizabeth visits with the two men when they come for meals and during the midday rest following the noon meal.

Speaking to Curley and Joe, Elizabeth says, "I understand the reason for burying the pipe far enough underground to keep them from freezing in winter. Please explain to me the reason for changing where the water storage tank will go. Mr. Gething is away often so I need to understand the way everything works in case there is a problem." Curley clears his throat and proceeds to answer.

"Yes, ma'am, the problem we're dealing with here is putting the storage tank high enough that the gravity will flow steady-like into your kitchen sink. This old windmill will pump about three gallon an hour and once we fill up the storage tank, you should always have plenty of water in your kitchen. We're waiting to open up the water into the pipe for your stock until this here at the kitchen is fixed."

Joe adds, "We'll put a cut-off valve on the stock tank so that you only need to add water every few days…enough to keep the tank out by your barn filled to a few inches below the rim.   Summer, you'll likely have to run it every day."

"We'll put a floater with a flag on it in your water tower," Curley says, "Now anytime you can't see that flag waving above your storage tank, you'll need to hustle down to the barn and cut off the water to the stock tank until you can see that flag waving above your water tower or you'll run out of water in the house."

"Joe, I understand what I must do to keep the water tower up by the house filled. You are warning me that during summertime when the cattle are especially thirsty and come to the stock tank often, I must be very observant and check both water tanks every day," says Elizabeth. Now, tell me why we could not have the water tower beside the windmill." Curley stretches and crosses his arms as he leans toward Elizabeth to speak.

"Ma'am, we could have set a twenty-five foot water tower next to the windmill, but you've got a nice little rise behind your place here. So that, it's gonna be the best spot for the water storage tank. Otherwise we'd need to build a twenty-five foot tower for your water tank to give you the same water pressure in your house. With the storage tank on the hill, it cuts the cost of building that twenty-five foot tower. But we're burying the pipe in a good deep ditch from there to under your dugout. It's more work now but less expense and there'll be less to go wrong this way. So, that's about it!"

Joe grins, "Curley and me will be here until we have a ditch digged from that tank to your dugout. And we gotta get back at it afore Mr. Gething starts yelling at us." *I ain't never seen a woman so curious to know about windmills, tanks and pipes.*

"Thank you for explaining this. It will be important to know if I need to tend to it. I believe you can never know too much about how things should operate because they can really spoil your day when they do not work as they should."

"Dead right! Mrs. Gething, we gotta get back to diggin' those ditches," says Curley.

No one is more dedicated to get water in the house than Arthur is. He stays at the dugout to cook and clean up after each meal. Doing this and taking his turn as the 'water mule' insures that work moves along at a steady pace. Arthur stretches out to rest in the cooler place—the dugout—before resuming the work with the hired men. Elizabeth chooses a shady place near the earthen tanks next to the springs and will watch the proceedings until evening. Then, Curley and Joe carry her back uphill to the dugout on a make-shift stretcher of two poles and a heavy wool blanket.

After the first week, she uses some crutches to get about on for short distances. Dr. von Brunow lent her the crutches that are stamped as 'Property of Fort Elliott'. He was given or bought crutches and some of the medical supplies he used at the military hospital before Fort Elliott closed. Dr. von Brunow is not continuing a career in the United States army, but he remains in the Panhandle. He is the only physician for miles in any direction.

With the men back to work, Elizabeth and Edward are alone at the pond. Edward stays a while and leans back on a tree next to Elizabeth.

"Mother, can I take a dip in the pond? It's awful hot!"

"Edward, you need to say, 'May I take a dip in the pond? And 'It is awfully hot!'

"Awh! Mother, nobody talks like that except you and father!"

"Speak the King's English like an Englishman, Edward."

Edward's eyes sweep upward in an arch as if he were following a bird in flight and asks, "Who's an Englishman?"

"Use proper English, Edward! No need to be cheeky! You will read to me from your McGuffey reader first. School begins in a few days. Reading last year's reader will improve your performance for the new teacher."

"I wish Miss Pennybacker was back," snorts Edward as he recalls her no-nonsense discipline and cheery ways. "She has a funny name! Miss Pennybacker was pretty and nice to everybody. We liked her!"

Elizabeth laughs, "Edward, if wishes were horses, beggars would ride! Run! Fetch your book and read for me! Besides, your teacher took a teaching job in Amarillo. They pay much better than our community can; plus, they pay for her lodging and meals in a boarding house where she will have her own room." At $35 a month plus board and room, Miss Pennybacker will be paid more than most cowhands.

Edward leaves telling himself he will swim sooner if he hurries to fetch his reader. He will go back to the Cottonwood School at Sand Creek east of the ranch. There will be school for four months and will probably end with the Christmas program if the new teacher continues putting on a program like Miss Pennybacker did. He will be home during the coldest months of winter, help his father with chores and help his mother with gardening in the spring. He spends more time with his father now. He loved going with his father and Emmett to buy the bull. He was the envy of his friends because he told that story when he started school his first year. Since then, he is doing more of the ranch work.

Edward thinks, *Someday I'll get to round and brand just like Emmett, but I can ride fence, mend fence—well, help anyway—and check the herd now.*

He comes back a little breathless with reader in hand. "I can read it easily. Just listen!"

He hesitates on words occasionally, but Elizabeth notices that he 'reads' the next page sometimes before he turns the page. *Hmmm, he needs something to read that he has not memorized. I have an idea.*

"Hand me your book and go for a swim. Your father will be needing your help this afternoon so go get wet!"

Let me think. *I can write a story for him to read. What will it be about? A boy named Edward who loves to swim in a pond... .* Once Edward comes back and is about dry, Elizabeth instructs, "Edward read this to me. Your reader is too easy for you." Elizabeth hands the tablet on which she wrote a story for him. He reads:

Ed wants to swim in the pond because he is hot and tired. He reads from his reader to his mother. He has to read the story she wrote before he can swim. When he jumps into the pond, something tickles his toes and he jerks but it is only a fish! If he sticks his nose in the pond, the fish may nibble it, too. Ed finds something better to do! He climbs on a huge log beside the pond and jumps into the pond to make a wave that will splash his mother. She needs to cool off. It must be dull to sit in that chair all the time with her feet up.

"You write better stories than McGuffey does! I'll take it to school to read to the new teacher," Edward snickers, "I want you to call me Ed, I hate Edward!"

"Ed, it is time to help your father with evening chores. I like 'Ed' best, too! Go along with you and find your father," Elizabeth chuckles; she is amused he prefers the name 'Ed' and that he likes the story she wrote for him. She congratulates herself on checking whether he could read words not in the reader. Edward enters the third form this year. He can join us in reading aloud to one another this winter.

Elizabeth call out to her disappearing son, "It is time to gather the eggs. Remember to check for snakes with a stick before you put your hand in the nests. Your father found one yesterday. Be sure to close and latch the chicken coop when you leave."

In the middle of the second week of her confinement, Perry LeFors stops by with a crate from the post office addressed to her. In early summer, she ordered a crate of dime novels from New York. The advertisement for them was in her magazine subscription for *Field and Stream* that keeps the family entertained during the winter. She loves western stories and she and Arthur read them aloud in the evening while Edward listens. Her favorite is *The Three Musketeers* which she special ordered several years ago; it is read within the family at least once each year. In the winter, they read every evening!

Elizabeth started their subscription to *Field and Stream* during the first few years it was published. The stories about hunting and fishing are always entertaining and occasionally there are recipes for preparing meals over camp fires which are easily adapted to frontier cooking and baking.

She wonders how many people have read *Field and Stream* before it is delivered to their post office. It frequently arrives so worn and dog-eared that they know the magazine has already been read many times. Reading is regarded highly in their home where letters, books, and magazines come along as infrequently as new clothing and shoes. They look forward to having this magazine for entertainment and no one minds that his postcards and magazines brightened some stranger's day.

When Elizabeth first arrived, Tilly Remington ran a boarding house and acted as postmistress. She handled the mail in Mobeetie before there was a proper post office. Tilly spread the mail out on her dining room table; everyone sorted through it to locate his and his neighbors' mail. Tilly was usually busy putting a meal on the table for her family, boarders, and anyone picking up the mail or traveling by stagecoach.

In that mindset, she begins daydreaming of other stories of mail delivery. Perry LeFors told the best one about Postmaster George Smith who followed George Montgomery as their postmaster. Elizabeth remembers how Perry told it.

Montgomery was accommodating in the way most postmasters are. He would open the post office whenever his services were needed. George Smith, the newly appointed postmaster, had other ideas. He opened the post office at 8:00 a.m. and closed it at 5:00 p.m. No one could influence him to take pity on cowboys who came into town after closing hours to pick up mail or buy postage stamps. Certainly not in the middle of the night!

These cowhands came from good distances away and usually had lists of supplies to get at the mercantile and other errands to do for their ranch bosses. Then they had the same distance to travel back to the ranches. It was a problem!

As it happened that winter, the merchants were stocking plenty of valentine cards which gave Perry an idea. The cowboys got together and bought every card in both mercantile stores and all the special delivery stamps the postmaster had. They waited until not a single horse was tied to the hitching posts along the street in front of the post office. Then the first cowboy took a special delivery valentine card into the post office addressed to some resident on the edge of town.

Postmaster Smith was a stickler for the United States Post Office policies. Because there were no horses hitched anywhere along the row of stores, he was unable to hire a horse and rider to make the special delivery so he had to walk to the addressee's home. As soon as he returned from this special delivery, another cowboy sauntered into the post office with another envelope stamped special delivery and addressed to a resident of Mobeetie or in the outlying area. This scheme continued for a week or more!

To make it more difficult there were no streets, only trails covered with grass burrs and weeds and uncut grass. To keep the prank going, they sent Jessie Wynne to the town of Clarendon to purchase an additional $10 worth of special delivery stamps. They kept this up until Postmaster Smith was worn out. He finally bought a horse but not before about everyone in town had been sent a special delivery valentine including the washer women on Suds Row.

Their new postmaster became more flexible about the established office hours at the Mobeetie Post Office.

A Spirit to Resist

How I admire those cowboys! They find many a way around a problem. I take lessons on how they operate.

At the end of the third week, Elizabeth is ready to walk about but unable to walk comfortably in her shoes because her feet are both wider and longer than they were before they were injured. She searches the pages of the Sears, Roebuck and Co. Catalogue for a comfortable fit in a pair of work shoes. The most practical pair sells for $2 and there is another pair of hand sewn felt slippers for $.75. She guesses at the size and traces her feet on brown wrapping paper to enclose with her order for her exact measurement.

Edward must have a new pair of shoes for school so she sits with him to select a pair from the catalogue. His feet are traced to go along with the order; his shoes cost $1.15. She will make-do going about inside in her stocking feet until the new ones arrive and with a razor blade, she cuts the toes out of Arthur's oldest pair of boots for wearing outdoors. Edward's boots still fit and are good for another month or more. By evening, the order is complete and the postage cost added; it will be sent with a post office money order.

This expense plus the shipping cost exhausts her egg money stash and she has the order ready for Perry and Emma to take to the post office when they stop by on their next trip to Miami. During the time Elizabeth is not walking to allow her feet to heal, Louella takes her eggs to sell to the mercantile in Miami along with her own.

While looking through the catalogue, Elizabeth notes that Sears sells an Acme eight foot windmill for $16.50 that can be used on either a wooden or steel tower. Two other Acme models sell for $23 and $35 complete with tower. She will ask Arthur to take a look at the advertisements so that he can compare these Acme windmills to the one they bought from the family in Amarillo.

She sighs over the elegant ladies' hats, but she seeks out pages of mechanical toys, baseball gloves, and books that interest her—*Story of the Wild West* and *Camp Fire Chats* by Buffalo Bill Cody. She thinks of Christmas. She needs to replenish her egg fund as soon as she can.

29 - A Shot across the Brow

The clank and whirr of the windmill are reassuring to Elizabeth, and yet it disturbs the silence in which she enjoys the call of birds in the early morning and the distant howl of the coyote late at night. There is a shift in the wind that sweeps to and fro across this arid land. During breakfast, Arthur accepts from his wife the Sears and Roebuck Catalogue and studies the windmill advertisements she brings to his attention.

"Kate," he says, "these windmills are good, but it costs as much, or more, to ship them as to buy them."

"I wondered when I looked at them" Elizabeth answers, "whether a new windmill might save money. Our windmill continues to cost more because of repairs the crew made and the new parts you bought."

Ed is interested in his parents' discussion and says, "Sir, the one you plan to put on the range, miles away, isn't going to be close enough so we can check it all the time.

"That is a good observation, Ed, but I doubt I can buy and ship a new one. I will scout about to find one that is already here and in excellent condition…the way I found this one."

"Mr. Gething, what are your plans then?" Elizabeth asks.

Hesitating, Arthur answers, "I will need to spend some time in Amarillo. New residents may sell for whatever they can get for their 'mills because they don't need them. Remember, I got this one because Amarillo is putting in a water system for all its residents."

Elizabeth steps to the stove for more coffee. *Arthur is predictable; he is eager to get away after being obliged to stay here until my feet mended, and I am able to do all the chores again. If he has an emergency while he is away, it invariably happens in Amarillo. That city has many attractions for him unlike isolated ranches or small towns.*

"Ed, check the wood pile and you and your father need to lay in a good supply for me in case there is a delay in Amarillo. Then, we will tend to the stock!"

Elizabeth takes the breakfast dishes to the sink, draws water into the sink with the hand pump, and adds hot water from the reservoir in the stove. She washes dishes, cleans the kitchen, and sweeps the floors. She thinks, *it is a comfort having a son who is willing and happy to work with me. He is a treasure of the heart. After school each day, we ride out together, check the herd, and share the jobs around the barn. If Arthur chops or splits any firewood, I will die of shock.*

Arthur packs his black bag with all his clean linen and business suits. It is still early morning when he bids them goodbye and he and Spider leave. It is not typical of Arthur, but he leaves wearing his high-crowned broad-brimmed western hat though he usually goes bareheaded.

Elizabeth and Ed split some wood before he leaves for school. After Ed leaves, she takes up her rifle and goes on foot away from the house. She heard gobbling this morning and hopes to locate the flock of wild turkey feeding in the corn fields. She intended to spend the morning in her garden turning the soil, but the day called her out into the fields. She carries cheese sandwiches wrapped and tucked into her apron pockets along with a tiny bottle of sweet pickles. This day is hers alone.

She takes a silent and listening walk far away from the windmill sounds so that they do not disturb her quest. Soft is the experience of the earth beneath her tender feet. The cushioned ground is the result of recent rains and the resurgence of plants that seemed dead but green up with a little moisture is a wonder.

Slipping into the cornfield, watching, and waiting, she bags two of the birds and she spends only one bullet for each fowl. With the rifle over her shoulder and the feet of the turkeys tied together and slung, one on each side, across the barrel, Mother brings home dinner. It is a routine matter. She learned to handle a gun in London along with other young ladies of her social class. It is a skill some of her women friends here enjoy but not all. She opens her pocket picnic when she is home, and she sits beside the earthen tank in the shade of the cottonwoods. It is cool here, and she relaxes and eats before returning to the house.

Once in the yard she plucks and cleans the birds. Inside, she bakes them one at a time because the oven will not accommodate both. The second one is in the oven when Ed arrives from school. She and Ed gather the eggs, feed the chickens, and check the water levels in their storage tank and the stock tank. They sit down in the kitchen to roasted turkey with dressing, green beans, and squash. Coffee for her; buttermilk for him. Canned peaches top off their meal.

"Tell me about your day at school, Son."

"We boys started a great game of horse wrestling. Bud and Wes are the best players, but I am good, too. Miss Allen put a stop to mumblepeg, and we all hate that. She says that the younger boys are the losers all the time, and it causes too many problems. Besides, she is afraid the knives will hurt someone. So we promised we'd stop."

"Good, Miss Allen is right, of course. Emmett taught you all the tosses, and it took you a long time with practice to do those well. I am proud you are respectful to your teacher.

What about your game of horse wrestling?"

"It takes four boys—two make a team. One boy rides the others' back and each team tries to drop the other team's 'rider' off the back of his 'horse.' Whichever team unseats the other team's 'rider' wins. Dan and me won three times."

Elizabeth lets the grammar slip go uncorrected while she hones in on a tear in Ed's shirt and grubby appearance of his shirt and pants.

She says, "That game explains the condition of your clothes?"

"Yes, ma'am," grins Ed.

"Tell me about your classroom work."

"Miss Allen taught a good geography lesson today; she showed us how water affects the land with a big pile of sand, a bucket of water and a dipper outside on the school yard. She told us about erosion. Our assignment tonight is to find places on our land that show how erosion has worked and tell about it tomorrow. I can do that while we check on our cattle

"How was your history exam?"

"We get our papers back tomorrow; I'll get a good grade."

That means a solid "C."

After they finish their visit, it is time to take her mare, Kate, and Ed's pony, Mischief, out of the corral and make the rounds of the herd. None of the cattle was sick, so they did not use the common medicines in their saddlebags.

There is time to ride about half of the fence line today and catch the other section tomorrow. Passing the new well, they inspect it; it is secure and will be until a windmill crew erects the tower and windmill above it. The wooden frame is in place. No cow can fall into the well. The grass will turn brown again, but it is as nutritious as green grass. There is a good stand of grass; it should last until the colder weather sets in this winter. Then they will haul hay and other fodder to the cattle.

"Mother, see that arroyo. It's a good example of erosion; so is our creek where it's washing away the dirt and exposing tree roots."

"Let me know what your teacher has to say about erosion in her lessons."

"Of course, Mother, we are studying this for maybe a couple of weeks."

Elizabeth reminisces, *I learned erosion soon after I arrived in Texas. That was before Ed was born. Leo, our neighbor boy, came to the dugout with the hoop skirt and bustle I buried weeks before!* She enjoys a chuckle remembering how Arthur and she explained it to the embarrassed boy who thought it was a rat trap. We still enjoy telling that story.

The land determines their day to day routines and chores, but it is a long time—ten days—that Mr. Gething is away. Elizabeth grows anxious for him to return; she is weaker than she was before the bones of her feet were broken. Their home windmill begins to make a metallic shrill sound and reminds her the gears need to be greased every week.

What is needed? The windmill crewman climbed the ladder to the platform with a stout pole and a beer bottle filled with grease. Then using the pole, he held the blades of the fan still while he reached above the gearbox to distribute the grease. Finally he put the beer bottle back into his belt before withdrawing the pole and positioning himself on the ladder to descend.

I am not equal to that task yet; Ed is not tall enough and also lacks the strength. Neither of us is experienced. If wasps attach their nest under the platform, it becomes a bigger problem. My better option is to let it go and hope Arthur arrives soon. She hopes the gears will not be damaged. Having to buy a new gear can endanger their shrinking resources.

Her anxiety turns to discontent and the anger within her rises and simmers. She thinks, *Arthur knows how difficult it is to tend to everything with only the help of Ed who is now in school most of the daylight hours. Arthur often complained of too much to do when Ed was home all day during the month I was not allowed to walk.*

Days later, and long after she and Ed are asleep, Elizabeth hears a rider approaching. With the windmill running, she cannot be sure, so she collects her rifle from its rack and peers into the moonlit night. It is a rider; but shadows are menacing and outlines of the horse and rider are blurred. She slips out into the shadows of the porch. A warning from a lone woman defending her home will send a message of indefensibility to an intruder. So, taking aim, she takes the shot. The rider's hat whips away and rolls down the road.

"Dammit, Kate," Arthur slurs, "you might have killed me!"

"If I intended to do that, you would be, I am a crack shot!"

Elizabeth walks back into the house, puts her rifle in the rack, tells Ed to go back to sleep, and she goes to bed. *You would think a man living in this country as long as Arthur Edward Gething has should know better than wander into a yard after dark without identifying himself.*

Arthur stumbles toward the barn leading Spider. Arthur is wide-eyed and a chill runs through his body. He puts his fingers through the crown of his hat in two places—entry and exit holes. The smell of sulfur and charred felt is on the air.

"Whew! Spider, it is just you and me tonight, old boy!"

30 - Fragile Relationships

Only Ed and Elizabeth seat themselves at breakfast. The porridge is lumpy and the coffee is cool. The house is as still as a poised cougar.

Ed asks, "What happened last night, Mother?"

"Your father came home. I thought he was either a horse thief or cattle rustler and took a shot," says Elizabeth. "He will join us later."

"You took a shot at him?"

"He was in his cups. He is not up this morning yet. Let it go, please."

"Yes, Ma'am."

"We will milk the cow and put her out to pasture. I will tend to the breakfast dishes afterward."

Elizabeth clears the table and sets the dishes in the sink. They go to the barn and see that Spider is in his stall. Once they turn out the work horses and the mules along with Spider, they milk the cow. Ed chops and splits wood while Elizabeth checks the water levels and tops off the water in the tank for the cattle.

Elizabeth thinks, Arthur must be sleeping it off in the hayloft. I'm surprised he was able to climb the ladder.

"Ed, wash and dress for school. I will saddle Mischief for you."

Ed says nothing to his mother but looks at her with quiet questioning eyes.

"It will be fine, Son. That late at night, your father was thoughtless not to call out to let us know he was back. Go on, get ready for school."

"Will you be all right?"

"Of course."

Elizabeth waves Ed off to school and then she returns to the kitchen and resumes her morning routine. She is sitting on the porch drinking coffee when Arthur approaches.

Elizabeth calls to Arthur, "Mr. Gething, you gave me quite a scare last night."

"Kate, you gave me a hell of a lot more than a scare and a ruined hat. Why in God's name did you shoot?"

"Do not ever do that again! Ed and I were here alone for two weeks. You came in the dark of night and did not announce yourself. Arrive in the daytime or shout down the stars if you ever approach this house at night again!"

"Ah, hell, Kate! A man ought to be able to come into his yard without fearing his wife will shoot him."

"You leave me to protect our home and with instructions to shoot at anyone who skulks about after dark. I did as you told me. That is all I will say about it."

"Damnation! Kate, bring me some of that coffee."

"It is warming on the back of the stove, Mr. Gething."

Arthur charges into the house and Elizabeth follows. She claims her rifle and leaves to hunt for turkey or quail. Mostly to calm herself.

Arthur is in no condition to grease the gears on our windmill, but the shrill sound of it is going to play the dickens with his headache.

She returns midday with enough quail to make a meal. At her outdoor kitchen, she scalds, plucks, and cleans them under the cottonwoods before returning to the house.

Arthur is asleep in their bed. He covered his head with pillows. She allows herself a chuckle.

Ed will be home from school soon. We can do the chores before I bake the quail.

She snaps the green beans and pares the potatoes and sets aside garden produce for a salad. The quail are rubbed with herbs and covered with sour cream. Then she hears Ed approach on Mischief.

"Ed," Elizabeth calls, "join me in the kitchen for a while. Fresh buttermilk is ready for you and cornbread is in the oven. Let us eat before we go to the barn."

"I'll be right in!" Ed answers.

Arthur comes into the kitchen making no noise and sits gingerly at the table. He eases into a limp slouch with random straws of hay clinging to his clothing and hair. Looking at Elizabeth with red-rimmed and bleary eyes, he growls, "Any coffee?"

"It will be ready soon," she says. "Ed and I are having cornbread and buttermilk. Do you want some?"

"I will wait for the coffee," he says.

"Did you find a windmill in Amarillo?"

"The quality ones I was looking for were gone; others had bought them up as soon as they were put on sale. I finally found a new one and made an excellent deal."

"A new one! How did you manage that?"

"The Circle Heart ordered an Aermotor of Chicago, but the company shipped the wrong model, and the ranch manager rejected it. I was able to buy it for the cost of the windmill.

"How did you avoid paying for the shipping?" asks Elizabeth.

"The customer usually pays the shipping, but, in this case, Aermotor, the windmill company, made a mistake in shipping the wrong windmill to the Circle Heart and was responsible for the shipping bill. The windmill company was in a bad situation because it would need to assume the cost of shipping the rejected windmill back to the factory or find a buyer in Amarillo."

"So, you bought it in Amarillo and saved them a further expense of returning it."

"Well, there is a little more to it than that. Aermotor wanted me to pay the shipping cost or part of it, but no other customer was standing by with cash for the windmill. It's a little like high stakes poker," says Arthur pleased with himself.

Elizabeth says, "Here is your coffee. That was shrewd of you. When will it be brought out?"

"The neighbors may give me a hand with erecting the tower, but we will not feed the windmill crew even if I they do the entire job. They will camp out on the range until it is set up. It's their normal practice."

Elizabeth takes the cornbread from the oven and sets it on the top of the stove only minutes before Ed comes in the door.

"Sir, how was it in Amarillo? Did you find a windmill?" asks Ed.

Arthur scowls and answers, "Ed, remember this. We small stock farmers survive by having connections in the right places and working with our neighbors. I learned that a windmill was sitting in a freight car on the siding from one of the railroad employees, a long-time acquaintance. Then, I was able to negotiate for the new windmill. I make this work by helping our neighbors and by knowing everything I can about what is happening in the region."

"Yes, sir," Ed says looking from one to the other of his parents.

Elizabeth says, "Mr. Gething, your son is learning about erosion from his teacher. He has been telling me about it during your absence. You will be interested in it, too."

"Tell me about it after we eat this evening, Ed. I am going down to the tank for a bath before then," Arthur says leaving with a towel and clean set of clothes.

Elizabeth and Ed enjoy the cornbread and buttermilk as they visit before leaving for the barn. She completes preparations for the evening meal: bakes the quail, cooks root vegetables, and slices fresh tomatoes, onions, and celery.

"This is turning out well, Ed. Your father will hear you out after we eat. He made an excellent bargain for the windmill. I suggest you ask more about how he accomplished it. Ask about the men he talked with and how he learned of this new windmill. He understands the other man's situation in order to negotiate for the best terms. Let him tell you about it."

"All right, but do you think he'll listen to what I've learned about erosion?"

"He will listen to you, but let him go first. Sharing what he does and how he does it is important to him...especially he wants you to learn how he bought our new windmill. What you can learn from him will be as valuable as what your teacher is telling you about erosion. He wants to guide you with your future," says Elizabeth.

"Does he?" asks Ed.

"Yes, of course, you are his son! I believe he is uncomfortable with fatherhood. It may reflect on his relationship with his father. Trust my judgment in this.

"Yes, Ma'am."

"Another problem we must deal with is the greasing of the gears of our windmill. I need to learn how to do this because you are not yet tall or strong enough to do it. The wasps are another concern. I will bring this up with your father as soon as I can."

"Let me ask Emmett to show me how. He won't let me go up if it's too dangerous. He'd teach you, too if you want."

"We cannot neglect those gears any longer. How soon can you contact him?"

"After school tomorrow, I'll ride onto the LeFors place before I come home."

At the evening meal, the family visits around the table.

"Sir, tell me more about how you found the new windmill. I'm glad it is not an old one."

"Ed, when I purchased the home windmill, there were several that were in good shape. In the short time since then, many small stock farmers realized the advantage of buying used ones. I could not find one as well suited as this one for the well we need on the range."

"How did you locate a new windmill?"

"It was necessary to make all the cafes and saloons to gather the local news. I explained to your mother that it was necessary to play some poker to get a lead. Poker is how I landed the first section of this property; I won it. Your mother never approves, but playing poker allows you to size up other men and, among friends, we talk about a wide variety of topics. In poker—and even among friends—you must never tell all you know, but you must share some information that you are aware is valuable to the others at the table."

"How did you do that?"

"Nick Blodgett sat in on one of the games; he has worked for the railroad a long time. Everyone at the table knew I was in town to buy a used windmill. After the poker game closed, Nick took me aside to let me know that a new one was still in the freight car on the siding. We traded information before and I trust him. He knew who to contact at the Aermotor company office in Chicago. The ranch that ordered the windmill refused it because it was the wrong model. Therefore, Aermotor is responsible for shipping it back to Chicago entirely at their expense.

"Then they were glad you bought it?"

"I contacted the company and proposed to buy the one already in Amarillo. The manufacturer wanted me to pay for the shipping. Of course, it eventually made sense to them to pay for the shipping because I was the only customer with cash to pay for the windmill. It saved them that additional expense and suited my purpose, too."

"You were very lucky, then."

"It was a lucky break, but a man must find and make his lucky breaks. It was necessary to make the right connections to pull it off. The money is often not as valuable as who you know and whether those with whom you do business trust each other. Having available cash at the right time is always convincing to those with something to sell."

"Mother told me you are a savvy stock farmer."

"Did she now?" Arthur grins and cocks his eye at Elizabeth.

Elizabeth smiles, "Of course, I did."

"Ed, you want to tell me about this erosion you're learning about?"

"We've studied it all the time you were in Amarillo. I think we could use what I've learned by building land dams across some of the arroyos. Our teacher showed us how water washes away the top soil. The grasses are important to hold the soil.

"If cattle graze off the grass and the roots die, then the water washes away the top soil. The water runs off instead of absorbing into the soil. But, I guess, that is a separate erosion problem." Ed takes a deep breath and continues.

"Sir, it makes sense to me that we can begin holding the top soil by making land dams to catch the water flows. It will also create more surface ponds for our cattle."

"We don't get a hell of a lot of rain here. I can't believe it would be worth the effort."

"You wouldn't think so, but when we do get big rains between here and the rivers and creeks upstream, we have flash floods. Then there is a huge loss of water and soil. It's easy to see along the creek beds."

"Well, you're right about that. Just how do you propose to build these dams?"

"My friends and I thought we could work together next summer to build one on each other's place. I think we can all have one…maybe two."

"I like the way you are thinking! That's the way to keep communities together by working together. It is the same as trading our bulls around among trusted friends. It strengthens everyone's herd and cost very little. Where will you put a dam for us?"

"I've got several in mind. Let me show them to you next time we ride out."

Elizabeth leaves the table during this discussion of ranch business and stands with her back to Arthur and Ed as she sets her kitchen in order. She smiles and listens to them talk.

When she returns to the table, she says, "Mr. Gething, I need your help with the sound of that windmill. Could you please grease it for me?"

"Sure, Kate, I'll take care of it first thing in the morning. It was a fine meal you put on the table."

"Sir," says Ed, "I'd like to go up with you to see how it's done. I could swat away the wasps for you."

"We'll take care of it before you leave for school in the morning," says Arthur.

The Gething family sleeps peacefully throughout the night.

Mrs. Perry LeFors (Emma): We had discussed where we would build a home to school the children and had decided on Clarendon. Perry had sold cattle for a good price and we were ready, but the home was never built. We got a doctor from Kansas but after he went back the doctor from McLean did as he had done before and not as the Kansas doctor had instructed, thinking he knew best but I do not think he did.

Millie Jones Porter: I respected Mrs. LeFors' reluctance to talk longer after she touched on her sorrow.

Millie Jones Porter, page 330
Memory Cups of Panhandle Pioneers

31 - Trouble Nearby

Chores and routines of this fall morning move the day along. However, a disjointed feeling prevails. The air sizzles, although it cools. The tall grasses are dry and brittle and they whistle on the wind that whips them this way and that. Edward leaves for school and Arthur returns to the kitchen for another cup of coffee. Elizabeth gazes out the window in a pensive mood with arms crossed at her waist. "I expected Perry to drop by to collect the mail we picked up for him."

"Unless he ran into trouble selling his cattle, he would be home. We can check with his family. Let's ride over and take their mail."

Elizabeth and Arthur are uneasy; they saddle up after leaving notes for Edward explaining they are visiting the LeFors family. Their instructions are to tend his after-school chores and homework. Elizabeth, who is invariably at home after school, knows that both ranch hands are working around the barn today and will be there when Edward returns.

As they ride out, Elizabeth reflects, "I cannot imagine how we will miss the LeFors family. We will not enjoy many more visits with them. I cherish the lilt of Emma's English and her cheery outlook." *She, transplanted from Switzerland; I, from England.* "Emma insists upon the best schooling for her children, so they move to Clarendon."

"That's their plan. Emmett, probably has everything well in hand during his father's absence, but I may be able to give him a hand with whatever takes the muscle of two men. He is surrounded by a bevy of women when his father is away."

No one enjoys a fast ride or race as much as Elizabeth, and she angles her head at Edward and lifts her chin. "I will race you to the knoll beside their old cottonwood tree on the creek."

"You will not win! Away!"

The race is on! When they pull up, Arthur wins again. He outmatches her on Spider against her sturdy mare, but she thrives on the challenge. Their horses settle back into a trot by the time they are in sight of the LeFors house. It is more than a mile before they arrive.

"Hello, the house, we bring your mail. Show yourselves!" shouts Arthur.

Emmett emerges from the house. "You're a welcome sight!" He comes onward to help with the horses. "Dad's home but...bad sick and Mom is not able to persuade him to call the doctor out. Maybe you can help. We've tried everything we know, but nothing puts him at ease."

"What seems to be the trouble?" asks Arthur.

"Dad doesn't eat and burns with fever and complains of a terrific headache. He keeps telling us it will pass. Mom is frantic because Dad engaged a military doctor down from Kansas, who told him to put a Lyster bag in our water well."

"What's the bag do for the well?"

"The doctor from Kansas says it's an effective preventive for cholera, typhoid, and diarrhea on military posts. It's used on Army forts and camps so that crystals of chlorine in a linen bag seep into the well or holding tank. It makes the water safe to drink. The doctor in McLean has never heard of such a thing and thinks it's another snake-oil cure. Mom doesn't know what's best, but she's in a state."

"I will go to Emma. Join me as soon as you can." Elizabeth rushes into the LeFors' house.

Arthur says, "We worried when no one came for your mail. When did your father return?"

"He came home a week ago and was already under the weather."

"Well, no need to put up the horses. We may need them to go for the doctor. Let's find out what my wife has learned." With a look of relief, Emmett leads Arthur inside.

The women are quiet, and Emma is tearful. Elizabeth says, "Setting Mr. LeFors' wishes aside, this seems serious enough to contact a doctor. Emmett, you can tell your doctor everything your father is suffering, but your mother tells me he also has a rash of flat rosy spots all across his torso. I will stay to help Emma with your father and your sisters."

The urgency in Elizabeth's voice convinces her husband and Emmett that it is time to take action. A wordless agreement passes between Elizabeth and Arthur: Emmett needs his father's friend on this mission. Without a word, Emmett and Arthur leave.

Elizabeth says, "Emma, you did all you could for your husband. My grandfather's advice with a very sick patient was to engage everyone in boiling water for drinking and make everyone in the family scrub with soap before and after meals. You and I need to scrub every time we tend to your husband no matter how little contact. Even if it does not help, it will keep us busy and our minds off fears."

"Elizabeth, I worry that Dr. Jackson is no good for Perry?"

"Why?"

"Typhoid fever erupts all about us; Perry contacted his medical friends searching for something to stamp out typhoid and cholera. The reason he brought that military doctor out of Kansas was to protect all our families."

"I think that you do not trust Dr. Jackson to treat your husband." Silently, Elizabeth ponders, *Is no doctor a good choice? Is the doctor you doubt better than none? Is there another choice? But, what?*

"Perry listened to the doctor from Kansas because he thinks Dr. Jackson is just a country doctor and does not know enough. Perry is forever studying medical and legal books and he believes our doctor is poorly informed."

"I understand that! You are in a very difficult position, Emma! Do you want me to ride after Arthur and Emmett to bring them back?"

"Having no doctor is bad, too. Dr. Jackson is nearby. I think I must trust him."

"Come then! We need a good fire going in your stove and water boiling in the kettle and as many pots as we can."

Elizabeth thinks, *If only Dr. von Brunow's office were in McLean instead of Pampa, I prefer him with his European training and the way he keeps up with medical advances. It is a medical conundrum. I wanted to encourage Emma to send for Dr. von Brunow, but he is two days ride away and could arrive too late and delay the treatment. On the other hand, Dr. Jackson is nearby but may not be the one to save Perry. What a dilemma! Not my decision.*

When the water boils, Elizabeth brings Emma's four young daughters, Freda, Eva, Mava, and Ersa, into the kitchen. With basins of hot water, soap, and towels, Elizabeth shows the girls how they must wash their hands while their Papa is sick. Emma tends to the baby, Molita.

When her husband stirs from a restless sleep, Emma indicates to Elizabeth with a slight motion of her hand the rash spread across her husband's chest. Perry acknowledges Elizabeth and thanks her for coming to his wife's aid.

Emma encourages Perry to drink the broth and eat the cooked vegetables with little success. He complains of painful stomach cramps and Emma gives him a dose of the dwindling supply of laudanum left by their doctor another time. When her husband sleeps, she leaves to wash her hands with lye soap and joins Elizabeth.

"Emma, you look exhausted. There is no need for both of us to stay awake. You must try to sleep. I will watch your girls and be here if your husband wakes up. We need to take turns resting and tending, or both of us will collapse."

"You offer the best thing to do and practical…like always. The baby will sleep for several hours before I must nurse her again. Call me when she wakes." Emma goes to her girls' bedroom to sleep.

Elizabeth thinks, *We are in for a long campaign with Perry. I believe he has typhoid fever. A death sentence for many! Dear God, let this fine man live. Amen.*

The LeFors girls are playing with their dolls in a shady spot outside. Elizabeth goes to see that they are all right and coaxes them inside. After they wash their hands, she serves the girls bread-and-butter sandwiches and glasses of milk. Then, she entertains them with nursery rhymes and children's stories. Finally, she promotes a pretend tea party and enjoys the delights of these charming stair-step LeFors' daughters. It helps pass the time while waiting.

Molita sleeps almost four hours before Elizabeth needs to get Emma for the next nursing. When Emma is awake, she prepares their supper and insists Elizabeth take a nap. The little girls make a game of the frequent hand washings, and they drink cups of boiled water from the kettle in the style of a tea party.

Elizabeth considers whether it will be best to send Emmett away with Arthur to help with the chores at the Gething place or keep him with his mother to join in the rotation she and Emma started. She decides it will be better to wait on word from McLean and hopes the doctor returns soon with Arthur and Emmett. Reminding herself that the longer days of summer allow enough daylight so the men can return this evening, she sleeps.

Elizabeth wakes to a racket from the kitchen and goes there. Dr. Jackson and Emmett are there but not Arthur. "Thank you for coming, Doctor! I am worried about Mr. LeFors. Did you examine him?"

"No, we just arrived," the doctor says.

"Emma is sitting with him. Please go to them. Where is Mr. Gething, Emmett?"

"He turned off toward your place to be with Edward and do chores. He'll come back in the morning."

"Your mother and I are taking turns watching the children and sitting with your father.

I take the next turn. Would you join us to help out?"

"You know I will. I'll follow you so that Mother can sleep for a long spell. I want to hear what the Doc has to say."

Elizabeth warms the evening meal for all of them and adds water to the boiling pots and kettle. We must keep a reserve of safe drinking water. They eat in silence.

Dr. Jackson comes from the bedroom with his hand on Emma's shoulder. He says, "Perry is in for a long struggle and so are you. I wish I were able to give you better news, but this is typhoid." The doctor turns to the others in the kitchen and says. "Mr. Lefors believes he contracted typhoid while on his business trip. There is no telling who will survive and who won't. I see you are boiling water for drinking and cooking. Everyone must wash his hands after tending to Mr. LeFors. All of you must scrub your hands thoroughly after using the toilet."

Emmett and Elizabeth overhear the conversation. While Dr. Jackson speaks, Elizabeth watches Emma and nods in her direction and makes eye contact, "I will stay with you, Emma, until you no longer need me."

"Mom, you can count on me, too," says Emmett, "Vera will come to help."

"Of course, your sister will come, but she and her husband live in Beaumont now—a long journey for them. I am so grateful to both of you! Words do not say what is in my heart."

"Mom, we need to send a telegram to Vera. I'll take care of it." Emmett sits at the table to compose it. "Doc, you won't mind sending it when you go back? I've included enough for the telegram with the fee for your house call and the laudanum."

"Be happy to says Dr. Jackson.

Elizabeth realizes that Emmett cannot be on duty in the sick room, and do all the chores at home. "Arthur will come over with Edward each day to do chores. Time for you and Emmett to rest! I will take the night hours. Emma, I hope your sleep will not be interrupted to tend Molita."

Dr. Jackson says, "Mrs. LeFors, you are doing all you can. I left plenty of laudanum to help with your husband's misery. Send someone if you need me again." He takes the wording for the telegram with him.

Arthur not only volunteers to do the farm chores at the LeFors place, he contacts their friends to get more help. Neighbors bring prepared food so that Emma, her son, and Elizabeth can give Perry and the children their full attention.

One day follows another in a desperate attempt to save him.

Perry develops diarrhea and daily loses weight and finally consciousness. Some neighbor women arrive each day to boil the soiled sheets out-of-doors in the black cast iron pot over fires. A foul stench clings to the sick room in spite of the washing, scrubbing, and cleansing.

The arrival of the LeFors' daughter Vera and her husband, Albert Doucette, lifts the spirits of the family and friends.

Elizabeth and Arthur believe it best to take their leave now so the family can take charge, but they join the neighbors to provide food and laundry for the LeFors family on a daily basis.

Perry does not regain his health and strength in spite of the dedication of family and friends. Diarrhea wastes his body and leaves him emaciated. September 9, 1909, Perry dies.

His funeral is attended by friends, neighbors, and business associates all around the eastern Panhandle, but everyone leaves right after the service because the grief-stricken family requests that they are too worn out for the traditional spread of food and offers of sympathy and assistance. Thus, the family enforces a quarantine without making an official announcement.

Emma struggles through the shock and grief of her husband's terrible death but carries on with the demands of caring for her family. She wakes one morning with Eva patting her face. "Mama, I'm ill. My head hurts."

Touching Eva's forehead, Emma says, "You run a fever. Maybe it's a cold." She gets up and tends to Molita while Eva clings to her nightgown. After bringing her girls to the kitchen, she begins preparing the oatmeal for their breakfast. The family gathers to eat as soon as Vera herds them to the table. The girls are grumpy and their mother guesses all of them may be getting colds.

Freda, just older than Molita, cries, "I want my Papa. When will he come home?"

Her brother's eyes flow a stream of tears, "Our Papa has gone to live in heaven, Freda. Just come here."

"NO! Bud," says Freda, "get my Papa! You can't make my headache go away! Only Papa can do it."

The two older girls—Mava and Ersa—join in the wail, "Momma, we need our Papa."

Emmett and Vera look at their mother in despair with looks that say, 'What is to be done?'

At that moment, Albert comes in from the morning milking. He consoles his wife and her mother.

In the space of three-or four days, the girls are lying about and going back to their beds. They are listless and demand the attention of their mother, brother, and sister. Mava and Freda suffer colds, and all four of the girls burn with fever.

In another few days, Emmett is alarmed enough to say to his mother that this may be typhoid fever. But his mother cannot entertain that idea. It is merely colds; she insists. In two days, none of the little girls fevers break. Instead, the skin of all is hot and dry.

Emmett assumes full responsibility and goes to the Gethings for help. Elizabeth returns with Emmett. Arthur rides to bring Dr. Jackson back and then alerts the neighbors for assistance as before. In no time, everyone in the community knows a second terrible crisis descends on the LeFors family, and they fall in to do whatever they can.

By the next week, the four girls develop diarrhea and stop taking water or any food. Their eyes are half closed with the typhoid stare. They do not respond and are wasting away from unchecked diarrhea. Still they linger for another week with bleeding gums and rashes on their chests and sores around their mouths.

On October 26, Elizabeth watches as first Eva, then Freda, Ersa, and Mava—all four girls—die of typhoid fever this day. Her friend, Emma, is numb with grief; she is inconsolable and slips into a black depression. Elizabeth takes herself to the barn to sob in anguish.

The family arranges the funeral and burial preparations. There is another outpouring of friends and neighbors to attend the funerals of these young girls. The LeFors' family buries the four little girls beside their father in Miami.

Emma tends her chores and takes care of the baby, but she seldom speaks and sits, spiritless, rocking the baby. Her typical cheerfulness deserted her weeks ago. Her two beloved older sisters—Anna Thut and Lina Schneider—

arrive to care for her through her period of extreme grief. Vera and Albert return to their home in Beaumont. Once the remaining family settles legal issues and leave the property in Emmett's care, Emma leaves with the baby to stay with her sister, Lina Schneider's family in Frankfort, Kentucky.

In this land of isolated homesteads and stock farms and ranches, one death creates a vacuum that fills with a painful loss. Five funerals in one family create insurmountable sorrow. These five deaths are felt in the Gething family as if it were in their own. Perry and his children were well-loved.

Together he and Emma had offered, with open hearts, their hospitality and encouragement to many settlers and friends. Of the LeFors family of nine, only the mother, Emma, and her three children—Emmett, Vera, and Molita—survive. A year later, Emma returns to the town of Lefors with Molita and their friends and neighbors welcome them home.

32 - The Great War

Elizabeth gathers her mail in the Laketon Post Office. The ubiquitous poster of Uncle Sam scowls and points his finger at her. Clearly, "Uncle Sam wants YOU!" This poster dwarfs everything in the Joneses side room where neighbors pick up their mail. Florence Jones, daughter of the Post Mistress, acts as postmistress for her mother and Florence may also ring up neighbors with their signature rings on the telephone.

Elizabeth sighs, "Well, we are in this damn war and I cannot believe it is a good thing. Ed talks with excitement about it and sings that infernal song, "Over There, Over There." His chums found sheet music and searched for a piano until they could set it to music."

Florence, busy at the switchboard, interrupts her conversation with Elizabeth. Waiting until the operator is free, Elizabeth opens the *Pampa Daily News*. On the front page, she reads: Atlas Stallings and John Hollis, two young men from the Laketon community, are the first draftees from Gray County. On down the article, she learns that every county in Texas must send two men to Camp Travis, San Antonio. Atlas and John, whom she knows, will set up camp and prepare to receive the other men drafted from Gray County. More will be called up.

Florence, free again of her switchboard, talks with Elizabeth about school and her desire to become a teacher when she grows up. Elizabeth encourages her to follow her dream. Then, she posts her letters to London.

Arthur and Elizabeth see their son off to the Wentworth Military Academy in August of 1917. He catches the train in Miami with a ticket to Kansas City, Missouri and he waves good-bye to his parents. Arthur has a coughing fit, and Elizabeth blots her eyes as his train rolls out of the station.

"He promises to write often," snivels Elizabeth.

"Aw, Hell! Kate, he will never give us another thought! Ed's a young fellow with a tough year of military school ahead and making new friends. Do not hang your heart on his promises! He is not going to forget us but do not set your expectations too high."

They made a good showing at the depot with smiles and easy chatter. His school chums came to see him off and also their friends, the Harrahs, the LeForses, the McEntires, the Webbs, Doc von Brunow, and Jake Dawson. There were several others that happened to be in town and just tagged along behind Ed, who was balancing his small trunk on his right shoulder.

Elizabeth is deep in thought. *I think I shall I ever stop looking up when someone is at the gate and expect to see that slim six foot, four inch son come through the door.*

When she climbs into their car, Elizabeth's mood is somber. *After this year, there will be no more saddling up together and looking over the range or sit about in the evening reading the news and discussing the day. Ed will not draw up his chair to the table for a meal. His friends will not hang about with him. The baseball games, picnics, and swimming parties with all those young people are forever a memory.*

"Come now, Kate," Arthur says taking her hand. "It is not the last we will see of him, but we are going to be fine until he comes for the holidays. The ranch is enough…to keep us…busy until then."

Arthur's words do not match his mood. His feels this as deeply as I do. He knows our son is as good as gone.

"Kate," Arthur says, "We are drawn into this damned European War in spite of President Wilson's commitment to neutrality. Ed signed for the draft in July; the draft board will notify him once he is twenty-one. I knew it would be war as soon as Congress passed the draft act."

Arthur's declaration confirms Elizabeth's suspicion that he has hidden his anxiety about Ed. That catch in his voice also tells her that he is as emotional as she.

Elizabeth thinks, *What would Ed say to us if he saw us this gloomy? He would always say, "Well, this is a fine pair! What if your faces were to freeze like that?" That is just what Ed would say to us throwing back at us what we said to him as a boy when things were not going his way.*

"Kate, old girl," says Arthur, "What will we do if our faces freeze like this?

Elizabeth says, "Both of us thought the same! Ed would challenge us with our very words." Elizabeth holds yet another thought.

Yes, Ed will be twenty this December, and after one year's time, he will be required to enlist for military service if this God-awful war continues. With the military academy training behind him, he can qualify as an officer. I hope this additional education is an advantage for him.

"Yes, he would." says Arthur. And a lighter mood prevails. "Guess we better put on a cheery front for ourselves!" Both chuckle and blink away tears from their eyes and settle to talk of more practical routines on the ranch. But the war in Europe has already intrude in their lives.

The bell on the train clings and clangs as it makes the last crossing out of Miami, and they drive back to the ranch determined to let him go with resolve if not enthusiasm. They stay busy with the chores of home and ranch. Something on the ranch always needs their attention. Elizabeth revisits a note she received in her Christmas card from her sister dated January 1915 after England declared war against the Central Powers.

Dear Elizabeth,

In 1914 when our young men went off to war, we were sure they would be home by Christmas. It was wishful thinking. Our presses picked up the story of an unofficial truce on Christmas Day when the German and English troops joined in the singing of Christmas carols. Their commanding officers ordered them to continue fighting as soon as it was made public. Our army and navy continue fighting. We English are bearing tremendous loss of troops in the trenches, and unavoidable sacrifices are being made at home.

The signature of that letter is her sister Alice's. Since then, Elizabeth opened many letters from Alice about the fighting and the progress of the Great War. This one tells about a friend both Alice and she know. Her brother-in-law was home on furlough:

Our mutual friend, Anita Seward, told me about her brother-in-law, Thurmond, who was on leave. Anita feels she witnessed his shattered soul. Although it was difficult for Thurmond to tell her about it, he confided some of the hell of battle. She, then, knew his fears. He told Anita the conditions in battle. Our press does not tell what happens in the trenches and on the front. Anita wonders why her husband's brother did not desert, but instead he returned to those horrors. Six weeks later, the Army notified his family of his death.

When Thurmond was home on leave, he did not hear well. There seems to be little or no medical treatment on the battlefield. Anita tells that his deafness started with a painful ear infection, and the only treatment was to fill his ear with warm urine. Its acidic content gave him some relief, but he lost his hearing in that ear. Hearing is essential on the battlefield.

Another letter from Alice tells of the battlefield conditions they are learning from various sources—Red Cross nurses, doctors, reporters and troops at home with debilitating wounds. She reads her sister's letter:

The common circumstances of our soldiers are—malnourishment, walking in feces-infested mud day after day, shoes worn out, infected feet and serious wounds and they share the trenches with some rats as big as small cats. Dead horses are all around, and the stench rises over the battlefields.
The soldiers are ordered out of the trenches to advance against the enemy with rifles to fight against German machine guns. They face great spirals of barbed wire between the trenches. The sickening odor of dead bodies is ever present. The loss of life on the battlefield is overwhelming. Influenza kills more troops than battle.

I fear there may not be any young men left in the country between twenty and thirty-five. For this reason, the country is losing its confidence in its political and military leaders.

Rose M. Hall

Your sister, Alice

Elizabeth is depressed for England and for the families whom she knows with sons fighting in this chaotic war. She thinks this war will not be over before Ed must go into battle with American boys. He will return home between semesters at the Academy. She yearns to see him.

After the United States declared war and unofficially joined the Allies on April 6, 1917, local officials plaster posters in all public buildings. In all of the Great Plains states, the message was the same: "FOOD will win the war!" Every region of the Great Plains—the breadbasket of the nation, including Texas—must support the military effort.

Elizabeth and Arthur scour the next issue of the *Pampa Daily News*. It has a photograph of about twenty young men drafted from Gray County. These are the first detachment going to Camp Travis, San Antonio. Another photograph shows their families and citizens giving them a big send-off at the train station as they leave from Alanreed. Now it begins!

For months, Elizabeth and Arthur read the war news. The Allies need wheat, and the United States is the only nation with plenty. India and England need all they grow; Argentina's crop rots in the fields. Except for a few months of every year, seaports of Russia freeze over and Russians cannot transport wheat overland because Germany blockades the Dardanelles. Australia suffers a drought. The United States government agrees to buy wheat from American farmers to aid the Allies.

Arthur says, "Kate, The U.S. Government encourages farmers and stockmen to produce whatever the Allies need by subsidizing those prices. Patriotic pressure grows;

Congress wants our young men to enlist in the army or navy. This jingoism plays to their desire to win the war for the Allies."

"It is effective with our son."

"And with farmers and stockmen. This war is a power struggle between dying empires and arrogant new jackanapes. It is young men who believe the illusory glory of war that pay the final price."

Arthur expands his fields for planting more wheat. There are spaces as vast as an ocean with few trees and those found only along the river and creek beds. However, most of Arthur's land is not flat—the ideal topography for planting and harvesting wheat—he dedicates most of his land for grazing cattle. The breaks—an undulating land filled with arroyos and sand hills—on the edge of the Llano Estacado is not level enough to grow wheat. He does his bit. Only a small amount of his land is suitable for growing wheat and will not improve his income. He is not enthusiastic. He uses most of his arable land for growing cattle fodder.

There is demand for beef, but it is modest beside that for wheat that goes for an inflated $1.20 a bushel due to the demand. Going to their banks, farmers with good wheat land borrow to buy gas or gasoline-fueled mechanical plows to increase their crops. They plow up the grassland as fast as they are able.

Elizabeth and Arthur read how war affects their families in Wales and England. They continue to receive letters about food, fuel shortages, and death; they send packages of non-perishable foods with words of comfort and faith. They never know whether their packages will reach their families because merchant marine ships must slip past the German U-boat patrols.

These, their former countrymen, are fighting in trenches. The death rate is unimaginable. For Elizabeth and Arthur, war is more personal for a longer time than for many of their American neighbors.

But Ed is still eager to join. His parents did not celebrate the official declaration of the war last April. Instead, they view it with anxiety for they know the tragedies of this war from their relatives.

Elizabeth cannot get the jingoistic ditty "Over There, Over There" out of her head. In public, posters plea to buy Liberty Loan Bonds encourage her to get involved. This morning she brings it to Arthur's attention.

"We can do that, Mr. Gething," she says. "We can buy Bonds. English boys are dying in trenches to the point they are exhausting England's population of young men."

"Kate, for a long time, American boys volunteered in Canadian, English, French, and Spanish armies and did so until America declared war. A number of them left Harvard to enlist. They are flying new air machines, driving ambulances and fighting in the trenches. It's in the news!"

"Mr. Gething, these bonds will make it possible to train, equip, pay, and transport American boys to the fronts. The American government estimates it needs two million young men. Young women are volunteering at Red Cross offices— even in Amarillo and McLean."

"Kate," he says, "it looks like the country will take our only child, our only son. That seems sufficient. President Wilson failed to maintain neutrality. German U-boats destroy any and all navies and merchant marine ships they can find on the seas. You forget; I lost two brothers in the Boer War. I will not put money into these bonds. We will never see a return from such an expense…only a sacrifice."

310

"Arthur Edward James Gething! Our relatives fight in this war and face German machine guns, armored cars, poisonous gasses, and flame throwers. Young men crawl out of trenches and go over the top with only their rifles and their lives in defense. Ed may face the same fight in a years' time. It is far better to send him and all who go into the trenches with better equipment and training than for you to sit on your money…even if you never get a penny in return."

"Oh, hell, Kate! You cannot imagine the stupidity of the English military leaders and government; the American politicians are no improvement. All of them beat the war drums about defeating the Hun, but who cares about our son, except us?"

"I gave birth to Ed and raised him. My contribution is equal to your toil on this ranch, and I want to give Ed every chance to come home alive. We ought to do more than raise more wheat. Upon my word, do you not remember that Germany offered to return all of Texas and more, to Mexico if it would only join as their ally? If everyone shares your opinion, none of our sons will come home."

"The damn English treat their countrymen—Ireland, Scotland and Wales—like their colonies. They send the 'colonists' to fight their wars."

"But America is not a colony and we are in this war whether we like it or not. If you want to keep my loyalty and my service to you and to this land, you will buy some Bonds."

"You and your damn 'tough biscuits'! And just what do you think you will do if I refuse."

"Mr. Gething, my loyal and dedicated friends will stand beside me! I survived more than an insufficient home and food before. And I can do it again!"

Arthur stomps out of the house, but Elizabeth is unmoved. *My friends will know of your refusal if it comes to that. War is hell all over! And has all the charm of a family feud.*

33 - Marmalade Christmas

Less than a week before Christmas 1917, Elizabeth moistens her Christmas fruit cakes with their final application of brandy. The sharp sweet fruity aroma trumpets the season. Red velvet ribbons and loops of paper chains and popcorn strands swirl about the dark green cedar tree. Ed cut and hauled it out of the breaks to stand in the parlor.

Ed is home from Wentworth Military Academy; he celebrated his twentieth birthday with his parents and his closest friends a week ago. Arthur and Elizabeth have followed English news since it joined the Allies. Ed expects to join the Army as soon as he is twenty-one, the minimum age for the draft.

Packages are wrapped in newspaper with bright, colorful fabric bows and surround the Christmas tree. She practices her solo—*I Saw Three Ships Come Sailing In*—for the Christmas service when she hears an automobile horn beep-beep-beeping. My, who can this be? She goes to the window and moves the lace curtain aside.

Whoever it is, its tail feathers must be on fire! A luxurious touring car kicks up dust and stops with a jolt.

Elizabeth is out and on the porch by the time the driver is stepping down from the running board.

"Lady Gething, Lady Gething!" says Mrs. Tolbert, "I'm so glad I found you at home. We need you in Miami! Can you come right away?"

Elizabeth, amused at all the bluster, asks, "What has happened, Mrs. Tolbert? Is St. Nicholas bogged down in Miami?" She motions her huffing-puffing visitor into the sitting room.

"A Santa Fe...freight train...derailed. I've come...to get you...to show us...how to make... marmalade!" says Mrs. Tolbert forcing her words between breaths.

"You put a bizarre picture in my mind. Let me make us cups of tea, and then you should tell me whatever goes between and the train derailment and making marmalade."

"My apologies! Give me a minute. Tea sounds perfect," says Mrs. Tolbert taking deep breaths.

"Will you have some of my fruit cake to go with it?"

"Oh, yes, your Christmas fruit cake is legendary."

Elizabeth brings the tea pot, the best china, and fruit cake. As she serves her guest, Elizabeth says, "I cannot wait to hear. Please go ahead."

"My husband came back to the house soon after he left this morning with news that a Santa Fe freight derailed coming down that steep grade into the canyon," says Mrs. Tolbert.

Elizabeth thinks, *I know that steep grade very well. It caused my team to run away years ago.*

Mrs. Tolbert continues, "Those refrigerator cars were hauling oranges. They were scattered all along five acres of our pasture before the cars reached Mr. Tolbert's grain elevator."

"This will be more than a dozen jars of marmalade; I think."

"Oh, Lady Gething! I never…" Mrs. Tolbert sputters and then breaks out into giggles. "Oh, just let me finish! Mr. Tolbert rode all around the area and then called on Santa Fe's division supervisor who Mr. Tolbert deals with for shipping our grain.

"The supervisor told him we can have all the oranges we can pick up. But, if the oranges are left in the pasture until after Christmas, they will spoil. To save them, we need to do something with them now. I know you can teach us how to make the marmalade. Will you?"

"You suggest a fair-sized job…and only five days before Christmas. Hmmm! What have you done besides getting permission to gather these oranges?"

"Grandfather Tolbert, Uncle Weimar, and our hired hands are loading up the oranges in wagons. Mr. Tolbert is headed to Miami and Pampa to buy all the canning jars, seals, canning supplies, and sugar that he can load into his Stutz Bearcat. I'm here to recruit you. Please?"

"We will have the essential canning supplies, then," Elizabeth says.

"Yes, Lady Gething," says Mrs. Tolbert. "We will have them by this afternoon."

She studies, for a moment, how to organize the workers. "How many people do you count on to make the marmalade?"

Mrs. Tolbert counts off on her fingers, "Mr. Tolbert and I, our six-year-old son Frank, Uncle Weimar, Grandfather Tolbert, seven of Mr. Tolbert's hired hands—twelve; you'd make thirteen."

"Are there plenty of cooking pots?" asks Elizabeth.

"Mr. Tolbert was a cook on chuck wagons; we have huge kettles and Dutch ovens. You and I will cook down the syrup in my kitchen; my husband and our hired hands will cook outdoors.

Then, Elizabeth adds, "We will need more people to prepare the oranges and cook down the syrup—but, I expect we could do it!

"Our son, Ed, is home from Wentworth and out on the range with his father now, so they will be hard to contact. I hope they will want to join us; if this good weather holds, they will be free."

"Lady Gething, our biggest concern is that Christmas is almost here. We don't want to spoil either—Christmas or these oranges. It will not be easy."

"It will be fun! Mrs. Tolbert, go out and honk that horn, and I will bring pots and pans to beat. Maybe we can bring them up to the house with the racket."

"Oh, I just love you; I knew you would!" says Mrs. Tolbert hugging Elizabeth.

They make noise for a long time with the horn and banging pans and do it with abandon. Both are laughing. They return to the house and load the touring car with the largest kettles and all the Dutch ovens in the Gething household. Bedrolls are made, rolled up and packed along with the cooking containers and utensils. They return and continue making racket as soon as they pack the car. They stop. Arthur and Ed ride into the corral as if they had exploded into it.

"Kate!" Arthur yells from the corral, "What is going on here?"

Elizabeth waves and motions him onward. Arthur has not been well. His gait is stiff as he leaves the corral fence and trudges toward the house. But he halts beside the packed touring car. "This is one impressive car!" he says.

Elizabeth meets her husband and announces, "Mr. Gething, we are planning a Christmas party in Miami and Mrs. Tolbert is here to drive us! We will be harvesting five acres of oranges spilled out of derailed Santa Fe freight cars. They were released to the Tolbert family. We are going to make marmalade with them. Do come with us. Ed will love it!"

"Christ's Blood!" Arthur expresses his relief, "I thought we had a crisis on our hands!"

Elizabeth laughs, "We are beneficiaries of an orange bonanza. Mrs. Tolbert came to ask me to show everyone how to make marmalade so we can preserve those oranges. With all of us working together, we can finish before Christmas. Will you and Ed go with us? It will be as much fun as an old-time taffy pull."

Arthurs shakes his head and says, "I thought this must be a joke, but the packed car convinces me that it is not. Let me see what we can do!"

He ticks off several of his obligations in silence. He thinks, *Five days to Christmas...the fence to ride...cattle to check...cows to milk...eggs to collect...windmills are greased...domestic stock to feed and water.* Finally, he answers, "If Dub and Parker are around anywhere, I trust them to stay and take care of everything here. Ed and I need to put a few things together before we can leave."

Ed took care of their horses and hurries from the barn up to the house. His father meets him. They talk for a few minutes before Ed lets out a whoop. Elizabeth turns to Mrs. Tolbert with a nod and a knowing look; they go to the car and sit on the running board waiting for Arthur and Ed.

"Mrs. Tolbert," Elizabeth confides, "Mr. Gething is not well. I'm not sure how much he can help, but I want him to get away for a while. Ed will more than compensate for him when we preserve those oranges."

"Lady Gething," says Mrs. Tolbert, "we are aware he has been in poor health. Mr. Tolbert and I will be sure he is not asked to do too much. How would it be to put Mr. Gething in charge of keeping my young son Frank entertained and engaged? Our son can run errands, collect the kindling for the fires and be our messenger-boy. Mr. Gething can do some of the lighter work in the kitchen. Frank loves a good tale, and Mr. Gething is a gifted story teller. "

"You are very gracious. I believe that will be a perfect solution." replies Elizabeth.

In half an hour, they are on the way. Miami is about thirty miles away, and the four of them reach it by midafternoon. When they spill out at the Tolbert house, Mr. Tolbert shows them that he stored oranges in every available space: in the kitchen, the barn, the grain bins, and the grain elevator. "Mr. Tolbert," says Elizabeth, "I should taste one of those oranges because not all oranges are Seville oranges."

"Lady Gething," Mr. Tolbert grins, "we've no shortage of oranges! Select from any of these."

"Thank you," she says, taking a nibble from the peel and a section of the orange. "These are sweet American oranges; Seville oranges are bitter. I need to improvise. Lemons can sharpen the flavor of the oranges and counter the sweetness a little. Were there any lemons in Pampa or Miami?"

"Yes," says Mr. Tolbert, "there were some. It means another trip in the morning. How many lemons do you need?"

"Only enough to counter the sweetness of these oranges. I can only guess, but I will try it with only a case of lemons."

"Lady Gething, do we need more sugar than we have? If we need more, I should get it tomorrow morning," suggests Mr. Tolbert.

Mrs. Tolbert interrupts, "Mr. Tolbert, I think you need to stay to organize the outside kitchen with your hired hands. I can make the trip for the additional supplies— lemons and sugar."

Mr. Tolbert agrees, "Right, that'll save us some valuable time."

"Sir Arthur," Mrs. Tolbert says, "I could use your help getting the additional things we need in the morning. Will you ride along with me?"

"I am at your service, Mrs. Tolbert. Another ride in your touring car is temptation enough," answers Arthur.

Elizabeth says, "We need equal amounts of juice, sugar, and the rinds of oranges and lemons according to weight. Are scales available?"

Mr. Tolbert says, "The smaller scales I use at the grain elevator will do the job."

The preparation goes on in the kitchen and outdoors. Mrs. Tolbert and Elizabeth begin washing the oranges and setting glass jars out for storing the juice and then everyone in the kitchen begins squeezing the oranges. Elizabeth shows how to use a spoon to scrape away most of the white membrane before slicing the boiled skins into slivers. They divide the crew. Half of it is squeezing the oranges; the other half, preparing the orange skins.

Meanwhile, Mr. Tolbert takes charge in the yard. His hired hands, mostly young men, dig fire pits or split and haul mesquite wood into stacks. A couple of the men gather kindling—cow chips, brush and twists of dried grass. Mr. Tolbert sets up kettles, Dutch ovens, and skillets for making syrup for the marmalade and for their evening meal. The Tolbert men—Grandfather, Uncle Weimar, and Mr. Tolbert—erect the scales for measuring the juice, citrus rinds, and sugar outside because the kitchen is too small for this equipment.

When Mrs. Tolbert returns with extra sugar and lemons the next morning, Elizabeth is cleaning containers and scalding the glass canning jars. Mrs. Tolbert and Elizabeth begin halving and squeezing the lemons. Arthur and Frank prepare and slice the lemon rinds so the syrup making can begin. Pots sit on the heated stove top and after the juices and sugar have been weighed and mixed together the cooking begins.

The syrup is stirred continually to prevent scorching even after syrup begins to thicken and the slivered citrus rinds added. Elizabeth guessed that the juice of two lemons in five gallons of juice with the citrus rind will make the marmalade both sweet and tart. She and Mrs. Tolbert sample and decide it is a tasty combination; then samples are given all around and approval is received. They take turns standing over the bubbling syrup kettles until the consistency is perfect. Finally, Ed and Uncle Weimar fill the jars with marmalade, seal and cap them. The kitchen is steamy. Brows are wiped. Everyone hustles.

For the evening meal, Mr. Tolbert made a Son-of-a-Gun stew with cornbread and finished it with apple cobbler. The workers eat with good appetites. Once the fires are extinguished and dishes washed and stored, they scatter their sleeping pallets throughout the house. No one has trouble sleeping after making the first batch of marmalade and establishing the outside kitchen. Whistles, whiffles and snores become an all-night concert.

Beginning the first full-day of cooking, the outside crew get a lesson on trimming the citrus rinds and using the ratio of lemons to oranges for the juice. Someone from outside is coming inside throughout the day to bring more fuel or appropriate weights of the ingredients. Someone from the inside steps outside from time to time to catch a cool breeze. Everyone is cooperative and there is good natured shifting and sharing.

Frequently in the next three days, Elizabeth catches herself singing favorite Christmas hymns and folk songs. Soon everyone joins her; they create their own a cappella choir. The house and yard exude the sweetness of oranges and the aroma of mesquite fires. Hearts are as mellow and sweet as the preserves.

By end of the third day, they are running out of canning jars and sugar. Grandfather and Mr. Tolbert suggest a way to put oranges to good use without more cooking. These two load up the Marmon touring car and the Stutz Bearcat and distribute Christmas oranges to every household in Roberts County—every square mile of it. The men visit every house, dugout, shed, sod house, railroad section house, and ranch house with prized Christmas stocking stuffers for the children—oranges.

Christmas Eve, the Gething family packs and Mr. Tolbert drives them home with a cache of marmalade and fresh oranges. Neither Christmas nor the oranges are spoiled! Christmas is sweeter this year than ever. Ed is home and not yet a soldier. This Christmas, all enjoy a fine memory.

Rose M. Hall

Elizabeth muses over the days before Christmas. *Lady Gething? Sir Arthur? No one doubts we are English. What form of flattery are those elevated monikers?* She chuckles. *I suppose my claim to royalty is that I know how to make marmalade.*

34 - Farewell Arthur

Elizabeth stands at the foot of Arthur's hospital bed in Canadian, Texas. The doctor pronounces Arthur dead on Tuesday, December 10, 1918. The head nurse stands with them.

Dr. Hamilton, the distinguished, white-haired physician steps to the foot of the bed and takes Elizabeth's hand. "Mrs. Gething, your husband is free of the pain of life. I offer my sympathy to you and your family," he says.

"Thank you, Dr. Hamilton, for your care and vigilance during Mr. Gething's final days," Elizabeth is dry-eyed and numb.

"Stay with him as long as you need and then give us your wishes for his final rest." The nurse in her crisp white uniform and cap steps aside, waits for Dr. Hamilton to pass and walks behind him from the room. Elizabeth follows them with her eyes. Everything seems white—walls, bed sheets, and professional uniforms.

Elizabeth looks on Arthur—at last, peaceful—and pulls the sheet up over his face. She empties herself into the nearby chair, closes her eyes, and allows her exhaustion to take over. The impersonal wind roars outside the window. It is no respecter of death or emotional depletion. For twenty-two years, she was the wife of Arthur Edward James Gething. He began failing three years ago. Only last Christmas, Arthur and Ed and she had a jolly time at the

Tolbert home. Their families and extra hands worked together making marmalade. They cooked over big pots right up until Christmas Eve, and the Tolbert men gave away oranges to every household in the county.

Before Ed came home from his first year at Wentworth more than a year ago, Arthur bought a house in Miami so that he could be under the constant care of his doctor, Dr. Abbot. Carbuncles erupted around his neck and over time opened, oozing bloody puss. Those growths—with the appearance of lumps—restricted his breathing and swallowing. He always had a volatile temper and became irritable and demanding; anger was the undercurrent of his being. Although the doctor increased the dosage of laudanum, it did not relieve Arthur's pain no matter how often he took it. At last, Elizabeth was unable to manage by herself and brought him here to the hospital in Canadian.

I will have time to reflect on our lives together. Now I must complete arrangements with the undertaker for burial. After that, there is nothing more inviting than finding a pillow and sleeping.

Elizabeth opens the door and summons the nurse. She hands her a written note with instructions for the undertaker and goes over them in order to answer any questions the hospital or undertaker may have.

Ed is on his way home from Wentworth; Elizabeth sent him a telegraph two days ago explaining that his father was dying and urging Ed to come without delay. Ed's train will arrive from Kansas City, Missouri, tomorrow evening. Before leaving here, she will go to the mortuary to make arrangements so that the undertaker can prepare Arthur's body and move the casket to Miami. Months ago, she made arrangements to hold his funeral in the First Presbyterian Church where she attends.

Daylight will expire before she can reach home today and nighttime travel is too cold and risky. She will keep her hotel room in Canadian this evening, but in the early morning, she will hook the team to the buckboard and travel thirty miles to Miami.

She enters her little house in Miami just past sundown after putting up the team and buckboard. She notes the time; it is five hours before she will meet Edward's train, so she makes herself a pot of coffee and busies herself about the house packing the supplies she needed to take care of Arthur while they lived here. Then, she packs his clothing and her own. She fears she may oversleep and does not allow herself a nap. She drinks a cup of coffee before stepping next door to Fudgie's house. This neighbor welcomed them as soon as they moved next door, and she gave Elizabeth her unflagging friendship and help during the time they were neighbors.

"My dear," says Fudgie, "whatever are you doing out? Come in out of the cold!"

"Arthur died yesterday morning. I am waiting for Ed to arrive," she says as Fudgie draws her inside.

"Oh, Elizabeth, you poor dear! I cannot think how you have managed these past months. Let me take your coat. Be seated."

"I was only able with your help. You will never know how much having you as our neighbor means to me. You are more than Dr. Abbot's nurse. You are my dear friend.

"Let me take you home and sit with you. You should take a nap, and I can stay until you leave to meet Ed."

Elizabeth embraces Fudgie and a ragged sob erupts as tears flood from her eyes. "Yes, I hoped you could."

"Dear Elizabeth, I will do anything you wish. Perhaps I can drive you to the depot and Ed can drive you to the ranch. What do you need me to do at your house?"

"Only keep an eye on it until I can sell it, I will handle other arrangements as I can."

Fudgie recognizes Elizabeth is not thinking of the things she must do right now, so she accompanies Elizabeth to her house and makes some mental notes of things she can put into motion. She plans to contact the neighbors to prepare a little supper here at Elizabeth's house. She will also insist upon driving Elizabeth to the depot.

Once inside, Fudgie takes charge, "Elizabeth, off to bed with you. When should I wake you up?"

"About an hour and a half will do."

With Elizabeth asleep, Fudgie calls in the neighbors, and they will cooperate to have a meal ready for Elizabeth and Ed to either take with them to the ranch or to serve them here this evening.

Fudgie drives Elizabeth to meet the train and sits with her until the train pulls into the station. They surge out onto the platform when the train comes to a stop and wait for Ed to debark. Ed puts his luggage down and puts his arm around his mother. "How are you, Moms?"

"Ed, you remember Fudgie."

Ed nods his recognition and extends his hand, "Of course, Fudgie! Thank you for taking care of Mother for me."

"She put me down for a nap as soon as I told her, took me home and managed my house. She takes care of everything!"

Fudgie says, "Both of you need a good rest before going to the ranch. We have a meal on the table, but we can package it for you if you feel you must leave tonight. I urge you to wait for tomorrow."

"Moms, Fudgie makes sense to me. Let's stay here tonight and leave in the morning. We can notify our friends and neighbors in plenty of time before the funeral and burial."

"I agree," says Elizabeth, "I need to rest."

They close the house the next morning and ride home to the ranch with Ed driving the team.

"Mother, how was Father in the end?"

"He was finally free of the pain."

"Did he ask for me or mention me?"

"The doctor did everything possible, but your father fought the pain and discomfort until near the end. By then, your father needed only release from his pain. Ed, he was beyond thinking of either of us. Neither you nor I would wish to extend his life even another minute. It was a blessing that he slipped into a morphine sleep."

"When will we have his funeral?"

"I plan it to be only two days…three at most. A Friday funeral is best, but it can be Saturday. Sunday is out of the question in order to engage the minister. The undertaker will have your father's body prepared today and brought to Miami. If we can arrange his funeral by Saturday, those who will attend have today and tomorrow to make their ways to Miami for his service. I will begin telephoning our friends as soon as we are home. Your father purchased burial plots for himself and me in the Miami cemetery before we left here and went to Canadian."

"Moms, I can ride out to the personal friends and neighbors starting this afternoon.

"Yes, our friends deserve to hear direct from us, but I will telephone the seven neighbors on our line. We do not have a central exchange as you have in Kansas City, but these friends will help spread the news to everyone."

"There are a few families I want to call on even if we can ring them." Ed twists his hat in his hands, hesitates and continues. "How well did Father provide for you?"

"You and I inherit the ranch equally; he provided well for us. Son, you must know: he was always impressed with you and your interest in the land and he was proud of you. He left his will in good order as you would expect."

"Yes, I know that. Are you able to manage and supervise it?"

"I have always taken an active interest in it as you know, but the problem will be getting the cowhands to take orders from me as they did from your father. For some time now, I acted as messenger from your father directly to our cowhands—even when he was no longer able to give any direction. That ploy is no longer available."

"You know I love the land. I cannot see myself doing anything except taking care of it. Just never thought he would die at fifty-six—almost fifty-seven! It's considerable I don't know about the business of running it."

"Do you intend to return to Wentworth to complete the second term and graduate?"

"Well, of course, that was what I expected I'd do, but it seems impossible now. Father, I thought, would be around for years to come."

"Ed, give some thought to taking over the operation of the ranch with me?"

Ed takes a long pause before answering. "I missed being drafted in the Great War when our country declared an Armistice last month. You know what this land and our friends and neighbors mean to me. It's a lot to take in and to take on. I planned to finish at Wentworth, but it seems the only thing to do is stay, in order to protect our inheritance."

The gate of choice clicks in place.

"Your answer relieves me the burden of how to go forward now. You can learn what you do not know. We have good neighbors to help us."

"Why would I go back to Wentworth? I'll stay, and we'll work out everything together."

"That settles it then. Thank you, Son."

The Presbyterian Church opens its doors for the family on Saturday. Louella Harrah McEntire and Fudgie will take charge of the hospitality that follows the funeral and burial. The sanctuary fills with their friends and the Reverend Mr. Ellis conducts the service. It is a touching testament to Arthur's life and service to his friends and neighbors. The minister recalls Arthur was one of the early pioneers to settle along the Cantonment Creek where they found good water sources in its wooded areas along the creeks, springs, and shallow lakes. He also recounts stories from Arthur's neighbors of his generosity to them: giving a helping hand or common-sense legal advice or loan of equipment and stock. Pastor Ellis says in summary, "Arthur was a man of sterling character who helped and encouraged friend and neighbor."

After the burial, the menfolk recall how he supported the mail carrier with extra teams in blizzards and bad weather. Many depended on his explanation of the changes in laws, and he guided them to understand their responsibilities and advantages within it. He took up the investigation of cattle breeds, new equipment—windmills, tractors, plows—and improved feed grains for cattle.

Palesteen McEntire urges her Grandfather Joe Harrah to tell about the time Mr. Gething's mule team ran away. Joe loves telling that story because Arthur's hair-trigger, hot-headed temper was legend.

"One fall day at the Gething place, we gathered to help harvest his hay and stack it to dry in the field. Arthur ran his thrashing machine over a hornet's nest. He lost control of his mule team, and it ran away with him. Some of the men rescued him and his team. Then, we expected him to explode with vile language. But Arthur simply said, 'Those dad-blasted bugs bit me.' Every time I think on it," says Uncle Joe in midst of rollicking laughter and with tears of mirth rolling down his face, "I..." His listeners join the hilarity because Uncle Joe cannot stop laughing.

Emmett LeFors recalls Arthur's farsightedness in acquiring their first Hereford bull to improve his stock. Ed tells about the long trip Emmett, his father, and he, still a boy, made to bring that bull to the ranch. M. K. Brown admires Arthur's ability to increase his land holdings and stock since he arrived. He started with twenty head of cattle and through sacrifice and smart dealing increased his ranch ten-fold and his stock even more. Some of the tales the men most enjoy is that of running Arthur's hounds, chasing coyotes. Before the end of the day, each man offers his hand to Ed with sincere offers to help him in any way. Many friends gathered today give quiet testimonies of how Arthur gave them advice or help when they asked or needed it.

The women bring food and beverage and sympathy to Elizabeth. Her circle of friends expands continually over the years. These ladies share the role of women and support widows and their children out of their common experience. They are as rock solid as the foundation of a well-built house. So they move ahead in faith and friendship. The women accept the essential routine and even drudgery of life; they embrace the birth of joy and death of dreams. They know how to offer comfort.

When the last person extends sympathy to Elizabeth and Ed, they return to their house with Fudgie. The three of them enjoy a simple supper—a variety of dishes and desserts left from the noon meal and sliced ham that Fudgie put away for them. They visit about the service and seldom seen friends and acquaintances. Elizabeth and Ed show their warm affection for Fudgie with hugs and embraces before she leaves. For a while, Ed and his mother sit about recalling conversations with their friends before they retire.

Elizabeth prepares for bed and brushes out her hair counting one hundred strokes of her brush before the dressing mirror. She takes inventory of her face. She sees her drawn face and dull eyes that tell of loss and bottomless weariness. She wonders if she will ever feel joy and have energy to be up and about again. Then she slides between covers and snuggles into her pillow, partially covering her head with the downy sleeve of her flannel gown. Sleep is not far off.

In her dream, she is dancing with Arthur at a London ball; he is teasing her with stories of her galloping over the Wild West prairie. She sees herself in his tale, free in space and time. She tries to control the dream; she looks for the Victorian house as she imagined it on the prairie while she lived in London, but it never materializes. She wakes herself with a groan and lies wakeful in the dark.

Then she muses. Arthur was insightful. She wanted adventure and believed she had married for it along with the expectation she would be cherished by Arthur. Well, it has been an adventure, but far from the life of adoration and luxurious hospitality she expected.

Arthur was always an enigma. He lived in a world of reality for the land, and he tended it, and he was loyal to his friends. He grew to have affection for their son and to be proud of him. Elizabeth never felt he had genuine feelings for her. Oh, he appreciated how accomplished she became at making a home for them and the comforts she provided. He was never able to show the sort of loving respect for her that she thought her husband should have had. She expected the sort of gentle loving commitment she observed between her parents and, after their deaths, her grandparents' gentle kindnesses to one another.

She learned early in the marriage that Arthur intended to use her for keeping his home and being a partner in the work of the ranch. He wanted children, and she was to be in charge of all that entailed. She often wondered what family life was at home with his parents, brothers and sister.

I believe we give our children what we have. Who can do more? An inheritance is perhaps the least valuable of the gifts we pass along.

She survives and thrives in this land by creating a loving family with friends. Each new friend taught her how to survive and trust and grow. She extends her chosen family as wide as the land itself.

Ed, she hopes, will be happy with his life here and with his decision to join her on this land they will toil on together. Her son is the light of her life; she will see him successful and content here if it is in her power. He was keenly disappointed that the war was over before he could join it. He will not know how relieved she was that it ended before his twenty-first birthday. She thinks he is as devoted to the ranch as she. Still, he is young to make such a choice. May he never regret it!

Elizabeth does again what she learned she must do. She recognizes what life offers her and makes the best of it. There is a vacuum in her life and Ed's; it will be a source of regret and loss for those days gone. There was both pain and pleasure. She and Ed will survive.

Well, I shall never again be addressed with the despised name *Kate* as if I were one of the stock! She smiles and drifts off to sleep. Tomorrow will take care of itself. Her faith says it is so.

HISTORICAL ENDNOTES
AND COMMENTS

There does not seem to be an established form to include historical documentation for family sagas and historical fiction. These endnotes attempt to braid together three elements: the Gething family's oral and written histories, various scholarly histories and lay histories and, finally, the author's considered imagination of how they might have occurred. For that reason in each chapter below, the following construct is provided for the interested reader.

Bold type is used to highlight the chapter numbers and titles and documented sources from books. Websites are also printed in bold type and underlined within parentheses. Since a number of friends, neighbors and people who lived and interacted with the Gething family are part of this novel, some sense of what events and relationships were fact and which were fiction is provided by the author. In the absence of a specific connection to fact, the reader should assume the event, action or dialogue is fiction.

PREFACE—When the newly-wed Gething couple stayed at the Astoria Hotel in February 1896, it is possible they were served the classic Waldorf salad. Walnuts were added later as part of this classic Waldorf salad. It was a combination of chopped apple and slices of celery within a salad dressing (British term: *salad cream*) of mayonnaise and served on a fresh lettuce leaf. Also, the maître d'hôtel, Oscar Tschirky, created this popular salad, the Waldorf salad, and he was better known than the proprietors, George and Louise Boldt, who managed both the Waldorf and the Astoria Hotels. (**www.kitchenproject.com/history/Waldorf_Salad.htm**.)

Rose M. Hall

It is possible that Arthur and Elizabeth Gething were some of the last guests before the Waldorf and Astoria Hotels were combined in 1897 since they arrived in New York City in February 1896. The history of the hotels is interesting as they came about due to a dispute between Astor cousins, millionaire, William Waldorf Astor and John Jacob Astor IV and John's mother, Caroline Webster Schermerhorn Astor. She might have been the Lady Astor in Elizabeth E. Gething's story of this Preface. Find more information on that history here: (www.en.wikipedia.org/wiki/Waldorf_Astoria_New_York.)

The author doubts that the title "Lady," especially in the United States, had the narrow meaning it had among the royals in Great Britain. Elizabeth Ellen Gething may have adopted the American connotation which meant *a woman of refinement* rather than one implying a family relationship to the English monarch.

CHAPTER ONE– One Face of Fort Worth

Descriptions of the Fort Worth Courthouse and U. S. Post Office are from two photographs taken in 1896 soon after it was built. See it: http://wwwfortwortharchitecture.com/forum/index.php?showtopic=2 369 on pages 4 – 7; The author viewed them on October 10, 2010. They are public domain photos from Jack White UTA Collection and from his accompanying notes in which he identifies the electric trolley, buggies, St. Patrick's Church and the drugstore. Also, in the photos, are utility poles and surrounding residences. The weather station is visible above the courthouse roof. This red sandstone courthouse was demolished and replaced.

Regarding Shakespeare's play and Kate's line from Act III, scene ii used for the title of this book, *A Spirit to Resist*, interpretations of *The Taming of the Shrew* vary. Author Rose Hall concurs with Richard Hosley, University of Arizona in his introduction to the cited volume of this play: "Directors of *The Taming of the Shrew* corrupt its meaning when they bring Petruchio on stage cracking a whip. Admittedly such stage business would be appropriate to an extra-Shakespearean literary tradition, conspicuous in medieval *fabliaux* and Elizabethan jestbooks, according to which the husband of a shrewish wife forced her to mend her ways by beating her or otherwise subjecting her to physical cruelty." Richard Hosley concludes his introduction as follows: "To a degree, each of us who engage in the War between Sexes must cope with the sort of problem faced the by

Petruchio or Kate. Like other of Shakespeare's plays, *The Taming of the Shrew* deals with an archetypal situation." Entire discussion may be found in the source below.

The Pelican Shakespeare, Alfred Harbage, gen. ed. 38 vols. Kingsport, Tennessee: Pelican Books, 1964-1990 [Hosley, Richard, ed. This volume-Introduction, pp. 14-25.]

CHAPTER TWO—Another Face of Fort Worth

Arthur E. Gething attempted to practice law in Fort Worth and ceased the practice according to his grandson W. E. (Bill) Gething because of the abuse he suffered from rough men of the era. Arthur had a partner, but 'Roger Stone' is a character of fiction. His partner, it is believed, absconded with the cash deposits in their fledgling bank and it forced Mr. Gething to sell his most-valuable real estate in Fort Worth. His property was located in Hell's Half Acre which is today's downtown Fort Worth.

He returned seventeen times to London, according to family and family history written for *Gray County Heritage*, and usually returned with a foxhound. In the same document, Elizabeth reported that her husband had a pack of twenty-five hounds for hunting, primarily coyote.

Birkes, Darlene, et al. eds. *Gray County Heritage*. Dallas: Taylor Publishing Company, 1985. ["Gething, Arthur and Elizabeth," (F356) pp. 277-278]

The author made no attempt to learn when Arthur made seventeen return trips to England. Fannie LaRue is a fictitious character. It is unknown how buyers for his property were contacted. Arthur lived in Gray County at the time, and his partner was responsible for their Fort Worth businesses while Arthur was in England. Arthur's properties were within Hell's Half Acre, and he won the first section of land in Gray County in a poker game in Fort Worth as reported by W. E. (Bill) Gething. It is possible, if not probable; he used some connection in the area that was helpful to him in the crisis.

In the 1880s, elected officials of Fort Worth established ordinances with the intent to shut down Hell's Half Acre; however, it remained little changed. The apparent reason was that the merchants depended upon the money spent by cattlemen and cowpunchers and undesirable characters. According to work cited below in chapter,

Rose M. Hall

"Refinement from the Ashes of the Vice and Violence," this quote was given: "It was all right for 'Long Hair Jim' [Courtright] to arrest a drunk, the town said—but not until he had run out of money and was worthless to the Fort Worth economy."

Pirtle III, Caleb. *Fort Worth: The Civilized West*. Tulsa, Oklahoma: Continental Press, 1980.

CHAPTER THREE—The Bride's Homecoming

It is unknown whether Arthur Gething abandoned his bride in the rundown shack for three days. However, Elizabeth Gething did expect a well-built and fine house and years later she recalled, "I cried enough to float the battleship Maine down the Cantonment Creek."

Birkes, Darlene, et al. eds. *Gray County Heritage*. Dallas: Taylor Publishing Company, 1985. ["Gething, Arthur and Elizabeth" (F356) p. 287.]

CHAPTER FOUR--Courage

This chapter is primarily my imagination at work creating the feeling of abandonment and loss that a twenty-six year old bride may have experienced when she had no one to whom to turn for help and found herself in that desolate, raw place. I drew on my familiarity with the eastern Panhandle of Texas where I lived more than twenty years.

CHAPTER FIVE—Breakfast – Texas Style

As a child listening to Elizabeth Gething's stories, I remember she said the cowboys taught her to cook. The process of brewing coffee and maintaining sourdough starter and making sourdough biscuits is borrowed from several sources including present day aficionados of Dutch ovens but relies primarily on the source cited below.

Adams, Ramon F. *Come an' Get It: The Story of the Old Cowboy Cook*. Norman: University of Oklahoma, 1952.

The fictitious character Jake Dawson is not based on any person, dead or alive. However, the idea for that character started after reading *Fifty-eight Years in the Panhandle of Texas* because J. E. (Jim) Williams came to the eastern Panhandle as a youngster and lived most of his life in Gray County. He knew the ranchers and many of the cowboys from when he first arrived in 1897 until his death. He specifically mentions the Gethings as follows: "…Ranching near is

Mrs. A. E. Gething and son, Edwin [sic] Gething. They own considerable landed interest in that Cantonment country. This [Cantonment Creek country] is the creek that the Fort was first established on and then moved to Fort Elliot [sic] near Mobeetie...."

Williams, J. E. (Jim). *Fifty-eight Years in the Panhandle of Texas*. Austin: Firm Foundation Publishing House, 1944. [p. 136]

CHAPTER SIX—Llano Estacado

Elizabeth (Nana) told this story of angrily turning a pan of sourdough biscuits onto the dirt floor and crushing them. The author heard the story more than once.

There are many explanations of the history of the Spanish term, 'Llano Estacado,' but there is no agreement of its origin. Spanish explorers possibly used the term, Llano Estacado, in 1541. *Llano* is 'plains' in English; *Estacado* is 'staked,' 'stockaded' or 'palisaded' in English. Most historians accept this explanation, but other theories are included in the source given below.

Robertson, Pauline Durrett, and R.L. Robertson. *Panhandle Pilgrimage: Illustrated Tales Tracing History in The Texas Panhandle*. 2nd ed. Amarillo, Texas: Paramount Publishing Company, 1976. [pp. 2-3]

Elizabeth, raised in the Church of England, sang from its hymnals. These hymns were included in the *Book of Common Prayer of the Church of England* and the *Protestant Episcopal Church of the U. S. A.* The author used both sources and they are provided below in the order in which they appear in this chapter.

Book of Common Prayer of the Church of England. London: William Clowes & Sons (no date). [Hymn 197]

Hymns of the Protestant Episcopal Church of the U. S. A. New York: The Church Pension Fund, 1940. [Hymn 177 – Prayer for Guidance, p. 103.]

This incident of losing her way and being found by cowboys happened to Elizabeth Gething, and it was recorded as she told it in the source below.

Birkes, Darlene, Eloise Lane and Elleta Nolte, eds. *Gray County Heritage*. Dallas: Taylor Publishing Company, 1985. ["Gething, Arthur and Elizabeth" (F356) p. 287]

Rose M. Hall

CHAPTER SEVEN—Community Church

This chapter is fiction, except for the lives of Elizabeth Gething, Emmogene and Louella Harrah, but it is based on the traditions of West Texas and the eastern Panhandle. The author read many other sources about pioneers, settlers, and ranchers. Louella Harrah became Elizabeth Gething's loyal friend and dependable source of advice and survival-type homemaking. The Harrah family settled on the west Cantonment Creek and the Gething family on the east Cantonment Creek.

Both the Harrah and Gething families attended community churches that were non-denominational in the sparsely settled region for a long period before churches of specific denominations were established. Itinerant preachers were typical. [Even thirty or more years later, my family attended a community church near the Webb Schoolhouse in Gray County where both my parents taught in its three-room, three-teacher school.]

The large ranches, including the XIT, sold parts of its land to families who engaged in stock farms. This selling-off of large ranch lands was a gradual process, and the White Deer Land Company that held land in Hutchinson, Carson, Gray, and Roberts Counties divested its last land holding in 1957. Some of the large ranches continue today, but none is as large as the XIT was.

The author read a number of books to recreate this period in the Panhandle and West Texas. It is contextual information only, and no attempt is to document common practices or experiences of pioneer families who lived in the Texas Panhandle at that time. A general bibliography follows.

Birkes, Darlene, Eloise Lane and Elleta Nolte, eds. *Gray County Heritage*. Dallas: Taylor Publishing Company, 1985.

Erickson, John R. *Prairie Gothic: The Story of a West Texas Family*. Denton: University of North Texas Press, 2005.

George, Louise Carroll. *Some of My Heroes are Ladies: Women, Ages 85 to 101, Tell about Life in the Texas Panhandle*. Baltimore: Gateway Press, 2003.

Hamner, Laura V. *Short Grass and Longhorns*. Norman: University of Oklahoma Press, 1943, second printing.

---. *Light 'n Hitch: A Collection of Historical Writing Depicting Life on the High Plains*. 1st. ed. Dallas: American Guild Press, 1958.

Kelton, Elmer. *The Good Old Boys*. 2nd ed. Fort Worth: Texas Christian University Press, 1985.

Whitlock, V. H. (Ol' Waddy). *Cowboy Life on the Llano Estacado*. 1st ed. Norman: University of Oklahoma Press, 1970.

Williams, J. E. (Jim). *Fifty-eight Years in the Texas Panhandle*. Austin: Firm Foundation Printing House, 1944.

Williams, J. W. *The Big Ranch Country*. Lubbock: Texas Tech University Press, 1999. [Reproduced from a 1971 Nortex Press edition copy and is published as part of the special series Double Mountain Books—Classic Reissues of the American West.]

CHAPTER EIGHT—Taking Stock

No one could enjoy biscuits as tough as hardtack—and without salt—as those Elizabeth served her husband. However, the method of preparing them provided in this chapter comes from lessons my mother and grandmother taught me about preparing biscuits made of baking powder—not sourdough starter. The method of sliding two knife blades across one another was a tip from a woman who organized a home demonstration club in Stinnett, Texas of which I was a member. This author was about ten at this time and has forgotten the name of that club leader. The two knives used as described in this chapter replaced the lack of a utensil called a pastry blender. Handling the biscuit dough as little as possible and blending the solid ingredients before adding the milk and then lightly mixing the batter is the key to fluffy biscuits. Carnation milk was a staple of many pioneer housewives until the family owned a milch cow. The family may have owned many cows, but not dairy cows. The cowboy cooks—referred to as 'cookies' or 'coosies'—usually called Carnation milk, 'canned cow'.

Other than this, the author imagined it would have been counterproductive for Elizabeth to hold onto her anger and resentment toward Arthur and also punish herself with tough and tasteless biscuits. In as much as Elizabeth had few options, she had to adjust according to her circumstances. It could have happened by remembering her grandmother's strategy of marital bliss and Louella Harrah's help which is documented in other written sources and confirmed by Elizabeth's grandchildren, Mary Ellen Gething-Jones and W. E. (Bill) Gething.

The knowledge of the small cast iron stove came from the late Willie Mae Mangold whose husband Otto had donated one of that type stove to the historical museum in Claude. It was called a 'bachelor stove' because it was often used by unmarried men who were striking out on their own with the barest of essentials that cost as little as possible. Willie Mae told me Otto had used it with his Boy Scout troops. Otto and Willie Mae Mangold worked and taught at Boy's Ranch for years before joining the faculty of Pampa Independent School District. Another source follows.

Floyd, Wells & Co. *Authentic Victorian Stoves, Heaters, Ranges*, etc. An unabridged reprint of the illustrated Floyd, Wells & Co. Catalogue, ca. 1898. New York: Dover Publications, Inc., 1988. [Lark model illustrated and described on page 155]

The Lark model (above) was similar in some ways to the 'bachelor stove' used by Elizabeth in this chapter because it was inexpensive in relation to other stoves this company sold and because it had but two covers (cook surfaces). It was also advertised as a "camp stove" which indicates it was used in tents, temporary shelters, and on wagons.

Most families during the time had copies of either the Sears & Roebuck or the Montgomery Ward catalogues or both. [When the new season's copies came out the previous one was sent to the outhouse and used just as toilet paper we buy for the same purpose.]

The author used the two following sources on clothing for women as well as photographs in *Gray County Heritage.*

Sears, Roebuck and Co.—Fall 1900 Catalogue (Catalogue No. 110). A miniature reproduction of the Sears, Roebuck and Co. catalogue of 1900. Northfield, Illinois; DBI Books, Inc., 1970. [See illustrations of women's skirts on page 723 and shirtwaists on page 732.]

Lester, Katherine Morris. *Historic Costume: A Résumé of the Characteristic Types of Costume from the Most Remote Times to the Present Day.* 3rd ed. Peoria, Illinois: The Manual Arts Press, 1942. [Reference to the 1890s, skirts on page 209—whether circular or gored; reference to popularity of shirtwaists on page 209; from the same source is information on the evolution of the paper patterns for women's and children's attire on pages 207-8]

CHAPTER NINE—Accident

Elizabeth's experience of her miscarriage was reported to the editors of *Gray County Heritage* cited in endnotes previously. The quotation: "Indeed [Elizabeth] did adjust to the harshness of the Texas Frontier. She lost her first baby with a miscarriage when she fell as a mule colt ran between her and the mare she was getting ready to mount" (Page 278).

The remainder of Chapter Nine is fiction except that Arthur did name all the domestic female stock, Kate, and always called her "Kate" rather than Elizabeth or Mrs. Gething according to Elizabeth's grandchildren Mary Ellen Gething-Jones and W. E. (Bill) Gething.

CHAPTER TEN—Coming to Grips

This chapter is fiction based on the characters of Arthur Gething and Louella Harrah. It witnesses to the many friendships Elizabeth made and kept. Elizabeth's granddaughter, Mary Ellen Gething-Jones, testified that her grandmother tolerated her husband out of necessity and learned to cope. Elizabeth confided to her granddaughter Mary Ellen Gething that Arthur frequently "packed his little black bag and left" for stretches of time, and she believed he was often away for personal entertainment and pleasure rather than ranch business. Louella was Elizabeth's staunch friend.

CHAPTER ELEVEN—Charles Rath's Mercantile

Elizabeth told this story on herself about the purchase of the entire bolt of calico and quipped that no one would then ever know when she had on a clean dress. This author and her sister heard it a number of times.

The information about Charles Rath was written by his daughter-in-law. He was broke when he left Mobeetie to go to Kansas and had to beg money on the streets of Denver, Colorado in order to buy his meals as he waited for a telegraph wire from his son giving him the necessary money to purchase his ticket to California where his son and daughter-in-law lived. Ida Ellen Rath began to collect information while her father-in-law made his home with them. Charles Rath's extraordinary life is noted in other books, but the information for this chapter is from this source. The time at which both Charles Rath and Elizabeth Gething lived in the Panhandle overlapped, but their meeting is entirely fiction along with the conversation at the café with Bertie, the proprietor. Historically speaking, it might have happened.

Rath, Ida Ellen. *The Rath Trail*. 1st printing. Wichita, Kansas: McCormick-Armstrong Co., Inc., 1961.

CHAPTER TWELVE—A Window in a Hole

Arthur and Elizabeth built and moved into the dugout in order to have more comfortable temperatures in summer and winter. W. E. (Bill) and Grace Gething took me into the basement of their ranch house in order to show me the dugout. The plastered and painted walls are just as Elizabeth prepared them with green paint on the plastered walls and the white floral stencil design she applied near the roofline. The stenciled pattern resembles a wallpaper border used in homes today. Bill and Grace use this space for storage, and it houses a deep freeze unit on a concrete floor instead of a dirt floor.

Dugouts were not typical beyond the manner of carving out a living space in the side of a hill, embankment or creek bank. How they were finished depended upon what materials were available and used. The Gething dugout had to have been well constructed because it remains in use today but without its original roof. Its earthen roof was replaced when it was converted to the half-human dugout.

Ladies of Elizabeth's refinement often kept journals, but the one of this chapter was created by the author. If Elizabeth ever kept a journal, the author believes she had little time or inclination to continue it due to the physical demands on her time and strength.

Otherwise, Chapter Twelve is written to reveal the demands of surviving on the harsh land and the dedication it demanded from the men and women who lived on it. The generosity of its people toward one another was part and parcel of the Panhandle culture then and continues.

CHAPTER THIRTEEN—Root, Hog, or Die

Before construction on the Gething's first dugout began, Arthur ordered the materials for the more desirable half-human dugout so that Elizabeth would have a 'window in a hole'. Chapter Thirteen is about the relationship between Arthur and Elizabeth. She puts to rest any idea of returning to London. The English culture was rigid about divorce and punished women who took that option. The same was true within the American culture at the time. Both were male dominated. Women in both nations had narrow legal rights and no influence on government legislation because they could not vote. Elizabeth, we think, was motivated to have a home and family. It must have been a difficult decision and one she took time to make. We only know she decided to remain—not what her struggle was.

The title of Chapter Thirteen is from an American folksong collection published by Alan Lomax because it expresses the plight of pioneers who had no choice but to work hard for their living or die. The Haywood and Winther books provided contextual and general information. Bob in this Chapter is a fictitious character as well as his claim to have been the cursing bull-whacker of the Lomax story collection.

Haywood, C. Robert (Clarence Robert). *Trails South: The Wagon Road Economy in the Dodge City-Panhandle Region.* **Meade, Kansas: Prairie Books, 2006. [1st ed. Published at Norman, Oklahoma, University of Oklahoma Press, 1986]**

Lomax, Alan. *Folk Songs of North America.* **Garden City, New York: Doubleday & Company, Inc., 1960. (Page 326, the story about a Christian general and the cursing bull-whacker; page 333, words of the song).**

Winther, Oscar O. *The Transportation Frontier: Trans-Mississippi West 1865 – 1890.* **New York, New York, Holt, Rinehart and Winston, 1964.**

CHAPTER FOURTEEN—Mule Train, Mule Train

This Chapter is based upon an incident in which Arthur fights with the mule skinner as told by W. E. (Bill) Gething. It is from Gething family's oral history. The sources listed above in "Chapter

Seven-Community Church" continue to guide the conversations that ensue between men and women who lived in the area and also the fictitious characters. The intent is as in Chapter Six (above), to recreate this historical period of the eastern Panhandle with Arthur, Elizabeth, Perry and Emma LeFors and the imaginary supporting characters in order to both entertain and educate.

At the end of this chapter, the Gethings have the materials to improve the dugout by constructing a half-human dugout above it. There is a photograph of the front of this half-human dugout in *Gray County Heritage* that is frequently documented previously. See it on page 278; it is the top photo. The author found many photographs of half-human dugouts and the one the Gethings erected, in comparison to those, is superior. Many dugouts collapsed or had to be rebuilt. This one is in use as the basement of the ranch house.

CHAPTER FIFTEEN—Elizabeth's Journal

The reader will recall the first days Elizabeth spent in the shack alone when she cried and felt she lost those days because it was a long time later that she recalled them. In this chapter, Elizabeth is isolated within the half-human dugout and experiences her first blue norther. She retreats to her journal and the pleasure of her ball gowns. Now she is committed to stay in the Panhandle and make it her home, but she recalls the forgotten past with some healing.

In view of the human tendency to deny unacceptable events, for example, the loss of loved ones through death. The author believes denial occurs when a tragedy of other sorts happen. In this case, Elizabeth has lost everything dear to her—pride, social standing, and her dreams of an ideal marriage. Here she comes to terms with that loss. The adventure is all around her including the fierce weather and the need to provide sustenance to the men who are rescuing Arthur's cattle—not her cattle—for she owns nothing because she is married. The author imagines, at this point, she had to accept the reality of her situation. She may have even embraced it.

Information on the location of the Holland House in Pampa, the cost of the room including meals and the presence of a grand piano in the lobby is located on page 126 along with an exterior photograph of the Holland House is from the source cited below and included in the journal entry. Elizabeth Gething did not leave a journal to our knowledge; the journal entries were created by the author.

Morris, John Miller. *Taming the Land: The Lost Postcard Photographs of the Texas High Plains*. **College Station: Texas A & M University Press, 2009. [Number Twelve in the Clayton Wheat Williams Texas Life Series]**

The information on the blue norther is the author's recollection of those experienced while living in the Texas Panhandle and oral stories of them. A 'blue norther' is written and spoken without a terminal "n" on norther. This usage is typical.

The manner of cowboys and cowhands working during and after a blue norther are common practice. However, W. E. (Bill) Gething explained the danger of cattle walking onto a snow drift across an arroyo and then falling through the snow breaking their legs and of the necessity of hauling feed to the bunches of cattle trapped by snow drifts in the breaks and in arroyos after a storm had passed.

CHAPTER SIXTEEN—Mobeetie on the Horizon

The author is indebted to Laura V. Hamner and Millie Jones Porter for this account, but the view point is changed to one Arthur and Elizabeth Gething may have had. Whether they went to Mobeetie with food and other assistance is fictitious, but tornadoes like this one were common, especially in the spring. However, they were inaccurately referred to as cyclones by many Panhandle residents. Perhaps this misnomer came about because tornadoes are essentially the same as cyclones which only occur over the oceans. The word, cyclone, may have been used for lack of meteorological knowledge and proper terminology or from its use by a seafaring people. This chapter is intended to include another climate and weather event that were and are typical in the region. In addition, it alludes to the willingness to give help and comfort to neighbors in need.

Hamner, Laura V. *Light 'n Hitch: A Collection of Historical Writing Depicting Life on the High Plains.* **1st ed. Dallas, Texas: American Guild Press, 1958. [Chapter 45, "Tornado at Mobeetie", pp. 291-296.]**

Porter, Millie Jones. *Memory Cups of Panhandle Pioneers.* **Clarendon Press: Clarendon, Texas, 1945. (p. 5l, pp. 409-410, and 481.)**

Rose M. Hall

CHAPTER SEVENTEEN--Expecting

The flash flooding included in this chapter is a recurring phenomenon in the Texas Panhandle. The headwaters for the region rise in the Rocky Mountains and its foothills or rise in the escarpment of the Llano Estacado. As either rapid snow melts or heavy rainfall occurs, the waterways carry surges of water that is first heard as a tremendous rumble before the wall of water—the flash flood—arrives. This phenomenon is also documented in the tertiary, secondary and primary sources given below.

Rathjen, Frederick W. *The Texas Panhandle Frontier*. 1st paperback printing. Austin: University of Texas Press, 1985. [Page 7 (map) and page 9 (quote)]

Gould, Charles N. *The Geology of the Eastern Portion of the Panhandle of Texas*. Pp. 42-43. [Rathjen quotes Gould who quotes the *U. S. Geological Survey. Water Supply and Irrigation Paper No. 154*. For the readers' convenience the quote follows the U.S. Government source.]

***United States. Geological Survey. Water Supply and Irrigation Paper No. 154*. Washington: Government Printing Office, 1906.**

"Canadian River is perhaps more treacherous than any other stream of the plains.   The stream is either dry or a raging torrent. The river may have been dry for weeks a time, when suddenly, without warning, a wall of water several feet high   rushes   down   the channel, sweeping everything before it, and for a number of days the river continues high, then gradually subsides. Following this period of abnormal flow the sand in the stream becomes "quick sand," or loose sand (bogs) which appears firm but gives way suddenly underfoot, rendering the stream extremely dangerous to cross. Many a herd of cattle has been mired in the Canadian River, and every year loaded wagons and even teams are abandoned."

The author notes that the Gething ranch exists along an abstract boundary between the Canadian River Basin and the Red River Basin as noted on the above cited the Rathjen book and its map (page 7). The east Cantonment Creek is arguably effected primarily by the Red River, but the flash flooding and resulting "quick sand" seems only moderately less dangerous to people and cattle than flash flooding in

348

the Canadian River Basin; it remains the same danger to cattle and the men who rescue them.

CHAPTER EIGHTEEN—Circle of Friends

This chapter is primarily fictitious, but Elizabeth did use a collection of pictures clipped from a variety of sources to create 'wallpaper' in her half-human dugout. The author heard her describe how she decorated the walls of the half-human dugout and that she called the bedroom portion of it her "pregnant room." She was an accomplished embroider and an example of her work is framed and on display in the home of W. E. (Bill) and Grace Gething. She made clothing for herself and young Edward. Quilting parties were a tradition all across the country from east to west coast. Therefore, Elizabeth may have participated in a quilting circle, for any community event engaged its isolated population—the women were especially brought together by sewing, cooking, and church activities. Needlework of all kinds were essential for mending, making clothing, and decorating the home.

The poke bonnet mentioned in this chapter was also called a sun bonnet or a slat bonnet. Cardboard was not the only stiffening material used. Thin slats of wood were sometimes used as well; those were called slat bonnets. Many patterns existed and the one set forth in this chapter is an example. When they were made of fine fabric like silk or satin, they were worn on Sundays and for other special events.

Sewing circles were social events and became opportunities to exchange information and offer many supportive and compassionate friendships so that women could help one another with personal issues, for example, general family health, pregnancy, and giving birth.

CHAPTER NINETEEN—Enter Edward James

This chapter is fictitious with several true-to-life portions. The following is quoted from page 278 of the *Gray County Heritage*: (cited previously) "On December 14, 1898, after trudging through two miles of snow to feed cattle she gave birth to Edward James born in a dugout and it is said she was alone. She wrapped him in cotton quilt batting, later she laughed when she said it dried on his skin and it took six weeks to get all the cotton off."

Dr. von Brunow was *not* the attending physician, for he came to Pampa in 1902 and Edward was born in 1898. However, for the sake of the story, he has been given the honor because he was a much respected doctor in Pampa for the remainder of his professional life.

Additional information is from *Gray County Heritage*, page 279, "Gething, Edward James Family" (F358). "When [Edward] was born Emmett LeFors came by for a visit and remarked, 'That's the longest baby I ever saw.'"

Because Emmett was only eight at the time and the author needed someone to fetch the doctor and it would be imprudent to send a youngster to Pampa in winter with snow on the ground. Therefore, that dialogue was given Emmett's father, Perry LeFors.

Granddaughter Mary Ellen Gething-Jones supplied the information that her grandfather, Arthur Gething cut the umbilical cord and this was told to her by her grandmother, Elizabeth Gething. Certainly, Arthur may have arrived after Edward was born and wrapped in cotton batting but was in time to do that important bit of surgery.

The remainder of the chapter is imaginary but buttressed with the medical expertise on childbirth from friend and fellow writer, Frances Lovett, RN. She confirmed the progression of childbirth but cautioned me that a regular pair of sewing scissors would not be adequate to sever the umbilical cord, but that stout, sharp scissors or surgical scissors would have been necessary.

CHAPTER TWENTY—Indomitable Women

Louella Belle Harrah operated a photographic shop in Miami. The author learned this from Mary Ellen Gething-Jones. In addition, it was confirmed by documentation as follows:

Morris, John Miller. *Taming the Land: The Lost Postcard Photographs of the Texas High Plains*. College Station: Texas A & M University Press, 2009. [From a set of books in the Clayton Wheat Williams Texas Life Series.]

According to the author, John Miller Morris, (above) the postcards of Miami were printed by a mysterious Shirley & Cheney that he was unable to locate; however, two photographs of street scenes of Miami are included in this collection. Your author wondered whether the photographs may have been taken by Louella Harrah and printed by Shirley & Cheney for sale as postcards. This possibility may have occurred to John Miller Morris since he included the information about Louella Harrah in his chapter on Miami, Texas. The names in *Taming the Land* seem to have been copied from the *1900 U. S. Census* and likely resulted in misspelling Louella's and Emmogene's names.

A photograph of Elizabeth and son Edward Gething is included in *Gray County Heritage*, page 277. It was used in creating the story in this chapter, but whether Louella Harrah was the photographer is unknown.

Midwifery was practiced by many women on the plains. Emmogene Harrah provided this service for the neighborhood; she died on November 11, 1902, and she probably instructed her daughter Louella to assist in midwifery. Following Emmogene's death, we know Louella remained at home with her father to raise her younger brothers and sisters. When she opened the photography shop, it is unlikely she was readily available to act as midwife to neighbors afterward.

Elizabeth's memory is recorded as follows in the *Gray County Heritage* on page 278: "Although [Elizabeth] did not plan to be a midwife, there was a dire need for doctors and nurses on the frontier, and Elizabeth once said, 'I've helped 50 babies be born and not one of them died.' She delivered S. B. and Ivey Morris and six or seven of the Ivey children."

One of Elizabeth's (Nana's) stories was about cutting off the trains of her ball gowns in order to make Edward clothing from them. I heard the story and was reminded of it by her grandchildren.

On the advent of telephones in the Texas Panhandle, the following sources document their earliest appearance.

Hamner, Laura V. *Light 'n Hitch: A Collection of Historical Writing Depicting Life on the High Plains.* 1st ed. Dallas, Texas: American Guild Press, 1958. [pp. 194-196, "The Barb Wire Telephone"]

Birkes, Darlene, Eloise Lane and Elleta Nolte, eds. *Gray County Heritage.* Dallas: Taylor Publishing Co., 1985. [Jones, Florence (F525) pp. 351]

CHAPTER TWENTY-ONE—Deep Wounds

This chapter is based upon a family story of Elizabeth killing one of Arthur's foxhounds. This author heard it from her sister, Judy Ann Smith, (who was at the time a student at West Texas State University). Judy spent one summer with Nana (Elizabeth) after her stroke so that she could stay on the ranch again. Usually, Edward came by in the morning for coffee and conversation; Judy asked once if he remembered Nana killing his father's foxhound. His typical taciturn reply was to ask her, "How could anyone forget it?" In the same conversation, Nana asserted, "He kept his hounds penned after that."

My grandmother, Mrs. Walter R. (Rose) Williamson, (and friend and contemporary of Elizabeth) talked to me when I was a girl because I was disturbed about Nana's killing the hound. As I remember, she told me that The Gething family might go hungry without her garden and flock of chickens. Elizabeth Gething was counting on a supply of chicks to maintain her flock. When the hound killed her rooster, she had no other rooster and would have to save her milk and egg money a long time to buy another one. While killing a dog continued to bother me, I learned how valuable the flock of chickens and the garden were to feed frontier families.

Whether Arthur was raised in an abusive family is unknown. He was trained as pugilist in college. He had a reputation for a quick and violent temper. Arthur was thrashing hay and ran his team over a hornet nest. An event that friends and neighbors expected an outburst of anger and foul language. Instead he made the mild reply in this story. It was a favorite story of the old frontiersman Joe Harrah and was recorded by Millie Jones Porter as follows:

Porter, Millie Jones. *Memory Cups of Panhandle Pioneers.* Clarendon: Clarendon Press, 1945. [241]

As an adult, son Edward met a Welshman in Denver while on business. Their conversation revealed to Edward that his grandfather, a capitalist, owned coal mines and Edward's fellow-traveler and businessman told Edward that his grandfather put his miners out of work when they started to organized a miners' union. He did this by flooding his mines. Taking this as credible (and Edward seemed to believe it), Arthur's father inflicted harsh measures against his employees. This information about the meeting of her father, Edward, with the unnamed Welsh gentleman in Denver, was told me by Mary Ellen Gething-Jones.

Arthur's father may have intimidated, bullied, or beaten members of his own family. Recent studies of how anger gets out of control suggest this is a possibility. That possibility became part of the shaping of this chapter. It is fiction.

CHAPTER TWENTY-TWO—Here Comes the Bride

Louella Harrah, Elizabeth's friend, married T. J. McEntire on the date given in this chapter. His daughters were from his previous marriage and he was a widower at the time. Other than that, the story is fiction. Palesteen revealed, as told in this chapter, that she loved Louella as if she were Kathleen's and her own mother. Palesteen was less than a year old when her mother died. It seems probable that Elizabeth took part in the wedding preparations, especially with Louella's wedding dress because of her ability with embroidery and dressmaking. Weddings were enjoyed community celebrations and everyone put forth his or her best gift for the married couple. Another purpose of including this event is to reveal the typical manner of celebrating a wedding at that time.

CHAPTER TWENTY-THREE—Proving Up the Stock

Arthur Gething bought a Hereford bull from Charles Goodnight and took Edward with him. Edward was about five at the time and he remembered sitting on Mr. Goodnight's knee according to W. E. (Bill) Gething. This is the family history and is the source from which this chapter was created.

The author visited the restored Charles Goodnight house in October 2013. Its Coordinator, Janeane White, gave me a tour and related its history and something of the lives of Charles and Margaret (Molly) Goodnight. At the end of the tour, Mrs. White gave me a copy of the floor plans and later sent photographs she took for me of the interior of the house for my use in writing this chapter. Mrs. White also told me Charles Goodnight referred to his office as the 'War Room."

Nana's grandchildren, Bill and Mary Ellen, enlightened me about Hereford bulls and the route that may have been taken, the time it may have taken, how the bull would have been trail broken, the manner of treating the bull, etc. I am, also, indebted to George Fischer, Arizona cowboy and ranch manager and fellow writer, for better understanding of the manner of handling bulls and ranchers' ways in arid Western lands during this period.

From reading J. Evetts Haley's *Charles Goodnight*, I knew that Goodnight was a keen observer of the animal life on the High Plains and that he picked up lost nails along the pathways around his home. I employed that information in the story knowing prairie dogs would appeal to a five-year-old boy. Edward's interest in the actual pocket doors in the Goodnight house was included for the same reason and the operation of pocket doors was demonstrated by Coordinator, Janeane White when I visited the Charles Goodnight Historical Center.

Fourteen-year-old Emmett was probably interested in the Goodnight College and it educated young men and women at that time. Also, his parents, Perry and Emma LeFors, took special care to educate their children. Emmett took advantage of several other educational institutions as he grew into manhood. Although Goodnight College closed later, it seems due to both the growing prominence of Clarendon College and West Texas Normal College and the Goodnights' inability to find a reliable administrator for their college. Charles Goodnight's financial situation declined around the same time and he was perhaps unable to continue supporting it from his own funds. It demonstrated Charles and Molly Goodnight's earnest efforts to educate young men and women in the agricultural economy of the Panhandle.

CHAPTER TWENTY-FOUR—Return Trip

This chapter was written to expand upon the contextual history of the region at the time with the goal to make it live again in readers' imaginations. For that reason the railroad entrepreneurs and magnates, their ever changing policies and struggles along with the lives of railroad employees; the typical foods eaten and dangers encountered when pioneers traveled light by horseback; and amusements enjoyed by men of the era are expanded. At the same time, the purpose was to illuminate the fictionalized and historical characters of Arthur, Emmett, Edward, and Charles and Margaret (Molly) Goodnight.

As before in the endnotes above, "Chapter Seven—The Community Church," this chapter relies on that same bibliography plus those in the previous endnotes, Chapter Twenty-three—"Proving

Up the Stock." The characters "Irish" and the railroad manager at the siding are fictitious. Animals walked on the tops of dugouts and fell into them on occasion. It happened often enough to be included in this story and to show readers one of the many drawbacks to living in a dugout. Snakes—poisonous and non-poisonous—were another concern and the source of stories about their cohabitation with dugout dwellers!

Mumblepeg has a number of pronunciations and spellings and a variety of knife-tosses and rules. Both depended upon the region in which it was played. The author used the following source.

Texas Folklore Society XLVIII, Abernethy, Francis Edward, ed.; *Texas Toys and Games*: Southern Methodist University Press, Dallas, 1989 [pp. 168-71].

CHAPTER TWENTY-FIVE—Unexpected Guest

Mr. M. K. Brown noted his visit to the Gething family not long after he arrived in Pampa. It is an oral family history and the same event is documented in Mr. Brown's memoir on page 10.

Recorded in M. K. Brown's memoir is his purchase of a horse named Waco that he bought from Mrs. Holland six weeks after he arrived in Pampa. He also stated he won a number of matched races riding bareback on Waco (page 17). There is a photograph of dogs on page 47 of the same memoir with this notation, "Will Wilkes, M. K. Brown and Charlie Tignor's hunting dogs which they used to hunt coyote on Sunday."

Brown, Montague Kingsmill. *M. K. Brown and His Legacy to the People of the Texas Panhandle*. 1st ed. Austin: Nortex Press, 2001. [p. 10, 17, and 47]

CHAPTER TWENTY-SIX—Put the Wind to Work

Windmills soon dotted the plains and drew water from the Oglala Aquifer. Many families of the prairie hauled water from creeks, streams, rivers, and playas before windmills were available. After the coming of the railroads, locomotives used great volumes of water and the companies set up windmills at standard intervals along the tracks; the various railroad lines allowed homesteaders to fill their water barrels at these windmills. Towns and cities who erected windmills also allowed people to draw and haul water from them. According to Walter Prescott Webb, homemade windmills were built as early as

1855 on the plains, but they were inefficient; the commercial ones that followed were constantly improved. The homemade windmills allowed homesteaders on an acre or two of land to recycle other farm machinery and survive for a low cost on their land. Find a thorough study of windmills by Webb, cited below from pages 333-348.

Webb, Walter Prescott. *The Great Plains*. **Paperback. 1st printing. Bison Books, 1981. [Original edition. Boston: Guinn, 1931.]**

CHAPTER TWENTY-SEVEN—Cost of Water

The run-away team incident of this chapter happened when Elizabeth returned the unused equipment to Miami where cowboys rescued her; she had chronic foot pain and difficulty finding comfortable shoes after her feet were injured. The runaway team incident happened as presented in this chapter, but the injury to her feet was the result of dropping a plow on her feet in the process of loading it on a wagon.

As a child, my parents visited friends who depended on windmills for water. They need constant attention and sand did cave into the water well which often meant the well had to be drilled deeper or in some other fashion the caved portion of the well was sealed off. However, no one who has fallen asleep to the whir and clang of a windmill ever forgets that soothing sound. After the 1940s, advanced designs made it unnecessary to grease the gears on a weekly basis and later gasoline or electric motors could be engaged when the wind was not blowing.

CHAPTER TWENTY-EIGHT—Watch and Wait

The earliest U. S. Post Office in Gray County was at Eldridge and was established March 20, 1886. Before then, the first inhabitants relied on military mail or freighters whose business was primarily supplying Fort Elliott and points south. Somewhat later the Concord stage carried mail from Wichita Falls through the Panhandle in a circuitous route and it terminated in Dodge City, Kansas.

Birkes, Darlene; Eloise Lane and Elleta Nolte, eds. *Gray County Heritage*. **Dallas: Taylor Publishing Co., 1985.**

Until the U. S. Post Office extended mail service in the frontier regions, civilians took responsibility for mail, or there was some merging of governmental and civilian handling of it. According to C.

A Spirit to Resist

Robert Haywood, P. G. Reynolds, a well-known mail contractor and entrepreneur in the wagon freight, kept the mail moving. Once a mail bag was delivered, it was poured out on a surface in a way station or designated location; people of the area came in and collected their own and their neighbors mail. They purchased postage stamps in the same casual manner.

Haywood, C. Robert (Clarence Robert). Trails South: *The Wagon Road Economy in the Dodge City-Panhandle Region.* Meade, Kansas: Prairie Books, 2006 [1st ed. Published at Norman, Oklahoma, University of Oklahoma Press, 1986]

Once the Rural Free Delivery Act of 1896 was passed by Congress, mail delivery improved.

Burright, Orrin Ulysses. *The Sun Rides High: Pioneering Days in Oklahoma, Kansas & Missouri.* Nortex Publications, Inc., Wichita Falls and Quanah, Texas; 1973. (p. 183)

Elizabeth (Nana) Gething habitually wore the woolen felt slippers because of the earlier injury to her feet as witnessed by her family, friends, and this author.

CHAPTER TWENTY-NINE—Shot Across the Brow

Nana (Elizabeth) Gething told this story to Lynne (Followell) Cline and me when we were in high school and visited Elizabeth in her apartment in the building above the Levine's Department Store, once owned by Dr. von Brunow. Lynne reminded me of it a few years ago or it would have been lost.

Elizabeth learned to ride sidesaddle at a London academy. It was in England she also practiced marksmanship. Both skills were advantageous for pioneer women and many women were accomplished. There is a photograph of Vera LeFors sitting on her horse, riding sidesaddle, in front of the porch of Elizabeth's house; Elizabeth stands on the porch. It is on display in the White Deer Land Museum in Pampa, Texas. By that time young women were also wearing split skirts and riding astride western saddles according to other photographs the author saw in print.

Horse wrestling was invented or reinvented by boys during school recesses or during periods of boredom. It required no playground equipment and few rules. It was ideal for the pioneer school's playgrounds on which there was no equipment. Similar

357

games are played in many countries and have evolved into other games.

Texas Folklore Society XLVIII, Abernethy, Francis Edward, ed., *Texas Toys and Games*: Southern Methodist University Press, Dallas, 1989 [pp. 116-118].

CHAPTER THIRTY—Fragile Relationships

This chapter is a solution to the relationship problem that must have resulted from Elizabeth's shooting Arthur's hat off his head. Without regard to Elizabeth's belief her husband was an intruder and possible thief, reparations might have been necessary. This chapter is altogether fiction because the author thought Arthur needed 'face-saving.' Thus, he secured the windmill for the far range in what was a characteristic and adroit move for him. We have no idea what followed the last chapter. This chapter is entirely fiction.

CHAPTER THIRTY-ONE—The Trouble Nearby

The Perry LeFors family was reduced from nine members to only four by typhoid. The sources of information were taken from the following sources. Albert and Vera Doucette moved to Beaumont after they married, but retuned to Pampa to make it their permanent home following the deaths in Vera's family. Albert Doucette took up his occupation as an independent surveyor in the Gray County area.

Birkes, Darlene; Eloise Lane and Elleta Nolte, eds. Limited Ed. *Gray County Heritage*. Dallas: Taylor Publishing Co., 1985. [LeFors, Emmett, (F592), pp. 380-381; Lefors, Perry and Emma, (F593), pp. 381-382, and Gething, Arthur and Elizabeth, (F356) pp. 277-278; Doucette, Albert and Vera, (278) pp. 245-246]

Porter, Millie Jones. *Memory Cups of Panhandle Pioneers*. Clarendon, Texas: Clarendon Press, 1945. ["Mrs. Perry LeFors," pp. 328-332]

Decades later when both Emma and Elizabeth near the end of life, Emma declined to talk of it when she was interviewed. On the event of her 90th birthday, Elizabeth simply stated in a newspaper reporter's interview that she served as nurse for ranch families and mentions taking care of neighbors with typhoid fever. None of the LeFors family who died of it in 1909—not even Perry Lefors—were named in either interview.

A Spirit to Resist

That raised my curiosity because Perry LeFors was Mayor of Lefors when it was the county seat of Gray County (1902), and he also served as Gray County Commissioner after the county seat was moved from Lefors to Pampa. Years before 1902 (the year Gray County officially became a county), Perry LeFors established a stage coach stand in Lefors, and a few years later he organized a post office. During that period, the coach lines and post offices functioned almost as one. Establishing a stagecoach stand was a civic duty rather than an economic advantage to anyone who offered to take the responsibility. A person did so in order to create dependable mail service. In other sources written about this time period, pioneers, who took on the job of postmaster, described it as a "thank you" job.

I based the story in this chapter on the close relationship between Emmett LeFors and Elizabeth E. Gething's grandchildren—W. E. (Bill) Gething and Mary Gething-Jones. My assumption is that loss of those dear ones who died so slowly and painfully was emotional, even long afterward, and too devastating to revisit.

Notably, an effective vaccine was developed in 1897 by Almroth Edward Wright. In the same year in which five of the Lefors family died of typhoid, a U.S. Army physician, Frederick F. Russell, developed an American typhoid vaccine. However, it took two years to implement a vaccination program so that immunization was provided throughout the Army. In the 21st Century immunization and public health hygiene are so well established that death by typhoid is rare in the United States and Canada, Western Europe and other developed countries, but typhoid is still rampant in much of the world today.

The name of the military doctor from Kansas referred to by Mrs. Lefors is unknown. However, by 1911, the preventive used in the linen cloth Lyster bag, a chlorination water treatment—calcium hypochlorite—became widely used not only on military posts and camps but also in public water supplies across the nation. This same Lyster bag was used by the military in WWI and WWII and beyond. The use of the Lyster (or Lister) bag [which is named for its inventor/discoverer, Army Doctor William J. Lyster] is a historic fact. That it played a part in this real event is my fictitious invention based solely on the possibility that some medical officers of the Army used it and spread its use prior to the time it was universally used in American Army camps and civilian water systems.

The division between civilian and military leaders was very informal on the frontier. Also, frontier leaders, like Perry LeFors and others, were self-educated in many fields and skills. In another chapter, "Root, Hog or Die" it is evident that wagon-freighters undertook many forms of labor and were considered 'jacks of all trade.' Frontiersmen, by necessity, needed many skills and this was true of all the successful people of the frontier—men and women.

CHAPTER THIRTY-TWO—The Great War

Edward Gething enrolled in Wentworth Military Academy in Kansas City, Missouri and attended for almost two years. This was documented by his story in *Gray County Heritage*, by Wentworth Academy from which an attempt was made to get a photograph of him without success because only group pictures were in their yearbooks during that period, and individuals were not identified in them.

During WWII, my uncle, Tom Cotton, was stationed in London, England, and Elizabeth gave him letters of introduction to her family. He was warmly welcomed by them. The author deducted that Elizabeth was in touch with her family during WWI (The Great War) and because both Elizabeth and Arthur emigrated from Great Britain. Surely, they had a different experience of that war than Americans whose families had immigrated to America generations ago. The factual information was taken from several sources as given below.

Florence Jones was not a fictitious character; she was the school girl acting as assistant postmistress for her mother at the Laketon Post Office to neighboring families: Stump, Gillis, Eller, Kenner, Hoffer, Gray, Benton, Gething, Elliott, LeFors and Smith. Mr. Stump, a neighbor, had brought telephones back from Chicago and the lines were strung along the barbed wire fence posts. As an adult, Florence Jones taught school in several communities in Gray County and retired from Pampa Independent School District.

The first two men to enlist from Gray County were Atlas Stallings and John Hollis who prepared for next detachment to follow them to Camp Travis, San Antonio. A photograph of the seventeen in the detachment and their names accompany a short article entitled "World War I, II Efforts."

Birkes, Darlene, Eloise Lane and Elleta Nolte, eds. Gray County Heritage: Dallas, Taylor Printing Co., 1985. [F525, p.

351—Florence Jones and "World War I, II Efforts (1917-1919, p. 46]

Documentation on the need for wheat and the demand for growing more wheat, the popular songs, and the posters displayed in U. S. Government buildings are given below.

Robertson, Pauline Durrett and R.L. Robertson. *Panhandle Pilgrimage: Illustrated Tales Tracing History in the Texas Panhandle.* **2nd ed. Amarillo, Texas: Paramount Publishing Company, 1978. ["World War I" (p. 333).**

CHAPTER THIRTY-THREE—Marmalade Christmas

Frank X. Tolbert was the six-year-old boy in this story. He became a journalist, writing for Texas newspapers, several books about the Texas Panhandle history, its characters and events including, *A Bowl of Red.* He was co-promoter of the Terlingua Chili Cook-Off. The source of this story is a Gething family oral history and appears in Frank X. Tolbert's book *Tolbert's Texas*.

The final paragraph of his chapter, "The Orange Christmas", Frank Tolbert wrote: "We had orange marmalade for years. We got tired of orange marmalade. But my folks never got tired of telling about the Orange Christmas. And that's why I remember it so well."

Tolbert, Frank X. *Tolbert's Texas.* **Garden City, NY: Doubleday, 1983 [pp. 155-157].**

CHAPTER THIRTY-FOUR—Farwell Arthur

The date of Arthur's death was not consistent in the printed sources; therefore, the author made a trip to Canadian to obtain a copy of Arthur Gething's death certificate to establish an accurate date for this chapter. The stated cause of death was paralysis of the heart. However, that may have been a secondary problem. The common term used at the time was carbuncles and today it might have been diagnosed as cancer of the thorax for which there was no known surgery, cure, or treatment when her grandfather had the disease. Granddaughter Mary Ellen Gething-Jones worked as a medical transcriptionist. Therefore, the author accepted her understanding of the differences of diagnoses from then to the probable present-day terminology. She also supplied the information that her grandparents took a house in Miami, but Elizabeth moved Arthur into the hospital in Canadian when his condition grew worse.

Rose M. Hall

Edward did not return to Wentworth Military Academy after his father's funeral, and he and his mother continued to operate the ranch together for over four decades until the death first of Edward (1961) and then of Elizabeth eighteen months later (1963).

Arthur's funeral service is assumed to have taken place in Miami because he is buried in the Miami cemetery.

The story told at the funeral by 'Uncle Joe' Harrah about Arthur's runaway mule team was previously documented in Chapter 21— "Deep Wounds" above and is in Porter's *Memory Cups of Panhandle Pioneers*, page 241.

ABOUT THE AUTHOR

Rose M. Hall is mother, grandmother, widow, and teacher with a passion for writing about women who live as equals with men.

Made in the USA
Middletown, DE
06 February 2017